MW00786263
Torah Day School
of Seattle

THE SHAAR PRESS

THE JUDAICA IMPRINT
FOR THOUGHTFUL PEOPLE

EYE

OF THE
STORM

A novel by

YAIR WEINSTOCK

translated by

Libby Lazewnik

First edition – First Impression / March 1999
– Second Impression / September 2002

This is a work of fiction. Names, characters, places, and incidents are either the product of the author's imagination or are used fictitiously. Any resemblance to actual persons, living or dead, or locales is entirely coincidental.

Published by **SHAAR PRESS**
Distributed by MESORAH PUBLICATIONS, LTD.
4401 Second Avenue / Brooklyn, N.Y 11232 / (718) 921-9000

Distributed in Israel by SIFRIATI / A. GITLER
6 Hayarkon Street / Bnei Brak 51127

Distributed in Europe by J. LEHMANN HEBREW BOOKSELLERS
Unit E, Viking Industrial Park, Rolling Mill Road / Jarrow, Tyne and Wear, NE32 3DP/ England

Distributed in Australia and New Zealand by GOLD'S BOOK & GIFT SHOP
3-13 William Street / Balaclava, Melbourne 3183 / Victoria Australia

Distributed in South Africa by KOLLEL BOOKSHOP
Shop 8A Norwood Hypermarket / Norwood 2196, Johannesburg, South Africa

ISBN: 1-57819-292-7 Hard Cover
ISBN: 1-57819-293-5 Paperback

Printed in the United States of America by Noble Book Press
Custom bound by Sefercraft, Inc. / 4401 Second Avenue / Brooklyn N.Y. 11232

Guard me like the apple of the eye;

shelter me in the shadow of Your wings.

—Psalms 17:8

1

New York, July 1983

The blue midsummer skies quickly gave way to a thickening cloud cover. One minute, the city was bathed in sunlight; the next, clouds galloped in from the nearby Atlantic to drench New York City with a warm, sticky rainfall. The rain poured down for precisely 31 minutes, leaving the city considerably damper than before, but just as stifling.

A long line of cars stood in gridlock along Manhattan's 43rd Street. The traffic lights changed color several times as frustrated motorists waited to continue their journeys home after the day's work. A truck had skidded on the wet asphalt and jackknifed sideways, blocking every lane. Drivers leaned on their horns. The noise was deafening. The truck did not budge.

On either side of the street rose enormous buildings, their roofs scraping the sky. One of these — on the right side, not far from the stalled truck — was a tall, rectangular office building. As a rule, street noises did not penetrate the 20th floor of this building. Its sheer distance from the ground muted all sound.

Today was different. After half an hour, the assorted furious honks and beeps had blended into one concentrated blare that assaulted everything within earshot. Although the windows of Aharon Flamm's office were shut tight — the air-conditioning vents supplying a steady stream of cold, clean air — he suddenly realized that he was unable to concentrate on his work. The incessant honking below had penetrated even this sanctum. He waited for the noise to abate, but it only grew stronger. Finally, he stood up and went to the window.

Pale peach miniblinds covered the window, protecting the room from the summer sun. Aharon raised the blinds and yanked at the window handle. At once, the appalling noise and a blast of heat simultaneously struck him full in the face. Manhattan in the summer was unbearable. The heavy, humid air off the Hudson River was suffocating, and when combined with the honking, the effect was something out of a nightmare.

"Aharon, shut that window!" Steve Mantel called from the other desk in the room. "I can't stand the heat and that infernal din. Why are they honking like that, anyway?"

"Looks like a stalled truck." Aharon closed the window and turned the air conditioning to its full strength. He returned to his desk, dismissing the traffic jam from his mind. This scenario, or one like it, was played out every working day in Manhattan, as thousands of office workers streamed homeward. It did not trouble Aharon much. He avoided the problem by remaining at his desk until 8 o'clock in the evening, sometimes 10 o'clock. By the time he drove home to Flatbush, the roads were emptier and the Brooklyn Bridge passable. Steve Mantel, who lived just on the other side of Central Park, was bothered even less.

Within half an hour, traffic policemen managed to unsnarl the mess in the street below. The noise lessened as cars crawled along their way. Aharon and Steve bent over their work again.

Their suite of offices bore the title "Flamm and Mantel, Statistics and Measurements." To one side of their building lay the placid stretch of Central Park, Manhattan's oasis of green; on the other side flowed the peaceful blue waters of the East River. The office employed 20 people, occupying seven rooms. The ambiguous name served as a cover for the office's real purpose. "Flamm and Mantel" was a subsidiary of the U.S. State Department.

Flamm, Mantel, and their assistants busied themselves with situational assessments, garnering and processing data, and drawing up statistical charts for comparison purposes. But their primary function was in the area of prediction. Aharon Flamm was an expert in geopolitical forecasting, having specialized for the past 20 years in the Middle East and the Arab states. His particular field was Iran, a fascinating hot spot that had drawn his professional interest from the start.

When Iraq's dictator, Sadaam Hussein, deported Iran's spiritual ruler, Ruhollah Almosowi Khomeini — better known as the Ayatollah Khomeini — from Iraq to France, Aharon Flamm had flown to France to follow developments among the core of fanatics surrounding the Ayatollah. He acquired every one of the Ayatollah's propaganda tapes and listened to them attentively. Two months later, he sent a secret memo to Jim Silver, head of his department. In the memo, Aharon had predicted the downfall of the Shah of Iran, Muhammed Riza Palavi, faithful ally of the United States, as well as the rise of a radical Islamic republic under the rulership of Ayatollah Khomeini.

"If we intervene now, we can halt the Islamic fundamentalist outbreak in Teheran," Aharon wrote in his memo. "But if we sit on our hands, as we generally do, we will see a significant lessening of American power in the region, and we'll be powerless to change the situation."

Jim Silver quietly filed the memo away. For the first time since they had met, he was convinced that Aharon was exaggerating the situation.

A year and a half later, in 1979, Flamm's prediction became a reality. State Department officials were caught by surprise and unprepared. Jim Silver began to harbor a renewed respect for his branch office in Manhattan — a branch that had been blessed, seemingly, with the gift of prophecy.

The ringing of the phone broke into the stillness of the room, and a green light flashed. Jim Silver was on the line from Washington.

"Aharon, I have a new project for you."

Aharon's ears perked up. The term "new project" generally meant a trip in the near future. This time, though, the timing was not ideal. In just a month, his son would be celebrating his bar mitzvah. Benjy was his oldest child, and Aharon did not relish being absent from home just when his family was gearing up for the big event.

"What are we talking about?" he asked guardedly.

"I have your latest memo in front of me. The Secretary is very interested in it."

Aharon felt a stab of pleasure at the compliment. The Secretary of State, Mr. George Schultz himself, had shown interest in his memo.

"Go on," he said, his voice betraying no sign of pride.

"You're taking this for granted," Silver chided. "Not everyone merits this kind of attention. All right, that's for another time At 8 o'clock tomorrow morning, my private plane will be waiting for you at La Guardia Airport to fly you to Washington. I'll meet you here."

Aharon replaced the receiver and raised a cup of mango nectar to his lips. From what he had managed to glean from Silver's hints, he was slated to meet with the Secretary of State tomorrow.

The prospect did not please him at all and he decided to make an early night of it.

◆ ◆ ◆

During his commute home to Brooklyn, Aharon spent time reflecting on his past.

The Flamm family had landed on American shores shortly after the turn of the century. Aharon's grandfather, Rabbi Shlomo Flamm, fled Kishniev with his family in the wake of the first pogrom of 1903. Leaving behind a sizable estate, he arrived in the United States with empty pockets. Within a few years, however, he established the realty offices of "Flamm and Sons" in the Jewish section of Manhattan's East Side. After his death, his sons Menashe (Mark) and Reuven (Arthur) continued running the firm under a new name: "Flamm Brothers, Real Estate." The firm became increasingly successful, eventually going public. Shares of its stock fetched a high price on Wall Street.

Aharon's father, Rabbi Reuven Flamm, had studied in yeshivah and remained dedicated to Torah study all his life. Every spare hour would find him poring over a small Talmud that he took with him everywhere, jotting down his thoughts rapidly on the pages of a slender notebook.

When Aharon was of age, he was sent to Yeshivah Torah Vodaath, where he excelled in his studies. From the first, his friends and fellow students were struck by Aharon's analytical powers. Mealtimes would find them mesmerized by his political dissections. Unlike the rest of his family, Aharon showed no predilection for real estate. It was politics and statesmanship that fascinated him. International diplomacy, political strategy, the logic that informed governments and rulers — these were magical things to him. The Middle East, in particular, drew his interest. Among his acquaintances, he was considered something of a political oracle.

At the tender age of 19, Aharon found the courage to write a letter to the-then Secretary of State, in which he outlined his analysis of the situation in the Middle East as it existed at the time and as he predicted it would develop. Miraculously, the letter found its way not into oblivion, as so many others are fated to do, but into the Secretary's own hands. He was riffling through the pages, about to toss the letter into the wastepaper basket, when one or two significant sentences caught his eye. They were wise sentences, shining a new light on old problems. They encapsuled a fresh point of view that drove straight to the roots of the matter.

Standing beside the wastebasket, the Secretary carefully read the letter from beginning to end. He was flabbergasted: the young writer seemed to possess keener analytical faculties than most of his own employees, graduates of prestigious universities. He was deeply impressed by Aharon's intellectual powers, and by his ability to see far beyond the present.

"Unbelievable! An intellect like this, and just a child?" He immediately set up an appointment to meet the young yeshivah student from "Torah Vodaath."

As expected, the Secretary was greatly impressed by the insightful young man. A year after his marriage, Aharon joined the team in the Manhattan office of "Statistics and Measurements," where he quickly climbed the ladder to ultimately become head of the division.

◆ ◆ ◆

Just last month, Aharon had submitted another memorandum to Jim Silver. It contained a possible scenario for the evolving relationship between the U.S. and the Arab states in the coming years. The scenario was based on a thorough and far-reaching study, and touched upon various highly sensitive issues. Aharon had developed a theory that drew upon different factors — a radical theory, to all appearances, although his earlier projections of the Shah's downfall and the Ayatollah's rise to power, of the peace process between Israel and Egypt, and a dialogue between Israel and the PLO had seemed radical in their times, too.

A great deal of water had flowed along the East River since Grandfather Shlomo Flamm had first crossed the bridge into New York. Now his grandson, Aharon, crossed it on his way home. He pressed the button on the car's tape player, and the car was filled with the vibrant voice of Rabbi Kalman Gold, explaining the *daf yomi* in fluent English. This was Aharon's preferred method of unwinding at the end of a long day's work.

Tonight, however, he found his attention straying after only five minutes. He was thinking about his son's bar mitzvah.

Benjy was already fairly comfortable with his *tefillin* and knew his speech by heart. The caterer had assured them that all was in order and the invitations had been sent — hundreds of them. The Flamm family was among the most respected and popular in Brooklyn's Orthodox Jewish community.

Everything was going well — and yet, anxiety gnawed at him. Something was going to go wrong with the bar mitzvah. He felt it.

"Nonsense," he told himself sternly. "There's no reason in the world why anything should go wrong."

His Buick entered Brooklyn and continued toward Flatbush. A pleasant warmth filled him as he neared his home. Waiting there for him was his wife, Margalit, and the children: Benjy, his oldest; Eli and Shlomo, the 11-year-old twins; Judy, 8; Dovy, 7; and Moishy, 5. Because of the upcoming bar mitzvah, the children had elected to stay home this summer instead of going away to camp as most of their friends had done.

Aharon pulled into the driveway and went into his house. Margalit met him on the second-floor landing with a sigh of relief after a long day.

"Thank goodness," she murmured.

Instantly, Aharon was overwhelmed by children. In short order he put together a colorful puzzle with them, then trotted around the rug with various small warriors on his back. After half an hour of rolling around on the floor to the music of his children's laughter, he went to find Margalit.

"Margalit, has something happened?"

She was busy with dinner preparations; a meat loaf on the counter was waiting to be popped into the oven. She tried to evade the question, but he persisted.

"Leave the food," he said quietly. "What happened?"

She turned to face him. "I've never interfered with your work," she answered carefully, "but this time I think I have the right to say a word."

"Even two."

"What have you been investigating recently?"

His throat went dry. "The usual trivia. The Middle East, Israel, nothing out of the ordinary."

She looked him squarely in the eye. How did she know he was hiding something? His last study had been anything but trivial....

"Don't go to Washington tomorrow, I'm begging you," she whispered suddenly.

Aharon was thunderstruck. "How do you know about Washington?"

"You see — I know. There's such a thing as a telephone."

"Who called?"

"About two hours ago, the phone rang. A voice I didn't recognize said in a hoarse, guttural accent, 'Tell your husband not to poke his nose into the secrets of the holy Arabs. He who tampers with Muhammed will be punished. He'd be better off not going to Washington.' Then he hung up."

Phone calls in the Flamm residence were automatically recorded by a machine in the master bedroom — yet another sign of the secret nature of Aharon's work. Margalit quickly slipped the meat loaf into the oven and followed him upstairs. Together, they listened to the recording of the sinister call.

"It's clear that he's an Arab," Aharon decided.

"So what?" Margalit countered. "Is he any less dangerous because of that? How did he find you?"

Aharon was silent. He was turning over several possibilities in his mind. Tomorrow, he would have CIA experts go through his office. Maybe his phone had been tapped. But even if they found something, the mystery would remain unexplained. His memo had been completely classified. Who was behind the anonymous phone call?

The aroma of cooking food reached them in the bedroom. Margalit excused herself and hurried back to the kitchen. In short order, the family was seated around the large dining room table. Benjy entertained the others with a rendition of his bar mitzvah speech, which he had researched and written himself. It focused on the question of a bar mitzvah that fell on Tishah B'Av, and Benjy was proud of it. It was a question that interested him in a very personal way, having been born on the afternoon of that special day. Aharon glowed with fatherly pride.

"When Benjy gets up to talk, I'm going to start singing!" Judy declared. The others laughed.

It was a calm scene, a peaceful scene, Menace seemed remote here. Aharon knew that nothing was going to stop him from traveling to Washington the next day. And right now, he was especially anxious to go. It was vital that the Secretary hear what he had to say, no matter what!

2

A small executive plane bearing the logo "Jet Commander" was waiting for Aharon Flamm at La Guardia Airport. The flight to Washington was short. Aharon hardly had a chance to look over the papers he had intended to review before the upcoming meeting in the capital.

Below, patchwork squares of green were dotted with rounded stands of trees and intersected by lines of black asphalt on which tiny cars glinted as they caught the sun. Though he knew those cars were traveling at highway speed, to Aharon's eye they seemed to crawl like tiny ladybugs. A steward tried to interest him in a fragrant croissant or a bottle of beer, but Aharon accepted only a glass of ice water.

"Oh, I just remembered," the steward exclaimed. "Everything has to be kosher, right?"

Aharon nodded and half-smiled. Then he bent his head over his papers once more, and the steward ceased to exist for him.

The Potomac flowed lazily south of the city, and the famous obelisk dedicated to George Washington pierced the sky as they approached the landing field. Aharon caught a glimpse of the Capitol's great white dome. The plane taxied smoothly to a stop. Aharon packed his papers into his briefcase and thought about what lay just ahead. The procedure was a familiar one.

He would be met at the airport entrance by a Lincoln Town Car, which would take him to his meeting with Silver. Today, for a change, that meeting would not take place in Silver's office or at Georgetown University, as it occasionally did. Instead, Aharon would be whisked away from Washington, to the Pentagon building located in Virginia.

◆ ◆ ◆

The Pentagon has its name because of its five-sided shape. At the time of its completion it was the largest office building in the world. Each of its five sides measures 281 yards, and the length of the entire building is over a mile. Multiply this by the four internal rows of buildings, and the result is a staggering *six* miles of offices! And that doesn't even begin to take the upper floors into account.

Jim Silver was waiting for Aharon in the Lincoln, and they traveled to the Pentagon together. Aharon permitted himself to be led along endless corridors, up an elevator to the third floor, and into a large, attractive office decorated in expensive teak in natural shades of browns and beiges.

He had not been mistaken. George Schultz himself was waiting in the room. He sat at his ease on a white leather sofa.

"So, here's our daring analyst," Schultz said, rising to shake Aharon's hand. "Two years ago, you predicted that Prime Minister Begin would invade Lebanon in at attempt to oust the PLO You were right. He did go in a year ago, though he got into a bit of a mess over there."

"I wrote about that, too, in my semi-annual report," Aharon replied. "Lebanon is something of a quicksand."

A short silence descended. Aharon waited tensely for some clue as to why he had been brought here.

"And now," the Secretary of State said, "you're talking about the quicksand of Jerusalem! I must tell you frankly, your forecast sounds exaggerated to me. It doesn't ring true. Only your reputation for accurate predictions is standing up for you right now. My friend, the President is convinced that you're way off base. The Iranians will never go as far as you're saying they will. It would clash with some of the fundaments of their faith."

So the President had read his memo, too. Aharon felt a small twinge of pleasure at the knowledge — although, in view of the high-powered nature of his subject, perhaps he shouldn't be surprised.

"The Iranians will be prepared for any sacrifice as long as the ultimate goal is justified in their eyes," Aharon said quietly. His eyes stung with sleeplessness. It had been a hard night; Margalit had been distraught over the telephone threat, and calming her down had not been easy.

The Secretary came closer to Aharon, so close that Aharon could see every line in his face. "Look me in the eye," Schultz ordered, "and tell me honestly: Don't you think your feelings as an Orthodox Jew have influenced this report? Your people tend to embrace the apocalyptic view. You're always talking about the End of Days."

Aharon was weighing his answer, when he became aware that the Secretary had not finished. "Also, frankly, I have to take into account your education and background. You never went to university or studied in any institution of higher learning. You're self-educated."

Aharon was surprised to catch a note of hostility in the Secretary's tone; the final sentence had been uttered with barely concealed contempt. Beside him, Silver took an uneasy step back. It was true that Aharon had not come to him from any academic institution. He had been catapulted into his department straight out of yeshivah. But everyone knew that Aharon Flamm had more knowledge in his little fingernail than 100 professors carried around in their heads.

Unconfirmed rumor had it that the Secretary had lately developed pro-Arab leanings. Upper-level Washington sources hinted at extended relations between American government officials and the Arab oil cartel. Aharon focused his clear blue eyes directly on Schultz's and said, "The answer is 'no.' A thousand times, no! My memo has both feet grounded in reality. If you don't do something to stop it, the extreme terror groups, or Iran itself, will seek to fulfill the goals I've outlined in the memo — in exactly the same way that my other predictions have come true."

"Maybe you're right," the Secretary suddenly capitulated. "Nuclear missiles have been trained on this building in their time. The Pentagon has never lacked for threats."

"If only one of those threats pans out," Jim Silver put in, encouraged by the new turn in the Secretary's tone, "the Pentagon won't be around anymore."

After that, the conversation flowed more easily. Aharon detected no further animosity in the Secretary's manner. The momentary tension was submerged in an atmosphere of conviviality. There were moments when Aharon was even relaxed enough to take in his surroundings: the ornate furniture, the expensive crystal fixtures hanging from the ceiling. The room was decorated in a modern style, except for the brown-and-burgundy Persian rug. "Maybe that rug has the power to change the mind of whoever stands on it," Aharon mused irreverently. "He doesn't like my forecast. Well, as far as I'm concerned, he can dance a *hora* with Khomeini!"

The conversation was over within half an hour. Flying back home to New York, Aharon gazed out the window and wondered what it had been about. Why had the Secretary really wanted to meet him?

The clouds floating below offered no answer.

◆ ◆ ◆

Less than 24 hours later, Aharon had his answer.

He was dumbfounded when Jim Silver called to inform him that Aharon was being transferred away from the Office of Statistics and Measurements. His new post would be in the Office of Industry — that is, the Far East division.

"But — why?" Aharon demanded, his whole world crumbling at once. He felt like a fish gasping on dry land, or an eagle with newly clipped wings.

"Are you so crazy about the Middle East, Aharon?" Silver said with an attempt at jocularity. "Stay in the East, but change the 'Middle' to 'Far.' What's the difference?"

Aharon gripped the table to stop his hands from shaking. "What's the point of joking? This is mid-July, Jim, not April first." He tried for a reasonable tone, but his suddenly thickening voice betrayed him.

Silver turned coldly businesslike. "Aharon, this is no joke. India is a developing nation with an eye to progress, but Sikh and Tamil minorities are raising a ruckus there. We don't need another Iran in the Far East. The Sikhs in India are just as extreme and dangerous — if not more so — than Khomeini's ayatollahs in Iran."

Aharon cleared his throat, but he could find no words. Exasperated, Silver burst out, "I don't understand you! Why are you taking this so hard? Haven't you ever heard of professional rotation? It's your turn now, that's all."

"Who's talking about rotation?" Aharon managed to locate his voice at last. "I'm a complete ignoramus in Far Eastern affairs, and — modesty aside — the most accurate forecaster of events in the Middle East. You might as well ask the President to become a traveling salesman!"

Silver — his sense of patriotism outraged, perhaps, by this reference to the President — reacted harshly. "May I remind you that you were a complete ignoramus in Middle Eastern affairs when you started working for us? If you don't like the way things are going, you can tender your resignation!"

Aharon saw his livelihood in danger of evaporating with the wind. He whispered, "Why are you doing this to me? Why uproot me from an area where I shine, and move me into one I find as interesting as a radish?"

"You're wrong, Aharon." The temperature of Silver's voice rose some two degrees. "India is a fascinating place. A month from now, you'll thank me."

"A month from now?"

"Aha!" Silver said with satisfaction. "Your first move in the Far Eastern division will be a trip to India next month! And not alone, but with your whole family. An adventure-filled trip that'll take you from coast to coast, boating up crocodile-infested rivers, visiting pagodas and one of the seven wonders of the world, the Taj Mahal, meetings with maharashas — and, for dessert, active participation in talks with armed, bloodthirsty Sikhs. Aharon, you don't know what's waiting for you. The adventure of the century!"

"Empty comfort," Aharon thought. India held about as much interest for him as the far side of the moon. Trips to India were a treat for children, not for him. The order had come from the highest echelons, there was no question of that — from the President himself, or his Secretary of State. He was being punished for that memo of his; it had been too daring.

"Aharon? Are you still with me?"

"Yes, of course."

"Well, why don't you answer?" Without waiting, he went on, "Accept my congratulations, Mr. Flamm. At 8 o'clock tomorrow morning you are to report for work at the 'Office of Industry' in the World Trade Center. You're going to like the work. It's just as exciting as the Office of Statistics and Measurements. Well, best wishes, and have a good day."

All of it was artificial. It rang of falseness, Aharon thought tiredly as he sank back in his chair. Silver had modulated his tone at every sentence, like a good actor, while letting the ax fall on his, Aharon's, neck, with the government's blessing.

"What's the matter, Aharon?" Steve Mantel turned anxious eyes on him. "You look awful. Who were you talking to, and what did they tell you?"

"Good-bye, Mantel. Starting tomorrow, you take over the Middle East desk. Best wishes, and have a good day," he ended bitterly, in imitation of Silver. He felt like crying as, in a few succinct sentences, he filled Mantel in on Silver's "good" news.

The news hit Mantel like a thunderstorm on a sunny day. He rubbed his forehead disbelievingly. "After 14 years in Statistics and Measurements, they're shuffling you off to India? Aharon, something smells fishy here."

Aharon stood beside his desk, staring bleakly at the piles of folders and loose papers. The personal computer, that had found its way into his office only a few years before, blinked monotonously. He looked around the room at the file cabinets, alphabetically arranged and filled with documents that, to the uninitiated, read like dry office business. Aharon knew what was hidden inside each file. Together, they contained the elements that fueled world events: power, dominion, chance, the secret international chess game — and now he was about to leave it all behind.

"Something certainly does smell," he agreed. "But it's not fish it smells of. It's oil!"

3

As the Flamm family got organized for Benjy's bar mitzvah, Aharon was busy preparing a big surprise of his own in honor of the grand event: the publication of his book, *The Complete Tosafos of Maseches Bava Kamma.*

It was a huge undertaking and had involved many years of work. Despite his position as a senior government employee for the State Department, Aharon had not neglected his Torah learning. Some time ago, he had begun a comprehensive study that had quickly become his life's work. It was a study of old, hand-written commentaries by the *ba'alei tosafos* on the tractate *Bava Kamma*. In a spiritual sense, Aharon felt that his learning was permanent and his job temporary; his daytime work for the State Department took a back seat to his nighttime labors over his Gemara. No one could take that away from him — not even the President.

Aharon flew to England to research the microfilm collections at Oxford and Cambridge Universities. After that he managed to part the Iron Curtain — something that only selected diplomats were granted permission to do in those years — to visit Leningrad University in the Soviet Union. Aharon Flamm was a considerable *talmid chacham* whose breadth of scholarship helped him to succeed where others might flounder.

Now, after all the years of research, he was nearly ready to publish his masterpiece. He showed the manuscript to his *roshei yeshivah,* who responded with joy. His work in unearthing the originals of the *Tosafos,* they declared, would shed light on many sections that had previously been difficult to understand.

The work was nearly completed, but Aharon was hesitant to publish it just yet. There was still a bit of work he wanted to do first. He had been able to find only one original manuscript on the *perek "Merubah,"* and without something more he was not completely satisfied that his volume would justify the title *The Complete Tosafos.*

On the day he was transferred from the Middle East desk, Aharon went home at noon, wondering how to break the news to his wife. After that difficult task was done, he decided to bury himself in his work. Benjy's bar mitzvah was moving inexorably closer, and he wanted to finish.

Late that night, the telephone rang.

◆ ◆ ◆

Thousands of miles from New York, in the city of Chandigarb, capital of Punjab, India, in a dilapidated hut in the foothills of the Himalayas, certain preparations were taking place.

"Do you see?" A swarthy man pointed at a large, color photograph. "You wouldn't believe how we got hold of that picture, but it's a good one. That's the couple. You know what to do with them."

Two other men, dark eyed, heavily bearded, and turbaned, spread the picture on the rough floor and studied it at length by candlelight.

"The Sikhs never abandon a friend," one of them said. "You say he's a Jew." He scrutinized the face in the picture once more. "He's shaven and wearing glasses... His wife also looks like a typical American. How will we be able to pick them out of the group of tourists?"

"Are you blind or stupid?" the swarthy man snapped. "What do you have eyes for? Look at what he's wearing on his head. A black head-covering made out of cloth. Jews call it a 'yarmulke.' It's an excellent way of recognizing him; he'll be the only one in the group wearing one."

The bearded man stood up and growled, "Said, you will not insult me. I have eyes as keen as an owl's."

"Of course!" The Arab took a hasty step backward. "All I wanted to point out, my dear — uh — "

"The name is Arjune Singh," the Sikh said angrily. "Don't be forgetting it again."

"Yes, of course. I only wanted to mention, my dear Arjune, that the man wears a special symbol on his head — something that is never removed. In the candlelight, I wasn't sure you'd noticed it."

Mollified, the Sikh stooped to the floor again, lifted the photograph, and held it closer to the candle. "Now I see it very well. They won't get away from me. I am Singh (a lion). All the Sikh are Singh." His chest swelled with pride.

"Good luck," the swarthy one said. He handed the Sikh a bundle of 10,000 rupees. "When you bring me a picture after the deed is done, you'll get another 20,000."

"Why don't you take care of them yourself?" the second Sikh spoke up for the first time.

The swarthy Arab was silent a moment, his eyes dilating in the flickering yellow light. "I am a gentle man," he answered finally.

The first Sikh asked, "When will they be here?"

"We'll keep you informed of all developments. According to the schedule they're supposed to be arriving a month from now, but it's not yet certain."

The bearded Sikh scooped up some dirt from the floor of the hut, letting it run through his fingers. "If you let us know when they are here, Rotek Singh and Arjune Singh will do with them like this." He let the last of the dirt run down to the floor.

◆ ◆ ◆

Aharon sat in his study, flipping through the pages of his draft manuscript. Though it was 3 a.m., he entertained no thought of sleep. Only he and his Creator knew how much work had gone into this labor of his, how many sleepless nights and treks across the world. How many hours painstakingly bent over faded manuscripts, how many meetings with Torah sages, how much thought, how much learning to get to the root of every *Tosefta*.

The phone rang. At night, Aharon muted the ringer, so that the sound was muffled. He never shut the phone down completely; more than once, the State Department had called him at just such an unearthly hour with some pressing new information. He picked up the receiver.

For a second, he expected to hear Jim Silver's voice, apologizing for the anguish he had caused, and letting him know that he was expected back at his old desk at "Statistics and Measurements" in the morning.

"Hello?" It was an unfamiliar voice, low and hesitant, unlike Silver's in every way.

"Who is this?" Aharon asked.

"Is it possible to speak with Rabbi Aharon Flamm? This is Yehoshua Schwartz, from Yerushalayim."

"Josh!" Aharon caught himself on the brink of a jubilant shout. "What's going on? Why have you suddenly remembered me at 3 o'clock in the morning?"

Rabbi Yehoshua (Josh) Schwartz was an old Torah Vodaath friend of Aharon's. After high school, he had gone to Israel to learn in the Mirrer Yeshivah, and had never left. He married there, began to raise a family, and eventually started his own small yeshivah for outstanding students.

"It's 10 o'clock in the morning here. Forgive me for waking you," Schwartz apologized. "I forgot all about the time difference — I was involved in a *sugyah* till this minute."

"Never mind, I wasn't sleeping anyway. How are you doing, Josh? And how can I help you?"

His friend began to speak. As he listened, Aharon's face turned grayer and grayer. Shock overwhelmed him as Josh Schwartz explained that he had been working on a project for some years... a huge project entitled *The*

Complete Tosafos... and the first tractate he'd selected for this monumental work was — how could it be otherwise? — *Bava Kamma*....

"I'm about to go to print," Schwartz concluded enthusiastically.

"So why are you calling me?" Aharon asked, amazed that he still had the power of coherent speech.

"I asked our *rosh yeshivah* for a *haskamah*. He referred me to you. He said you could help me."

Shock finally silenced Aharon. His old friend was working on the same project, unwittingly competing with him. In one fell swoop, Josh had swept all the cards off his, Aharon's, table. Their former *rosh yeshivah* had doubtless been in a quandary when Josh appealed to him for an endorsement of his work. He was depending on his two former students to work things out between themselves.

"Tell me, what did you do with the *perek 'Merubah'*? Did you manage to track down all the original manuscripts?"

"Interesting that you should ask about that *perek* in particular," Schwartz said in surprise. "As a matter of fact, that one seemed hopeless for a long time — and then I managed to get my hands on a fantastic manuscript from a private collection. The book's going to be perfect!"

Aharon felt a stab of envy. If only *he* had laid hands on that manuscript, what he could have done with it! A moment later, he was ashamed of himself. Everything was decreed from Above. No man can touch what has been set aside for his friend, and nobody so much as bruises a finger unless it has been ordained in Heaven.

As they continued talking about Schwartz's work, Aharon found some measure of comfort in discerning that it was considerably less sophisticated than his own. Schwartz had not had access to many of the manuscripts that Aharon had located, especially those he had found in Leningrad. His footnotes were lacking the depth of Aharon's, and he had none of the supplementary commentary of present-day Torah greats which Aharon had obtained through voluminous correspondence and personal visits.

"Do you know why the *rosh yeshivah* told you to talk to me?" Aharon ventured finally, battling a confusing mix of feelings that resulted in considerable inner turmoil. "And how do I know about the difficulty with the *perek 'Merubah'*? The two questions go hand in hand. Josh, I've been working on the same project for 10 years now. I'm also on the verge of going to press."

"*What!*" Schwartz cried. Aharon heard the thud of a far-off chair as his friend leaped up and knocked it over. "You mean to tell me that you — "

"Exactly," Aharon whispered.

"So — so what do we do now? There's no point in two identical books coming out at the same time." Josh sounded downcast, as though his beard was turning white even as he spoke, over there in Jerusalem. Just as Aharon's hair was probably in the process of changing color from the various shocks he had received that day.

"M-maybe —" Aharon began, with an uncharacteristic stammer that betrayed his confusion.

"You want to say that there's nothing to worry about, because we're talking about publishing in two distant countries." Schwartz sounded slightly cheered for a moment, but depression quickly returned. "No, that won't do it. The Torah world is too small for that. We'll both end up looking silly and petty."

"I meant to say something else," Aharon said, the words bursting uncontrollably from him. "I'll send you my manuscript — as a gift — and you can print whichever work is better, more complete. The main thing is that the Torah world and yeshivah students don't lose out. They deserve the best that there is."

There was a long silence at the other end. Josh Schwartz could not believe his ears. "You're kidding, right?" he asked in a strangled voice.

"Definitely not." From moment to moment, Aharon found himself growing stronger in his resolution. "What did we learn, all those years? To study Torah in order to observe it. *'Lo hamidrash hu ha-ikar, ela ha-ma'aseh.'* The main thing is not the learning, it's the doing. 'Don't be like servants who serve their master in order to receive a reward.' Either way, *Hakadosh Baruch Hu* will be praised. I'm sending you the manuscript tomorrow — as a complete gift."

"But you've worked so hard on it," Josh cried. "How can you throw it all away like that? I've never heard of such a thing!"

"My father raised me to act this way," Aharon said. "My grandfather, Rav Shlomo Flamm, instilled a motto in our family that's lasted through the generations — 'To give your all without expecting anything in return.' That's the kind of person he was."

Josh was silent. At last, he said hesitantly, "Aharon, maybe you're being hasty. Think it over again."

"All right. I'll think it over again tomorrow morning," Aharon consented. He was not prepared to change his mind, but maybe, this way, Josh would feel better about accepting the fruits of his labor.

◆ ◆ ◆

"Who was that? Someone from the State Department?" Margalit asked sleepily when Aharon finally went up to bed at 4 o'clock in the morning.

"No, just an old friend from my yeshivah days." Maybe he would tell her about it in the morning; maybe not.

"The important thing is, it wasn't another threat to your life," Margalit sighed. "I fell asleep just half an hour ago, and you haven't been to bed at all. We have to take ourselves in hand and not break down. I know you've had a bad shock, but why don't you check out this 'Office of Industry' tomorrow? It could be interesting, like Silver told you."

"Baloney," Aharon said, just before his head hit the pillow.

Margalit fell asleep a few minutes later, but not Aharon. He mulled over his phone conversation with Josh, dissecting his decision from every angle and finding it good. Maybe Margalit would agree with him. She, too, had been tested over the years in the area of "giving all you've got without expecting anything in return." Two years ago, she had given a favorite recipe to an old friend. The friend had baked the cake and entered it in a contest — where it won first prize. Praised and congratulated, the woman had kept all the credit to herself. The name Margalit Flamm never crossed her lips.

"An *eishes chayil,*" Aharon thought drowsily, but with satisfaction. "My father would have been proud of her. She rejoiced with her friend with all her heart, and even phoned to congratulate her on winning the contest.

The ungrateful woman had hardly known how to answer."

Aharon had lately been noting similar signs of good character in his oldest son, Benjy. It was a thing that ran deep, its roots far back in the family's history. In *Gan Eden,* his grandfather and his father were doubtless rejoicing.

4

They took up seven Pan Am seats.

Aharon Flamm conversed pleasantly with his son Eli, who appeared older than his 11 years. At the moment, the boy's blue-green eyes were very serious. He was deeply attached to his brother Benjy and had not wanted to take this trip without him; but Benjy had remained behind in New York. Both his parents and his *rebbeim* had felt that a jaunt through India was not suitable for a boy just taking on the burden of mitzvos. As for Benjy, he had been eager to spend the summer weeks in camp with his friends before their dispersal to different high schools. Eli seemed far more dejected at his big brother's staying behind than Benjy himself did.

Behind them sat Shlomo and Judy, craning to see out the window and exclaiming almost continuously at the beauty of the mountainous terrain far below. Margalit Flamm sat with Dovy and Moishy in the middle row. Margalit silently blessed the missing passenger whose empty seat gave her some extra elbow room.

"I see the airport!" Shlomo cried. "Welcome to the land of elephants and cobras!"

The plane descended. As it taxied to a gradual stop, the stewardess recited the local time and weather conditions: 40 degrees Celsius, or over 100 degrees Fahrenheit — in the shade.

"Welcome to the oven," Judy quipped. Dovy said, "I don't want to get off the plane."

"The monsoon rains will start falling soon, and then things will cool off," Aharon promised. "In India, the winters are dry and the summers wet. The monsoon is late this year."

"I learned that in Geography," Eli spoke up. "But what good is the monsoon to us? We're going to Punjab, where the climate is dry all year round."

Aharon explained that they would first be experiencing the sights of India: rickshaw rides, boating on the River Ganges, visits to stunning palaces. His voice was filled with an enthusiasm that was infectious. No one could have guessed how far from happy he was with this whole trip. He wanted nothing more than to see them all on the plane back to the United States.

◆ ◆ ◆

A young American diplomat in suit and tie awaited them in the terminal at the New Delhi airport. Despite the air conditioning, the strength of the heat outside penetrated the concourse, causing his immaculate clothes to stick damply in spots.

"Welcome," He shook Aharon's hand vigorously. "You are Aharon Flamm, if I'm not mistaken, and this is your beautiful family. I'm sure you'll represent America with honor in this country."

"We'll respect every cow we meet!" Dovy assured him.

The diplomat grinned. "That's good. By the way, I'm Charles Seymour. People call me Charlie. And you?"

"I'm Dov." The boy extended his hand. "But everyone calls me Dovy."

"Hi, Dovy." Charles shook his hand, then twisted it slightly so that

Dovy yelped with surprise and pain. "Teach that to your friends back at school," the diplomat suggested. He gestured to Aharon, who followed him to a corner.

The air conditioning was much weaker here. Immediately, both men broke into a sweat. Charles coughed, groping for the right words.

"Go on, talk," Aharon urged good-naturedly. "That's the special art of diplomats, isn't it?"

"All right. There's been a change in your itinerary. We received a telegram from the State Department."

"We return to the States at once?" Aharon felt like dancing.

"The opposite is more like it," Charles said, dabbing beads of perspiration from his forehead with a folded handkerchief. "Your department head is very concerned about heightened tension in the city of Amritsar. Sikh elements have been attempting to take control of the Golden Temple. He wants you to fly there immediately to investigate the extremist Sikh group that goes by the name of 'Yadawindara' — a gang that's threatening local stability."

Aharon stared at him. "I understand what my job is. But to do it together with my family? You can't be serious."

"Yes, with your family! They provide the best cover you could ask for. You'll fly directly to Chandigarb, where you'll hook up with a group of American tourists. From there, you go on to Amritsar and go sightseeing in the Golden Temple region. At that point, you'll receive further instructions."

Aharon was a man of sound common sense. The study of Gemara had further sharpened his critical faculty. He exploded, "They've all fallen on their heads in the Far Eastern division! Is this the way to investigate something — together with children 7 and 5 years old? I was supposed to tour India with my family and travel to Punjab alone later, after the rest of them had gone home."

Seymour pulled off his tie, which had turned into a limp rag in the humidity. From his jacket pocket he extracted a slip of paper. "Here's the telegram we received at the Consulate just two hours ago."

Aharon read the telegram attentively. Its contents matched the diplomat's instructions almost word for word. It also included the words "extreme urgency." He refolded the telegram and handed it back to Charles Seymour.

Years of work for the State Department had taught Aharon how to mask his emotions. The children would be disappointed. Margalit, watching him from the distance, would not like the change in plans any more than he did. But his superiors had made their decision. As a senior State Department employee and a representative of the United States, he would swallow his feelings and accept his orders.

"What comes next?"

Seymour sighed with relief. The hard part was behind him. "Believe me, you'd be best off getting out of this steambath before the plane's wheels ignite on the tarmac." He handed Aharon a long, blue plastic envelope. "In there you'll find all the necessary papers: airline tickets, new visas, entry permits for you and your family. There's also a very nice sum in rupees; feel free to spend it. An Avis car will be waiting for you at the car-rental office at the Chandigarb airport. And here are a couple of phone numbers to be used in case of emergency."

"They've thought of everything," Aharon said heavily, taking the envelope.

"Good luck." Charles smiled, his face gleaming with the heat. "On your return from Punjab, you'll be taken on the sightseeing tour of India that you were promised. The State Department is putting together an itinerary that I think you'll find unforgettable."

"I'd gladly forgo it," Aharon snapped. "And I don't mind if you pass that on to your precious superiors!"

◆ ◆ ◆

The children, as expected, were keenly disappointed. Aharon just barely managed to prevent Moishy from throwing a full-blown tantrum in middle of the terminal. He dragged his unwilling brood after him to the Air India desk.

From the second-floor concourse, two olive-skinned men watched through miniature binoculars. One was very young. Their position in a narrow recess between the wall and the glass railing kept them out of sight.

"Hada el Yahud ('Those are the Jews')," the older man whispered, without moving his eyes from the binoculars. "The man looks exactly like the picture we saw."

"And that's his family. What do we do with them?"

"Patience, Kamel. What are you so worried about?"

"They can complicate things, Said. Think about it," Kamel insisted.

"*You* don't think about anything," Said returned in a hard voice. "Only one of us has to do the thinking — and I've already thought of everything!"

Kamel kept quiet. For a few minutes longer they continued to observe the family below them.

When the two slipped away, one five minutes after the other, no one so much as glanced their way.

◆ ◆ ◆

The Flamms flew to Punjab on an Air India flight. They did not touch the meal that was served, munching instead on the last of the homemade sandwiches they had brought with them from New York. One Indian steward smiled and said, in fluent English, "What a lovely family. Are those twins?" He pointed at Shlomo and Eli.

"Yes, they are," Margalit confirmed.

"You can tell right away!" The steward's smile grew even broader. "The same facial structure, the same intelligent blue-green eyes, the same chin and forehead. They are completely identical."

"Thanks for the compliments. Actually, all my kids have the same eyes." Margalit dropped a light kiss on Judy's and Dovy's heads.

The overly friendly steward did not know when to stop. "This one," he gestured at Dovy, "has deep blue eyes and a wider forehead. And this one," here he patted Moishy's head, "has the eyes of a boy who likes to see what is happening around him. He does not miss much."

"Well, you certainly win the prize for most gracious steward," Aharon cut in, terminating the conversation. Still smiling, the steward nodded, and hurried away to the kitchen at the front of the plane.

"I hope all the Indians are as gracious as he was," Margalit remarked dryly.

"But they're not," Dovy said. "They say the Sikhs can be very wild. They all wear turbans and have long beards, and they never drink wine. They're scary."

"You're generalizing!" Judy scolded. "Besides, how do you know all this?"

"I know everything." Dovy stuck out his tongue. "The Sikhs are anti-Semites."

"Not true. They don't even know what a Jew is...."

The debate raged a while longer. Margalit stayed out of it. She spent the second half of the flight sunk in thoughts of her own: Benjy's successful bar mitzvah; the manuscript, ready to go to press, that Aharon had given to his old friend Josh Schwartz. Schwartz had wanted to render effusive thanks in print, but Aharon had not consented to anything beyond a brief, unspecified acknowledgement for his "help." She thought, too, of the tedious weeks her husband had spent in the "Office of Industry" before embarking on this visit to India.

But what she wondered about most of all was the sudden change in their travel plans, turning what was supposed to have been an exciting pleasure trip into something much less interesting — an official foray into a remote hot spot. Soon now, the plane's wheels would touch down on asphalt, and they would find themselves in the northern Indian state of Punjab — a place she would willingly have omitted from their itinerary, had the choice been left up to her.

Unfortunately, it was the State Department that got to make that decision.

◆ ◆ ◆

Chandigarb surprised them. They had expected ruins and antiquities, and found instead a modern city built just 40 years earlier. Their State Department liaison — a benevolent, white-haired man — was on hand to greet them at the airport. The weather seemed to smile upon them, too: in contrast to New Delhi's baking temperatures, the heat was at least bearable here.

The elderly man was pleasant and full of good will. He was also voluble. "Welcome to Chandigarb, capital of two states: Punjab and Hariyena. You'll find Indian Punjab a flowering area, as opposed to Pakistani Punjab. Even if you don't speak Punjabi, the native tongue of some 21 million of the population, you'll find an English speaker here and there who will make the going easier for you.

"The capital, Chandigarb, is divided into 47 numbered zones, called sectors. The sectors are separated by broad avenues. The central bus station is located in sector 17 — as is a modern shopping mall...."

Aharon listened courteously for a time, until he finally broke in with a firm, "Thanks, but we're not interested in Chandigarb. We need Amritsar."

The man instantly switched gears. "Very good. You're right," he agreed enthusiastically. "Most tourists are not interested in this city, but rather in its neighbor, Amritsar, because of the Golden Temple. I'm afraid you'll find the hotels rather damp, with a persistent smell of wet towels."

"Where can we find the Avis office?"

The man led them out of the building. The gleaming car-rental office and the courteous service they were accorded there reminded them sharply of the West they had left behind, and filled the family with optimism about the trek ahead.

"Be careful around the Golden Temple," the white-haired man warned. "Lately, gangs of nationalist Sikhs have been rampaging there." For the first time, he stopped smiling. "I understand that you are Orthodox Jews, but it would be a good idea for you to remove your skullcaps. Cover your heads with a cap or hat of some kind instead. Jews are not very popular around here."

Aharon nodded, and switched on the car's motor. "Many thanks. We'll be seeing you."

The man stood and waved genially until their car disappeared around a bend in the road.

In the window of an apartment building opposite, four small flames flickered: the sun reflecting off the lenses of two pairs of binoculars. The men who were watching did not lower the binoculars until the car was out of sight. Then they met each other's eyes and exchanged an evil smile.

A radio transmitter hung by its strap from the doorknob. One of the men fiddled with the controls until he found the frequency he wanted.

"This is your neighbor speaking, from the mountains. The man in the picture is on his way."

The communicator crackled. Arjune Singh, at the other end, was not well versed in the ways of electronic devices. At last he pushed the right button.

"I heard you, Said. I am ready."

"If you mention my name in connection with this, you won't get another rupee!" The older Arab screamed. *"I have no name!"*

"Okay, Said, forgive me. I understand you. All is excellent."

The connection was broken. As Said folded up the low footstool he had been using, he fumed about Arjune. If the Singh was as stupid as he sounded, then the man in the picture was liable to return to New York as healthy as when he had arrived. But the one who had recommended Arjune had praised him as tops in his field. The price he exacted for his work spoke for itself.

Kamel, his partner, burst out laughing. "Tomorrow, in the Hari Mandir (the Golden Temple), the Singhs will give them a tour they'll never forget."

For the first time, Said laughed, too.

5

The road wound through breathtaking mountain scenery. The children drank it all in through the car's windows. To the right, tall green trees nodded in greeting, while the left featured slopes of dramatic tumbling rock. From time to time they passed through a drab Indian village, where farmers walked up and down the fields harnessed to primitive wooden plows, curved blades biting into the dry brown earth. Youngsters hauled water from ancient wells and filled tin pails to the brim. The car drove past rows of bushes bearing green tea leaves, and wheat and rice fields whose yield did not reach half the height of their counterparts in the more developed Western countries. A herd of cows rested on the road, blocking traffic.

"Here's where we start seeing the 'holy cow' syndrome," Aharon explained to his children. "In the eyes of the Indians, the cow is a holy creature, the way sheep were to the ancient Egyptians. They attribute heavenly powers to the animal. That's why it's forbidden to remove a cow from the road."

"So we have to wait here until Her Majesty the cow decides to get up?" Shlomo asked.

"Abba," Dovy advised, "let's throw rocks at them."

"Only the Jews in Egypt had Hashem's permission to rile up the Egyptians by taking their sheep to the slaughter. If we harm a single cow, or even treat it disrespectfully, the Indians will be very angry!"

"But it's so stupid!" Judy protested. "How can they believe something so silly?"

"That," her father replied humorously, "is a little-understood aspect of the 'holy cow syndrome.' "

The lead cow chose that moment to lumber to her feet in search of grass at the roadside. The other cows quickly followed suit, and the car was able to continue on its way.

"Yay! The road to Amritsar is open!" Dovy crowed. "I wonder what kind of adventures we'll have there."

The road was long, and afforded the family more picture-postcard views of soaring, snow-capped mountains, verdant green valleys, herds of sheep grazing under the supervision of 10-year-old shepherds, fields of red poppies, flowing streams.

Then the terrain began to change. The further south they penetrated, the more barren the countryside became. Maintaining control of the car became difficult as the uneven road wound in sometimes tortuous curves. Time and again, Aharon stopped to ask natives the way to Amritsar. The Indians gave them a clue: the closer they got to the city, the more tourist restaurants they would see, all carrying the names of birds.

"We're getting close to Amritsar!" Aharon decided presently.

"How do you know, Abba?" Judy asked.

"Look around. We've arrived in the 20th century."

The natives had been accurate. Restaurants — many of them advertising air-conditioned sleeping accommodations for tourists — lined the roadside: the Flamingo, the Blue Crow, the Starling, the Kingfisher, and more. Apart from the menus posted outside each eatery, the restaurants vied for tourist dollars in open competition. The touted attractions were varied and numerous: sulfur baths, steam rooms, swimming pools, playgrounds, exercise equipment, and the crowning glory of them all — elephant rides!

This drove the children into a frenzy of excitement. "An elephant ride! Abba, Ima, please?"

Aharon and Margalit could not refuse. They all eagerly mounted the gray Indian elephants, shrieked with delight and terror, and had themselves photographed beside the most kingly of the huge beasts.

As dusk approached, they finally encountered a large blue sign that proclaimed in gold letters:

The holy city of Amritsar — 5 kilometers. Please drive respectfully.

◆ ◆ ◆

Preparations were being completed near the Golden Temple. Said and Kamel had outpaced Aharon and his family on the express train, and arrived in Amritsar hours ahead of them. They kept a close watch on the operation.

They found 300 Sikh extremists in full dress waiting in an adjacent building. The armed militants were pitched to a fever of nationalist pride. They were planning to try to take over the Golden Temple the next day. Further instructions were whispered into their ears, and a picture of the American tourist couple was passed around.

◆ ◆ ◆

That night, the family stayed at a medium-priced hotel opposite the train station. The desk clerk tried to talk them into renting a good motorcycle, only desisting when Aharon showed him the keys to the Avis car. After a light meal of fruits and vegetables, the family went up to their room.

"What are we doing here?" Margalit fretted. "Golden temples, gurus, krishnas — it's pure *avodah zarah* in the starkest sense of the word! We can't even eat here. Why did we come? To sleep in two-star beds, when we have much more comfortable ones at home?"

"This is where the State Department sent me," Aharon sighed. Suddenly, something snapped inside him. Throwing caution to the winds, he confided in his wife the contents of the telegram that had rerouted the family from New Delhi to Amritsar.

Margalit heard him out in silence. When he was finished, she said grimly, "Too bad you didn't tell me this right away. I wouldn't have let you change our plans."

Aharon was startled. "Why not?"

"Call it women's intuition. I suspect that telegram's authenticity. The original trip to India had some logic behind it, but that so-called diplomat, Charles Seymour... Aharon! Someone's laying a trap for us!" She was near panic.

"Margalit, calm down. You're still upset from that phone threat back home. Your fears are not rational."

"I wish they weren't." Margalit wrung her hands. "I have a very bad feeling about this. Aharon, let's get away first thing in the morning."

"And what do we do with them?" Aharon pointed at the children ranged in beds and armchairs, sunk in the deep sleep of exhausted travelers. "We came all this way and won't even show them the city? They'll never forgive us."

"The kids will be happy with anything we show them, as long as it's not home," Margalit pronounced with a mother's wisdom. "Let's get out of here. Please!"

"I can't go back to New York empty-handed. We'll tour that silly Golden Temple for a few minutes tomorrow, and I'll see if I can sniff out any scent of revolt or violence in the air. That much I'll do — even if only as a formality — for the State Department. Then we can go right on to Chandigarb."

Reluctantly, Margalit consented to the plan.

◆ ◆ ◆

"The Golden Temple that you see before you is known in Indian as the 'Hari Mandir.' It is the most beautiful building in Amritsar. The name means 'pool of nectar' and it refers to the large pool around which the building was erected. While Amritsar itself is only another dusty Indian city, this spot is outstanding in its beauty and tranquillity."

The tour guide stood beside the gates of the marble palace, droning his spiel into a powerful megaphone. Listening to him was a group of nearly 100 American tourists. The Flamms had mingled with the group in the hotel lobby, then followed the bus in their own rental car. They listened as the guide began to describe the building itself, starting with the copper and gold dome which gave the temple its name. He spoke of internal bridges, of architecture that blended Hindu and Moslem design, of marble walls in the style of the Taj Mahal. Then he went on to tell of the *prasad*, a sweet dough that was distributed to the priests inside the temple.

Aharon whispered to Margalit, "They stole that from us. All the world's religions have taken something from Judaism. I don't need to travel to India to find out that they've imitated the *lechem hapanim* of our own *Beis Hamikdash, lehavdil elef alfei havdalos*. It's a superficial and pathetic imitation. Why do we have to stand here hearing this? Not even the State Department can force me to listen to this stuff."

He and Margalit decided that, at the point when the rest of the group began entering the temple — a place which they, as Jews, were halachically forbidden to enter in any case — they would slip away quietly and return to their hotel.

After an hour of explanation, the guide finally began letting the group pass into the courtyard. Vendors hawked their sweet dough to the tourists, who snapped up packages of the *prasad*. Eli Flamm giggled at the sight of the Americans shedding their shoes preparing to enter the mosque. "That's stupid," he whispered to Judy. "When they come out they'll never find their own shoes again. It'll all be one big jumble!"

"Not true," Judy countered. "Everyone's putting his shoes in his own separate corner, see?"

"Oh look at that," Eli said, grinning mischievously. To his sister's alarm, a small Indian boy stole into the courtyard through a back entrance, and emerged a few minutes later heavily veiled, a thin branch in his hands. Thus camouflaged, he mingled with the crowd, sweeping the floor lightly with his branch as he moved ever closer to the place where the shoes were lined up. After six circuits of the courtyard, the orderly rows of shoes were — as Eli had predicted — a huge jumble.

Their father, who had gone to get the car, tooted his horn. "Eli, Judy, come on. We're leaving."

The two children ran toward the car. At that exact moment, a roar rose behind them, rhythmic as the tom-toms of the jungle. From the watch-tower and the Sikh museum, robed and turbaned figures came marching in a horde.

The Sikhs were climbing up to the Golden Temple.

Aharon started the engine, made a U-turn, and drove toward the edge of the road. Suddenly, for the first time, he noticed the locked shops and the empty marketplace. Apparently, the shopkeepers were in on the secret of the day's agenda, and had fled for their lives.

Hundreds of armed Sikh militants converged on the spot. With exultant faces they shouted rhythmic slogans in voices that aroused terror in every heart.

"That must be the Yadawindara and their mantra," Aharon murmured to his wife, as they watched the progress of the operation from the car at a distance of a hundred yards. The Sikh extremists wore red togas and purple turbans embellished with semiprecious stones. All had beards — black, brown, gray, or white. They chanted continuously, monotonously, eyes closed for the most part in an ecstatic frenzy, except when the marchers opened them for a few seconds to see their way.

"Margalit, you owe Charles Seymour an apology. The State Department was right. Something *is* slated to happen here today — some bloodletting, it looks like."

"I see," Margalit whispered back, as though afraid the Sikhs on the other side of the road might hear. She never removed her eyes from the unfolding scene.

Abruptly, the uproar ceased. Hundreds of Sikhs stood facing the gates of the Golden Temple. Their leader, in resplendent robe, jeweled turban, and white beard, began shouting an oration. His sentences were short and rhythmic. After each one, the crowed roared in repetition. The effect was terrifying.

"That's all?" Dovy asked, disappointed. "No action? No shooting? Just a lot of shouting?"

Aharon roused himself. "I want to go out and see from up close," he told his family. "Maybe take some photographs. I need to do that to make a full report to my office."

"Aharon, don't go!" Margalit cried.

"Just for a minute," he said, stepping out of the car.

"I'm coming with you!" his wife screamed. "You're not going alone. Kids, I'm going with Abba just for a minute. No one is to leave the car, not even for a second. Understand?"

Before the children could react, their mother was out of the car and running after her husband. They neared the group of Sikhs listening to the orator. Careful not to expose themselves to the eyes of the fanatic horde, Aharon and Margalit slid into a covered alley. The alley was dark, and fragrant with the aroma of exotic spices.

◆ ◆ ◆

Arjune Singh did not mix with the masses of Sikhs gathered at the mosque entrance. He and his cohort, Rotek Singh, passed silently through the marketplace and the square, searching for the man and woman in the picture. According to the last report they had received, the couple had been standing near the temple when they had suddenly disappeared.

They moved from street to street, alley to alley. The Sikh extremists were silenced, on orders from above, to allow the fish to swallow the bait. Arjune himself was responsible for the order.

The two were nowhere to be seen.

Singhs have great reserves of patience. "We haven't looked in the spice alley," Rotek pointed out. They went into the dark alley — where, at a distance of some 30 yards, they spotted the two Americans crouching to photograph the scene at the mosque gates. Silent as a pair of cats on the prowl, the Singhs moved closer to the unsuspecting couple.

"It's no use. It's not them," Arjune said, exhaling in disappointment.

"How do you know?" Rotek whispered.

"The man is supposed to be wearing some sort of black cloth hat on his head. This guy's wearing a regular American baseball cap. It's not him."

Rotek threw his partner a disgusted look. "Arjune, you know something? Even a mosquito has a bigger brain than you. Isn't it possible to switch hats?"

Arjune's forehead wrinkled in the effort to think this through. At length, comprehension illuminated his bearded face. He nodded.

◆ ◆ ◆

The children waited in the car for more than an hour. Their patience was wearing thin.

"What happened to Ima and Abba?" they kept asking one another. "They went out for a minute and forgot to come back!"

Shlomo opened the car door. "I'm tired of waiting here, doing nothing. I'm going to scout around near the mosque."

"Shlomo, no!" his brothers and sister shrieked. "Ima said not to!"

Shlomo paid them no heed. Nimble as a mountain goat, he began running fearlessly toward the main street. He had no more than 70 yards to cross before he made it to the darkened alleyway that seemed to him the most logical place for his parents to have gone.

He did not emerge from the alley.

Some two hours later, it dawned on the waiting children that the Flamm family was in deep, deep trouble.

6

The gang of Sikh extremists stood at the tall stone walls surrounding the Golden Temple, waiting for the signal to storm the Guru Bridge into the temple courtyard. They were growing restless. At fever pitch, they needed only a spark to ignite them.

Suddenly, there was a wail of sirens. Police sirens. The stampede began. Hundreds of feet pounded the streets as robed and turbaned figures fled in every direction, like a pack of frightened rabbits. Scores of Sikh militants ran past the rental car where the Flamm children cowered in a desperate attempt to avoid being seen. They need not have bothered. The extremists were too busy fleeing for their lives.

The demonstration, then, had been no more than a show of unity. The Sikhs had not come prepared for actual battle, as in the past, when they had taken over the mosque and departed only after a bloody clash with the Indian army. A hidden hand was pulling the strings, and that hand had scattered the hundreds of fundamentalists without action.

Someone, apparently, had been interested only in a little playacting — in creating a superb diversion.

◆ ◆ ◆

Moishy was the first to start crying.

"Where's Ima? I want Ima and Abba!"

Dovy came next. Eli and Judy tried their best to calm the younger ones, but they themselves were on the verge of hysteria. They, too, were only children. Their parents had disappeared — and also their brother, Eli's twin, Shlomo. They were hungry and thirsty, tired, confused, and bewildered. The sight of the frenzied Sikhs pounding directly toward their car had roused a terror so real and so deep that they were genuinely traumatized. Up until this point, they had remained imprisoned in the car by choice. Now they wanted to get free of it and move on to safer ground. In other words, wherever their mother and father and Shlomo were.

Gradually, the tumult died down. The frightened tourists were permitted to leave the mosque and return to their hotels. For good measure, the children waited an extra half-hour after that, just in case the Sikhs should decide to return for an encore performance.

At last they felt secure enough to leave the car. They began walking up and down the streets, searching for their parents and brother. It was Eli who wandered into the spice alley.

The covered alley was dark and gloomy. From the doorways of the little shops, tantalizing scents tickled Eli's nose, changing every few feet to a different spice with a different aroma. Each shop specialized in spices and its derivative fragrant oil. The perfume of rose petals and lavender permeated the area outside one shop; a few steps further on, it mingled with and then changed to the scent of jasmine, followed closely by chamomile, then refreshing mint. Eli walked on, entranced even as he fought down his fear.

"Ima? Abba? Shlomo?" he called again and again. His thin voice echoed off the metal bars and rolled up to the vaulted roof that covered the alley. But neither Ima nor Abba returned his calls, and Shlomo had vanished as though swallowed up by the earth.

He had seen all three enter this alley and not come out. Fearfully, he searched for a clue to their fate. Without admitting it to himself, he was looking for a bloodstain or a scrap of torn clothing — witnesses to the possible violence that might have occurred here....

Instead, at the very end of the alley, he glimpsed something very different, and the sight of it made him gasp.

It was Shlomo's tiny *Sefer Tehillim.* On the inside cover was a dedication in his father's handwriting, written on the day he had presented the *Tehillim* to Shlomo as a reward for an excellent report card. Holding the *sefer* in his trembling hands, Eli read:

> *To my dear son, Shlomo,*
>
> *Tehillim has accompanied our people since the days of King David. In its merit, we have never lost our way. It will stay with you all your life, in times of joy and in times of sorrow, on cloudy days and sunny ones. It will be your signpost should you ever lose your way — and your guide to bring you safely home again.*
>
> *Your loving father,*
>
> *Aharon Flamm*

Blinking back tears, Eli read and reread the dedication. He, too, had received a *Sefer Tehillim* from his father, but his message had been slightly different. He had slacked off in school toward the end of the year, and his father had included several pointed hints about how to do better.

Here was proof that Shlomo had been on this spot. How had he lost the *Tehillim?* Had it fallen to the ground in a struggle with a surprise attacker? Had his brother dropped it in his wandering and lost his way? Had Shlomo found their parents, and were the three of them together, searching for the other children? Maybe it was best that they return to the hotel. Why, Ima and Abba and Shlomo might be waiting there this very minute! But even as the hope crossed his mind, Eli knew that it was only wishful thinking.

Besides, how in the world *could* they return to the hotel? None of them knew how to drive a car!

He ran back to the car, overcome by an urgency that grew out of his realization of how very serious their situation was. "Judy, Dovy, Moishy," he called as he ran. He found his siblings sobbing quietly beside the rental car. He pulled at them. "Get in — now!" he commanded.

Abba, he reasoned, must have some sort of cell phone in the car. He always did. Where could it be? Eli searched the glove compartment but came up empty-handed. It wasn't resting on the dashboard, or beneath the front seat. Tears of despair welled in his eyes. Everything was going against them today.

Then little Moishy groped under the back seat and handed his brother a blue plastic envelope. Rummaging inside, Eli found all the papers his father had received from Charlie Seymour at the New Delhi airport. But what good were these papers to the children? What use had they of permits for unlimited travel in India? What good were airline tickets without Abba and Ima and Shlomo?

Beneath the official documents lay a single sheet of stiff plastic. In large letters were the words *Emergency Phone Numbers,* followed by the numbers themselves. There were also several coins: tokens for the public telephones.

Taking Judy and Moishy and Dovy with him as he got out of the car — Eli was taking no further chances of getting separated — he walked until he found a telephone booth. With trembling hands he dialed the first number on the plastic card. It rang in an office in New Delhi.

"American Consulate," a woman's voice said. "The Consul's secretary speaking."

Eli's throat grew suddenly dry. "This — this is Flamm," he managed to croak.

"Who?"

"Eli Flamm."

The secretary's voice grew warmer. "Flamm? Then you must be one of Aharon Flamm's children. Where's your father?"

Eli spoke slowly, forcing himself to say the words out loud for the first time.

"Our father and mother, Aharon and Margalit Flamm, have disappeared. And our brother Shlomo, too."

◆ ◆ ◆

Members of the consulate staff, together with some police officers, soon came to collect the children. The police instituted inquiries and set up roadblocks, performed house-to-house searches, and closed off streets. Investigators checked out whatever there was to investigate. They visited Sikh strongholds in the neighboring villages, planted agents in various locations, and closely followed any and all unusual developments.

Aharon, Margalit, and Shlomo Flamm had vanished without a trace. The circumstances of their disappearance were hidden in a thick cloud. Not a clue to their whereabouts could be found anywhere, and not a single witness came forward in all of Amritsar or the surrounding countryside. The police were at a loss.

After two weeks of fruitless searching, it was decided in the top echelons that there was no point in detaining the remaining four frightened and overwrought Flamm children in India. They were returned to the United States in the company of a heavy contingent of embassy and security personnel. At the airport, waiting for them with the reddened eyes of one who had been weeping copiously, was their 13-year-old brother, Benjy.

There they were, five children alone, with the fate of their parents and brother shrouded in a dense, impenetrable fog.

◆ ◆ ◆

The American social work agencies began finding suitable foster homes for the Flamm children until such time as their parents would return — *if* they would return — from India.

The problem was a complex one. Aharon Flamm had been an only child. Margalit had one sister who lived in Los Angeles, and a younger, unmarried brother.

"Abba would never forgive us if he came back and found out that we went to live in Los Angeles without his permission," Benjy maintained. The boy had, overnight, found himself in the role of father and mother to his younger siblings. It was a heavy burden for his young shoulders.

The search for a proper home continued. At last, as the month of September and the Jewish holidays approached, one was found.

Mark and Adina Goldenblum were longtime friends of the Flamms in Flatbush. Mark was a rising star in a flourishing industrial concern, and money flowed freely in the Goldenblum household. After 15 years of marriage, the couple had not yet been blessed with children of their own. Though they longed desperately to start a family, the doctors held out little hope.

In September, they welcomed the five Flamm children into their home.

The children were grateful, though they were all waiting with painful yearning for the day they would see their father's beloved face as he descended the airplane steps onto American soil, when they would feel their mother's warm embrace as she hugged them to her in joy. And they waited for their Shlomo to wave eagerly at them, and run straight into their open arms.

Maybe it would happen in the form of a phone call: "Come get us, we're in the airport with our luggage." Or a telegram from the State Department: "Your parents and brother have been found in India and will be returning shortly."

On the other hand, there might be a very different sort of call: "We've kidnapped your parents and brother, and demand a ransom in return for their lives."

But nothing happened. No phone call, no telegram, no shred of evidence about the whereabouts of their mother and father and Shlomo. It was as though someone had drawn a big, red "X" right through the three of them.

Day followed day. Summer vacation ended. Benjy entered yeshivah high school; Eli, Dovy, and Judy returned to their own schools; Moishy went to kindergarten. Their teachers tried to be extra kind. Adina Goldenblum visited the younger children at school nearly every day.

On the surface, life went on in its normal way. But it was a life as flat and empty as a pricked balloon — like a canvas painted with an illusion of life instead of the real thing. There was none of the happy, carefree feeling they had known in their parents' home, until a trip to mysterious India had cut it off so cruelly.

News came from the State Department, only occasional apologetic phone calls from their contact there, who took the trouble to update them from time to time on the progress of the search in India. The investigations were continuing, he assured them. "We'll find something," he promised. "People don't just vanish into thin air without leaving behind some kind of clue. It's just a question of time."

Steve Mantel and others from the Office of Statistics and Measurements stayed in touch, dropping in now and then to see the children in person. So did some of the staff of the Office of Industry. The children received visits from social workers, who came to see how they were adjusting to life at the Goldenblums. The press hovered curiously. They smelled a story here, only no one knew what kind of story it would turn out to be. Mark and Adina Goldenblum did their best to ward off the media and keep them out of the children's private lives.

Everyone agreed on one thing: the children had made a remarkable adjustment. Mark and Adina spared no effort to make them feel completely at home. The children appreciated this. Still, there was nothing to take away the awful emptiness, and the fear that gripped them as they wondered what had become of their mother, their father, their brother. Where were they now, this very minute? What was happening to them? Were they even still alive?

Long months of disappointed hope and tension had emptied the children's storehouse of tears. Their eyes were dry, their hearts filled with despair. They returned to their routines, their schoolwork. Eventually, the ringing of the phone stopped making them jump. Their expectation changed to stoic patience, a wait filled with question marks.

One day, Mark took them all to a lookout point to enjoy the beautiful sunset. They stood and watched the red ball of the sun sink lower and lower, toward the horizon. Orange stained the sky over the sea. The clouds were shot through with crimson and purple in a panorama no camera could adequately capture. The water turned to gold.

The sun set in New York.

7

1996 — Thirteen Years Later...

Rav Anshel Pfeffer left his house at 6:30 a.m., as he did every morning, and set out for the yeshivah. For 20 years, Rabbi Pfeffer had been delivering a *shiur* in Yeshivas Chochmei Provinzia in Jerusalem. His job included some of the duties of a *mashgiach*; hence, his obligation to be present at *Shacharis* services along with the students.

He turned up the collar of his coat around his ears for the 10-minute walk. The weather was very nasty, with a cold rain whipping his face on the wings of the shrieking winter wind. From the ground rose the scent of rain — the scent of earth thirstily drinking its fill.

"If only a car would stop, one with a driver that has a friendly face," he thought hopefully.

As if in response to his wish, he heard the squeal of brakes beside him. A white Subaru pulled over to the side of the road. The driver — a yeshivah *bachur* whom the rabbi didn't recognize — was rubbing at the inside windshield in a futile effort to defog it. Putting down his rag, he rolled down the side window. "Rabbi Pfeffer?" he shouted above the wind and rain.

"Yes!"

"Can I offer you a ride?"

With a grateful smile, Rav Anshel walked around to the passenger side, opened the door, and sat down. "Thank you. I need to go to Yeshivas..."

"Chochmei Provinzia," the other finished for him. "I know where that is. But first, Rabbi, there's something I need to talk to you about."

◆ ◆ ◆

Rebbetzin Breina Pfeffer went out to the landing to collect her laundry. The rain had been coming down for two straight days, and with a family of 10 children, the laundry had to be a more or less continuous operation. On sunny days, Breina hung out large quantities of wash to dry, then took the clothes in, folded them, ironed where necessary, and put them back into their respective closets and drawers. With the steady downpour, she was left with great mounds of wet laundry on her hands. Ingeniously, she had strung clotheslines out on the landing. What dried in two hours under the fierce Israeli sun took two days on the landing. With Rabbi Pfeffer's income placing him among the lowest 10 percent in the country, a gas dryer was only a dream.

She was stepping back into the house, a huge pile of towels and sheets in her arms, when the phone rang.

"Someone has the knack of calling at just the right time," she sighed. She dashed into a bedroom, dumped the dry clothes on one of the beds, and ran into the living room to snatch up the phone.

"Rebbetzin Pfeffer?"

"Yes."

"We're calling from the yeshivah. "Now she recognized the secretary's voice. In growing dismay, she heard him continue, "We wanted to find out why Rabbi Pfeffer hasn't shown up today. His students are waiting for him. Isn't he feeling well?"

Breina Pfeffer reeled. "What are you talking about? My husband left this morning like he always does! He still hasn't reached the yeshivah?"

"No," the secretary said hesitantly. "He usually *davens Shacharis* with the boys, but he wasn't there today. We assumed he'd turn up in time for his *shiur,* but he's late for that, too."

"I don't know what to tell you." Worry darkened Breina's face. "I'm sure he'll show up soon. He's a very responsible person."

"I know that," the secretary said sympathetically. "Well, I'll call you the second he comes in."

Breina froze, listening. "Don't bother. I think that's him now, coming through the front door."

She heard the secretary exhale in relief. "Well, as long as he's all right...."

Anshel Pfeffer did not walk into the apartment; he staggered in. He appeared completely dazed as he went to the kitchen and put three heaping teaspoons of coffee into a mug.

" What exactly are you doing?" he wife asked, bewildered. "And why aren't you in yeshivah? Your students are waiting."

"Are they? Then I'd better be going to them." Anshel took a sip of the bitter coffee, spat it quickly into the sink, and ran out of the kitchen. Breina hurried after him, calling, "Anshel, where did you *daven Shacharis?"*

"In a special *minyan,"* he called back, never slackening his pace. "I'll tell you about it later!"

Confused, Breina watched from the window as her husband flagged down a taxi. In short order, Rav Anshel was running up the yeshivah stairs. Though he tried hard to deliver a coherent *shiur,* his students picked up the same thing his wife had sensed earlier. This was not their usual calm, collected rebbe. Something had taken hold of Rav Anshel's thoughts and set his spirit in turmoil.

Lunch was the main meal of the day, and once a week Rebbetzin Pfeffer served a special one to her children on their return from school.

Consequently, Tuesday was — apart from Shabbos — their favorite day of the week.

Today she set down a platter of stuffed cabbage, followed by a rich vegetable soup, stewed chicken, and a chocolate mousse dessert. Rav Anshel, always conscious of the passing time, kept his eyes fixed on a small *Mishnayos* during most of the meal, but always remembered to look up and thank his wife for the delicious food. Breina had learned over the years that even when her husband seemed most detached, he was never quite out of touch with what was happening around him.

Today was different. The children giggled to see their father gulp down forkfuls of chicken and spoonfuls of chocolate mousse together. "I'm in a rush today," he explained. "Would one of you kids bring the *mayim acharonim?*"

Chanie, 9, shouted with glee, "But Abba, you didn't even eat bread!"

"Oops, you're right." Rav Anshel laughed along with his daughter.

Breina was waiting in the bedroom as Anshel came in for his customary 15-minute rest before returning to yeshivah.

"Anshel, can I know what's happening with you today?"

He paused, hands halfway to his shoelaces. "It's a long story, and it's not over yet. If it continues, I'll tell you everything."

Breina had to be content with that. After 20 years, she trusted her husband's judgment implicitly. Twenty years is a respectable amount of time in which to get to know a person. She had seen Anshel during hard moments and difficult decisions. But she had never seen him in the state he was in today.

Twenty years ....

◆ ◆ ◆

Anshel Pfeffer came from a simple Tel Aviv family. His father, Shlomo Zalman Pfeffer, was a Holocaust survivor of Hungarian descent. The liberation forces had found him at Buchenwald, near death's door. But the young man had proved stronger than he had appeared. With a fierce desire for life, he had rehabilitated quickly and arrived in Israel on one of the refugee ships that managed to slip through the net of the British Mandate.

On his arrival, he stayed as a guest at the home of Aryeh Hecht, a very religious Tel Aviv carpenter whose craftsmanship had turned the name"Hecht" into a synonym for quality. His closets, tables, and beds found their way into the best Tel Aviv homes, at affordable prices.

Aryeh Hecht was seeking a husband for his only daughter, Penina. The young refugee struck him as a man of integrity and *yiras shamayim.* He saw in Shlomo Zalman Pfeffer a fitting heir to the Hecht carpentry business when the time came.

Shlomo Zalman married into the family and into the business. In due course he took over the management of "Hecht Carpentry" and ran it profitably for many years. He sent his son Anshel to a local yeshivah for eight years, and then to a famous yeshivah in Jerusalem. He hoped for great things from the boy.

He was not to be disappointed. Anshel soared beyond anyone's hopes. His diligence and piety knew no bounds. But he himself was not satisfied.

In an almost surreptitious fashion, he formed a group of his fellow students into the *Va'ad Hashomrim.* The group set lofty goals for itself. On the 10th day of every month, beginning with Yom Kippur, they dedicated themselves totally to the study of Torah while forbidding themselves to speak any word unrelated to their learning. Their paramount concern, in fact, was with matters of speech. They took it upon themselves to be especially cautious in avoiding any sort of gossip or slander, and to distance themselves from those who did engage in these practices.

A little later, Anshel expanded the group's goals to include an operation that he dubbed *Tovas Ayin.* The members struggled hard against the jealousy and divisiveness that besets so many communities. In its first stages, they tried to view others' success without envy. In the next stage, they sought to uproot their egos completely. For example, one student might labor for hours or days over an original *devar Torah,* then hand it over to someone else — who would recite it as if it were his own, while the actual author didn't blink an eye.

They aspired to great heights, and they nearly succeeded. The "Va'ad," as it was known, became a symbol of integrity in the yeshivah. Sadly, however, the group dispersed as its members married. Family life was not conducive to the kinds of goals they had in mind, at least not in an organized fashion.

Anshel Pfeffer was the only one who promised himself that the *Va'ad Hashomrim* would never leave him. He turned away from the routine and the habitual, imposing ever more stringent practices on himself. " Man was born to toil," was his motto. A person is not born into this world in order to indulge himself in good food and luxurious sleep. He was born in order to work — hard. Wasn't this world only the entrance to the next? In that case, if he didn't prepare adequately he would find himself barefoot and naked in the Eternal World.

"Imagine," Rav Anshel would tell his students. "We're investing all our energies in worrying about this world, for a matter of 70 years or so. In the end, we'll all pass on. Out of every four people, four will die."

His voice soared. "What will we do in the Eternal World? For eternity — endless years — we will be poor. What kind of sense does that make? We've got our heads on backwards! All we're busy thinking about is getting away to the beach for a swim and a little sunbathing!"

For a while, the students would feel inspired. Gradually, however, routine would encroach on their fervor, dissipating it. In his heart, Rav Anshel yearned for the old days of the *Va'ad Hashomrim,* and dreamed of opening a yeshivah of his own run along the same lines. He would personally groom 10 top boys to become the next generation's *gedolei hador,* men of piety and uprightness who would be embarrassed to stand beside the great luminaries of 200 or 400 years ago.

Rav Anshel also dreamed of making a good match for his oldest daughter, Ayala — a girl of many fine qualities. She was an excellent student, noble in her bearing and in her behavior. The father awaited the day when he would see her engaged to a truly superior young man.

In his vocabulary, "superior" meant a thorough grounding in all of *Shas,* a great breadth of knowledge in every aspect of Torah learning, and a soaring ambition for personal growth. He could spot a true *ben Torah* when he met one, and knew the value of the kind of marriage such a man could lead with his wife. He wished nothing less for his daughter than a spiritual *Gan Eden* in this world.

Rav Anshel did not have the wherewithal to buy the young couple a three-bedroom apartment in Bnei Brak or Jerusalem, and he certainly could not afford what was known in yeshivah circles as *"siddur malei"* — meaning, apart from the apartment, the purchase of all its furnishings, a wedding with all the fixings, and other lordly gifts.

As long as Shlomo Zalman Pfeffer was alive, Rav Anshel's children had lacked for nothing. The devoted father handed over half his monthly income to the son who had dedicated himself to a life of Torah. In recent years, however, the fortunes of "Hecht Carpentry"had been undergoing a reversal. What had been chic in Tel Aviv in the '40s and '50s was old and humdrum in the '90s. Modern furniture factories were replacing the old, sturdy carpentry shops. Furniture was fast becoming — like everything else these days — instant, disposable, and cheap. Buyers were more interested in cutting costs than in solid workmanship. To his sorrow, Shlomo Zalman Pfeffer had witnessed the heavy inroads made by modern competition. His business was fighting for its life.

With Shlomo Zalman's passing, "Hecht's Carpentry" passed on, too. And from that day, the Pfeffer family in Jerusalem began to taste poverty in earnest. They subsisted meagerly, and with difficulty, on Rav Anshel's yeshivah salary and on *Bituach Leumi* (National Insurance) stipends for the children. Breina was a thrifty housewife who managed to spend what money they had wisely, shopping assiduously for the nicest clothing at rock-bottom prices. "Thriftiness, not stinginess," was her motto. Due to her efforts, the Pfeffer family still enjoyed a reasonable quality of life.

But, reasonable or not, what a leap from this to marrying a daughter off well, especially with nine brothers and sisters waiting their turn after her! This was completely beyond Rav Anshel's capabilities, or even those of his thrifty wife.

Rav Anshel was a realistic man. He did not deal in false hopes. He knew that he would have to set aside his dreams of a son-in-law who stood head and shoulders above the rest, and settle for what was available: a good boy, a good learner, and a *mechutan* who would be willing to divide the cost of a modest apartment in one of the new developmental towns.

And still, the dreams would flare up in him from time to time, forcing the words of a heartfelt prayer onto his lips: *"Oy, Ribbono shel Olam,* maybe a miracle can happen. Maybe I could win the lottery. Maybe my Ayala could marry a true *ilui* one day." He would try to choke down the wish even before he thought it, lest the price of his disappointment prove too steep.

But today, something had happened.

It had begun with the young driver who picked him up in the rain.

"Where do you know me from?" Rav Anshel had asked curiously.

"Ah!" The young man's eyes burned. " I have the honor of speaking to one of the best-known *talmidei chachamim* in Yerushalayim. Who is Rav Anshel Pfeffer? What a question!"

"No flattery, please," Rav Anshel murmured. "Really, how do you know me?"

The youth laughed. He drew a yellowed paper from his suit pocket. "Do you recognize this?" he asked, spreading it open in front of his guest. Rav Anshel's eyes widened.

8

av Anshel's eyes opened even wider as he recognized the document. It was a declaration he'd written along with his *Va'ad Hashomrim* some 22 years earlier. The statement was dated the 23rd day of Sivan, 5734, in Jerusalem.

In the presence of all members of the "Va'ad Hashomrim" :

We have gathered here, all 22 members, after deliberations that have lasted a day, a night, and a day.

Two years ago, with Hashem's help, we established the "Va'ad Hashomrim. "With thanks to the Creator, we have seen that he who comes forward to purify himself is helped from Above. We have succeeded in establishing a committee devoted to improving our characters through introspection, refraining from slander and gossip, and strengthening our ability to view others favorably and without envy. We have guarded not only our tongues from evil, but also our eyes as well as our thoughts and motivations — in the most stringent ways possible. We are continuing into the next stage of our efforts — that is, to be like servants who toil for their master with no desire to receive a reward; for example, to perform a good deed for someone who has done us wrong.

Knowing the power of the evil inclination, and knowing how it will try to pull us away into different directions after we marry, we have decided to sign this letter obligating each and every one of us to continue, bli neder, to observe everything we have managed to observe as a group, after we marry as well.

The letter was signed by Asher Anshel Pfeffer, leader of the group. His signature was followed by that of the 21 other members.

◆ ◆ ◆

"Where did you get that?" Anshel shouted. He kissed the page, tears flowing. "There were only 22 copies made. My own copy was lost years ago, when we moved."

"And did you do what you promised to do in the letter?" the youth asked, evading the question.

Rav Anshel sighed. "Heaven is my witness. Every day that I don't walk in the path I forged as a young yeshivah boy burns me up inside. I was better then than I am today."

"Rav Anshel," the young man said energetically, "I want to make a suggestion. But I need to ask you to keep it strictly confidential. Don't tell a soul."

"Well?" Rav Anshel was curious.

"Why don't you open a yeshivah for outstanding *bachurim,* like this *Va'ad Hashomrim* of yours."

"A wonderful fantasy." Rav Anshel waved a dismissive hand. "I appreciate the suggestion. You probably know the son of one of the people who signed this letter. But I think you're chasing a dream. I don't have a penny to my name."

"But I do." He turned the wheel, expertly making his third circuit of the block in the pouring rain. "Or rather, my father does. He's a rich man. He has a high-tech factory in the Western Galil. With his *ma'aser* money alone, he could support a yeshivah."

"You're a professional fantasizer!" Rav Anshel cried. "All right —

enough. Do me a favor and take me to the yeshivah already. I'm late for *Shacharis.*"

"Rav Anshel! You won't regret this. There's a good chance that such a yeshivah can be opened, and I want you to head it. There'll be plenty of money, believe me. You'll even be able to provide everything you want for your daughter."

He had struck gold.

Rav Anshel was thunderstruck. This boy had certainly done his homework. Where did he get his nerve?

"Who are you?" Rav Anshel demanded.

The young driver stopped the car. Turning to look deeply into Rav Anshel's eyes, he said, "I'm Mark Goldenblum's son."

"Aha! Your father is the famous millionaire Goldenblum, who owns Gold Hi-Tech?"

"That's the one," the driver said. "Just one small correction. He's my adoptive father. My name is not Goldenblum, it's Flamm. Eli Flamm."

◆ ◆ ◆

Night fell on Gaza.

It was a wintry night, cold and damp. A strip of light, miles long, zigzagged through the dark sky to the accompaniment of a mighty explosion equivalent to thousands of tons of TNT. Immediately, a heavy rain began to fall. Large droplets fell forcefully, then bounced up from the ground to meet their brothers. All was a chaos of water mingling with water.

A sunstruck city; a city of small fishing boats, tangled orchards, hills of sand, twisted streets and alleys. Israel saw the place as a nest of trouble, and had departed after years of bloodstained rule. Gaza was turned over to Arafat's Palestinian Authority, who began building the city anew.

On this dreary night, the streets were empty. Most of the shops had locked their doors before their usual closing time of 7 p.m. Gaza was plunged into another night of tedium and hatred.

Issam Abu Rabia stuck his head out the door of his small grocery store for a minute to watch the play of the storm in the sky. His hair was instantly soaked. As soon as the rain let up a little, he would close up shop. No one would be coming here tonight. Even without the rain there were few customers — perhaps 10 people had stopped into his store that day. Contrary to all of Yassir Arafat's rosy promises, he thought sourly, conditions in Gaza had not improved a whit from what they had been under the Zionist oppressor. They were, in fact, much worse.

His sad-eyed gaze swept the shop. The place was attractive and well-stocked. Most of the products offered for sale were Arab in origin, though here and there some fine quality goods from the Israeli side were masked with an Arabic label.

The storm outside abated to a slow, gentle rain. Keys jangling in his hand, Issam went to switch off the lights and lock up for the night.

"Issam?"

A tall man stepped into the shop. He wore a genuine mink coat that glistened wetly — the kind of coat rarely glimpsed in Gaza. His face was intimidating: heavy black brows meeting in an almost unbroken line over eyes of dark brown, a crooked nose and mustache pointed at the ends, thin lips, and a swarthy complexion. Issam reacted to the sight of that face with pleasure.

"Ya, Yusuf my brother, welcome! How are you?" They embraced.

Yusuf Abu Rabia was Issam's younger brother. Since being deported from Israel along with hundreds of terrorists like himself, he had resided in Syria and Iran. Good luck had always followed Yusuf; he had attained great prosperity in Iran. This was his first visit back to Gaza since that city had passed into Palestinian control.

Yusuf studied his older brother. "Ya, Issam, it's good to see you. How is our father?"

"So-so. Such a pity our mother died without seeing you. What's the matter, did you miss our father too much?"

Yusuf boomed, "I missed all of you! But you, especially, Issam. I miss you the way I'd miss my right hand. I'll never forgot how you made a man of me."

They fell silent, letting memories of their childhood together wash over them. Two brothers out of a family of 10, a poor Gazan family. Everyone in the city hated the Israeli conqueror, but their father, Daoud Abu Rabia, hated them with a special fervor. He had deliberately raised a generation of terrorists. Four of his children — including one daughter — were killed in the course of various terrorist operations, two others were sentenced to life terms in Israeli prisons, and the rest were scattered in various countries. Only Issam had remained in Gaza, former terrorist turned struggling shopkeeper.

Yusuf looked at the shelves that had obviously been untouched by customers' hands for some time. Even the cartons of freshly baked bread were almost full.

"How's business, Issam? Never mind, I know the answer. The shelves are full and your eyes are empty," Yusuf said mournfully. Issam responded by bursting into hysterical tears. The two embraced again.

"What am I to do, my brother? My wife and children are hungry, and I am a beggar."

"I have a suggestion you won't be able to turn down," Yusuf told him.

Issam listened attentively to what his brother had to say.

◆ ◆ ◆

Two crazy days passed for Rav Anshel Pfeffer.

His students whispered that something must have happened in his home. What else would explain the fact that their eminent rebbi had turned into a dreamer? As long as he was delivering his *shiur* he managed to maintain his concentration; the minute the students began asking questions, he lost it.

One of his students launched a long, complicated query about the explanation of the *Taz* on a certain part of the Gemara. Rav Anshel watched him, nodding his head from time to time, and wondering why he could see the boy's lips moving but could make no sense of the words coming out of them. In his mind's eye he could see himself in front of a class of outstanding students in the yeshivah of his dreams. Not that there was anything wrong with the boys he was teaching now — each and every one of them was precious — but Eli Flamm had ignited his old aspiration."A yeshivah for the créme de la créme." The words called to him, and Rav Anshel responded to the call with a yearning that had lain dormant for 20 years. And, apart from the possibility of the yeshivah, a new window of hope had opened in regard to *shidduchim* for his children. Imagine, being able to make really respectable matches without financial worry!

It had all sounded like a foolish, young man's fantasy at first. Then, later that night, Eli Flamm's words had echoed and re-echoed in his head. Every craftsman knows his field, and Rav Anshel was expert at judging yeshivah boys. He understood their problems, loved their enthusiasm, participated in their agonies. He learned with the same youthful energy that his students invested in their own learning. "I'm a *yeshivah bachur* who happens to have also married, "he would joke about himself: a man of 45 whose mind was as youthful and whose spirit was as enthusiastic as a boy of 17. He sensed that Eli Flamm was cut from a different mold than most others. He was a superior young man, in the truest sense of the word. And now, this crazy proposal of his.

He had to hear more!

"Maybe it's a good idea to call him up, to ask exactly what he meant," he mused aloud.

"Call who? The *Taz*?" the bewildered student blurted. The other students glanced pointedly at one another, exchanging smiles and winks. Rav Anshel closed his eyes for a moment, then said, "Repeat the question, please."

This time, he provided the necessary answer, and the class moved on. Still, the students knew something was up. Rav Anshel walked and thought, ate and thought, even — to his sorrow — prayed and thought. He thought about the young man who had succeeded in bewitching him in one short meeting.

After two days of hesitation, his resolve to get in touch with Eli Flamm solidified. But trying to put that resolve into action proved more difficult than he had anticipated. He knew that Flamm was learning in Yeshivas Vilna in Jerusalem, but Eli's friends told him that Eli had not been seen around the yeshivah in several days.

He waited in vain for Eli to call.

Four days of doubt and anxiety ate away at Rav Anshel's nerves. Finally, he succumbed and looked up the Goldenblum's home number in Jerusalem. His face lit up as he heard the phone ring, then fell as the cleaning woman answered.

"There's no one home," she informed him.

"When will they be back?"

"I don't know." She hung up.

◆ ◆ ◆

The phone rang —10 times.

Rav Anshel jumped up at the ninth ring. He had been so absorbed in what he was learning that the sound hadn't penetrated till then. "Hello?"

"Rav Pfeffer?" asked a familiar voice. "Eli Flamm!"

"I've been waiting. What happened?"

Eli sounded hesitant. "I can't go into details. Tomorrow you'll receive a letter stating specifically where we will meet." He sounded as dispassionate as if he were concluding some business with the postal service.

In anyone else, such an arrogant and disrespectful tone would have caused Rav Anshel to hang up at once. But he recognized in Eli Flamm a refined character, not given to such displays. He must have a reason for this behavior.

"You sound mysterious," Rav Anshel said mildly. " What's all the secrecy about?"

"Rav Pfeffer, don't ask me now. When we meet in person, you'll understand everything." Gently, the receiver was cradled.

Eli Flamm was a young man of gentleness — and courage. He had captured Rav Anshel's heart from the first. He possessed unusual qualities, true, but the teacher found it hard to pinpoint exactly what it was that he liked so much about Flamm. There was a sharpness of wit combined with a certain purity, even innocence; practical sense alongside a soaring idealism. These contradictions confused Rav Anshel, and intrigued him.

Tomorrow he would receive the letter, Eli had promised. Who would have believed that, four days ago, he had not even known Eli Flamm — and now he waited impatiently for the chance to meet him again.

His yeshivah for superior students might actually become a reality!

9

As promised, the letter arrived next day — hand delivered. Eli Flamm, apparently, placed no great reliance on the postal service.

The letter's contents were brief:

I am in a settlement called Tzofnat, in the western Galil. Rechov Harakefet.

Eli Flamm.

Rav Anshel debated the matter long and hard. Was it right to abandon his students for a full day, in pursuit of a fanciful project? His real-life students stood on a scale opposite his imaginary future ones — and the future ones triumphed. Rav Anshel went.

The western Galil offers some of the most breathtaking views in all of Israel. Rav Anshel drank in the meadows and forests, the wooded valleys, winding roads, and rolling hills, and silently blessed Eli Flamm for dragging him out of his routine and up to this part of the country. To his good fortune, the day was clear, with no sign of the rain that had poured down for the past several days. It was possible to see for miles through the crystal air.

Tzofnat was a small, pretty settlement. Scores of shingled roofs dotted the central hill like wildflowers. Rav Anshel wandered through the terraced streets and among the picturesque cottages, searching for Rechov Harakefet. At length, just past a flowering playground filled with children sliding and swinging in delighted abandon, he found it. The first house he saw was a two-storied structure, surrounded by beds of brightly colored chrysanthemums and petunias.

Eli Flamm was waiting for him.

He opened the door at the first knock, clearly impatient to greet his guest. For the first time, Rav Anshel saw him fully and clearly: a face that radiated goodwill; intelligent, smiling eyes; a wiry build dressed in clothes that were in the best of taste, neither too flashy nor too plain. "Thank you for coming," Eli exclaimed in open joy. "And please accept my apologies for dragging you all the way up here."

"Because of you," Rav Anshel answered, smiling, "I've had the privilege of seeing the beauty of the Galil once again. It is I who should be thanking you."

The front hall was lined with pictures of famous American *roshei yeshivah* and a large oil portrait of the Chafetz Chaim. Rav Anshel walked across a beautiful oriental rug and gazed with pleasure upon delicate ceramic figurines and exquisite wood cuttings. This was clearly the home of a rich man, one who possessed excellent taste in art. Though the weather outside the large windows was cold, inside all was snug, with warmth radiating from the large, built-in fireplace.

"This isn't our regular home. We live in Yerushalayim," Eli explained apologetically. "My father stays here for long periods, though, to keep an eye on the factory. He's here now."

"And why are *you* here, so far from Yerushalayim?" Rav Anshel asked.

Instead of answering, Eli asked a question of his own. "Do you know anything about high-tech?"

"Not a thing."

"Then I'd like to invite you to come with me to my father's factory. I think you'll be surprised." Eli issued the invitation with an enthusiasm that brooked no refusal.

◆ ◆ ◆

"Izzadim-el-Kassam, the Islamic Jihad, the Palestinian Authority — forget about them! You can throw them all in the garbage. Their imagination is limited. All they can think of is suicide bombings, 20 or 30 casualties. They're babies."

"Issam Abu Rabia bit his lip to contain his rising anger. This was his first meeting with members of the Hizballah, and already he despised them. He found these men insufferably conceited and hard. They were presently meeting in the huge basement of Issam's house in Gaza's Shiekh Raduan neighborhood. He had turned it over to the Hizballah at his brother Yusuf's request — in return for $10,000 in crisp green bills.

Ten men sat in comfortable eastern-style armchairs, sipping sweet coffee or spicy tea from small enameled mugs. The speaker was Mahmud Talel Nedir, a giant of a man with enormous, iron-hard muscles. After dismissing Yassir Arafat as "backward," Talel attacked the Islamic Jihad and its military arm. " The way they're going, we won't be free of the Zionists even a hundred years from now," he shouted. "Arafat is worried only about his bank account and does nothing practical. His people are good friends with the Israelis. Something else is needed — something big!"

Issam shook with rage, causing drops of hot coffee to spill onto his hand and the carpet. He set down the cup and leaped to his feet. "How are you talking about Yassir?" he cried, ignoring his brother's frantic signals to sit down and be quiet. No one was going to tell him how to think in his own house! "Yassir is smarter than any of you," he continued vehemently. "You'll do something wild and you'll fail. He'll finish off the Israelis with wisdom. A few more years and there'll be no more Israel, you'll see!"

The 10 men stared at him without speaking. Issam gathered renewed confidence from their silence. "You, Hizballah, what do you know how to do? Another ambush in Lebanon, another hand grenade. You're not serious!"

A balding man with a face more refined than the rest cut him off coldly. "And just what will Yassir Arafat do to finish off the Israelis?"

Issam recognized Faud Halil. He had known for some time that Halil was a Hizballah man, as did his friends in the Palestinian Authority police, but Arafat had chosen to ignore that fact. Halil and his cohorts moved freely about Gaza with no interference.

"Just you wait," Issam said proudly. "The first thing he'll do is accept, on a silver platter, everything that Israel gives him. Why waste energy when you can easily take it?"

"And after that?" Halil goaded.

"He'll get East Jerusalem, will establish his capital there, and will declare a Palestinian state."

"And after *that*?"

"What's the matter with you, Faud?" Issam flashed. " You keep repeating the words " And after that?' like some sort of senile parrot. After that, we wipe out the State of Israel. That's what!"

"How?"

"Once Jerusalem is ours, we'll destroy the Jews easily."

Faud Halil's voice was cold as ice. "How?"

At last Issam fell silent. How, in fact? Israel had a powerful and well-trained army and air force, and the atom bomb. It also had a population that could devour itself in strife during peacetime, but it would stand together in awesome unity against a common enemy — the unity of the Jews was an incomparable secret weapon.

Halil laughed, victorious. "Issam is quiet because he has nothing to say."

"And what would you suggest?" Issam asked between clenched teeth.

Faud Halil stood up from his armchair and made a fist for all to see.

"*Har Habayit*," he said quietly.

◆ ◆ ◆

Gold High-Tech did surprise Rav Anshel Pfeffer. He had never been in a plant devoted to the production of higher technology, and had expected the roar of machinery to assault his eardrums from as far as a mile away. The silence he encountered — instead — astonished Rav Anshel, and made him suspect for a moment that Eli was trying to trick him.

The building itself was impressive, six stories high and sprawling over thousands of square feet. The outside of the structure was encased in smooth, white stone. On the roof was a tall, circular dish antenna. Rav Anshel's curious gaze spotted a lookout on the roof. Why would a factory need guards?

They entered the facility through the front gate, using Eli's magnetic identity card. Rav Anshel glanced at his watch. It was lunchtime. Apparently, the workers were all off duty; that would account for the uncanny silence.

At the door of the building itself, two guards stopped them and instituted a thorough security search, not exempting even their employer's son. "They have to do it," Eli explained as he pulled a metal comb from his pocket to silence the beeping of the security scanner. "This place is classified."

"What do they make here — bombs?" Rav Anshel joked.

"Other things that have to be guarded: computer components, electronic parts, microprocessors."

Rav Anshel admitted, "It's Turkish to me."

"I can explain everything to you, but it's probably a good idea to visit the plant first." They crossed a narrow hall and rode an elevator up two floors.

"Now we enter the factory itself?" Rav Anshel asked.

"Forget that; the production floor is off limits. We can view it from up here."

"Why all the secrecy?"

Eli didn't answer. They entered a side room in which one entire wall was transparent glass on one side and a one-way mirror on the other — the factory — side.

"Avi, I've brought a guest," Eli said to a pleasant-faced man who stood by the glass watching the workers on the floor below. In addition, four closed-circuit monitors mounted nearby disclosed everything that was happening in the production line. From time to time the cameras would zoom in for a close-up of some worker's hands manipulating a minute electronic part.

"Welcome," the man said, without removing his eyes from the monitors. "You're a friend of Eli's?"

"He's an important rabbi from Yerushalayim," Eli said, disregarding Rav Anshel's dismissive gesture. "I wanted to show him what a high-tech plant is like. Rav Pfeffer, meet Avi Goshen, work supervisor at Gold High-Tech."

The two men shook hands. Avi Goshen tore his eyes away from the monitor screens, but continued to glance down at the production floor through the window.

"Do the workers know that you're watching them?" Rav Anshel asked with interest.

"Naturally."

"But how can they work that way? Doesn't it bother them to be under constant scrutiny?"

Avi Goshen pointed at Rav Anshel's black hat and said mildly, "You are obviously a religious man, as I am. We are also under constant scrutiny. "An Eye sees and an Ear hears and all your deeds are recorded in a book. '"

"You're right," Rav Anshel nodded, although several questions still remained in his mind.

They watched the floor. Dozens of workers, dressed in pale-blue smocks and sterile masks, handled tiny components and operated machines. Black elastic lines separated the rows of workers from gleaming mechanical arms. "Computerized robots," Eli explained. Rav Anshel finally understood the silence. The plant's machines were robots, exacting, efficient, and quiet.

A man in white strode onto the production floor, exuding authority. He passed among the workers, exchanging a few words with each. The mask he wore could not conceal the friendly relations he enjoyed with them.

"That's my father," Eli said with a modest smile. "He's a good boss, and the workers like him. He's never fired a single one. Despite his easy-going approach, none of his employees has ever caused him trouble."

"What do you manufacture here?" Rav Anshel asked.

Avi Goshen pointed at one of the monitors, which showed a worker handing a minuscule electronic part to one of the robots. The robotic arm accepted the component, swiveling around to place it on a gray transistor board. The arm then pressed the part into the board in a circular motion, like a screwdriver. One of the mechanical fingers ran two electric wires to the attached component and away from it. The entire procedure was an exercise in precision, and took just seconds.

"That's the answer to your question about the supervision," Avi Goshen smiled. "The truth is that I'm not responsible for the workers' output as much as for coordinating it. Everything is automated or semi-automated, but hitches can crop up. My job is to prevent the hitches." He paused. "As for what we make here — all kinds of things, including electronic parts for Israel's industrial-security sector. From here, the components pass on to computer and digital equipment plants. The specific part you just watched, for example, is called a microprocessor."

"Invented, no doubt, by a tiny academic called a Micro Professor," Rav Anshel quipped, making Eli and Avi laugh.

They parted with another friendly handshake all around, but not before Avi explained a little more about the sophisticated production line below. Rav Anshel offered several insightful comments, leading Avi to murmur, "A pity such talent is wasted." The comment brought a sharp rejoinder from Rav Anshel about the critical role of Torah study in the upkeep of the world, and the true nature of "wasted talents." Eli and the rabbi rode back to Tzofnat in Mark Goldenblum's BMW.

Eli drove. Both were silent, immersed in thought. Finally, Rav Anshel turned to Eli and asked, "So tell me, why have you dragged me up to the Galil?"

Eli turned the wheel and carefully negotiated a turn. "I wanted you to see my father's plant. It's the pride of the Galil, with 180 high-tech employees who were desperate for work before we came here."

"Did you think I wouldn't believe you?"

"I didn't think — I knew." Eli had driven this route many times before, but his eyes never left the road. "A perfect stranger comes along with a proposal — why should you believe him? Now I hope you'll weigh that proposal in a new light. Hearing is never as strong as seeing with your own eyes. Now you've seen for yourself that Mark Goldenblum is on a sound financial footing. There's a basis for establishing a yeshivah."

"True," Rav Anshel said, raking his beard with his fingers until it stood out in all directions. He glanced out the window at the passing wooded hills gleaming in the sun. "You picked a good spot. Against a background like this, everything seems rosier. It's so peaceful and quiet."

Eli nodded, but didn't answer. Presently he pulled over to the side of the road. The two sat for a moment in silence, listening to the call of wild birds in the woods. The Galil's spell was powerful.

When Eli spoke, his voice was low. "The yeshivah, under your leadership, will be something really special. I've already located the perfect area in the hills outside Jerusalem — a place with a stunning view. Rav Anshel, my father has promised to support the budget fully. There are 30 excellent boys waiting impatiently for you. Come with us to build a bridge to the next world."

On the bus back to Jerusalem, Rav Anshel replayed Eli's parting words. They brought him to the brink of tears. It wasn't a fantasy, after all! It was no illusion, no dream. He was going to establish a yeshivah that had no equal — a yeshivah for the truly superior and spiritually aspiring student.

Eli watched the departing bus until it disappeared down the highway. "If Rav Anshel knew the whole truth..." he thought sadly. Then he shrugged. " But what he doesn't know can't hurt him."

10

A score of inflamed Arab youths hurled stones and burning bottles at the Israeli soldiers. Hebron's shops were locked, hidden behind their heavy metal grilles. Clear plastic masks protected the soldiers' faces from the fumes. Rubber bullets had little effect on the advancing teenagers, led by Mazuk Osman, a 19-year-old firebrand.

Osman incited his cohorts with repeated battle cries. Glimpsing a spark of fear in the soldiers' eyes, he was roused to greater heights. Under his encouragement, the youths moved closer, the constantly flying stones acting as their advance guard.

Some 20 yards away, the street led into a narrow, winding alley. The alley appeared deserted; it was not. There, behind a pile of fallen stones from a semiruined building, several of Osman's friends crouched in ambush. Armed with small but powerful explosives, they waited for an Israeli soldier to unwittingly appear at the end of the alleyway.

The mob moved closer. Four youths, injured by the flying rubber bullets, were moved to the side, screaming with pain. The rest pressed on. The noise of their shouts was deafening.

The Israeli captain spoke urgently into his communicator. "We're in danger!" he insisted. With a face like a sweet child's, he looked far too young to be in his present predicament. But his commanding officer was adamant: the men were forbidden to use live ammunition unless the danger was imminent.

The young-looking captain gritted his teeth and gestured to his men to continue defending themselves with rubber bullets. The mob was now just a short distance away.

Under a protective umbrella of flying stones, it moved even closer. The Israeli captain stepped into the mouth of the alley, leveling his gun. Suddenly, from behind him, a figure shot out of ambush. He threw something at the Israeli and tore back inside the alley.

With an ear-splitting crack, the explosive went off at the captain's feet. He fell heavily, badly injured. Producing a steady hail of rubber bullets to screen them from the hostile Arabs, the soldiers ran to where their fallen leader lay in a spreading pool of blood. Two of his men dragged him to a more sheltered spot.

On the roof of an adjoining building, an Israeli media team was busy recording the entire episode — a reporter scribbling furiously while his companion — a younger man, wearing a small black yarmulke — worked a video camera. His face twisted at the sight below. All at once, he flung the camera straps off his shoulder. "Enough already! We have to help him!"

The reporter tore his eyes away from the small notebook in which he had been jotting down details of the scene, and grabbed the photographer's shoulder. " Chemi, where are you going?"

Chemi shook off the restraining hand. "Leave me alone, Tzachi! I'm a paramedic. I'm going down there to help that soldier!"

The reporter, whose full name was Yitzchak, tightened his grip. "You're not going anywhere! Pick up your camera and get on with the filming. You're a photographer, not a nurse."

With a mighty shrug, Chemi shook off the other's hand and cried, "You should be ashamed of yourself, Tzachi! That wounded boy could be your son. I should stand here filming when I could be saving someone's life? Look at those young soldiers down there. They're near hysteria. In the state they're in, they're not going to be able to apply the most basic elements of first aid. He's going to die!"

The reporter's chest heaved angrily as he shouted, "What I care about right now is my story. You idiot, you're ruining the scoop of the year! Not even CNN was able to get a photographer out here today."

But Chemi wasn't listening; he was already running down the steps.

Muttering furiously, Tzachi picked up the camera and began operating it himself. To his rage, the focus had been lost and all his efforts could not locate it again. "You'll pay for this!" he screamed at the steps, as he tried again and again to work the camera.

Meanwhile, Chemi burst through the door into the blazing sun. Surprised, none of the mob had the presence of mind to throw a stone his way. He darted toward the knot of soldiers and, as the Israelis kept up the barrage of rubber bullets to hold off the mob, he knelt by the injured man. He was instantly splattered with the blood that spurted from the young leader. Quickly and efficiently, Chemi tied two arterial tourniquets. Thanks to his swift reaction, the young captain's life was saved.

His heroism was of no use to him at all when, two days later, he was called into his employer's office and informed that he was fired.

Chemi (Nechemiah) Maimon — in the opinions of those who knew him, and in his own opinion as well — was a rising star in the field of electronic communications in Israel. Being fired was a severe blow to his ego and wreaked havoc with his family life. He appealed the decision to the administration of the station that he worked for. When no response was forthcoming, he turned to the courts. The matter was endlessly postponed and delayed. No one else offered to hire him.

Chemi sat at home, a prey to gloom and dejection. With eyes welling, he asked himself for the thousandth time, "What happened?"

He reached for a tissue. "It's 8 a.m. The whole world is leaving for work. Only Chemi Maimon is sitting at home." He was frustrated and angry, hurt and depressed, near despair.

It was about an hour later that the phone rang. Chemi snatched it up. "Hello?"

"Good morning, Chemi. We know everything about you." The voice was deep and soothing. "We believe that an injustice was done to you."

Chemi was instantly suspicious. "Who is this?"

"Call me Dekel. I have a surprising proposal for you, Chemi. It would be worth your while for us to meet."

"When?" Chemi had nothing to lose.

"At 8 o'clock tonight."

The deep voice was mesmerizing, calming. Chemi agreed to the meeting.

◆ ◆ ◆

"Do you want to rise to great heights?" Eli Flamm asked.

"What?" Yoel Goldfinger stared at him.

"Do you want to be a really aspiring *ben Torah*? By that, I mean a person who's prepared to forget about the rest of the world — whose desire to grow and rise spiritually is not just part of his identity, but his *whole* identity!"

"I understand the term," Yoel said. "You just surprised me with the question."

The two were talking in a clearing among the trees near the yeshivah. From time to time, a half-moon peeked from behind the clouds, bathing the students' heads with silvery radiance. Eli had already signed up 30 boys who were interested in attending the new yeshivah he hoped to found, but he would not rest until he'd recruited *the* genius of his yeshivah. There was no one who better fit the description of the type of student Rav Anshel Pfeffer was looking for than Yoel Goldfinger. Knowing this, Eli had decided to try to ensnare Yoel in with a series of provocative questions.

But Yoel was proving to be a hard nut to crack. He responded to each of Eli's questions with one of his own.

"What exactly is a yeshivah for aspiring students?"

Eli leaned against a cypress tree and said, "It's a furnace for creating the next generation's *gedolei hador.*"

"And without your yeshivah there won't be any *gedolim* in the next generation?"

"Look, Yoel," Eli said earnestly. "We're all products of our generation — the instant, silicon, digital generation. We've forgotten what it means to really delve into something. We're too caught up in the present, too tied into cell phones and beepers. The yeshivah we want to start will be located in a remote settlement in the hills, far from civilization, almost without transportation or communication with the world outside. Someone who wants to forget that world will be able to do it there, easily. Someone who wants to learn till he drops — two days at a stretch or more, like the Steipler did, and Rav Chaim Shmulevitz — can do it!"

He paused for breath, but Yoel stopped him. "Don't get so excited. I assure you, the regular yeshivos are producing great *bnei Torah* without any tricks, without hiding in the hills. Right here in the heart of the city, with phones ringing and computers blinking and buses roaring and threats of war and terrorist bombs, the next century's Chafetz Chaim and Rabbi Akiva Eiger are learning just fine, *baruch Hashem.*"

Eli searched his mind for an answer, and came up with five possible ones. In the end, however, he kept quiet. He felt the words,"I have something to say but I'm not saying it," trembling on the tip of his tongue, then had to smile at the absurdity. As the two began walking tiredly back to the yeshivah, Eli said only one thing. "If you ever change your mind, you'll find the yeshivah's doors open for you."

Yoel shook his head. All the same, for days afterwards, he could not shake the impression that the light he had seen in Eli's face as they parted had been more than just a reflection of the moon.

◆ ◆ ◆

That particular winter morning did not start out differently from any other. Rafi Gamliel and his partner, Shalom Tzanani, made their third circuit of the Old City walls. Rafi had little confidence in the weapon he carried or the uniform he wore. The Israeli Defense Forces had lost much of its glamour. The Arabs sneered at its soldiers and engaged them without fear. During recent years, the soldiers themselves had become nervous and fearful. They watched each other's backs, eyes darting at every suspicious sound.

Rafi remembered strolling through the Old City's Arab *shuk* with his older brothers as a child of 10. In the period after the Six-Day War, such an excursion was routine and easy. They would bargain with the stall vendors, extracting packets of pencils from them at a third of the market price, ceramic pitchers and drums for ten *agurot,* fresh apricots and grapes for next to nothing. On the way home, they would kid around fearlessly with the small Arab boys playing in the streets.

"And today," Rafi sighed, "we're afraid that each hour will be our last. Hey, look at that guy over there. He looks suspicious."

An Arab youth in a black sweater was approaching them at a rapid clip, one hand hidden behind his back. His black eyes blazed with hatred. Tzanani pointed his gun at the youth and called out for him to stop.

The Arab's reaction was too swift for the eye to follow. The hidden hand shot out from behind his back, and hurled a bottle at them. It was a clear bottle, in which a small blue flame flickered. The bottle missed the two soldiers by inches, landing on the pavement near their feet with a mighty flare of fire. The acrid smell of benzene filled the air. The Israelis leapt back.

"Did you see that burning bottle?" Rafi cried. "It nearly scorched us!"

Even as he spoke, his legs were pumping with all their might in pursuit of the Arab. Twenty seconds later, the chase was over. The Arab youth lay pinned on the ground, the two soldiers frisking him for weapons.

In a reaction to their fear, the Israelis punched and kicked the prone youth mercilessly. A newspaper photographer snapped pictures of the soldiers beating the young Arab, as well as photos of the Arab's limp figure sprawled helplessly on the ground. The photographer conveniently neglected to include any pictures of the burning bottle.

The next day, a nationwide furor arose over the beating. The Israeli media were quick to condemn the two soldiers, dragging "public opinion" along after them. Spokespeople from the far left made many pompous speeches that were faithfully broadcast and printed in the media. Rafi Gamliel and Shalom Tzanani were sentenced to prison terms of a year and a half each, plus community service. But the important part came after their release.

Tzanani, through family ties to an influential government figure, managed to overcome the stigma attached to his name and to rejoin society. But Rafi Gamliel had no such pull.

Six months after his release from prison, Rafi found himself in a situation very similar to that of photographer Chemi Maimon: out of work and shunned by his peers.

A deep voice, identifying itself as "Dekel," spoke to him over the phone and invited him to a meeting at 8 o'clock that night.

Rafi Gamliel was only the second name on "Dekel's" list.

11

The copper tray gleamed in the candlelight. Ten cups of strong black coffee were arranged on it, covering the decorative pattern in the center.

For Daoud Abu Rabia and his sons, the tray was a prized possession. Daoud had inherited it from his grandfather, Sufyan Abu Rabia, who bought it in Mecca's antique market on his pilgrimage to that city some hundred years before. Sufyan had had an active imagination, and he would while away the hours traveling back to Gaza on camelback, weaving stories about how the tray had passed from the "Prophet's" own hands to the Mecca market place.

Sufyan's descendants embroidered the story after him, until they believed that the Prophet Mohammed had drunk only from cups proferred to him on that tray. The women of the family contributed their share by keeping the "holy tray" polished to a high gloss. It was used to serve important guests.

Only the tray's holy status prevented Issam Abu Rabia from flinging it and its contents at Mahmud Talel Nedir's head. Issam had never been so angry in his life.

"That is blasphemy!" he shouted, the veins protruding in his neck. "You are a man without principles. I will stop you from carrying out your evil plan. Israel must be destroyed — true. But there is a limit to what we should pay for that goal. Your price is too high!"

Talel Nedir remained impassive. His cold eyes raked Issam's crimson face for a moment. Then he turned to Yusuf Abu Rabia. "Your older brother."

Yusuf leaped out of his chair. "Yes!"

"Make sure he causes us no problems," Talel said mildly. "You might offer him some water right now, to help him calm down."

Yusuf all but dragged Issam from the room and escorted him to his bedroom.

"Has the fool quieted down?" Talel asked upon Yusuf's return.

"Sssh," Yusuf beseeched, a finger to his lips. "He might hear you."

"Let him hear! Advise your brother to stick with sensible people. Maybe that way, he'll be cured of his idiocy." Talel spoke in a voice deliberately loud. "We're dealing with serious matters, and that little fool takes it upon himself to scold me! I'm as zealous a Moslem as he is, and more! But it is sometimes necessary to sacrifice that which is most holy and precious."

"For the sake of the ultimate goal," Faud Halil breathed reverently.

Another conspirator, Faouzi Ajimi, whispered, "With all respect to this marvelous plan -- how is it possible to carry it out? It's not practical."

"Meaning?" Talel's manner was mild, but his eyes appraised the speaker carefully. Was Ajimi going to cause problems, too?

Ajimi wiped beads of perspiration from his brow, answering nervously, "Who will volunteer for such a filthy task? Every Moslem would react the way Issam just did."

To his relief, Talel did not get angry. He merely threw Ajimi a cold, disdainful look, and snapped, "We have many brave volunteers among the noble Arab nation. However, as always, there is no one who could do the job better than — the Jews themselves!"

◆ ◆ ◆

Akiva Tamiri's life was divided into two distinct periods: the period up until the age of 12, and the one after.

His father, Yossi Tamiri, was a skilled electrician who earned a respectable living for his wife and six children. A warm and emotional father to all his children, Tamiri was especially close to Akiva, his oldest. Father and son shared many a long talk, in which Yossi would open gates in Akiva's young mind. Neither Akiva nor his siblings knew just how happy they were until the black day, in Akiva's 12th year, when their father failed to come home.

His tardiness in returning from work that evening roused an ominous sense of dread in Mrs. Tamiri. She was fearfully reciting *Tehillim* when the phone rang, its shrill sounding just like a raven's cry. One of the children answered, but the caller wanted to speak specifically with their mother. They saw her grow pale in the space of a second, and needed no words of explanation. The heart already knew.

Yossi Tamiri had been electrocuted while replacing the wiring system in someone's apartment. He was a careful and professional worker, but a neighbor had mistakenly turned on the main electrical current at the moment Yossi was touching wires with unprotected hands.

It took the family a long time to recover from the tragedy. Akiva never really recovered. He had inherited his emotional nature from his father. He remained raw and wounded, sorely missing his best friend. Twelve-year-old Akiva could not be comforted.

He knew what was to blame in his father's death. Electricity! Electricity had killed his beloved father. From the time of his father's death, Akiva would run in a rage to switch off any electrical appliance that happened to be running, and to turn off the lights in the house.

"Abba died because his time had come. The electricity was only the means," his mother tried to explain. She was afraid of what she saw happening to her oldest son — this pathological hatred of anything electrical in particular, and of modernization in general. But Akiva would not listen. He believed with all his heart that electricity was a bad thing, a thing that produced only pain, a curse. In the boy's mind, the word "electricity" became synonymous with death.

This marked the beginning of the second period in Akiva's life — the "primitive period," in the terminology of the psychiatrists who attempted to swerve the boy from his fixation. Akiva would ride only on bicycles, would read at night only by candlelight, and would not listen to music from any electrical device. Every trip involved a prolonged tug of war with his mother before Akiva would grudgingly agree to ride in a bus or car. Mrs. Tamiri resigned herself to waiting, believing that time would accomplish what reason could not. With the passage of time would come the inevitable lessening of the pain, and that surely would turn the tide for Akiva.

She was wrong. The older her son grew, the stronger grew his love of the simple, old-fashioned life. He longed to live in the bosom of nature, as his forefathers had done before him. "If I could only establish a settlement in the hills, surrounded by woods, without electricity or running water, I would be happy," he would tell his friends.

They would nod as though they understood, then shake their heads slowly behind his back.

But these friends had other friends, and one day Akiva received a letter.

> *I've heard about you, and I agree with your views. Electricity and modernity are a curse. If you want to wake up every morning to the sound of birds singing and to live in the place of your dreams, in the bosom of nature, without electricity or running water, in a settlement in the hills far from civilization, with clear water and green trees — come meet with me tomorrow, at 8 p.m.*
>
> *Dekel*

◆ ◆ ◆

The final days before the yeshivah opened were a nightmare for Eli. He had no idea how many details were involved: office equipment and furniture, dormitory beds, kitchenware, transportation, housing for the teachers.... The list was endless.

The staff was still tiny. They had hired Rav Menashe Segal, a young and talented teacher, to be the *maggid shiur*. Rav Segal had already informed them that he intended to continue residing in Jerusalem, and that he would require transportation to and from the yeshivah each day. Rav Michoel Salzburg, the *mashgiach,* was a man his students had dubbed a "walking *Mesillas Yesharim.*" He, too, would remain in Jerusalem and commute in each day. As for Rav Anshel, he was still undecided, but was leaning toward a home close to the yeshivah.

"Ever since my visit to the Galil, I've had a great yearning for green scenery," he told Eli, as they drove from location to location searching for a suitable site for the yeshivah. "But this area is even more beautiful than the Galil."

"Beautiful? You'd have to travel far to find a place as primitive," Eli laughed.

"That's its whole beauty. It looks as though no man's hand has ever touched it."

After lengthy deliberations, they selected Anafim, a bucolic settlement in the heart of the Jerusalem hills, at the edge of the Ben Shemen forest. Anafim had been founded by a group of nature lovers in the '50s, eventually abandoned as a failed dream, then revived six years later by a group of 40 idealistic new immigrants from Michigan who wanted to till the holy soil of Israel with their own hands. This group of farmers had finally been defeated by the Israeli bureaucracy. For the past three years the place had been deserted — until Eli Flamm and Rav Anshel Pfeffer came along to rescue it.

Fortunately, the settlement was still connected to the country's electrical network. That, however, was the extent of its links to civilization. The homes were primitive stone structures, some without electricity or running water. But the breathtaking physical beauty of the place weighed heavily against these deficiencies. A natural spring gurgled up among the date palms. The village was surrounded by flowering trees; the whole area was dressed in green. The birds sang, the sky was a strong blue, the air was pure and clear.

"The boys will be happy here, that's for sure," Rav Anshel exclaimed in satisfaction. "All we need to do is cut the grass a bit, and this place will be a taste of *Gan Eden.* The clean air will help their concentration, and as for the beauty... Ah, truly elevated students will develop here, close to the heart of nature. I know from experience that half the distractions to learning come from the boys dreaming about getting out of the city, about taking trips and hikes in the countryside. Here, we'll be bringing the countryside right into the *beis midrash.* You sit and learn, and just outside your window a bird perches on a branch, singing its own song to Hashem — the two songs blending in perfect harmony."

"Yoel Goldfinger doesn't know what he's missing," Eli sighed. He had told Rav Anshel about his conversation with the yeshivah's *ilui.*

"Don't fret about it," Rav Anshel advised. "That which is barren will yet bear fruit. When he hears about what we have here, he'll come running!"

◆ ◆ ◆

They returned to Anafim a week later. Eli led the way directly to the site of the *beis midrash,* which was undergoing renovation. At the edge of the settlement, in a spot surrounded by lush greenery, stood a large house that had served as a social center for the back-to-nature group. Rav Anshel and Eli had designated this building as the new *beis midrash.* It needed only some minor repairs and a good coat of paint. The work was being done by a team of Romanian workers who had come to them highly recommended for their speed and efficiency.

Climbing the steps, Eli sensed something amiss. He paused, listened a moment, then took the rest of the stairs at a run.

The paint cans stood unopened. The highly recommended laborers were carrying on a heated debate in Hebrew with several men — all of them strangers to Eli. They appeared to be religious, though there was something odd, even bizarre, about the unusual garb, the strange-looking yarmulkes, and especially the bright glitter of their eyes.

The construction foreman, Costel Bulgia, broke away from the group when he saw Eli and Rav Anshel.

"Sir, please not to be angry. These men" — he gestured at the strangers — "they do not let Costel and his friends to work."

"Who are they?" Eli asked.

A youth approached him, stammering, "Uh — Uh, we were here before you. We want to learn here. You surprised us."

Rav Anshel glared at him. "Who are you?"

By this time, the rest of the strangers had drifted over. One of them, a young man with a moustache and an indefinable air of authority, appeared to be their leader.

"We are 'Friends of the Mikdash.' We were thinking of using this building to learn about the laws of the *Beis Hamikdash* and *korbanos.*"

Rav Anshel tugged at his beard. *"Oy, vey.* Even before we begin, there are problems. "

"Not necessarily." Eli Flamm was prepared. He reached into a pocket and pulled out the sales contract confirming Mark Goldenblum's undisputed ownership of the property and every building on it. Eli's adoptive father had sunk a considerable sum into the purchase and had had the transaction legally documented and notarized.

"And now," Eli concluded in a tone that brooked no opposition, "you'll find yourselves another place and let my men get to work."

The youths went without protest, though they cast several lingering backward looks at the spacious, sun-filled hall. Their moustached leader shook his head in open frustration as he left.

"Costel starts to work at once!" the foreman announced, dragging a paint-splattered ladder into the center of the hall. "In two days, you will have here a beautiful place."

He clapped his hands briskly to signal the onset of the work shift. His men scurried over to their equipment. For the next 10 minutes, as Eli and Rav Anshel watched, the room was transformed into a humming, clanking, scraping hive of activity. Eli sniffed the smell of fresh paint with pleasure.

Rav Anshel stood at the window, watching the departing figures. "Out of all the madmen in the world, it's this group that decides to camp out in this spot."

"You know them?"

Rav Anshel didn't answer. His eyes were still glued to the window. "I'm afraid they really are camping out at Anafim. Look, they're wandering around inspecting the place as though searching for a more hospitable spot. They don't look like people who are getting ready to leave."

"Does that worry you?" Eli sounded slightly amused. "They don't seem especially dangerous to me."

Rav Anshel swung around to face Eli sternly. "You want neighbors like that?"

"Why not? They'll keep us amused. We'll never be bored here."

"No, no! Under no circumstances! We want to found a yeshivah for boys seeking spiritual elevation. Those people will disturb that process." Rav Anshel stared back out the window, continuing grimly, "Now I know that what we're doing is a good thing — a holy thing. If the Satan sets up obstacles right at the start, it's the best sign that we're on the right path. 'Yerushalayim — hills surround her.' When a Jew tries to go up to Yerushalayim, to the *Beis Hamikdash*, hills stand in his way."

"The *Beis Hamikdash* is exactly where those guys are trying to go," Eli said with an attempt at a smile. With a look, Rav Anshel speedily quelled the attempt.

"You're right," Eli apologized. "I was just kidding."

Rav Anshel remained extremely serious. "Those young men have strayed from the straight path. The minute you start straying, you never know where you'll end up."

12

It was the middle of the winter semester when the new yeshivah for aspiring students opened in Anafim. It was named "Yeshivas Aish Aharon," in memory of Aharon Flamm. (In Yiddish, a *flam* is a flame, or fire.) Mark Goldenblum's nobility of spirit, in so generously endowing a yeshivah in honor of his adoptive son's birth father, garnered a great deal of respectful comment.

On the day before he left Yeshivas Chochmei Provinzia, Rav Anshel's students threw a modest party. They made no attempt to hide their distress at seeing their beloved rebbi strike out on a new path of his own. Rabbi Nosson Karo, the *rosh yeshivah,* blessed Rav Anshel warmly, though he, too, was sorrowful. "Rav Pfeffer, I have seen superior students, and they are few," he quoted the Gemara sadly. "If there are two —" He pointed at Rav Anshel's two top students, Dudu Klein and Simchah Tauber, who were transferring to Aish Aharon along with him. The *rosh yeshivah* stopped, his throat too choked to utter another word.

Rav Anshel answered, "Rav Karo, please don't be angry with me. You know that this is a lifelong dream of mine. The ambition to help create a certain type of student has burned within me for a long, long time."

Rav Karo inclined his head. No one knew better than he how it had pained Rav Anshel to abandon his dreams. The *rosh yeshivah* overcame his emotion and repeated his blessing for success. "This is a time when the other side of the Jewish nation is sinking spiritually. A yeshivah for aspiring students will help tilt the balance a bit."

At long last, Rav Anshel and Eli could breathe easier and regard what they had built with satisfaction. The yeshivah's premise had been met with some raised eyebrows at first, and interest in registration had been correspondingly small. But the two had not given in to discouragement. They explained, they demonstrated, they coaxed, and they persuaded. The hardest part was recruiting the core group. Once they had acquired the first dozen top boys from the best yeshivah, the idea gathered momentum like a rolling snowball. Now, excellent students were knocking on Rav Anshel's door. Rav Anshel joyously and carefully separated the finest from the fine.

On the day before the yeshivah opened, someone was waiting for Eli in his room at the yeshivah.

"Don't laugh," Yoel Goldfinger said, sheepishly. "I haven't changed my mind. Regular yeshivahs are also busy raising future *gedolei hador.* But I sense that your yeshivah has *siyata dishmaya,* Heaven's blessing, and it's not hard to sense the *kedushah* of the group you've gotten together. Please, let me be a part of it."

Eli flung out his arms and hugged Yoel. He made no effort to mask his joy as he said simply, "You're in."

◆ ◆ ◆

They arrived at Anafim in a rented bus at noon. In the bus sat Rav Anshel Pfeffer, Rav Segal, Rav Salzburg, and 32 outstanding boys. The bus fairly vibrated with excitement as it rumbled into the settlement.

Eli had the idea of fasting to mark the yeshivah's inauguration. "I once heard that when the Ponovihzer *Rosh Yeshivah,* Rav Yosef Shlomo Kahaneman, laid the cornerstone for Yeshivas Ponovizh, he cried so hard that his tears wet the foundation sand," he told Rav Anshel. "The Chazon Ish saw this, and said that a yeshivah that is founded on tears from the heart will grow and flourish to ever greater heights. We are about to open a special kind of yeshivah, so there are sure to be plenty of forces opposing us. The Satan won't remain silent in the face of this kind of operation. Let us open the yeshivah with a fast. All the boys will fast on the first day, and *daven* for the yeshivah's success."

Rav Anshel considered the idea, gave his consent, and introduced the idea to the boys themselves — who embraced it enthusiastically. They rode in the bus now, a little weak from fasting, but imbued with the special glow reserved for important moments.

The sun added its light to theirs, bursting through the clouds just as the bus entered the settlement. Sunshine bathed every tree, every leaf, every stone. The boys, taking in the scene, drew a deep, emotional breath. No one spoke a word.

On this special day, they had also undertaken to refrain from speech. The students of the new yeshivah were prepared to sacrifice a great deal for success!

The dormitory buildings were old, neglected apartments that had received a rapid face-lift. The former granary was converted into the yeshivah's dining hall. Its walls were paneled in oak, its floors laid with a sturdy and attractive linoleum, and the old chipped ceiling replaced with a far more sightly one. The *beis midrash* was to be the jewel in the crown of Yeshivas Aish Aharon. It was impossible to recognize the former dilapidated structure through the new marble-covered walls and modern banks of lights, a giant chandelier at the center. A brand new ark graced the eastern wall.

The first days felt like a holiday. Everything was sparkling and new, both physically and spiritually. Every boy had a *shtender* fresh from the carpenter's shop and a new Gemara with the scent of fresh ink on the pages. The very air was fragrant with newly sawed wood.

On that first day, there were no parties or speeches. The boys recited psalms with great fervency as Rav Anshel, wrapped in his *tallis* and choked with tears, stood before the ark and led the prayers. *Minchah* lasted twice as long as usual, after which the boys thirstily set upon their Gemaras. The voice of Torah filled the *beis midrash* like a great outpouring of water.

Rav Anshel wanted to push off the official festive party until Rosh Chodesh Iyar, after the experiment had been seen as successful. "The true test is not over a piece of chicken and a slice of cake, but in the *beis midrash*," Rav Anshel told his students. They, in turn, did their best to justify the trust laid upon them.

Yitzchak Winogradski, Tiberias born, pored continuously over his Gemara for stretches of up to seven hours at a time — while refraining from speech — and saw nothing unusual in it.

Shmuel Abrams, from Bnei Brak, took upon himself to learn through the night — twice a week.

Dudu Klein, of Jerusalem, undertook to study 500 *blatt* of Gemara, over and above the yeshivah's regular curriculum.

Yanky Pinto, from Haifa, was the student authority on halachah, having memorized all six sections of the *Mishnah Berurah*.

Tzvika Sofer, of Petach Tikvah, would remove his shoes at the dormitory door at night and walk barefoot on the cold floors so as not to rouse his sleeping classmates. Yoel Goldfinger decided to stop relying on his innate talents and to throw himself into a program of really diligent study. He would learn to the point of physical exhaustion, when he would collapse on his bed fully dressed. Later, he purchased a pair of slip-on shoes to save himself the two minutes needed to tie his shoelaces. Those two minutes could be dedicated to Torah!

As for Eli Flamm, the oldest student in the yeshivah and the catalyst behind the yeshivah's establishment, word had it that he was as well versed in the tractates of *Nashim* and *Nezikin* as "someone who'd studied in a *kollel* for two years," according to Rav Menashe Segal. But Eli never spoke about his accomplishments.

Thirty-two aspiring students, all on an upward spiritual track — "32 paths to wisdom," Rav Anshel fondly called them. He thanked his Creator for every day he was able to spend with these marvelous boys. The program was more successful than he had dared hope.

What really astonished the staff was the smoothness with which the yeshivah functioned, despite the extreme individuality of the boys. They saw, also, a growing sense of unity among the student body. Despite the differences, in many ways it was a yeshivah like all other yeshivahs, with the same kind of social structure and developing friendships. The boys were not above complaining about overdone meat or lumps in their cereal. There was some criticism, too, about various aspects of the dormitory. Eli Flamm hastened to contact his adoptive father. The students soon got to know the true "father" of their yeshivah. Millionaire Mark Goldenblum's BMW became a familiar sight as it sped into the settlement on a regular basis.

Mark toured the dorm with all the quiet modesty of a shy visitor. Still, he could not escape being recognized and warmly welcomed by the boys he supported.

Mark loved these boys. The more he gave to them, the more he loved them. "At first I had no children. Then I was lucky enough to get the five Flamm kids. Now I have 32 more."

The primary problem in the dormitory was the intense cold that made it hard for the students to sleep on winter nights. The uninsulated walls were no match for the keen mountain winds that buffeted them. Mark Goldenblum drew up plans for a comprehensive heating and air-conditioning system.

Dudu Klein approached him. With an engaging smile, he said, "I'm a Yerushalmi. If I can't stand the cold, how can anyone else?"

Mark nodded sympathetically. "Hm... You're absolutely right. Unfortunately, we can't do much about it this winter. We can't overhaul the whole dorm in a day — "

Someone interrupted: "The cold at night keeps us from sleeping and thus from learning well during the day!"

"Don't worry," Mark said, holding up a hand. "Let me finish, please. Even as we speak, my men are bringing over new electric heaters for all the dorm rooms. Starting tonight, you'll all be enveloped in warmth."

◆ ◆ ◆

Yonah HaKohen Pinter was a weak little boy who always seemed to have a head cold. Then again, 50 years ago, many Jerusalem children suffered the effects of poor nutrition. He attended a *cheder* like all his little friends. When the class began to learn *Chumash Vayikra,* the portions dealing with sacrifices kindled Yonah's imagination. While most of the other boys found the laws and details hard going, Yonah was fascinated. He could practically see the *Kohen Gadol* in the *Beis Hamikdash,* and the other *kohanim* offering up the various *korbanos* and sprinkling the blood on the altar. The minutiae of the procedures were clear as day to him.

"If the Rebbe will let me," he begged his teacher, Efraim Richtman, one day, "I can explain the laws to the class."

Richtman had been ready to tear his beard out in frustration. He beamed at the 10-year-old. "Certainly. Give it a try!"

Yonah pulled a tangerine out of his lunchbag and walked to the front of the room. "Who has a knife?" he asked.

"What do you need a knife for? You can peel a tangerine with your fingers," Richtman asked in bewilderment. "And what's the connection between a tangerine and the *korbanos*?"

"Please," Yonah pleaded. "Just give me a minute."

Reluctantly, the rebbe produced a knife, then stood back to watch Yonah's presentation.

Yonah proceeded to peel the tangerine in leisurely fashion. Then he separated the sections of fruit and spread them over the teacher's desk.

"Here are the *korbanos,*" he announced to his mesmerized classmates. "Now we'll see what the *kohanim* do in the *Beis Hamikdash.*"

He picked up a tangerine section and held it up. "Here's a chicken that the *kohen* wants to sacrifice on the *mizbei'ach.* The chicken doesn't like that idea very much." Yonah made some squawking noises. "The *kohen* holds it tight and uses this knife to cut its throat."

The other boys watched him slice carefully through the tangerine section. In like fashion, Yonah "slaughtered" seven other sections. Then he squirted tangerine juice onto the corners of the desk, explaining each move as he went along. The ritual became crystal-clear to every boy in the room.

When Yonah had returned to his own seat, the rebbe congratulated him. "Good work, Yonah. You made only two mistakes. First, chickens are not brought as *korbanos* — just *torim* (pigeons) and *bnei yonah* (turtle-doves), in the bird family. Also, the *kohen* doesn't slit the bird's throat; he uses a special procedure called *melikah*. But it was a terrific presentation, and I thank you — the whole class thanks you — for the explanation." Richter glanced around. "Is there anyone who didn't understand?"

Nati Milner, the class clown, raised a hand.

"Yes, Nati?"

"If the *kohen* breaks the *yonah's* neck, why doesn't the Rebbe break Yonah Pinter's?"

The class burst into a long, sustained bout of pent-up laughter. Even the rebbe was hard put not to smile. But Yonah sat stiffly, scorning his classmates and their mockery. In his 10th year, the course of Yonah's life was set. He gave himself over completely to studying the laws of the *Beis Hamikdash*.

One day, at the right time, he intended to become the next *Kohen Gadol.*

13

Like a guided missile, Yeshivas Aish Aharon took flight. The *beis midrash* rocked with intensity, night and day. The boys soared in their studies, in their personal growth, in their fear of Heaven. The yeshivah seemed to have garnered Heaven's own blessing, and the students were quick to seize the moment and not let it pass. For Rav Anshel Pfeffer, it was a return to his youth. These days, his eyes shone with purpose and contentment. It gave him great joy to see young boys who, just a short time earlier, would devote endless attention to details like the width of their hatbands, now willingly pass up a good meal in favor of an extra *shiur* in *Tanach*. Later, they would grab some cold soup and a morsel of chicken, or forget about eating entirely.

But he had not yet achieved his main goal. He wanted to restore the *Va'ad Hashomrim* to its former glory, to see his boys working on the trait of viewing others favorably.

"This is our generation's illness," he would explain to his students. "There are many people who are unable to bear the sight of another's success. Who knows how many tragedies might be averted if we were able to change this trait?"

Eli Flamm seemed to epitomize the character that Rav Anshel was eager to promote. He rejoiced in his fellow students' accomplishments, never betraying a shred of envy or competition. Even more — and only Rav Anshel knew this — he would take it upon himself to learn together with certain boys who were not gifted with originality in Torah. In a yeshivah such as Aish Aharon, such a deficiency was liable to cause a student some discomfort. Eli tried to prevent this by guiding these boys along the path to creative thought — all with extreme tact and a great deal of practical help.

Rav Anshel made sure his boys got fresh air, encouraging them to spend at least part of their lunch break, on sunny days, out among the fields and trees. On one such day, three boys were seated on a bench beneath a large, spreading tree. An underground spring bubbled up between two boulders, feeding into a pool where goldfish darted and swam.

"Spring is coming," Simchah Tauber exclaimed happily. "Nature is coming back to life. Soon we'll be hearing a thousand frogs singing to us at night."

Eli Flamm grinned. Tzvika Sofer said, "The *Zohar* tells about Dovid *Hamelech,* who was once walking along a river and asked *Hakadosh Baruch Hu* if there had ever been another man who praised his Creator the way he did. Immediately, a frog leaped out of the river and told him, 'Dovid, don't be so proud. You do not sacrifice your life for the sake of your Creator, as I did in the plague of frogs in Egypt. Besides,' the frog added, 'I do more than you. I praise Hashem both day and night, and croak without stopping.'

"So," Tzvika continued, "when you hear frogs croaking in the spring, you should know that they're singing praise to their Creator and are ready to sacrifice their lives to fulfill His will."

"That's nice," the others said admiringly. "Very nice."

Suddenly, a figure appeared in the path. It was a bearded youth with long, uncombed hair. He wore a pair of *tzitzis* with some blue fringes, short red pants and a green shirt. His feet were bare.

"Ho, my brothers, that's very nice," he greeted them.

"What's nice?" Simchah Tauber asked.

"Everything — nature, the view, your story, Dovid *Hamelech.*" His eyes glittered. "Dovid was the father of King Shlomo. He built the *Beis Hamikdash.*"

"Ah, you're one of the 'Friends of the Mikdash,' " Eli said. "Are you really settled down here?"

" 'Friends of the Mikdash'?" Simchah asked. "What's that?"

Eli explained, "They're learning the *halachos* of the *Beis Hamikdash.*"

The bearded youth waved a hand. "Learning is only a small part of it. Soon we'll be *building* the *Beis Hamikdash*!"

Simchah glanced hurriedly at his watch. "Oops, we're running late. Eli, Tzvika, we've got to get back to yeshivah."

Tzvika followed Simchah at once, but Eli lingered to chat with the youth. He learned that the 'Friends of the Mikdash' had indeed found lodging in one of the larger buildings on the other side of the settlement. The group numbered 20 men and was led by the charismatic David ben Avraham, for whom the others would walk through fire and water. At the moment they deemed proper, they were planning to rebuild the *Beis Hamikdash.* From time to time they would travel to Jerusalem to receive inspiration from the greatest of all the 'Friends,' a man by the name of...

"... by the name of — of — Yes! Now I remember! His name is Rabbi —"

"Eli, it's late!" Simchah called back anxiously. He returned to escort Eli back to the yeshivah. What in the world could he have found to talk about with that strange guy?

They hurried back to the *beis midrash.*

◆ ◆ ◆

Yonah Pinter dreamed day and night of a third *Beis Hamikdash.* He spent every spare moment poring over the laws of the Holy Temple and the sacrifices until he was word perfect. He consulted a number of leading rabbis, many of whom praised the young man for his diligence and the intensity of his desire for the final redemption.

Then, at the age of 22, he slipped on a figurative banana peel. He began to believe that the *Beis Hamikdash* was meant to be built by men, just as the first and second had been built by King Shlomo and Ezra *Hasofer,* and that until that time it was proper to bring sacrifices on *Har Habayis.* From that minute, both his students and his teachers distanced themselves from him — though not without many a long and heated debate.

"What do you want?" Yonah would scream. "The Rambam clearly states that it's a positive mitzvah to build a house for Hashem and to bring sacrifices in it. Where does it say that that house has to descend from Heaven? The Rambam also says that it's necessary to bring *korbanos* even if there is no house built. What do you have to say to that?"

"We're forbidden to go up to *Har Habayis!*" his friends shouted. "Yonah, stop this nonsense!"

"But there are places where you are allowed to go," he shot back.

As long as eastern Jerusalem remained in Jordanian hands, the debate was theoretical. No one was happier than Yonah Pinter when, in the course of the Six-Day War, old Jerusalem was freed for the Jews. The cry "*Har Habayis* is in our hands!" echoed through his very bones. Yonah shone like the sun as he hurried to immerse himself in the *mikveh,* ready to be summoned to *Har Habayis* to bring an offering. For three days he remained in his room, practicing his *shechitah.* It was summer and tangerines were not in season, but Yonah, undaunted, practiced first on apple quarters — he found them too hard — and then, more successfully, on bananas. As he "slaughtered" the fruit he clucked quietly, in imitation of the long-ago chickens he had sacrificed on Rebbe Richtman's desk at *cheder.*

Sruly Egozi was a normal boy, with strictly average talents. His tragedy lay in his father's ambition. Rabbi Levi Egozi sought to turn his son into the pride of his life. Refusing to recognize Sruly's lack of special gifts, he pushed the boy far beyond his capabilities.

Each parent-teacher's meeting was a source of fresh agony. "Are you sure?" the father would ask that year's teacher. "My son is only average?

You must be mistaken. I learn with him and I see how talented he is."

"The teachers don't understand our Sruly," he would sigh at home to his wife, Bella. "Sruly — average? Why, only yesterday he asked a really outstanding question when we were learning Gemara together. Average? Ha!"

This state of affairs continued until Sruly was in the seventh grade. His new teacher was a young man who fervently believed in the powers of positive feedback. A boy who is praised, he believed, would work harder. Levi and Bella Egozi came to the first parent-teacher's meeting, burning with eagerness to meet the teacher who had sent home a string of complimentary notes with their son.

After an hour's wait, their turn came. The teacher greeted them warmly. "You're Sruly's parents? What a wonderful boy!"

The parents' hearts swelled with joy.

Ten minutes later they left, heads swimming with all the marvelous things they had heard about their son. The teacher had rained a veritable shower of praise on Sruly's head. Levi Egozi went home filled with higher expectations of his son than ever before. Neither he nor his wife noticed that none of the teacher's flowing compliments touched upon their Sruly's actual abilities.

The seventh grade passed in a roseate dream. Encouraged, Sruly worked hard in the eighth grade to justify his new image. His father was convinced that his son would win one of the coveted few seats in the "Korman *Yeshivah*" high school, headed by the famous Rabbi Zalman Korman. There were, indeed, some grounds for this conviction: Zalman Korman was Levi Egozi's brother-in-law.

When the time came, Rabbi Korman tried to gently persuade his brother-in-law to look elsewhere for Sruly, but Levi was adamant. So Sruly was enrolled in the yeshivah, where he managed to survive only by virtue of an enormous investment of time and energy by his uncle. As for his father, he was already certain of Sruly's next step: the great *yeshivah gedolah*, "Vilna."

Rav Zalman called him in for a talk. "Levi, understand me. Sruly is a good boy, but an average one. He's suffered great difficulties here and has felt inferior to the other students. He's managed to get by only because of me. But Vilna Yeshivah? Enough already!"

"Why?" Levi demanded.

"Do you want to destroy your son?"

Rav Zalman succeeded only in insulting his brother-in-law. Levi Egozi's goal remained fixed in his mind. Pulling every string he knew, he succeeded in getting his son accepted into Vilna Yeshivah.

That was when life started getting really difficult for Sruly Egozi.

Without his uncle's help, he found himself swimming in waters far too deep for him. After six months, he began to drown. The very fact that he was competing with outstanding youths doomed him to a sense of failure. He began coming late to *davening,* then cutting *shiurim,* then skipping full days. In short, he was on his way out to the street.

"What will happen to your learning?" the *mashgiach* would rail at him. "Okay, so you'll never be another Vilna Gaon. But to waste full days like this?!"

Sruly had lost the last shreds of motivation. He shrugged. "I'll admit it, I can't learn. *Bittul Torah* is a serious thing, but I'm just not capable of learning."

The *mashgiach* invited Levi Egozi in for a talk one evening. He strongly urged the father to send his son to a "suitable yeshivah" — meaning, a yeshivah where the young man would learn half the day and work the other half — or risk losing Sruly entirely.

Levi Egozi was shocked and bewildered. He felt like crying bitter tears. His poor Sruly just had no luck. Apart from his seventh-grade teacher, no one had ever really understood him! Levi chose to ignore the *mashgiach's* advice. Sruly sank daily. He began wandering the streets and making friends with the boys who hung around there.

On the brink of dismissing Sruly from the yeshivah, the *mashgiach* made one last attempt to save him. He hooked Sruly up with an older student, a veteran of Vilna — one Eli Flamm. Eli gave himself over to the younger boy, sparing no effort to endear him to learning.

It was too late. Already, in the yeshivah's halls, the word had gone out that Sruly Egozi was about to be kicked out. Sruly lost heart. "Whatever I do, they'll keep talking about me," he said in deep discouragement. "I have no chance here. I'm lost." Eli was not successful in changing his mind.

The next morning, Sruly showed Eli a strange letter he had received:

Dear Sruly,

I have heard about you from friends of mine. I think you're being treated unfairly and that no one understands you. In the right environment, you could have grown to unbelievable heights. Come meet with me at 8 p.m. tomorrow on Rechov Yafo, at the corner of Rechov Halu'ach. I have an interesting proposal for you.

I'll sign my name, "Dekel."

The letter struck Eli as suspicious. "Go to the meeting," he told Sruly, and equipped him with a tiny concealed tape recorder. "We'll listen to the recording afterwards and decide what to do."

This was at the start of the winter, several months before Eli left Vilna Yeshivah for the newly established Aish Aharon. Sruly Egozi left at the same time.

He, too, went to Anafim, where he joined the group that called itself the "Friends of the Mikdash."

14

Arkady Bogdanov sat in his room, head in his hands.

"No! Under no circumstances!" he told himself angrily. "I won't stay here one more day!"

On a tray on the table near him was a tempting lunch, prepared by the talented chef at the "Golden Towers" home for the aged. The nursing home was built along the lines of a five-star hotel, and Arkady's 16th floor room had a stupendous ocean view. But Arkady's mood was sour.

"You'll be able to see the sunset over the water," his son, Yefim, had remarked just before he left. "People would be willing to give a fortune for such a view."

"Wonderful," Arkady grumbled now, remembering the comment. "I raised an only son with the sweat of my brow, and now he throws me out." He glared around the spacious and lavishly decorated room as though it were a prison cell. He felt like a caged bird.

At 72, Arkady felt as young as he had at 40. All his senses were sharp and functioning. He could see without glasses, his hearing was excellent, and his legs still carried him wherever he wished to go.

Two years earlier, his wife, Vera, had passed away. Ever since, his son and daughter-in-law, Galina, had hounded him about entering an old-age home. "The loneliness will eat you up, Father," Yefim had said earnestly. "In the home, you'll get to know lots of other nice people. They'll keep you busy all day long. You won't be alone for a second. You'll love it!"

Without waiting for his father's consent, Yefim had started the ball rolling. For two years, Arkady fought with him, clinging to his house and his old life by his fingernails. Finally, yesterday morning, Yefim and Galina had simply put him in the car and driven him to the home.

"Traitors!" he hissed, blood boiling. "Galina wanted the house and Yefim does whatever Galina says."

The house was an expensive villa in Herzliya whose value was estimated at some $800,000. Arkady had purchased it with money he had secretly brought with him from Russia. Yefim and Galina were prepared to shell out $1,500 a month on this place, just to get their hands on the stunning house and enormous garden.

The food on his tray was cold. Arkady had lost his appetite. He sat in an armchair, brooding. The hours passed, with the sun sinking lower toward the sea and painting his room with an orange glow. Arkady roused himself to go to the window to "see the sunset," as his son had urged. Remembering, his anger spurted up anew.

"I'll teach them a lesson they'll never forget," he promised the red fireball dipping into the calm waters. Here and there, at the horizon, tiny ship's lights began to flicker. A breeze played on the ocean, raising blue-orange mists. Small waves rushed to the shore, exploded there, and fell back. On the boardwalk, seated on benches facing the sea, elderly men and women from the nursing home savored the sunset. The sound of children's laughter floated up to Arkady's window from far below.

The enchanting scene did nothing to cool Arkady's rage. His mood was exactly opposite that of the peaceful scene outside. "Yefim and Galina will regret the day they threw me out of my own house," he vowed.

When the sun had disappeared, he left the window and sat at the desk to write something. Several times he erased a word and then plowed on, until he had a final product that satisfied him. Then he flipped through the phone book and dialed a number he found there.

The next day, two major newspapers contained a small advertisement, all but hidden on one of the inner pages. It read:

Russian atomic scientist interested in having his exciting biography written. Excellent pay. Thrilling work for an extended period. Experience required.

◆ ◆ ◆

Yonah Pinter insisted on his right to climb the Temple Mount. He was certain that Israel would seize the historic opportunity to rebuild the *Beis Hamikdash* before the world had recovered from its stunning victory in the Six-Day War.

"Fools! Idiots! A government of defeatists!" he shrieked in the *shtieblach* of Meah Shearim, when Moshe Dayan handed control of the Temple Mount over to the Moslem Wakf. "We've lost our chance to build the *Beis Hamikdash* and bring *korbanos,* to light the Menorah and offer the *ketores.* They're afraid of the Arabs, worried about what the *goyim* will say."

The adults did not bother answering him, but youngsters flocked around him with interest — and considerable amusement.

"Yonah, how can we go up to *Har Habayis* if we have no *parah adumah* to purify us?"

Yonah had done his homework. "I feel there are places on *Har Habayis* where one is permitted to go. I know exactly how far we can go."

"Yonah, not a single *gadol* agrees with you!" scoffed a bold-faced youth who had just joined the circle. "And you have no *parah adumah!"*

Yonah flushed angrily. "Maybe you want to volunteer for the job?"

The other boys laughed. Yonah continued, "I'm as well versed in the laws as anyone. We will all be severely punished for not building the *Beis Hamikdash."*

He went on to clarify various halachic positions throughout the ages, *Rishonim* and *Acharonim,* and told anyone who would listen that most of the Torah greats throughout history agreed that the Jewish people are obligated in the building of the third *Beis Hamikdash*.

In the years that followed, Yonah passed from word to action. Together with a group of his Friends of the Mikdash, and after immersing in running spring water, he went up to prostrate himself on the Temple Mount. Each time, they were chased away by the Israeli police. And each time, they left behind an angry Arab mob — a mob that constituted only the tip of a vast iceberg, a hundred million Arabs throughout the world, who viewed a Jewish presence on the Temple Mount as an affront and a challenge, and who wanted nothing more than to destroy the State of Israel and every one of its Jewish inhabitants.

Some time later, Yonah came to the conclusion that only a cohesive group like the Friends of the Mikdash would actually be capable of doing the deed. He began gathering idle and disaffected youths. They studied the laws of *korbanos* and practiced on tangerine sections and tomato quarters before graduating to miniature stuffed cows "sacrificed" on a rubber altar. From time to time, they would gather in Yonah's house to light a seven-armed, gold-plated menorah, an imitation of the one that stood in the *Beis Hamikdash*.

◆ ◆ ◆

Yonah Pinter sat in a shul in his Beis Yisrael neighborhood one afternoon, wrapped in his *tallis* and *tefillin*. Apart from him and the white wooly lamb licking his shoes, there was not another soul in the place. His spirit was raging as it had not raged in a long time. That morning, he had attempted to climb up to the Temple Mount alone and had been ignonimously chased away by the Moslem Wakf, who seized the opportunity to beat him soundly with fists of iron. To Yonah's mind, this was the height of effrontery. Seeing the Arabs in control of *Har Habayis* inflamed him. "Soon *they'll* be the ones saying, 'The Temple Mount is in our hands,'" he thought bitterly.

Fighting back tears, he rose and went to the *aron kodesh*. The tears flowed as he pulled aside the curtain and fervently embraced the *sifrei Torah*.

"*Ribbono shel Olam!* he cried. "How long will Your might remain in hiding and Your glory be concealed?"

He wept copiously and long, one hand caressing the lamb that — on sudden inspiration — he had led to shul after the morning's devastating experience on the Temple Mount. The shul being situated no further than 10 steps away from his home, no one noticed him or the animal. Now, before the open ark, with one hand resting on the bleating lamb, he said in a trembling voice, "I, Yonah Pinter, am prepared to sacrifice this animal here, in this sanctuary, as an atonement for all of Israel. May it be Your will that we will soon be able to bring *korbanos* to the great Sanctuary, the third *Beis Hamikdash.*"

His limbs worked automatically; he refused to let himself think about what he was doing. His right hand drew a sharp knife from his pocket — the same knife that had slit the throats of so many toy cows — while his left hugged the frightened lamb.

He was in the act of lifting the knife toward the animal when a heavy hand fell on his shoulder. "Stop! That is forbidden."

Yonah whirled around in confusion. "Who are you? Who dares try to stop me from bringing a sacrifice as an atonement for all of Israel?"

"I am Daoud Abu Nimar."

"You're an *Arab?* But — but you're wearing a *kipah!*"

The young man laughed. "Trust me, I'm an Arab."

Yonah's confusion was complete. A young Arab had been with him in the shul all along, listening to him pour his heart out in front of the *aron kodesh!* "Why is it forbidden?" he asked, when speech became possible again.

The young Arab grinned at him. He had a small mustache. His eyes were large and luminous, his deep voice soothing. "I know all of your Torah and understand what you're doing. Your childish games are not respectful of the holy ark. Since when do you slaughter sheep in a synagogue? Besides, the people will be coming in to pray later — how will you explain the blood and the mess?"

Yonah's eyes bulged and his mouth hung open. "Who are you?"

"I already told you. My name is Daoud Abu Nimar. I'm from Shechem, and I'm interested in converting."

The lamb's life was spared. It was returned to its meadow quickly, before people came into the shul to ask embarrassing questions. That night, after *Ma'ariv*, Yonah brought the young Arab home.

Wearing his yarmulke, the youth resembled a Jew in every respect. In Yonah's kitchen, lit by an old kerosene lamp, Daoud spilled out his life's story. A son of a well-connected Shechem family, he had been drawn to Judaism and the Jewish Torah ever since he could remember. Hounded by his fellow Arabs for his betrayal of their religion, he had fled Shechem for western Jerusalem. For the past year he had been trying, without success, to convert.

Daoud Abu Nimar was naive, it seemed. He had told the judges at the religious court the truth: that is, that he was interested in converting in order to marry a Jewish girl he knew. The *dayanim* rejected his petition, explaining that a conversion for the purpose of marriage was unacceptable. Daoud had tried to argue, but the judges — none too pleased with problematic conversions, and especially not those involving Arabs — had closed all doors to him. In desperation, he had sought out unscrupulous types who peddled questionable conversions; in the end, the price they demanded was too steep for him.

Yonah Pinter's soft heart felt Abu Nimar's pain. "You see? Our meeting is straight from Heaven. I'm prepared to set up a *beis din* and convert you — if your intention is not only to convert for the sake of marriage."

Daoud chuckled. "My relationship with that girl ended the day she heard they wouldn't convert me. I want to be a Jew. That's all."

The very next day, Yonah put together a special *beis din* for the purpose of converting Daoud Abu Nimar. Two friends from the upper echelons of the Friends of the Mikdash agreed to serve with him. They put Daoud through a conversion ritual that ended with immersion in a *mikveh*. Daoud Abu Nimar was proclaimed David ben Avraham. Circumcision was unnecessary, as Daoud had already undergone one at the age of 13. All that was required was the letting of a small amount of blood, which David bore stoically. He was prepared to bear a great deal more in order to become a Jew.

◆ ◆ ◆

After he had converted Abu Nimar, Yonah made him a confidant. For a number of weeks, David ben Avraham lived in Yonah's house and was plunged into a crash course in Friends of the Mikdash thinking.

David proved to be a student who outshone his teachers. His young mind grasped concepts with a facility that astonished Yonah. David urged his mentor to re-establish his Friends of the Mikdash, this time as a group that would be unrelenting in its adherence to its goals.

"I'll gather a nucleus of real zealots for the cause," he promised.

"Where from?" Yonah demanded. "Are you planning to go out into the street and call, 'A 10th for the Friends of the Mikdash *minyan*'?"

Years of being on the receiving end of scorn and mockery had turned Yonah Pinter into an incurable cynic. His sneering words hurt David at first, but the convert was quickly mollified. He outlined his plan: "We have to look for young people who have become embittered and disillusioned — kids who have been shoved to the fringes of society. They will form a faithful nucleus, a group prepared to go up to the Temple Mount, to bring sacrifices, even to carry up sacks of cement to pour the foundations of the third *Beis Hamikdash.*"

Yonah was electrified. He leaped out of his seat, sending his glasses flying into the air to crash on the floor. "You're a genius!" he cried, embracing David. "From the first minute we met, I knew that Heaven had planned it all. It was no coincidence."

David began working that same day. He read all the newspapers, listened to all the news broadcasts, sniffed out rumors in the streets. He found people like Chemi Maimon, the heroic photographer. He found Rafi Gamliel, the inflamed soldier. He found Akiva Tamiri, hater of electricity, Sruly Egozi, newly dismissed from his yeshivah, and 15 other disaffected youths. They were young people in despair — people who had nothing to lose.

He presented himself to them as "Dekel," and believed that no one knew about him.

But Eli Flamm knew everything.

15

Arkady sat beside the phone in his room, waiting impatiently for it to ring. He knew two people who would definitely *not* be calling in response to his ad: Yefim and Galina could not read one word of Hebrew.

The hours crawled. Arkady did not leave his room. When trays with his breakfast and lunch appeared, he pecked at them like a bird.

It was 6 o'clock when the phone finally rang. Arkady pounced on it like a snake in attack mode. "Hello?" he quavered.

"Good evening," replied an unfamiliar male voice. "I'm calling about your ad in the paper."

Arkady nearly broke into a dance. His heart pounded wildly as he asked, with enforced calm, "What ad?"

Unruffled, the man gave him the name of the newspaper. "I'd like to meet with you."

"Can you write? Do you have experience?"

"A great deal."

They arranged to meet on the boardwalk at sunset next day. Arkady would carry a rolled-up copy of *TIME* magazine in his left hand, and the caller would wear a gray baseball cap.

At the appointed hour on the following day, Arkady prepared to leave his room. He was opening the door when the phone rang.

"Father?" It was Yefim, his voice dripping honey. "I just called to find out how you're enjoying your new home."

"Of course I'm enjoying it. I'm just thrilled to pieces that my son threw me out of my own house," Arkady answered bitterly.

Yefim ignored the comment. "Father, go down to the boardwalk and see the sunset. It'll cheer you up."

"That's exactly what I'm about to do." This time, Arkady sounded genuinely happy. What he hoped would occur on the boardwalk would certainly improve his mood. But Yefim hadn't a clue....

The bench where they had agreed to meet was empty. Arkady sat, read his magazine for a while, then rolled it up in his left hand, with the word *TIME* showing. Five minutes passed.

A man wearing a gray baseball cap strolled down the boardwalk and stopped, as if on impulse, by the bench where Arkady sat. "May I sit here?" he asked politely.

Arkady's heart thudded in his chest. He recognized the voice from the telephone.

For several moments the two sat silently, watching the red ball of the sun slide slowly beneath the horizon. A cool breeze blew at them off the water. Arkady shivered.

"It's getting cold," the man in the baseball cap remarked. He appeared about 40 years old, with the eyes of a sly fox.

"Yes. I didn't dress warmly enough."

"Do you live far from here?" The small eyes bore into Arkady's.

Instead of answering, Arkady cleared his throat and countered with, "What is your name?"

The man shook his head. "My name is irrelevant at the moment. Tell me about yourself."

Arkady began to spin out his biography, starting with his childhood in the Russian city of Mitishi, near Moscow, through his being drafted into the Red Army, his admission into Leningrad University, and his rise to overall manager of the nuclear plant at Tura.

"Tura?"

"Tura is a city in the western Siberian mountains, near the lower Vekhnyaya River. Nobody knows about the nuclear plant there. Officially, it does not exist. Only the American spy satellites have photographed it.

"I understand." The man paused. "If you were to travel to Russia and visit Tura — or anyplace else, for that matter — how would you be received? And what is your attitude toward nuclear devices these days?" Though he faced the darkened sea, he was alert to gauge the former scientist's reaction.

Arkady's breathing quickened. The conversation was going exactly where he wanted it to go! He answered cautiously, "If I were to travel back to Russia today, I'd be received royally everywhere. They were very upset when I decided to move to Israel — and believe me, I'm sorry, too. If I'd been a Jew... Well, that's water under the bridge. My wife insisted that we come. She suddenly remembered that she had a Jewish grandfather."

"Spare me the details," the man said coldly. "I want you to go to Russia and bring me back two 'dolls.' Can you do it?"

Arkady felt his skin grow damp. Beads of perspiration sprang up all over his face, despite the chill ocean breeze. "Are you talking about the real thing?"

"I'm talking about what you think I'm talking about."

"How serious are you?"

"Very serious. You'll be handsomely rewarded."

"How much?"

"If you supply what we want, you'll get a million dollars."

Arkady stood up as though prepared to leave. "You're not serious," he sneered. "You're babbling like a child. Two 'dolls' are worth twice that amount. I'm not bringing you a piece of junk from the marketplace, something worth maybe half a million that will never explode. I'll get you brand-new goods, direct from Tura — with a guarantee. It will cost hundreds of thousands of dollars in bribery alone."

The man tugged at his sleeve. "Sit," he ordered curtly. "You'll get two million. A quarter-million dollars will be paid in advance, the rest when you return. In new, unmarked bills."

Two women, pushing strollers and chatting animatedly, walked slowly past their bench. They had scarcely passed when a couple of policemen came into view. The uniformed pair strolled along the boardwalk in leisurely fashion, throwing a curious glance at the elderly man and his companion. Arkady grew white as a sheet. The other man maintained his granite composure, though he, too, paled slightly. They watched the policemen walk slowly away, conversing quietly, until they were no more than two specks in the distance. Arkady and his companion drew a simultaneous sigh of relief.

"Israel's almost as bad as Russia; you can't say a word without the police showing up!" He turned to the other man. "Okay, who's behind you?"

The man told him. As he listened, Arkady's expression changed once or twice. When the man had finished, Arkady chuckled. "Do whatever you want with the goods. Just pay me in cash."

They stood to go. Beneath a lamppost, the man in the gray cap suddenly said, "We need one small 'doll,' with limited power, and another standard one."

Arkady was surprised. "Explain yourself!"

"You will receive detailed instructions within the next few days. You asked me my name. For you, it's 'Gray Cap.' That's my name."

The man handed him a small bundle of bills. "That's your first advance — a hundred $100 bills. Ten thousand dollars. The rest will follow."

Arkady extended his hand to shake the other man's, but the stranger had already turned away and was flagging down a passing cab.

As Arkady watched the cab move off into the night, he felt a thrill of fear. Gray Cap knew everything about him, but Arkady did not even have the other man's phone number. Who was he, and who was really behind him?

As he passed through the well-lit lobby of the Golden Towers, Arkady wondered why they needed a "doll" of limited power. On the other hand, what difference did it make to him? The main thing was for Yefim to see what his father was capable of, even at his age.

The reception clerk welcomed him cordially. "Good evening, Mr. Bogdanov. I see that things are beginning to look up for you here. You're smiling."

Arkady laughed. "Yes, things are looking up."

"Will you go to the dining room now? There's an interesting lecture about to be given in there: 'The End of the Atomic Age.'"

"Atomic age? Brrr, that scares me!"

The young woman smiled as Arkady walked over to the elevator bank and pressed the button. He rode up alone and entered his empty room. Closing the door behind him, he pulled the wad of bills from his pocket and burst into laughter.

"End of the atomic age? If that naive girl only knew what new epoch the atom is about to enter — If she knew what an embittered old man, thrown out of his home, is capable of — If she only knew — "

Eli Flamm and Dudu Klein sat by an open window late one night, lost in heated debate on a point in the Gemara that they were learning. The rest of the world faded away. Their voices cut through the silence of the sleeping settlement, floated past lawns and trees to a small wooden cabin where Akiva Tamiri tried in vain to fall asleep.

In the dark, he twisted restlessly. He had recently discarded his modern digital watch, and until he bought himself a simpler one, he had no way of telling the time except by his own biological clock — which told him that it was about 1 a.m.

His love of nature had led him to leave his window open despite the night chill. Even curled up beneath a down quilt, he was shivering. "In another minute I'll get up and close the window," he told himself. "Just another 60 seconds of fresh air — ah, what wonderful air, clean, clear, pure as wine. It was a great idea to leave everything and come here to Anafim." Dekel — that is, David ben Avraham, the righteous convert from Shechem — had not lied when he had promised Akiva a veritable *Gan Eden* in the heart of nature.

The voices of the two yeshivah students, muted for a moment, flared up again. "What are they arguing about so loudly?" Akiva thought with a stab of envy. He had never realized it was possible to learn Torah that way, so clear headed and with such a high level of positive energy.

"We're also learning," he scolded himself. "The laws of *korbanos,* of the *Beis Hamikdash,* how to build a *mizbei'ach*... But the gang here is a motley crew, each one odder than the next. They're involved in fantasies and absolutely fanatic on the topic of the Temple Mount, destroying the mosques there, and building the third *Beis Hamikdash.* How will they destroy the mosques? Are they planning to bring a tractor up to the Mount? A childish joke. As for rebuilding the *Beis Hamikdash,* right now that's just another dream." Dekel had begun procuring vast amounts of cement and sand for pouring the foundation. It would be interesting to see which contractor he would hire.

An amusing picture rose up in his mind's eye. If Yonah Pinter and Dekel had their way, people coming to pray at the Western Wall would come up against a surrealistic scene. Signs at the entrance to the Temple Mount, warning, "DANGER — CONSTRUCTION IN PROGRESS." The Wall itself, featuring a huge billboard, listing the project's details. *Architect: Yonah Pinter. Construction Foreman: David ben Avraham. Cement work: Chemi Maimon. Destruction of mosques: Akiva Tamiri. Infrastructure: Rafi Gamliel,* and so on.

"There'll never be a sign like that," Akiva told himself. "Yonah and Dekel are chasing a fantasy. First the *Mashiach* has to come, then the *Beis Hamikdash* will descend from Heaven, built from stones of fire."

Akiva turned on his other side. He was too lazy to get up and close the window, or perhaps he was mesmerized by the arguing voices reaching him from the yeshivah students. Though the debate showed no sign of letting up, there was a world of friendship and affection in the two voices.

There was nothing personal in their argument, just a mutual love of Torah. Let the discussion end, and the two would be the best of friends again.

"Maybe they're the ones who are really rebuilding the *Beis Hamikdash,* and not us?" Akiva thought wistfully. Every midnight debate over their Gemaras was adding another stone of fire up above, and hastening the redemption. Interesting, the yeshivah was called Aish Aharon. Perhaps the name referred to Aharon *HaKohen,* and the fire of the altar and Menorah?

He abandoned his efforts to court sleep, letting his mind wander back to his first meeting with "Dekel."

They met, at Dekel's suggestion, in the broad plaza at the Western Wall. Akiva waited at the edge of the plaza. He glanced nervously at the huge searchlights pouring brilliant white light onto the concourse.

"What was so bad about the days before electricity?" he whispered to himself. "Once upon a time, holy Jews sat here and prayed, saying *tikkun chatzos* by candlelight. Do we need searchlights in order to pour out our hearts to Hashem? The heart sees everything, without any light from the outside."

"You're right," a quiet voice agreed. Akiva jumped.

He opened his eyes and saw a youth standing beside him, with deeply tanned skin and soft, luminous eyes. He was wearing a light-blue shirt with long *tzitzis* dangling nearly to his knees.

"What am I right about? Who are you?"

"I'm Dekel," said the other, extending a friendly hand in greeting. "Forgive me for startling you, but you were speaking the truth. Electricity is unnecessary, and I have an idea for abolishing it from the whole world!"

Suddenly, Akiva shrank back. "Wait a second. Are you an Arab?"

A flicker of sadness came and went in Dekel's eyes, telling Akiva that this was not the first time he had encountered this kind of reaction. "I was born an Arab. Today I'm a Jew — I converted. They called me Daoud Abu Nimar; today my name is David ben Avraham, a son of our father Avraham, who was the first man to convert people to Judaism."

Akiva felt the blood rush to his face. "I'm sorry. I didn't intend to hurt your feelings."

Dekel chuckled and said, "It's nothing, I'm used to it. Twenty, thirty times a day, I come up against name-calling, curses, insults — and that's only from the Jewish side. As for my Arab brothers, they have already passed a death sentence on me, as a traitor to Islam."

"How do you cope?" Akiva asked with interest.

Again Dekel smiled. It was a warm smile that made Akiva feel as though they had been friends all their lives. Small groups had gathered at the Wall for the *Ma'ariv* service, their voices rising and falling in a continuous, cacophonous hum.

"How do I cope? Just like you do. Don't they reject you for your hatred of electricity and modernity?"

A flood of warmth went through Akiva. For the first time in a very long time, he felt he was not alone. Here was a soul mate, a man who understood.

Then he remembered the psychiatrist his mother had sent him to. For a while, in that man's office, he had also felt this sense of comradeship, of being understood — until he realized that the psychiatrist had empathized not with *him*, but with his mother's pocketbook.

"How do you know about me?" he asked cautiously.

"Trust me, I do my homework."

"What's your method for getting rid of electricity worldwide?"

At that moment, the *chazan* of a nearby *minyan* intoned, "*Bayom ha-hu yiheyeh Hashem echad ushmo echad — On that day, Hashem will be One and His Name will be One.*"

"You've got your answer," Dekel said quietly.

"What do you mean?"

"On the day Hashem's Kingship rules the world, the light that He has saved will shine down on us and there will be no more need for electricity."

Akiva trembled with rage as he hissed, "I've known that since I was a little boy. *I* was *born* a Jew. What did you bring me here for?"

Dekel refused to be insulted. "We are going to help establish Hashem's

Kingship in the world. We'll chase the foxes out of *Har Habayis* and build the third *Beis Hamikdash* with our own hands. We will bring the *Mashiach!*"

16

The following night, Akiva listened for the arguing voices he had heard the night before. They came again, still debating hotly, but on a different topic this time. The voices aroused a strange yearning. Akiva longed to see the yeshivah's students, and to speak to them.

To think was to act. He sprang out of bed, dressed rapidly, and left his cabin.

It was an unusual cabin, consistent with Dekel's early promise to him. Built all of wood, there were no pipes or electrical wires — "just like it was 2,000 years ago." The other Friends of the Mikdash were crowded into a dilapidated, four-room apartment at the edge of Anafim, close by a thick stand of cypresses, where they enjoyed all the benefits of modern life: electric lights, appliances, and even — in Dekel's office — a computer.

This computer caused Akiva no end of distress. To his mind, it embodied two evils: it functioned electrically, and it had come to symbolize progress and modernity. Sometimes, when Dekel was away from his office, Akiva would sneak in on tiptoe, turn off the machine and yank the cord out of its outlet. Then he would run away and hide in anticipation of Dekel's return, and the outburst that had become a standing refrain: "Who's been tampering with my computer again?!"

Listening, Akiva would smile. Each small triumph over electricity filled him with joy. He dreamed of the day when electricity would disappear entirely from the world — when the clock of progress would move backward. Then there would be a true paradise on earth.

Akiva walked carefully in the dark, following a dusty trail at first, then crossing two fields and rounding the natural spring with its attendant firs. The path to the yeshivah was not easy, but Akiva was helped in its final stages by, ironically, electric light. Illumination streamed from the *beis midrash* windows. No expense had been spared here: scores of long, fluorescent bulbs turned night into day. Akiva climbed atop a boulder beneath one of the windows and peeked inside.

The debaters were quiet now, each absorbed in a thorny passage in his Gemara. First one, and then the other, would read several words aloud in an attempt to understand. Akiva listened intently to references to *shechitah* and the sprinkling of blood. His own blood quickened.

"I knew it! That's what *we're* learning! They're studying the laws of the *Beis Hamikdash!*"

In another corner of the vast room, a boy was learning alone from a large volume. Narrowing his eyes, Akiva read the words on the binding: "*Talmud Yerushalmi, Maseches Bikkurim.*" It was one of Shmuel Abrams' regular, twice-weekly night sessions, which he had dedicated to that tractate.

"They're completely involved in the *halachos* of the *Beis Hamikdash*! *Korbanos, bikkurim* — an entire yeshivah of Friends of the Mikdash!"

The big clock on the *beis midrash* wall read 1:15 a.m. Akiva began to climb the steps, silent as a cat. Passing the building's electrical board, he paused. The temptation was irresistible. He checked: the metal door covering the board was unlocked.

With trembling hands, Akiva opened the door. He peered at the fuses and switches inside. This was the horrible thing that had betrayed his father and sent him to his death. With a single, convulsive motion, Akiva yanked the main switch. The *beis midrash* was instantly plunged into total darkness.

"What is it? What happened?" voices shouted in alarm.

Akiva was filled with satisfaction. "Some big heroes," he called into the darkness. "Lose your precious light for a second, and you panic. You're children of an artificial world."

"Who are you?" Eli Flamm called back. With arms outstretched on either side to encounter obstacles, he threaded his way along the lines of *shtenders.*

"I want to talk with you — but without electricity."

"What do you have against electricity?" Dudu asked in amazement. This must be one of the zanies from the group camping out on the other side of the settlement. One is wackier than the next.

Akiva pulled a packet of matches from his pocket, along with a candle he kept for just such times as these. With the candle lit in his hand, he advanced deeper into the *beis midrash* toward the boys who huddled there, still slightly alarmed. "Are you willing to talk to me?"

"Well, we weren't intending to go to bed just yet anyway," Eli answered quietly.

They studied the stranger by candlelight. Akiva was about 20 years old, of medium height. An enormous yarmulke covered most of his head. Beneath, his hair was shorn close to the scalp, with long *peyos* hanging down on either side. He had a broad face, high cheekbones, and eyes that were both intelligent and sad. In the flickering light of the candle, there appeared to be dark rings under his eyes.

"Does this feel strange to you?" Akiva scoffed. "You can't manage without electricity!"

Eli said mildly, "For the second time — who are you?"

"Akiva Tamiri. I belong to the Friends of the Mikdash. I heard the way you were arguing as you learned. Why all the shouting?" He paused. "To tell the truth, I envy the way you learn together."

Gently, Eli asked, "Did we keep you from sleeping?"

"I couldn't fall asleep anyway. Tell me, are you learning about *korbanos*?"

"We're learning *Maseches Zevachim.*"

"Because you're looking forward to the rebuilding of the *Beis Hamikdash?*"

Dudu spoke up. "Of course. Every Jew believes in *Mashiach* and the third *Beis Hamikdash*. Today, or tomorrow, the *Beis Hamikdash* will be built."

Akiva's whole face lit up. With a joyous smile, he exclaimed, "Then you're just like us!"

"Like you?" Shmuel Abrams asked, bewildered. "Who are you, and what brings you here?"

"I want to tell you a story that starts about 10 years ago. Will you give me a few minutes?"

"Even an hour," Eli said.

Akiva related the story of his childhood, orphaned and bereft of his beloved father. "It was electricity that killed him. Ever since that day, I've hated electricity. It brings death to the world."

"You're mistaken," Dudu Klein said. "Electricity also brings life to the world. If everyone got rid of electricity, the way you want, people would die on operating tables. Sick people who are attached to respirators would stop breathing. There are a million good things electricity does every minute. Just think of the millions of wasted hours of darkness each night, all over the world, if there were no electric lights. True, it's artificial, but it's also a gift from Hashem, Who put the potential for electrical power into water, into coal, into the atom, and gave men the wisdom to figure out how to use it."

Akiva tasted the sourness of failure in his mouth. "Where were you all those years?" he whispered in pain. "Why couldn't I have heard such logic before, instead of all the stuff those psychologists kept babbling at me?" He sighed, then looked up. "Still, you have to admit that life was nicer a couple of thousand years ago. Nature wasn't destroyed yet, there was no pollution, the forests weren't decimated and the ozone layer wasn't depleted." Seeing his audience intent on his words, Akiva found an unexpected eloquence. "Life was more harmonious when people studied by candlelight instead of artificial light. Electric lights are too bright — too scary. It doesn't lead to closeness between people. In the days of the *Tanna'im* and the *Amora'im,* people went to bed when night fell, and woke up to the rooster's crow at dawn. Wasn't that a nicer existence?"

Eli said, "You're describing nice things. It's certainly a good thing to get up early and *daven* with the sunrise. But the world has changed a little, my friend. Have you ever heard about the guy who yelled, 'Stop the world, I want to get off'? The world is changing at an amazing pace, and you're trying to stop it with nothing but — but a broomstick. Look at you tonight, for instance. So you managed to turn off the lights in one *beis midrash.* So what? Have you changed anything? Until you've managed to flip the master switch of the world and plunge the whole globe into darkness, you've accomplished nothing!"

These words put Akiva on surer ground. "With Hashem's help, we're getting closer to the moment when we *will* rule the master switch of the world."

Dudu leaped up. "What are you talking about?"

"We'll be going up to *Har Habayis* soon," Akiva answered, eyes shining. "We'll recapture it, the *Mashiach* will come, the *Beis Hamikdash* will be built, the world will be righted — and electricity will be abolished!"

"You're waiting for the *Mashiach,*" Shmuel Abrams burst out, "in order to abolish electricity?! You expect the *Mashiach* to actualize your infantile fantasy? I feel sorry for you."

"Shmulie, stop!" Eli cried. But he was too late. Akiva had been wounded to the core. Bitterly, he shot back, "Is that the way an 'aspiring student' talks? Only scholarship is important to you — outside of that, anything goes? Where are your *middos*, your relationship to other people?"

Eli sensed that the situation was slipping out of control. He wanted to hear more from Akiva, especially the part about how his group planned to go up to the Temple Mount. Something in the way the electricity-hater spoke touched an uneasy nerve in Eli's mind.

But Akiva had already turned to run back outside, leaping with amazing agility over benches on his way. Just before he reached the door, however, his long legs tangled with a chair, and Akiva crashed to the floor.

Dudu and Eli hurried to him, but Akiva was more adept at moving in the dark than they were. As if a hidden mechanism was propelling him, he jumped up and ran to the steps. Eli's final call accompanied him through the night: "Feel free to come back and talk whenever you want. Don't be afraid, and don't be insulted."

Without pausing or even turning his head, Akiva raced forward into an open field.

Eli was furious. A tenuous connection had been forged, and then Shmuel had ruined it with his hasty and ill-considered remark. In his plan to find a link to the Friends of the Mikdash, Eli was back to square one.

He did have a mole hidden within the ranks of the group — Sruly Egozi. But Sruly wasn't much help yet. The group operated on a need-to-know basis, so that none of its members possessed more than a few details of its operations. To date, Sruly had heard nothing about future plans. All he was able to report to Eli was that they were learning about sacrifices and immersing daily in the natural spring. And he had also supplied one more piece of information: Akiva Tamiri was practically the only one whom Dekel trusted absolutely. Akiva knew how to keep his lips sealed. "Apart from his nuttiness about electricity, Akiva has a good mind and lots of talent. Dekel tells him everything," Sruly had reported.

Akiva was high up in the Friends of the Mikdash hierarchy. There was a great deal Eli could learn from him.

◆ ◆ ◆

At an hour of the morning when his fellow inmates at the Golden Towers old-age home were busy with a gentle exercise class, Arkady packed a small suitcase, covered it with a blanket, and explained to the clerk at the front desk that he was planning to take advantage of the mild winter sun to do some sunbathing on the beach. Smiling her cool, impersonal smile, the clerk wished him a pleasant morning.

Some five minutes later, Arkady spread his blanket in a quiet spot on the beach and opened his suitcase. He pulled out a bundle of clothing and arranged them on the blanket: shirt, pants, shoes, socks. To the casual observer, it would appear as though he'd taken off his outer clothing in order to take a dip. He padded barefoot up to the edge of the boardwalk, where he put on a different pair of shoes.

The car "Gray Cap" had sent for him arrived promptly. Briefcase in hand, Arkady stepped inside. Two hours later, he boarded an El Al flight to Moscow.

He had met with Gray Cap the day before to receive his instructions. Along with these, he was given a quarter of a million dollars in thousand-dollar denominations. "And that's just the advance," Gray Cap promised. "My people have decided to up the ante."

"How much?" Arkady asked, trying unsuccessfully to keep the excitement out of his voice.

"Three million."

A broad smile nearly split the old man's face in half. Thinking of it now, his spirits soared as high as the plane he was traveling on.

Arkady missed his native land. It would be a pleasure to walk Moscow's snow-covered streets once again, just as he had in the good old days. From there, he would travel to the Ukraine to visit the nuclear plant at Zaporozh'ye or Zhdanov. If he didn't find what he wanted there, he would continue on to Gelivinsk to spend a few days with his friends at the Mayak plant, where he had worked for decades as assistant manager, right up until his move to Israel. The nuclear plant he had told Gray Cap about, at Tura, was purely a work of fiction. Such a plant did not, and never had, existed. Gray Cap had swallowed the story without blinking.

Arkady was an ardent Communist. He knew how to guard Mother Russia's secrets. He would never divulge the location of the secret nuclear facility Stalin had established at the foot of the Urals. The facility at Mayak had been a well-kept secret for many years, and the place where Arkady Bogdanov had enjoyed great prestige and a pay scale to match. Had the former Soviet empire still been standing, he would never have been permitted to leave. Arkady bitterly regretted having ever decided to go. There was just no substitute for one's native land. He whiled away the four-hour flight immersed in pleasant memories and some conversation with Dmitri, his seatmate, a friendly young man who had given up on Israel and was returning to Russia. "Ah! To taste those meat-filled piroshki again!" Dmitri laughed, smacking his lips. "And some borscht, washed down with Volga vodka — just like the good old days!"

When the plane touched down, Arkady had to restrain himself from bursting into song. His plans had been made and perfected. He knew exactly what he had to do next. The results of his actions mattered little to him. His primary concern was with the money he would be paid on completing his mission successfully — money with which to end his days in luxury in his beloved Russia. What devastation might be wrought by the "dolls" he procured for his anonymous backers meant little to him: he would be many miles away from Israel by then.

True, Yefim and Galina would remain behind in the danger zone, but in his great anger at them Arkady did not let that bother him, either. Maybe — maybe — he would give them warning — just enough time to run. But only if they expressed regret for what they had done to him. A frigid wind enveloped them the instant they stepped off the plane. "And to think," Arkady remarked to Dmitri, "that just four hours away, the sun is shining."

"The sun's always shining in Israel," Dmitri replied. "It's the faces of the people that are cloudy. All Israelis are nervous wrecks. Here, a smiling Russia awaits us!"

"You exaggerate," Arkady protested. "Smiles have been pretty scarce here, too."

They stood in line at passport control. Arkady anticipated a royal welcome. As a top atomic scientist, his name had been famous throughout Russia for years, and his picture had appeared frequently in the newspapers. He had been photographed shaking hands with Soviet leaders Khrushchev, Brezhnev, and Kosygin, and later on with Andropov and even Gorbachev. The name Arkady Bogdanov had been a well-known one in Russia.

To his surprise, he found the airport personnel indifferent to both his name and the sight of his face. Not so much as a smile or a wink did they express in their joy at seeing one of the country's top scientists — a man who had brought much honor to Russia — returning to their borders. His passport was stamped by clerks with faces as frozen as the wind outside.

"So much for the world's praise. Less than five years after I left, and already I've become anonymous." Arkady grew bitter again, as Moscow's ice entered his heart.

A taxi took him into the city. The driver, a gregarious fellow, would have enjoyed a chat, but Arkady's stony expression chilled him into silence. They drove past a long industrial stretch at the outskirts to the city, even bleaker than usual under the gray skies. "Where to?" the driver asked. "We're entering Moscow now."

"Go on," Arkady ordered, "until I tell you to stop."

It began to rain. The taxi skidded slightly on the wet asphalt as, on Arkady's instructions, the driver turned into Karl Marx Avenue.

"Stop," Arkady snapped.

He handed the driver a large bill and didn't wait for the change. He knew he was taking a risk in deviating from usual practice. A man who wishes to remain in the shadows does not call attention to himself by doing something unusual. With a shrug, Arkady stepped out of the taxi and onto the snowy sidewalk. He stood facing a gray and unattractive apartment complex. Old Svetlana lived here. She had been his assistant at Mayak, and today worked as assistant manager at the Zaporozh'ye nuclear plant. His advance research had unearthed the information that Svetlana was home on vacation now.

Arkady flipped through his small telephone book until he found the name he wanted: Svetlana Shesuyov, Karl Marx 243-G. He would call her at once. She would rejoice at seeing her former employer again, and would open every locked gate for him. After that, all would flow as smoothly as the Moscow River.

17

The phone rang 10 times before it was picked up. Arkady would have given up, except that he knew his secretary of old: Svetlana never hurried to answer a phone. Years of working with a bank of shrilling instruments had inured her to their summons.

When she did pick up the phone, he recognized her voice immediately.

"Who is it?"

"It's me — Arkady Bogdanov."

There was silence for several long seconds, as though the elderly woman was processing what she'd just heard. Suddenly, she emitted a shriek. "Arkady! How wonderful to hear your voice again after all this time? How is your life in Israel?"

"Excellent. Can I come up to see you?"

Svetlana was bewildered. "What did you say?"

Arkady gave a bark of laughter. "I've come on a quick visit to Russia and at the moment I'm about a hundred meters from your house."

Svetlana reverted instantly to the practical and efficient secretary. "Where are you staying?"

"I've just arrived."

"Go check into the Russia Hotel near Red Square. Call me from your hotel room and we'll set up a meeting in Red Square or Alexander Park."

The line was disconnected.

◆ ◆ ◆

The Russia Hotel was the largest in the world, capable of accommodating 6,000 guests at one time. Located just behind Red Square, the place resembled a giant office building. Arkady descended into the bowels of the Metro, Moscow's underground subway system, for the ride to the hotel.

Thousands of workers were hurrying home at this time of day. Preoccupied, they had no eye for the beauty around them. Arkady, on the other hand, was in no hurry. He allowed himself to dawdle, touristlike, and gaze at the grandeur that was the subway station. Its architectural style had been influenced by the Czar's palaces, the ceiling curved and adorned with many chandeliers. As Arkady stood and gazed, he became aware of several other people, obviously tourists, who were as moved as he by the beauty and on the point of engaging him in conversation about it. He quickly moved away.

The train brought him to the Russia Hotel, and a repeat of the depressing welcome he had encountered at the airport. No one recognized him.

"It's better this way," he tried to assure himself. "I'll have complete freedom of movement."

The reception clerk took his passport and handed him a card on which his room number and floor were printed. "You will get the key from the chambermaid in charge of your floor," she explained. "Whenever you leave the hotel, you will give her the key, and she will give it back to you when you return. When you wish to enter the hotel, you will show the doorman your card."

With a thin smile, Arkady thanked her for the instructions and went to find his room. He phoned Svetlana at once. This time, she answered on the second ring. As soon as she had identified his voice, she spoke one sentence.

"We meet in Red Square at 10 o'clock tomorrow morning, near Lenin's tomb."

◆ ◆ ◆

Lenin's tomb was a massive mausoleum made of marble and concrete, in which the mortal remains of Vladimir Ilyich Lenin, founder of the Soviet Union, rested in a glass coffin. Arkady came early and spent the waiting time recalling the way Communist leaders used to meet here on the 7th of November, to review the troops in honor of the Revolution. Svetlana did not put in an appearance until after Arkady had endured, in boredom, the hourly spectacle of the changing of the guard.

"Welcome to our beautiful Red Square," she said from behind him.

She had arrived just after 10 o'clock, wearing a heavy black coat and hat. Svetlana looked exactly the same as she had on the day Arkady left Russia. The eyes in her lined face were as penetrating as they had always been.

"Very few people know that this place was called 'Red Square' a long time before Communism," Arkady remarked.

"It's enough that the two of us know," his former secretary replied patiently. Comments about the name "Red Square" were an old password from their Mayak days.

Arkady smiled broadly. "Svetlana, what happened? What is this fear in your old age? You're afraid to let me in to have a good, strong cup of tea?"

"Let's walk over to Alexander Park," Svetlana said. "I'll explain there."

"She's still afraid that the room might be bugged," Arkady thought with amusement. Decades of living under a repressive regime had instilled a lifelong fear in all its citizens. He inclined his head in agreement. "Let's go."

They passed between the historical museum and the Kremlin walls and turned left to enter the park. Slowly, they strolled along the snowy paths until they came to a small wood cabin. The cabin was heated.

"I arranged for the heat in advance," Svetlana explained, "and bribed the guard to leave for an hour. That's why I was late."

Arkady sat down in a simple wooden chair and rubbed his raw, red hands to restore some warmth to them. "I had forgotten how cold our Russian winters can be. In Israel, the sun always shines."

Svetlana gave him a shrewd look. "What brings you here?"

"Lack of intelligence has never been one of your faults — but cowardice apparently is. What has made you as frightened as a rabbit?"

"Lately, several members of our Mafia have tried to get their hands on some cute little atomic bombs, straight from the reactor. They bribe scientists with huge sums of money. The government has heightened its vigilance, watching every scientist and worker who has ever been employed at a nuclear reactor. That explains my fear. I've noticed the way they've been watching me lately, and I'm not taking any chances." She paused. "Speaking of cute little bombs, do they have anything to do with your sudden visit to Russia?"

Arkady held his breath. She was smart, very smart, her shrewdness, like fine wine, only growing more pronounced with age. With a sphinxlike expression, he said, "Our Mafia heads are experts at assassination using machine guns. What do small-time criminals need with nuclear bombs?"

Fat white flakes began falling outside the window. Svetlana answered, "Our criminals have matured a little since you left, Arkady. First of all, Communism has died and the criminal classes in Russia are celebrating. Second, I'm not talking about the Russian Mafia. It's Iran.

"Iran?" His voice remained impassive, but above his turtleneck sweater, Arkady's face began to perspire.

"Aha!" Svetlana cried triumphantly, as though able to read the fears in his mind. "The road from Iran to the destruction of Israel is short. They don't have the patience to wait until they'll be able to develop nuclear weapons on their own. They're prepared to pay our Mafia people millions for a working nuclear missile."

Arkady chewed his lips. Could he trust her? Could she be bought?

"Look, Svetlana," he said gently, "I want to make a deal that will allow you to live comfortably for the rest of your days. You'll even be able to leave your Boris an inheritance that will make him bless his mother all his life."

"A deal? What are you talking about?" Svetlana's forehead was furrowed, her eyes darting suspiciously.

Summoning all his powers of persuasion, Arkady said, "It concerns the very subject you were just talking about. You were right — I'm also interested in purchasing a 'cute little bomb,' straight from the reactor. I'll give you half a million dollars if you can get enough material from the plant at Zaporozh'ye to make two small bombs. I'll worry about the rest. And don't try to deny it: I know that you're assistant manager at Zaporozh'ye."

Svetlana's eyes nearly bulged out of their sockets. "Arkady, you too? I wouldn't have believed it of my honest boss. You've become an atomic pirate — like our Mafia?"

"Don't preach at me," Arkady snapped, rising from his chair. "I haven't come all this way to sit and listen to that. I remember very well how, at Mayak, you squirreled away heavy water and plutonium and sold them to Iraq for $100,000." His voice grew very quiet. "By the way, I have a couple of papers that document that deal very nicely. Do you want to see them?" He placed his briefcase on the table, opened it, and began rummaging inside.

Svetlana was silent. Her face had grown waxen and her eyes moved constantly. She checked her watch; the guard would be back any minute.

"Listen, Arkady," she said hoarsely. "Maybe there's something to talk about. I need to think."

"No! There's not enough time. I know that it's possible to buy you off with money. The only thing we need to discuss is price. So let's start at the end. How much do you want?"

"Arkady, it's not the money. Security at the reactor has hermetically sealed the place. It's impossible to take out so much as a glass of water without official permission — and you're talking about enriched uranium and plutonium!"

Arkady was fast losing patience. "This talk is going nowhere. Svetlana,

I'm going back to the hotel. I'll call you tomorrow. For your own sake, I hope your answer will be positive."

He left the cabin before her. As he did, he pulled a document out of his briefcase and left it on the table. It contained a transcript of a conversation in which Svetlana had taken part at the Mayak reactor, just a short time before Israeli Prime Minister Menachem Begin sent his air force to blow up the nuclear reactor in Iraq. The transcript spoke for itself, and testified to 100 witnesses to Svetlana's role in passing heavy water and enriched uranium from Mayak to French scientists working for Iraq.

When he stepped outside, he saw the guard standing there, shivering with cold and shaking pipe ash down onto the newly fallen snow. Had he overheard their talk, or part of it? Arkady hurried away. The situation was becoming more complicated by the minute.

◆ ◆ ◆

Three days later, as he lowered his weary body onto his hotel bed, Arkady felt the full weight of his years. He was old and worthless. The aura that had surrounded him once was gone. No one recognized him any longer. In the dining room, he had approached a table of older guests and introduced himself. Expecting enthusiasm, he was shattered by the depths of their indifference. One of them even said, "So you were a great scientist. Where did that get you? Russia is drowning in vodka, everyone's drunk here; drunkenness is our country's curse. Do you have a cure, or can you carry nothing but atomic particles in your head?"

The other diners had agreed with the speaker. "We used to be proud of you and our other scientists — until our eyes were opened. For all her achievements, Russia is a land dying of hunger. We were the first to orbit outer space, even as millions of our countrymen were starving for bread."

They had scorned him — literally, scorned him! He, Arkady Bogdanov, who had lived his life believing that he was serving his motherland and sacrificing himself for her.

He had felt the same when he reached retirement age. In his naivete, he had expected to be begged not to abandon his important work for

Russia. But no one had begged, or even asked. On the contrary, young career men, beneath him on the ladder of success, had waited impatiently to take his place. In his bitterness, Arkady had begun threatening to leave Russia for Israel. Again, no one had reacted. So Arkady had left, vowing never again to set foot on the soil of the land that had taken everything he had to give, and then ungratefully spurned him.

He had remained true to that vow until Gray Cap came along with his staggering offer. Three million dollars! And now, Arkady was beginning to worry that he would return to Israel empty-handed. During the past few days, he had sent numerous coded messages and telegrams to old friends: reactor supervisors in Zhdanov, Zaporozh'ye, Kerch, Pnepropetrovsk, Chernobyl. Two didn't bother to answer, while the other three sent back the same reply: "With all due respect to the past, the situation is different today."

That morning, he had heard on the radio that Professor Leonid Pozorski, manager of the Ribna reactor, was staying at the Metropol, Moscow's most luxurious and expensive hotel. Arkady had gone there at once, requesting a meeting. Pozorski had let him cool his heels for two hours before condescending to a short talk — in which he strongly rejected Arkady's proposal.

Arkady was furious. "Leonid, I'm not asking for any favors. I'll pay!"

"Money doesn't solve everything," Leonid had answered coldly. "You've been in Israel five years now. Perhaps you were sent here by the Israeli Secret Service?"

"Are you crazy?" Arkady leaped out of his chair. "Israel has an ample nuclear arsenal of her own. Do you think they need to send an old man like me to shop here for materials?"

Leonid shrugged. "What do I know? After five years there, I no longer trust you. You've been brainwashed!"

"Leonid!"

But Pozorski tapped impatiently on his wristwatch, to indicate that the meeting was over.

And his former secretary, Svetlana, had phoned him yesterday to inform him that the incriminating documents he brought with him were no use as a weapon after all. The present government was very forgiving of such transgressions from the past.

So Arkady twisted and turned in his hotel bed, beside himself with rage and frustration. Everyone was against him: Russia, Israel, his friends, his son Yefim and Yefim's wife, Galina. He knew what was really behind their so-called patriotism. They were all liars, willing to sell their souls for money. Therein lay the problem: he wasn't offering them enough. If his offer was more attractive, they would be listening to him. He had heard rumors of nuclear warheads being sold for ten million dollars. In comparison, his own offer was laughable.

But with no more than three million to look forward to, how much could he offer? A quarter million? A quarter million here, a quarter million there, and he would have nothing left!

He jumped out of bed and yanked at the curtain drawstring. His rage was directed at Gray Cap now, who did not understand the mentality of the people he was dealing with. Money, money, money, that was all they understood.

After several days of steady snowfall, Moscow's skies had partially cleared. As Arkady stood looking out the window at the white street below, he realized how completely his plan had failed. He would never succeed in getting the goods straight from the source — fresh from the reactor.

At that moment, he decided to forego his pride and call one of his old friends about trying to obtain what he wanted in Russia's black market. Hundreds of nuclear bombs had drifted around the Soviet Union in the past. Gray Cap would be just as happy with the results. While it was true that the destructive power of any of those explosives was not equal to one big bomb, it was still nothing to sneer at. General Alexander himself had talked of the hundred thousand people that would die if one of those "small" bombs — stolen from the reactors in years past — should explode.

The men who had sent Arkady would be satisfied.

◆ ◆ ◆

Yefim Bogdanov was disturbed. He sat opposite the police inspector at the precinct house in Bat Yam, and pounded a fist on the desk. "I'm positive he didn't drown!"

Inspector Dani Devash studied Yefim's crimson face with interest. Years of experience had taught him that the reactions of family members to crimes could bring him useful information.

"Why are you getting angry at me?" he asked mildly. "We're doing the best we can."

Yefim lowered his voice a notch. "But it's impossible. An old man walks out of a nursing home with a blanket over his arm, walks down to the beach just 300 meters away, and suddenly disappears — with only his clothes left on the sand. I tell you again, my father is an excellent swimmer and has remarkable physical strength, more like a man of 20."

"What is such an old-young man doing in a nursing home?" Devash asked quietly.

Yefim cleared his throat, embarrassed. Devash made a mental note to investigate this point further. Aloud, he said, "We'll continue to check into the matter," and stood up to shake hands.

After the heavyset Russian had left his office, Devash went through Arkady Bogdanov's file once more. It included a picture of the old man, and Devash spent a few minutes studying the eyes. They reflected a fierce independence and stubbornness. This was a man who was capable of moving walls. Devash read through the file carefully, and this time his attention was caught by a line he had missed before: *Previous Profession: Atomic Scientist.*

A red warning light began flashing on and off in Devash's brain. The light seemed to surround the words he had just read.

Devash promised himself to pursue this case to its conclusion.

18

Early in the evening, when the *beis midrash* lights at Yeshivas Aish Aharon were ablaze, an unusual visitor arrived. He had apple-red cheeks and a remarkable paunch. His forehead was deeply lined and his eyes, behind thick glasses, were deep and penetrating. He wore a thick cashmere coat, with a dark scarf tossed carelessly around his neck.

The boys, deeply immersed in their learning, did not notice his entrance. But Yonah Pinter took no umbrage. He checked the Gemaras on the *shtenders,* and nodded to himself. "Akiva was right. They *are* learning *Maseches Zevachim.*"

At that point, one of the students left his *shtender* and came over to extend a warm welcome. Eli Flamm shook Yonah Pinter's hand vigorously. Rav Anshel observed the two as they moved into a corner, where they engaged in lively dialogue. A few words reached Rav Anshel's ears.

"You're the yeshivah's founder? Ah, a fine young man you are, tall and good looking, very impressive. If I had a daughter, you'd be my son-in-law." Rav Anshel saw Eli cringe under this onslaught of flattery.

"I just don't understand Eli," Simchah Tauber told Dudu Klein. "Why is he so attracted to those nuts? Why can't he just tell them 'no!'?"

Both shook their heads. If Eli wasn't such an outstanding Torah scholar, if he didn't possess the stature he enjoyed at Aish Aharon, he would be getting quite a tongue-lashing from these two. To their minds, Eli's willingness to consort with the group camping out in their settlement showed a disturbing tendency toward fanaticism.

Yonah Pinter, meanwhile, sighed with satisfaction. "I see that you're learning the laws of the *Beis Hamikdash.*"

"Yes." Eli kept his expression impassive.

"How long will you continue to dance at two weddings?" Yonah scolded. "Why won't you take this all the way? Why don't you bring all your friends to prostrate themselves on *Har Habayis?*"

"Don't put the cart before the horse," Eli said, smiling.

Yonah leaned closer. "Listen to me, my friend. You're a young man after my own heart. We need more like you in our group. We can accomplish great things together! Soon, the whole world will be talking about us. We are about to chase the foxes off the Temple Mount!"

"How?" Eli was eager for more information.

Yonah's eyes grew sly. "You want all the secrets at once? If you become a member of Friends of the Mikdash and prove your loyalty for two months, you'll hear a great many details from me."

With that, he abruptly took his leave.

"Two months," Eli whispered to himself. "He's trying to fool me. It's going to happen much sooner than that. Apparently, he came here now to try to sow misleading information."

If Akiva Tamiri, that hater of progress, only knew what sort of electronic devices were hidden in his room! Just yesterday, Sruly Egozi had brought him a tape recording of a meeting that had taken place in Akiva's room:

Dekel: Judgment Day is coming nearer. The mosques of Omar and of El-Aksa will fly off the Temple Mount and no trace will remain, not even a memory of them. We'll clear the way for the *Beis Hamikdash.*

Akiva: I want to understand, once and for all. Are we going to build the *Beis Hamikdash* ourselves, or is it going to descend from Heaven?

Dekel: Of course we'll build it — we have a positive commandment to do so. Many of the early halachic authorities count it as a commandment that obligates all of Israel.

Akiva: Dekel, you sure know your stuff! By the way, how do you plan to destroy the mosques?

Dekel: We'll sweep them away with the broom of destruction!

Akiva: Dekel, really!

Dekel: We'll blow them up.

Akiva (scornfully): The Jewish underground already tried that — and failed.

Dekel: The poor Jewish underground... Where are they, and where are we?

Akiva: Where *are* we?

Dekel: The earth will tremble, and the mighty mosques will come tumbling down like a house of cards.

Akiva: Dekel, stop speaking in riddles!

Dekel: I know the mosques at the Kosel like the back of my own hand. I can find my way down to the Well of Winds' beneath the Mosque of Omar. From there to an earthquake is not far at all, my friend!

Akiva: And how do you propose to create an earthquake? You'll pray for one?

Dekel: It's not necessary for you to understand everything. Just make a note of this: In a few weeks there will be an earthquake that will remove the mosques from the Temple Mount.

Akiva (giving up): I just don't get it!

But Eli did understand, and he was very worried. Sruly had told him about the huge pen that the Friends of the Mikdash had built at Anafim. It housed some 200 milk goats and a similar number of lambs. They'd brought in an expert to teach them a special method of making salted goat-cheese. The dairy farm was bringing in nice profits, but Eli knew that profit was not the group's primary goal. They were raising cattle to serve as sacrifices from the moment the *Beis Hamikdash* was built! The young lambs were slated for a *chatas* and also as *asham, shelamim* and *olah*. At the moment the Friends were content with sheep, but soon they would be investing in calves as well.

"From where did Dekel get hundreds of goats and lambs from?" Eli had asked in astonishment. But Sruly had been unable to enlighten him. Dekel was a man of mystery, and the group saw him only from time to time. He never returned empty-handed. Each time he set out for Jerusalem he returned with impressive booty. On top of his other qualities, he was apparently an outstanding organizer who had all the Friends of the Mikdash following him blindly.

"He has something," Eli admitted in the privacy of his thoughts. "He's charismatic and smart and has natural leadership ability, like someone who's been groomed from birth to lead others."

All the same, Dekel's dangerous talk had Eli very worried. He had a theory of his own about this "earthquake" of Dekel's. As much as he hoped that his fears would prove groundless, the more he thought about it, the more convinced he was that they were not. His theory could certainly be based on reality. And that made Eli very, very afraid.

◆ ◆ ◆

Arkady's next trip took him to Leningrad, which was once again called St. Petersburg. He flew there on a night flight from Moscow. Looking down indifferently on Moscow's lights, spreading out in their full glory as his plane gained elevation, he realized that the sight would have, in the past, filled him with a sense of heart-bursting patriotism. Not anymore.

"Good-bye, Moscow — *au revoir*. I won't be coming back."

When he had his money he would buy himself a dream house on one of the Caribbean islands and would spend the rest of his life sunbathing and fishing in the gentle breezes that blew off the ocean. He would have enough for four lifetimes, and he would use it well. He would not be back to Russia. Mother Russia had plunged a knife into her son's back.

There was one thought that afforded him some comfort. This time, he was traveling to a sure destination. He had arranged matters in a series of more than 20 phone calls. Without any display of shame, he had contacted several shady figures at the acme of the Russian underworld, people he once would not have deigned to look at. He hated himself for having to do it, but he was left with no choice. It was the Mafia or nothing.

The magic words, "a million dollars," opened all doors. These people demanded a considerably lower tariff than the reactor supervisors. In fact, the business proved astonishingly easy to conclude. People had always joked around, saying that laying hands on an atomic weapon was child's play in Russia; Arkady was now seeing the truth of this with his own eyes. It really required almost no effort at all on his part. All he had to do was get off the plane at St. Petersburg, take the metro to the Leningrad Hotel, and phone his contact man. Members of the St. Petersburg branch of operations would visit his hotel room to confirm his identity before handing him a specific set of instructions as to how and where he would receive his two "dolls."

It would all go according to plan. There was nothing to worry about. And yet, Arkady *was* worried. He kept feeling that he had forgotten something, something vital, but he did not know what it was. The troubling thought gave him no peace.

◆ ◆ ◆

The Leningrad Hotel was beautifully appointed in Western style. It was modern, the service was sophisticated, and there were none of the restrictions that Arkady had found at the Moscow Hotel. He was free to come and go as he pleased.

He lolled at his ease in the suite he had taken, drinking in the view, determined to enjoy his stay to the fullest. St. Petersburg is a much younger city than Moscow, and 70 years under Communist rule had altered it almost unrecognizably. Still, the city commanded a stunning view that drew even the discerning Western eye. Had it been summer, Arkady would have enjoyed the "white nights" of St. Petersburg, when tourists flock to the rivers to sail under bewilderingly bright night skies. Now, in the grip of winter, the city lay blanketed, white and still.

When he had had his fill of the view, Arkady picked up the phone and punched in the number he had been given. One ring, two, three, four. The receiver was picked up.

"This is Anatoly."

"Arkady here."

"I'll be there in half an hour. What's your room number?"

"Ninth floor, room 954."

"I'll be there."

Arkady opened the door of the minibar and poured himself a glass of Golden Vodka to strengthen him for what lay ahead. Anatoly arrived sooner than he had promised, knocking on Arkady's door in just a quarter-hour's time. He was obviously armed, with bulging biceps, greasy hair, and eyes that were like two dark holes. Arkady offered him a drink, but Anatoly refused. "Where's the money?" he barked.

"What money?"

"Are you trying to make a fool of me? I want to see the million dollars with my own eyes before I bring you the goods!"

Arkady gasped. He squeezed his head between his hands. *This* was the point he had overlooked. The money! Anatoly wanted to see the million dollars, while Arkady had — barely — a quarter of a million in hand.

A speechless rage engulfed him — rage at Gray Cap, for expecting him to fill a basket with nuclear goods for pennies.

The two black holes were following him suspiciously. "So where's the money?" Anatoly asked again.

Arkady was perspiring profusely, but he managed to maintain his outward composure. Coldly, he said, "I received a small advance. By the time you get me the materials I'll have received the rest from Israel."

Anatoly said angrily, "What are you talking about? The stuff's ready — just hand over the money!" His eyes raked the king-sized bed and the ornate chandelier that hung above their heads. "I see that you have plenty of it. You're living high."

Anatoly walked to the door, and toyed with the chain latch. Arkady was seized with a sudden fear: If Anatoly left this room without the money he had been promised, Arkady's life would be worth less than an onion peel. The Mafia could be unforgiving.

"Wait!" he screamed. "Let me give you something on account."

Anatoly returned to the center of the room, beginning to smile. "Let's see what you have for me," he purred. Arkady clenched his fists; there was a time when he would not have hesitated to slap this kind of scum across the face. But the wheel had turned, and top scientists had to bow and scrape before such creatures. He counted $100,000 into Anatoly's hands, and was given a receipt with a scrawled signature that he doubted the criminal ever honored.

After Anatoly had gone, Arkady sighed with relief and changed into a cool, cotton T-shirt. He took a few minutes to recover from the encounter before picking up the phone. Gray Cap answered on the third ring. Arkady threw all the force of his personality into his ultimatum: "Either give me all the money at once, or I will stay in Russia!"

Gray Cap hung up, promising to call back within the hour. When he did, he said simply, "On the day after tomorrow you will receive $2 million by special messenger. You'll get the rest when we meet in Israel."

◆ ◆ ◆

Dear Benjy,

I know that you're angry at me. You have no idea what happened — why your sister suddenly stopped writing. We've been corresponding for such a long time, and now, such a long break without any letters! I'm sure you've been judging me favorably, knowing how busy I am in school. I wish that were the reason.

Benjy, what's new in New York? How is your work coming along? Ever since the day you opened your "People's Clinic," we hear very little from you. Dovy keeps complaining; he says that ever since Ima and Abba disappeared in India, you're his father figure. And now you hardly ever write or call. Benjy, even a fax of two sentences can lift all of our morales.

I'm sure you're asking yourself, "Okay, what's doing with Judy? Does she know how to do anything except give orders?"

Benjy, out of all the people in the world, only you can understand what's in my heart. There's only one ophthalmologist in the world who's also my oldest brother. You know that my left eye has always been considered my weaker one. Well, now the weak one is saying, "Hey, I'm stronger," because my right eye — the healthy one — is wearing a giant bandage.

What happened, you ask? Nothing special. We didn't want to worry you, so no one told you anything. Eli, Dovy, and Moishy kept it to themselves, and agreed to let me tell you about it in my own way.

The Goldenblum's garden has some ornamental bushes growing in it, and also some kind of cactus. It has green leaves that end in thin, sharp, brown spikes. Adina was always saying that we ought to snip off the sharp tips, that they're dangerous. Too bad we didn't get around to doing it. I'm usually careful when watering the plants. This time, I wasn't careful enough. I bent over too far when watering the cactus, and before I knew it, a horrible pain shot through my right eye. I jumped back, but it was too late.

As you can imagine, I screamed to high heaven. They took me to the emergency room by ambulance, where my eye was treated on the spot. Now they're waiting to remove the bandage to see what shape my eye is in. I overheard some of the doctors talking — they didn't know I speak English. They think there's been damage to the retina or maybe some other part of the eye.

Abba and Ima always taught us about having a good eye." These days, I find myself praying, "Hashem, I've lived with a 'good eye' all my life. I've tried to live by what my father and mother taught me. Today I'm pleading with You to deal with me with a 'good eye,' and return my eye to health and vision."

As an ophthalmologist, what do you think my chances are? I feel a burning pain. Does that say anything about the seriousness of the injury?

I'll stop now. Everything's starting to swim in front of my eye, including the writing on this paper.

I miss you,

Judy

◆ ◆ ◆

Dear Judy,

I'm shocked by what happened to you! And why did you think you had to be strong after that?

Eli, Dovy, and Moishy — why did they keep quiet about this? You all know that you're always on my mind. Everything I do, my work, my career, is secondary to the main thing — my dear brothers and my dear only sister, all of you so far away in Israel. I'm the only one who chose to stay in New York, not to be dependent on Mark Goldenblum's support. But I do think of him and his wife with great appreciation, every day. Like the song says, "I'm in the west, but my heart lies in the east."

Judy, please fax me copies of your medical file, and we'll see what can be done. One thing's for sure: medicine is more advanced here than in Israel. Mount Sinai Hospital, where I work, has an excellent ophthalmology department. If you should need an operation, I want you to fly over here immediately! In my opinion, every day you delay is a pity.

Much love to Dovy and Moishy. A special note to Eli: I understand that you're learning well in your yeshivah. Your descriptions of the Friends of the Mikdash group made me laugh — total nut cases! I hope they aren't holding you back in your learning. Speaking of your yeshivah, how I envy you. It sounds wonderful — though the name hurts my heart. "Aish Aharon" — how fitting. Abba was all fire: the fire of chesed, of yiras shamayim, of love for his fellow Jew. Why did he, Ima, and Shlomo have to disappear in such a tragic way? I know we mustn't ask such questions, so I'll stop. But sometimes I feel weak.

Judy, let me know immediately what's happening with your eye and what sort of rehabilitation has been taking place. I hope that it will be restored to full strength and that we'll soon see both your blue eyes laughing with joy, as they always used to do.

I'm davening for you,

Benjy

P.S. FOR ELI'S EYES ONLY — CONFIDENTIAL!!

Your suspicion was right. Abba wrote this a month before he disap-

peared. I have the file I found in a hidden drawer in his desk years ago. At the time, I thought it was only an abstract theory. Today, I'm beginning to appreciate Abba's long-term vision.

I'm very worried about Judy. Her injured eye may get worse without the proper treatment. Please send her to New York as soon as possible!

Yours,

Benjy

19

A massive gray Volga picked him up at the hotel. Equipped with powerful front-wheel drive, the car dealt easily with St. Petersburg's snow-covered avenues. It traversed a number of icy side streets on its way to Anatoly and his friends' "bunker," situated almost at the edge of the city. Riding in the darkened back seat, Arkady felt as though this nightmarish journey would never end. Even in his most pessimistic moments, he had never envisioned his trip to Russia taking such a turn. Depressed thoughts scratched at his consciousness like wolves of prey.

"You wanted an adventure," Arkady told himself. "Well, you got what you wanted." And it was not over yet — not by a long shot. Waiting in the wings was a thrilling ride to the port, and then a pleasure trip in the company of two suitcases of nuclear explosives.

His bones ached. This was not an experience for a man his age. And the money was melting as quickly as ice cream in the sun. There wouldn't be much left of the three million that Gray Cap had promised him. Anatoly and his friends would take a million, and who knew how many hundreds of thousands more would disappear along the way? It would have been simpler by far to board a plane — but that would be sheer madness. Imagine trying to pass through customs with the cargo he would be carrying!

"What do you have in there?" the airport official would ask.

"Nothing special. Just an atom bomb or two."

No, only the sea route was open to him with this particular cargo. The Mafia had set him up with an old smuggler by the name of Clement Breinan, captain of the Norwegian ship, the *Charlotta Simpaya*. Breinan had demanded an exorbitant sum in payment — $50,000, in advance, to smuggle Arkady and his cargo out via Finland and the North Sea. How many times would he have to switch ships en route? The Strait of Dover and the English Channel awaited him, and a journey through the Atlantic, rounding France and half the Iberian Peninsula, before entering the Mediterranean through the Straits of Gibraltar, and on to his distant port of destination.

The car made its way down a narrow lane bordered on both sides by tall, dense bushes. The ice on the bushes formed weird shapes. Behind, two rows of trees caged them in. The atmosphere was sinister.

"We have arrived." Alex, the driver, killed the motor.

Stepping out of the heated car into air some 60 degrees colder took Arkady's breath away. "Quickly, get me inside," he gasped. "I'm dying."

"And I'm not cold?" Alex threw back over his shoulder, as he began to lead the way.

They passed through a snowy courtyard. Someone had left his footprints there before them. The distinctive mark was recognizable: it came from a pair of "Salamandra" boots. The sight gave Arkady a sharp pang of nostalgia for his pre-Israel days in this, his native land.

Up ahead stood a four-storied mansion, all of pale gray marble, built in the style of the Russian Czars. Each corner boasted a tower with its own gate. Long rows of windows ran along each side. Arkady was able to spot at least five guards, armed with Uzi submachine guns, on the flat roof. They were protected from the frigid temperatures by well-insulated jumpsuits.

The driver rang the bell at the front door, which opened a moment later. A stream of warm air burst into their faces, causing Arkady to gasp again. He glimpsed a gorilla of a man holding a pistol. He appeared at least seven feet tall, with arms and legs like tree trunks. Arkady wondered why such a fellow needed a gun; his fingers looked strong enough to break bones without the slightest trouble.

They entered quickly, then crossed a large foyer into an inner room where Anatoly was waiting with two of his cohorts. The room was large and lavishly furnished, the sofas upholstered in a dull-rose color. A white brick fireplace exuded life-giving warmth.

These men had money, and were not afraid to flaunt it. They sat in garish, rose-colored easy chairs, smoking expensive cigarettes, flanked by ornaments of crystal, silver, and 24-karat gold. A giant crystal chandelier hung in the center of the ceiling, emitting a thousand glints of brilliant light. Arkady was certain that these men had no artistic appreciation for the original paintings on the walls, all by Eastern European masters. The suits they wore were the last word in Western fashion, purchased no doubt in some of London's finest shops.

Every pair of eyes was fixed, with the frank interest of hungry wolves, on the briefcase in Arkady's hand. A sudden fear took hold of the old man: What if these criminals simply stole his money and, then, — did away with him? They were conscienceless, after all. Why hadn't he planned for such a contingency?

"I'm too honest," he mused. "I'm not used to dealing with crooks." Even as the thought crossed his mind, he came up with a simple solution.

They shook hands. Arkady was invited to sit. Masking his distaste for the gaudy furniture, he did as he was told. The oldest of his three hosts — he appeared in his middle 40s — spoke in a gravelly voice, a thick aura of smoke and alcohol surrounding him at every breath. A long red scar ran from beneath his ear to his throat.

"I am Victor Maximov, head of operations in this neighborhood. This is my right-hand man, Sasha Smolani." He thumped the shoulder of the man seated beside him, whose paunch stuck out in front of him like a small mountain.

Sasha rose fractionally from his chair, affording Arkady a glimpse of his gargantuan proportions. He was surely one of the world's 10 fattest men. Arkady estimated his weight at about 500 pounds, and wondered how the fellow's heart managed to keep pumping under such a load, and how the chair beneath him remained in one piece.

"And this is our liaison man, Anatoly Sarmatiev, a direct descendant of the noble family of Sarmatiev," the boss continued, gesturing at the man Arkady had already met in his hotel room. "Anatoly, did you tell him about your lineage? The Sarmatievs were Russia's Rothschilds, and he keeps it to himself!"

The friendliness, Arkady knew, was calculated to throw him off his guard. He nodded once, then carefully uttered the sentence that he hoped would keep him alive in this company. "Pleased to meet you. I am Arkady Bogdanov. In the past, I was supervisor of the nuclear reactor at Mayak. Today I live in Israel. Before I left, I told my cohorts where I would be met and they are tracking my whereabouts. I gave the people who sent me here an exact itinerary of where I'd be going and who I'd be meeting with."

The three exchanged silent glances. Arkady sensed that his gamble had worked. His life would be spared — for the moment, at any rate. He took advantage of the momentum to add, offhandedly, "My backers are tracking my every move. I'm supposed to report to them every six hours."

"Anatoly, get the barrel," Victor Maximov ordered abruptly.

Arkady's heart began thumping wildly. The moment of truth had arrived. His breath came short and ragged as he waited tensely to see what they would bring. Would it be what he wanted?

Anatoly returned a few minutes later, accompanied by the gorilla who had opened the front door to Arkady. The powerful arms were lugging a lead barrel, painted green. Arkady recognized it from his work at Mayak. The barrel, he knew, was coated on the inside with anti-radioactive material. The gorilla set the barrel down some three feet from where the other men sat, then turned around and left the way he had come.

"Where are the trumpets?" Victor joked dryly. He turned to Arkady, all business now. "Inside that barrel are two 'dolls,' each one 10 kilotons in strength — several times more powerful than the atom bombs that fell on Hiroshima and Nagasaki. Each 'doll' is capable of an explosion equivalent to 100,000 tons of TNT. I think that even our friend Sasha here, for all his bulk, would vanish in a puff of smoke if anything happened here."

"We spoke about one limited bomb," Arkady protested. But Victor ignored the comment, saying only, "You don't have to believe me. Check the contents for yourself."

Arkady did so. With each of the bombs was a brown envelope, held firm with stiff cardboard. Inside was a detailed instruction manual for arming the bomb — along with colored illustrations that would lead even an amateur step by step through the procedure.

Arkady knew who was responsible for the manuals. It was Professor Dmitri Koznitzov and his assistant, Dr. Tanya Nievski, from the reactor at Pibadno in the Ukraine. They had sold their souls to the Mafia in exchange for $3 million — a million and a half apiece — and then vanished without a trace. Up until then, the material had been useless except to a handful of knowledgeable individuals. An unarmed bomb is about as dangerous as a toy gun. Once the contraband atomic bombs began to be accompanied by instruction manuals, however, they were transformed into the lethal weapons they had been in potential — and a headache for world leaders everywhere.

Arkady scanned the manual. On the first pages, he found instructions for unlocking the nuclear "package." This was accomplished by spinning certain numbers on a combination lock, waiting 10 minutes, and then spinning other numbers. Twenty minutes after that, the package could be opened. This security measure was calculated to give a hothead time to cool off before using the devastating weapon that had fallen into his hands.

While they waited, the three Mafia men and Arkady sipped brandy and fine Scotch, chatting to mask the tension that underscored everything that went on in the room. Zero hour arrived at last. A final combination was followed by a ringing reminiscent of an alarm clock. Despite the drink, Arkady's mouth was dry. His head felt close to exploding, and his hands betrayed him by trembling like a sick man's. With a knowing smile, Anatoly approached the barrel, and, with the skill of a surgeon, opened the inner case.

Arkady came closer and looked inside.

They had not tricked him! It was a genuine atomic mechanism. Everything was there: boxes of heavy lead containing the uranium and plutonium pellets, charged with molecules of U-235. There were the ingredients required for setting off the atomic chain reaction: ditrium, beryllium, and graphite. When the fuse was introduced into the plutonium and thorium and activated digitally, the U-235 would be split, releasing neutrons and setting in motion the famous chain reaction. Each neutron would split another atom, releasing more neutrons, and so on down the line, until PU-239 was formed. In a hundredth of a second, an enormous amount of energy would be released, at a temperature of tens of millions of degrees at the explosion's center. The sheet of air formed by this sudden heat would destroy everything within a radius of at least 30 kilometers.

The fuses were neutralized, of course, and the "cigar" — that is, the tube that would activate the explosion — was packed in a separate box, wrapped in two sheets of red wax. All that was needed to turn these disparate elements into a horrific bomb was a simple following of the instruction manual.

Arkady inspected each of the two cases carefully, then relocked them. A feeling of deep satisfaction stole over him. The hard part was behind him.

"And now," Sasha said, "your part of the deal."

Arkady looked up. "Of course. I'm going to give you $1 million — in cash!"

"What are you talking about?" Victor said furiously. "You're paying us $2 million right now!"

"*What*?! We talked about a million. Not a cent more!"

Sasha's deep bass laughter shook the room. "Mister scientist, maybe you did not understand. The price is $1 million — *each*."

Arkady heard the other's raspy breathing. Sasha *was* suffering from his obesity, with a shortness of breath that might bespeak a heart problem. Arkady noted this even as his mind churned wildly. He had no idea what to say next. His satisfaction was gone, his world destroyed. He would leave this place with nothing!

"You have a choice," Victor offered. "You can take only one of the cases if you want. But a price is a price. It's two million for the two of them — not a cent less."

Arkady took a strong stand. "One million, and that's final!"

Victor shouted, "No one tangles with me, old man. Get out of here!" He raised his voice still higher. "Grisha, come and take the barrel away! Where did Alex go?... Alex, take Arkady back to the Leningrad Hotel."

Alex had come running at his boss's call, still holding a cup of hot tea. In his agitation, he tipped the cup and the steaming liquid poured onto the rug. Sasha uttered a Russian expletive. Alex fell to the floor and began trying to wipe up the spill with his sleeve.

"Leave the rug alone!" Victor screamed. "Take our guest to his hotel — now!"

The tension in the room was thick enough to slice with a knife. Arkady cursed the day he had ever gotten involved in this stupid business. He was surrounded on every side by poisonous snakes, and would end up with no money, to boot! With lightning rapidity, Arkady reviewed his options. To return to Israel with just one bomb was out of the question; Gray Cap would destroy him.

He decided to stand firm. "I want to call my boss," he said, "to report on this breach of contract. You know who he is and what kind of operation backs him. They're as vengeful as the devil and they have a million eyes and hands — plus nerves of steel."

Victor and Sasha engaged in a hurried consultation. Arkady broke into their muttering to clear his throat and ask, "May I interrupt for a minute?"

Victor turned. "What is it?"

"I had spoken to Anatoly about one regular bomb and another one of limited power. Why have you brought me two regular ones?"

Sasha exhaled with relief as he realized that Arkady was offering a way down the ladder of their dilemma. He boomed, "Anatoly, you didn't report this correctly! He wanted one small bomb. Why did you say two regular bombs?"

Anatoly stammered, "I-I-I d-don't know m-much about atom b-bombs."

"I forgot how limited your intelligence is, cretin," Sasha said scornfully. "A limited bomb is something else entirely. Grisha, go bring the other barrel."

Arkady knew this for the pretense it was. The whole episode had been a ploy to try to extort more money from him. When that failed, the second, limited-strength bomb was ready in the wings.

A second barrel was trundled into the room. "Here's a bomb that's approximately one-third as powerful as the other one," Victor told Arkady. "The price is fixed accordingly: $300,000."

Arkady was all too willing to back down from the ladder himself. "That's a reasonable price. I agree."

The deal was concluded after Arkady inspected the contents of the second barrel and found them in order. He handed over $1,300,000. The barrel, containing the two bombs packaged carefully between thick layers of cotton-wool padding, was placed in a cargo crate waiting behind the mansion.

"How will you travel to Lebanon?" Victor asked.

Arkady said confidently, "I'll sail on the *Charlotta Simpaya* from St. Petersburg, as we agreed."

"Do you think you can pass through harbor customs with that crate? You must be drunk!"

Victor's words were blunt as a hammer. They took Arkady's breath away.

Sasha stepped in, saying soothingly, "One of my men will transport you and the crate to Kronshtadt, near Petersburg. Our operation has excellent ties to the dock authorities there. You won't have to deal with customs."

"An excellent idea!" Victor approved. "No one will ever know where you disappeared to or how you left the country. This will completely cover your tracks."

The truck set out, its huge tires encompassed in chains to combat the icy roads. Arkady sat up front, beside the driver, wrapped to the nose in his scarf and trembling with cold. Silently, he blessed Sasha for his idea, which would baffle any Israelis who might be sniffing at his heels. He had no way of knowing that Sasha had been protecting his own skin, and that the notion of using the Kronshtadt port had been put forward as a means of preventing police scrutiny into the Mafia's operations in St. Petersburg.

The ride was very long. The truck rumbled slowly along the slippery road. Arkady was exhausted, but he couldn't fall asleep. He was consumed with bitterness about the millions of dollars that were fast slipping through his fingers, and wondering if there was a chance of coercing Gray Cap into replacing the $300,000 extra dollars he'd just had to shell out. He was doubtful.

20

Dani Devash, Lieutenant Commander of the Bat Yam police, wore a troubled look as he climbed the steps to the station house at 9 a.m. He rubbed his eyes several times, passing his hand over the stubble on his chin. When he crossed the hall on the way to his office, his steps were not as brisk as usual. Several police officers moved aside as he passed, wishing him a good morning with unctuous smiles. Devash nodded back, with no idea whom he was greeting.

"A penny for your thoughts," a voice said from behind.

Ari Naot, Dani's second in command, caught up with him and added, "Dani, you're late this morning, and you don't look well."

There was always a certain underlying tension in the relations between the two men. Naot was the cause of a constant pressure at Devash's back, waiting impatiently to inherit his position. But Dani Devash was only 50 and had no intention of retiring yet. Dani was not enamored of his second in command, and every dialogue between them was liable to degenerate into a verbal battle.

"I have a stiff neck this morning," he said in a tone of mock-complaint. "And a speck in my eye, a hole in my pocket, and water on the knee — and you to deal with, on top of everything else!"

Naot stopped walking and exclaimed in surprise, "What are you saying? It sounds like you need a complete overhaul. I have the number of an excellent handyman. Want it?"

"What I really want is to build a wall in our office, to separate the two of us."

"There's no need for a wall. A sheet of glass would do the job."

Dani's tone swiftly changed. "Ari, call an urgent meeting of all senior staff in one hour." Ari Naot opened his mouth to make some rejoinder, but Dani held up a finger in front of his face. "In one hour, Ari."

He went into his office, where he sank into his leather desk chair and spread open the newspaper to reread the ad Arkady had inserted there.

Dani had not slept well the night before. Just as he was about to go to bed, the words "atomic scientist" had flashed into his brain. He had seen an ad with those words somewhere recently. Lucky he tended to hold onto newspapers for a couple of weeks. He had begun to go through every old paper and magazine, searching for he knew not what, until he found it — an ad tucked into the back pages of a newspaper. At 6 a.m. he had dialed the number in the ad, but there was no answer.

After that, he had paid a visit to the Golden Towers old-age home.

An hour later, the senior police staff filed into the conference room at the police station and found seats around the large table there. At each place there was a legal-sized yellow pad. The officers jotted notes as Dani Devash summarized the case of Arkady Bogdanov, the former atomic scientist who had disappeared at the beach a few days before, and whose body had not yet been found.

"His body's probably stuck between some boulders somewhere," Sergeant Ruby Albert opined.

Dani rejected this. "I don't believe it. The old man was an excellent swimmer, with outstanding athletic ability in general."

Chaim Nachmias protested, "We've all heard about superb swimmers who have gotten caught in the undertow. Such things do happen."

"I'd like to put aside, for the moment, the theory that Bogdanov drowned, and to focus our efforts on locating a live person," Devash said firmly. "He was a senior atomic scientist. I suspect that he faked his drowning."

Ari Naot spoke up for the first time. "That only makes the case stronger against his being alive. An atomic scientist who came here from Russia and became an ordinary citizen — maybe he *wanted* to die!"

The other officers grinned, and began exchanging stories of Russian musicians and orchestra conductors who had been reduced to performing menial labor to survive after coming to Israel. Dani felt the meeting was getting away from him. He slapped his hand on the table.

"I visited the Golden Towers old-age home this morning. I spoke with the administrators. The overwhelming impression I got there was that Bogdanov was a man in full possession of his faculties and strength, a man who was locked away in the home against his will by his son and daughter-in-law, who have taken over his villa in Herzliya, valued at approximately $1 million." Dani pulled the newspaper clipping from his pocket. "Bogdanov was very bitter. He wanted to get out of there. A week ago, this ad appeared in two major newspapers." He read the contents of the ad aloud. He now had the full attention of every man present.

Ruby Albert was the first to break the silence. "So you think he's missing?"

"Yes."

"Wonderful. This past year, the Israeli police dealt with 3,300 cases of missing persons throughout the country. About 70 percent of them returned home within 48 hours. Another 20 percent returned within a month, and 9 percent by the end of the year. Only in 1 percent of the cases did we fail to find any trace of the missing person. Let's see into which category your scientist will fall."

Dani leaned forward. "Gentlemen, we are dealing with an atomic scientist with a desire for revenge." He felt the hopelessness of impressing the men with what he saw as the gravity of the situation.

Ari Naot picked up the phone near his elbow and punched the speaker button. Immediately, the sound of a dial tone filled the room. Consulting a small phone book he had taken from his pocket, Ari dialed a number.

"Ari, who are you calling?" Dani asked over the noise of the ringing of the phone.

Naot placed a finger on his lips, just as the ringing broke off and a voice said, "Ben Gurion Border Police. Vice-Inspector Pinchas Menashe speaking."

Ari waved a hand to shush the sudden murmur of voices around him. Into the phone, he said, "This is Second Lieutenant Naot with the Bat Yam police department. I want to ask you to check if the name Arkady Bogdanov is on any of your outgoing passenger lists."

"The date?"

Dani came nearer to the phone. "Menashe, we're interested in the 15th of January."

"Just a minute, I'll check the computer." Menashe's voice was superimposed over the sound of announcements in the airline terminal. The Bat Yam conference room was enveloped in a taut silence as the men waited for Menashe to get back with the information.

"Yes, the name Arkady Bogdanov — male, non-Jewish, 72 years old — appears on our departing passengers' list on the 15th of January of this year. He took El Al's flight 614 to Moscow at 2:25 p.m. Is there anything else I can do for you?"

"That's all for now, thanks." Naot pressed the speaker button again and hung up. With a half-smile, he announced, "And so, the man is neither drowned nor missing. He's run off to Russia, to end his days there."

Worry lines appeared on Dani's forehead. "A minute ago, when you took the initiative and phoned Ben Gurion, you shone. Now you're tarnishing that shine. The atomic scientist didn't fly off to Moscow to rest on his laurels."

"What then?" several voices asked at once.

Dani filled his lungs, then let his breath out in a sigh. "I have a sneaking suspicion that we're dealing with something big here — big and terrible. That's what my gut tells me. I haven't felt good about this case from the beginning. But now, after the information that Ari's just unearthed for us, I'm literally panicking." He looked around soberly at the assembled police officers. "The information we have at this point, gentlemen, is only the tip of the iceberg."

◆ ◆ ◆

To my dear sister Judy,

You asked me to send a fax and I'm hurrying to do your bidding. How are you, Judy? How's your eye? I don't mean to threaten, but if you don't come to New York, I'm coming to Israel. Without boasting, I can say that as an ophthalmologist I have some knowledge of my field, and I'd like to talk to your surgeon.

Take care of yourself.

Benjy

◆ ◆ ◆

For Eli — Extremely Urgent!!!

I really don't get you! Why haven't you put Judy on a plane and sent her here? You're playing with fire, don't you realize that? You know as well as I do that Judy is practically blind in her "lazy" left eye, and that the only reason she was able to see as well as she could was because her right eye worked especially hard and functioned almost as well as two eyes. Only her depth perception was affected by her left eye, which can only make things out up to two or three yards away, at most.

Eli, I don't intend to try and teach you in minutes what it took me years to learn, but I want to educate you a little in the field of ophthalmology, so that you'll understand how serious Judy's situation is.

Judy thinks that her retina was pierced when the thorn entered her eye. In other words, the foreign body reached all the way through to the back of the eye, tearing everything along the way. She's mistaken. If that had happened, she would not have been able to write me a single word without undergoing a complex surgical procedure whereby the eye is entered through the pierce-hole, beneath the retina and all the way down to its back wall, which is lifted. No one should ever know of such things.

You won't like all my medical lingo, but it seems to me that in Judy's case we have a "perforation with a traumatic cataract." In other words, the perforation by a foreign body reached the liquid part of the eye and created a leak. In such an occurrence, the cornea "runs" forward and is drawn toward the hole. I'm afraid that the thorn injured the cornea and the lens, leading to a cataract. This cataract, in turn, leads to a clouding of the lens, partial loss of vision, or even complete loss. In other words, blindness — may Hashem preserve us from such things.

I'm worried, Eli, and I'll tell you why. Even if my optimistic diagnosis is correct, Judy should have been operated on immediately for removal of the cataract and implantation of an artificial lens. Instead, the emergency room sent her home. Does this make any sense to you?

There are about twenty patients waiting in my "People's Clinic." I must start seeing them. Don't phone me; I'm too busy to talk. Send me a fax — quickly!

Benjy

◆ ◆ ◆

Dear Benjy,

Forgive me for not writing sooner. I think there's been a misunderstanding here, though I'm not sure how it happened.

Judy, being in pain and distress, apparently didn't explain herself well. She was injured three days ago, in the afternoon. She was taken immediately to Hadassah Hospital, where she is still a patient now, on the fourth day. She was NOT sent home the way you think. She received emergency first aid on the spot, and was admitted into the hospital directly from the emergency room. She insisted on writing you herself, though it was very hard and painful for her, while I haven't yet written a word. I feel like such a worm! Abba always said that your neshamah is embroidered with silk and golden threads. Your diagnosis is absolutely correct. Judy's eye was pierced to the lens, including the lens but not past it, baruch Hashem.

There's been no operation yet. The surgeons say that it's impossible to operate immediately because the intruding thorn also seriously infected her eye. Judy is bursting with antibiotics, administered intravenously. As an ophthalmologist, I'm sure you're aware of the complications that arise from an infection of the eye through injury; the eye itself has hardly any blood vessels, making absorption of antibiotics minimal at best.

The operation is slated to take place tomorrow, Thursday. I plan to take all the boys in my yeshivah up to the Kosel to recite the entire sefer Tehillim together during the operation.

The doctors here are excellent, and maintain Western standards of medicine. I'm sure they'll do a good job. It might be problematic to get hold of Judy's medical records from the hospital and send them to the States with her.

I'm not sure how best to proceed. If you still insist on her coming to New York, maybe you can call her surgeon and speak with him directly?

Regards to the wife, and a million kisses to little Dovid in honor of his first birthday.

Eli

◆ ◆ ◆

The hospital room was shrouded in gloom. In the place where the window should have been, Judy saw only a gray rectangle. She didn't know whether the darkness came from outside — was it nightfall already? — or inside herself.

Her "lazy" eye had made a mighty effort to compensate for the injured one — such an effort that, after several days, it had ceased to see entirely. The doctors had calmed Judy with the diagnosis that the weakness was temporary, and that in a few days she would once again be able to see with both eyes.

In the meantime, she saw nothing.

She was afraid. A thousand butterflies fluttered constantly in her stomach. Tomorrow she was due to undergo a complex operation to restore her vision. Would it be a success?

The doctors in New York had explained to her mother and father that her lazy eye did not send stimuli on to the appropriate part of the brain during the critical years from birth to six. "It's very unusual for a lazy eye to revive and begin to see well after the age of six or seven," they had said. All these years, her right eye had functioned very nicely for both of them. Now it had been injured.

What am I left with? she wondered. Hashem, I'm not asking a lot — just to be like everyone else. Please, restore the vision to both my eyes, and let me see again.

21

"Judy."

"Yes."

Adina Goldenblum entered the room quietly and shut the door behind her. She was a permanent fixture in her adopted daughter's hospital room, except for the few brief hours of rest she managed to snatch at home.

She approached the bed. "How are you feeling now, dear? Does it hurt any less?"

"*Baruch Hashem,* I'm all right."

"The operation is tomorrow. With Hashem's help, it should go well." Adina's hand smoothed the hair on Judy's head. Adina could not read emotion in the girl's bandaged eyes but she could feel her body trembling beneath the thin sheet. Adina was very anxious about the impending surgery, but she kept her fears to herself. Pressing Judy's hand, she said warmly, "Be strong, my girl. You're always a pillar of strength for the rest of us. You're not allowed to crumble."

The trembling beneath the sheet increased. "I — I'm afraid I'll be left blind."

Adina's heart was leaden. Blindness was indeed a very real possibility. The doctors assured them that the operation would go well, but it was not they who determined these things. There was Someone above them Who decided a person's fate. He was the only One Who could restore sight to the unseeing.

Who else knew the secret of vision? Hashem imbued the eye with His spirit, transforming a simple soft mass into a window on the world. Everyone was born with two eyes, yet no one knew why one person opened his eyes in the morning to see the blue sky, while another opened his eyes to darkness — lifelessness.

Adina Goldenblum shook her head to dispel these black thoughts. She must not let Judy sense her apprehension — no, her terror. Feelings such as these could be transmitted even without the help of a seeing eye.

There were voices in the corridor. At the door, they heard one voice say, in English, "I've got to talk to a girl in here who's having eye surgery in the morning. She has to be emotionally prepared for the operation."

A second later, Dr. Matof Abu Suria walked in. He was the Lebanese-born second in command in the ward hierarchy, assisting chief surgeon Gideon Levinstam.

◆ ◆ ◆

Dr. Matof had nearly succeeded in shedding all evidence that he was an Arab. He had acquired his medical training at major American universities, where he cultivated a rolling Western accent. His external appearance, also, betrayed no sign of his origins. He looked like a typical American doctor. Only the occasional stressed "p" — sounding on his lips like a "b" — exposed him from time to time despite all his efforts to banish it.

"Hello, Mrs. Goldenblum," he greeted Adina pleasantly in fluent Hebrew. "I've come to talk to Judy, but I'm actually pleased that you're here, too. Do you have a minute?"

"Certainly."

He pulled up a plastic chair and sat at his ease beside the bed. "Judy, are you worried about the operation?" he asked directly.

Judy answered, just as directly, "Very."

"That's natural. I'd be surprised if you weren't. Who's not afraid of undergoing surgery? Especially eye surgery. It sounds very scary."

His words struck home in two vastly different ways. Adina Goldenblum found herself trusting the doctor who spoke so compassionately to her daughter. Judy, on the other hand, picked up the faint trace of an Arab accent, and was thrown into an even deeper gloom than before.

The doctor unrolled a cloth poster which bore a diagram of a cross-section of the eye. He hung it on the wall, saying, "In a few days, when you're able to see again, you'll be able to see this poster, too." Turning to Adina, he explained, "This is how the eye looks on the inside. I'll start with the outermost layer — the protective layer — which consists of the white of the eye and the cornea. The cornea itself has five layers, the outermost of which is called the ephithelium. All five layers of the cornea together measure just half a millimeter across, or 500 microns. Each layer is 100 microns, or one tenth of a millimeter. And this thing actually sees!"

He went on to talk about the eye's anatomy in scientific terms, until Adina's head swam. Here and there she caught a word she understood and she nodded politely. After a while, Dr. Matof sensed that his speech was going over her head, so he downgraded it to laymen's terms.

"And this is the famous 'pupil,' or '*ishon*' in Hebrew — 'little man.' When the thorn pierced Judy's eye, it invaded the cornea and the front chamber, causing a leakage. If it had stopped there, the situation would have stabilized itself, because the liquid in the eye renews itself constantly. But the thorn pressed onward, destroying the lens. We're going to implant an artificial lens into Judy's eye tomorrow."

Judy spoke up for the first time. "What's an artificial lens, exactly?"

Smiling, Dr. Matof replied, "It's nearly as good as the natural one. It has the refractive capacity of 20 diopters and is made of plastic." The word emerged as "blastic." The doctor instantly corrected himself. "Of *plastic*. It's a special material, actually, called polymethyl methacrylate. Have you ever heard how they discovered it?"

"No."

"During the Korean war, some American planes were downed in battle. The hoods of these planes were made of polyethylene, and when they exploded, fragments entered the pilots' bodies. The doctors noticed that, as opposed to metal fragments, these plastic fragments caused no infection. They investigated further and discovered that polymethyl is a material that is not rejected by the human body. Ever since, it has been bobular — excuse me, popular — in delicate implants. That's what we use in forming artificial lenses."

"And she'll be able to see as well as before?" Adina asked intensely. "To see the sun shining, to recognize people and colors, to read?"

"Everything," Dr. Matof promised. "She will still have to wear reading glasses, though. An artificial lens can't read and view distances with the same flexibility as a natural one. But apart from that, it's every bit as good."

Both Adina and Judy were silent, digesting the doctor's words.

Matof continued, "Imagine — simple polyurethane — made from the same thing gasoline is made — will give your daughter vision! Just a drop of petroleum, and everything will be fxed as good as new."

This last sentence aroused Judy's panic. "No!" she screamed. "I don't want it! I don't want to have the operation here!"

Adina and the doctor tried to calm her. "I was just kidding," Dr. Matof said. But Judy stood firm. "I don't want it."

Adina poured her a cup of water. "Drink, honey. Drink, and calm down. The staff here is excellent, and this is not the first time Dr. Levinstam will be performing this procedure."

Judy's hand shook as she brought the cup to her lips, and a rivulet of water dribbled down her chin. "Ima," she whispered in a choked voice, "I want the doctor to leave the room."

Embarrassed, Adina's cheeks turned pink, but the doctor rose understandingly. "This is a normal reaction before surgery. I've seen it before. There are many fears at a time like this. She'll soon settle down." With a final smile, he left.

Adina pressed her daughter's hand warmly. "Judy, I'm surprised at you."

Judy leaned back against her pillow. Quietly, speaking as though she had little strength left, she said, "I don't trust that doctor. He's an Arab. I recognized his accent."

"Nonsense. Israeli hospitals have many excellent Arab doctors. Besides, he's not going to operate. Dr. Levinstam will be your surgeon tomorrow."

"I don't care. I don't want to have the operation here — period! Benjy says he can arrange for me to have it at his hospital, Mount Sinai, in Manhattan."

"You want to leave a day before your operation? No doctor will authorize that!"

The argument raged on. Meanwhile, at the nurse's station, a phone rang. A nurse picked up, answered in Hebrew, and switched to English. "Yes, yes — Judy Flamm? Immediately." She called down the hall, "Long-distance call from New York for Judy Flamm."

"It's Benjy!" Judy's face lit up. "My thoughts actually reached him."

With Adina guiding her on the right and a nurse pulling her I.V. pole along on her left, Judy made her way down the hall. The receiver was placed in her hand. "Hi, Benjy," she said, with a catch in her voice.

From across the ocean, Benjy made a valiant effort to control his emotions. "Judy, how are you? You sound excited."

Judy burst into tears. Trembling, she leaned against the nurse's desk for support. A nurse brought a chair over and helped Judy sit.

"Benjy, I want to fly to New York right away. Do me a favor and ask the doctors here to release me and my records."

"That's what I'm calling about," Benjy said urgently. "Who's your surgeon?"

"Dr. Gideon Levinstam."

"Levinstam!" Benjy repeated incredulously. "He's an excellent eye surgeon. I've heard of him here at Mount Sinai."

"Then — then there's no reason for me to go to New York?" Judy's heart sank.

"I want to talk to him first. Then we'll see."

◆ ◆ ◆

Dr. Levinstam spoke angrily into the phone. Some young doctor from New York was questioning his abilities? "I understand that you're her brother, Mr. Flamm, and that you're also an ophthalmologist. But why drag your sister to New York? That would be a foolish move, to say the least."

Benjy was undaunted. "It's not a simple procedure, and it's my sister's right to have the operation anywhere she wants. Here at Mount Sinai I'd be able to arrange for optimal conditions for her. I'm her brother and I'm also a senior physician, for your information. If it only contributes to her morale, that would be sufficient reason."

"I disagree! To release a patient on the eve of surgery? We've already had to delay the operation too long because of the infection in her eye. And you want to delay further?!" Levinstam was furious.

Benjy continued talking, trying his best to get the surgeon to see the situation his way. At last, Levinstam barked, "It's beneath my dignity to debate this nonsense any longer. If you insist on having your way, if you don't have enough faith in what we can do here, then it's not worth our while to treat her." He was about to slam down the receiver when his sense of responsibility as a doctor prompted him to ask, "Who will be performing the surgery at Mount Sinai?"

"Dr. Schneider." Benjy stifled a sigh of relief.

"Dr. Schneider? H'mm — I know him well. In fact, he's a good friend of mine." Levinstam unbent even further, asking, "By the way, where are you calling from?"

"From Dr. Schneider's office at Mount Sinai."

"Is he there?"

"Yes, he is — and he'd like to speak to you."

The two top surgeons exchanged greetings. Then Dr. Levinstam said, "Look, Schneider, the girl has undergone a severe traumatic injury. I hope this foolishness of flying her to America won't prove harmful. I don't wish to interfere with your method of treatment, but I was planning to operate under a general anesthetic. She has an additional problem — her cornea is torn in an unusual way, requiring a special type of suturing to prevent leakage."

Dr. Schneider responded, "Naturally, the operation will take three to four hours instead of the usual hour and a half. I had a similar case just yesterday. Don't worry, Levinstam, I also have my suturing methods, plus a few of my own twists in the operating procedure that minimize the patient's suffering in recovery."

Dr. Levinstam's ears perked up. As he began to mentally plan a short trip to New York to study the famous eye surgeon's methods, he said, "Actually, I have some things I could show you in operating on premature babies' eyes."

"I'd love to hear all about it," Dr. Schneider said heartily. The Israeli Levinstam had earned himself an international reputation for his innovative surgery on extremely premature infants, often preventing blindness. In the past, the retinas of such underdeveloped babies had become irreparably torn when new blood vessels, growing after the premature birth, burst and leaked into the eyes.

Dr. Levinstam said, "Well, may the surgery go well. I'll prepare all the necessary paperwork, and she can take off tomorrow. I will also assign a nurse to fly to New York with her."

"Thanks, Doctor."

"No problem. Good-bye."

A secret meeting was taking place in the Prime Minister's office. Present at the meeting were the heads of the Mossad, the General Security Service (GSS), and the relevant police departments. The topic: Russian atomic scientist Arkady Bogdanov.

Everyone listened quietly as Inspector Dani Devash outlined the situation. From time to time he threw a triumphant glance at his second in command, Ari Naot, who tried unsuccessfully, more than once, to interrupt with a description of his own role in tracking down the missing Russian.

The security people took Devash seriously. Their own intelligence sources confirmed the bleak truth of the scenario he was handing them.

"In my opinion, some extreme terrorist faction is backing Bogdanov," said Shimi Tzipori, a very senior Mossad man. "The retired scientist was sent to Russia to get hold of an atomic bomb. I predict that the bomb will be brought back to Israel, in order to involve our government in a nuclear bomb threat. The question is: Who's behind this, and what do they want? We've never reached this level of threat before, though I suppose it was to be expected."

Ari Naot jumped up. "Nonsense! Would a terrorist group rely on a chance to make its move? What if Bogdanov hadn't been forced into an old-age home against his will, or if he hadn't put that ad in the newspaper?"

Devash cast a furious look at his underling. "My assistant has extensive experience in the field of espionage," he said, thumping Naot's shoulder in a mock-friendly way. "His grandfather was in charge of reading the section of the Torah that deals with the spies."

Tzipori looked at them over his bifocals. "The first lesson in espionage is ferreting out the moles."

"W-what?" Naot stammered.

"That's a word that the intelligence community has coined. In short, your scientist was planted in this country to await the appointed day. A story was conjured up of a hostile family and an enforced move to a nursing home. He's been waiting for instructions."

Papers rustled on the conference table as Tzipori searched for the newspaper clipping. Here, listen." He read the ad aloud. "I'm certain that one or two of the words in this ad were prearranged signals. I speak from experience."

Naot gasped in surprise. Pleased with the reaction, Tzipori continued, "The groundwork was laid back in Russia, even before Bogdanov came to Israel. The terrorist organizers were waiting for an ad like this. They contacted the scientist and no doubt identified one another via additional passwords. For example, Bogdanov might have asked,'Do you have experience?' and his contact would have answered, 'Vast experience,' or something similar. Contact was thus established, and thereafter all proceeded according to the prearranged script."

"The question is, what do we do?" The questioner was Benny Turiel, head of police intelligence.

Tzipori answered without hesitation, "We complain to the U.N.!"

"Why the sarcasm?" Turiel snapped, stung. "I only asked."

"And I only answered. You still need to ask what we do? We're already four days behind Bogdanov — four critical days. We must send an experienced Mossad team to Russia immediately, to follow Bogdanov's trail — and capture him."

These words spurred a heated debate. No one wanted to miss out on a chance for glory.

"With all due respect to the Mossad," the GSS man said, "we have a long record of success in this type of affair."

"The Russian police won't cooperate with anyone but the Israeli police," Turiel shot back.

"Police," sniffed the Mossad man. "Only trained, Russian-speaking espionage agents will be able to track down the scientist."

The debate grew stormier. None of the three interested parties would give up its right to run the operation. It was up to the Prime Minister to intervene.

"All three of you will go. Three representative agents will leave Israel tomorrow."

The selected agents were Yossi Katri of police intelligence, Yoni Dor of the GSS, and Uzi Saraf of the Mossad.

Armed and eager, the three entered Russia determined to stop Arkady Bogdanov in his tracks.

22

A heavy fog covered the city of Kronshtadt as the truck rumbled slowly toward the port off the Baltic sea. As the salt tickled his nose, something made Arkady think of the Golden Towers home. He was troubled in mind and terribly tired in body. Neither the Israeli police nor the intelligence community were stupid. It was entirely conceivable that someone had seen through Arkady's feigned drowning. Were security forces on his heels at this very moment?

His lips moved soundlessly. "Impossible! How can anyone know about my connection to 'Gray Cap'? The ad I put in the paper was minuscule. Probably not more than two or three people even noticed it. What am I so worried about?"

The driver, glancing sideways, noticed the moving lips. "Are you praying? Matter of fact, so am I. I want to get rid of that barrel as fast as I can. I'm still young — too young to go up in smoke."

Arkady smiled mechanically. The truck came to a stop near a gate of green metal that blocked its way. Floodlights poured powerful white illumination upon several cranes engaged in loading ships. Beyond the gate a conveyer belt moved endlessly, its poorly oiled gears setting up a screeching that was painful to the ears. Drowning in the noise, neither Arkady nor the driver was aware that they had company until a voice shouted: "Do you have permission to enter here?"

The speaker was one of a pair of khaki-clad harbor guards. Hastily, the driver produced a plastic card. The guard scanned it briefly, then leaned over to whisper to his companion, "It's the organization from Petersburg." No one wanted to get tangled up with the Mafia.

"You may enter."

A dock employee pressed a button and the gate yawned open. The truck passed through.

An approaching ship blared its horn deafeningly. Arkady could just make out the silhouettes of cargo ships berthed along the pier. Large blocks of ice floated between the ships on the greasy black water. At the thought of the journey that still lay ahead, Arkady felt the last of his strength drain away. He was limp as a wrung-out rag.

A tall man in a black overcoat suddenly appeared before him. "Arkady Bogdanov?"

"*Da.*"

"Clement Breinen, captain of the *Charlotta.* I got a call from Sasha Smolani, asking me to help you. I like Sasha; a man after my own heart. Luckily, the ice has thawed enough for us to break into open sea this very day."

Arkady's frozen blood began flowing again at this happy news. "Where's the ship?" he asked.

Breinen pointed into the fog. "She's over there. If our luck holds, she'll take us across this puddle, all the way to Beirut."

Arkady peered in the direction that the captain's finger pointed, and made out a hulking mass with the words *Charlotta Simpaya* painted across the bow in slanted letters. He asked, "Is this a civilian or a military port?"

"This is where Russian arms are sent out to the rest of the world," the captain winked. "There are some things you don't want to know too much about."

An hour later, Arkady sat in a warm cabin inside the *Charlotta Simpaya.* At his insistence, the lead barrel had been placed in the cabin with him instead of in the cargo hold. He felt he had the right to demand that in return for the $50,000 he was paying for the trip.

Captain Breinen had objected strongly. "I have a good name in every port, and I've never once smuggled cargo in a passenger cabin."

"There's always a first time."

"But what if there's an inspection at one of the ports?"

Arkady waved this away. "This barrel doesn't leave my room."

"Yes, it does!"

"No!"

Breinen was about to storm out of the cabin in a rage when he suddenly relented. Coming back to Arkady, he hissed, "Okay. The barrel stays here. I don't care what you have inside — gold, diamonds, drugs, or a genie in a bottle. But the price is doubled to $100,000."

Arkady fought a sinking sensation in his middle. "Seventy thousand," he tried.

Breinen's eyes narrowed to two slits. "The crane that lifted the barrel up here can lower it again just as easily. Let Sasha Smolani worry about it."

"Such a cruel world," Arkady said sarcastically. "How soon we forget our friendship for poor Sasha — a man after our own heart."

The captain shrugged. He cared nothing for Arkady's barbs as long as he received the money. Before he left the cabin, he handed Arkady a single sheet of paper, typed on an old-fashioned typewriter, outlining measures for emergency evacuation of the ship. Breinen was an old sea hand who did not believe in taking chances.

Left to himself, Arkady reviewed the situation. "A hundred thousand," he sighed. "I knew this was going to happen. Still, I'll have a little money left over. Just let Breinen get me safely to Beirut."

Not more than five minutes passed before there was a deferential knock on the door. A young waiter came in bearing a covered tray, which he set on the table. Arkady lifted the cover, then licked his lips. There was half a sugared grapefruit and his favorite type of fish in lemon sauce. It was almost as if someone had filled the captain in on Arkady's gastronomical preferences. As he sat down to enjoy the meal, Arkady's glance fell on the lead barrel. The sight tugged at the corners of his conscience, and he knew why.

◆ ◆ ◆

Judy arrived at the airport the next day by ambulance. Dr. Levinstam had stood by his promise, providing her with Tami, a nurse experienced in accompanying surgical patients abroad.

"Do you have 10 hands?" Judy protested, as Tami whisked a small suitcase away from her. "Let me."

"The slightest exertion could hurt your eye," Tami replied. She seemed indeed to have 10 hands. She managed to guide Judy's walker forward while juggling two suitcases of varying size plus a briefcase containing all the medical documents bearing on Judy's case.

"You look better," the nurse told Judy as they approached the plane. "Still a little pale, but not as frightened. Your family will be pleased."

The large bulky bandages had been replaced by a more aesthetic dressing that just covered one eye. Dr. Levinstam had granted Judy permission to have limited use of her "lazy" left eye until the operation — "Just for seeing, not for reading" — and had liberated her at last from her enveloping darkness.

Her family had been permitted to accompany her to the steps of the plane. They were all there to see her off: Mark and Adina Goldenblum, her adoptive parents, and Eli, Dovy, and Moishy, who came from their various yeshivahs. The nurse stepped aside to give them a moment of privacy for their farewells.

"What do you know, I can see again," Judy glowed. "Dovy, I like your new hat. Moishy, you never told me you got new glasses." Her lazy eye provided her with limited vision — only for a distance of two yards or so, but Judy was satisfied for now. It was infinitely better than the murky twilight that had been her lot in the last days.

Dovy and Moishy blinked away a surreptitious tear or two. Eli appeared his usual self-contained self, but was actually more moved than any of the others. Biting his lip, he told his sister, "You'll soon be using both your eyes again."

She turned to him. "What?"

"With Hashem's help, you'll soon have two good eyes to use in good health." His voice grew thick as his throat constricted.

"From your mouth to His ears. Amen."

She looked at her family with love. "Watch out, soon you'll all be bawling," she smiled. "I'd better hurry onto the plane before you melt completely." For an instant her face crumpled, as her own emotions grew too strong to control. She turned hastily and started up the stairs to the plane.

She hadn't climbed two steps when Eli stopped her. He motioned for her to step aside. When they were out of the others' hearing, he whispered, "Abba wrote an important security memo before we left for India. He hid a copy of it in the house. Benjy found it in a secret drawer in Abba's study. When you return to Israel, I want you to bring the memo back with you. *Don't* fax or mail it. And remember..." He put a finger to his lips.

"I understand," Judy said, though it was clear she did not understand much. She was tired and muddled by the events and emotions of the past few days. All she wanted was to board the plane and sink into her seat. With a hug for Adina and a final flurry of waves for the others, she followed Tami onto the jumbo jet.

The stewardesses helped make her comfortable in the first-class section on the upper deck. Judy's seat leaned so far back it was practically a bed. Dr. Levinstam had thought of every detail. It wouldn't do for a patient meant to be on the operating table that very hour to travel economy class.

"Your parents were very emotional," Tami remarked as the plane flew through the clouds. "Why didn't they travel to New York with you?"

Judy pulled down the window covering; the brilliant sunlight hurt her one functioning eye. "How could they? The trip was decided on only yesterday, very suddenly. They had no time to get organized. But even if they could have come with me, I wouldn't have let them. My father runs a large high-tech firm and I know he's under tremendous pressure at work. And my mother cooks for a yeshivah and —"

"Your mother's a cook in a yeshivah?!" Tami echoed in astonishment. "Excuse me for prying into your personal life, but — a cook? If they have a high-tech company, they can't be too poor."

Judy said tranquilly, "It all depends on your point of view." She went on to explain about Yeshivas Aish Aharon, recently opened by her brother. "My mother was once a home economics teacher. She's also a great cook, and she's taken it upon herself to cook for the yeshivah with her own hands. That's how she expresses her love for Torah. She travels from Jerusalem to Anafim every day." She paused, smiling inwardly in recollection. "You should see her in her apron, surrounded by those enormous pots. Her face shines like — like — oh, I can't find the right comparison."

"Like a lottery winner," Tami offered. "Believe me, that's a shining face. An ear-to-ear smile."

"You're right, that is enormous happiness — but it's a material happiness. My mother's joy is spiritual. It's solid and real, and it comes from deep inside. Have you ever seen the faces of yeshivah boys dancing on Simchas Torah? It's on a whole different plane."

Tami was quiet for several moments, then said, "I have to admit, your ladder of priorities manages to surprise me time after time. You people have really got it right."

"We try," Judy said simply.

"You know, I had a religious grandmother. When I was a little girl, she taught me that there's a law and there's a Judge."

Judy started to say something, but Tami continued musing aloud. "She used to talk about sins and their consequences. Whenever there's a tragedy in our land, some of you people start talking about the sins that brought about this punishment. But what sin could a young girl like you have done? You don't believe in pure coincidence, Judy. You didn't just happen to lean over and get a thorn in your eye. You must have sinned. How?"

Judy was beside herself. Just a few minutes earlier, she had tried to take a small suitcase from Tami, and the nurse had refused for fear it would damage her. But what about the damage her words were causing? "What are you saying?" she wanted to scream.

But her father, Aharon Flamm, had always taught his children: "I believe with all my heart that Hashem does everything. Do you hear me, children? It's not we who make things happen, but Hashem. We're like puppets on a string. He does everything — everything! But He doesn't reveal Himself. He hides in nature. We live within the framework of the natural world, forgetting that we can find Hashem behind every occurrence. All we have to do is move aside the curtain that we call 'routine.' Sometimes," Aharon would add, "Hashem has to punish us. Then we get angry at the stick that beats us, not understanding Whose Hand is holding that stick."

Judy, she thought now to herself, Heaven obviously wants you to suffer. Her accident surely wasn't by chance! Maybe the pain was the minimal price she was being asked to pay in order for the operation to succeed. If she felt anguish at her companion's words, she must remember that Tami was only a stick.

"You're right," Judy said quietly. "I've sinned. I think I know the reason."

"I — I'm sorry!" Tami gasped, startled. "I really am."

"You have nothing to apologize for. I needed the reminder."

The nurse sank into a confused silence. Judy continued speaking, haltingly.

"I was born with one eye that was lazy, nearly blind, and a second eye that did the work of both. My vision was fine. But I was always complaining. 'Why do I have a lazy eye?' I'd cry to my father. He was a very wise man. He would answer me, 'Judy, you don't have a lazy eye. You have a good eye. The soul peeks out of the eyes, and Hashem has given you a beautiful soul and a good eye. You get this trait from your Flamm ancestors: the ability to rejoice in others' happiness, to nurture others, to view their success without jealousy — even to give others the fruit of your own labor without talking or boasting about it. A good eye.'

"To give everything without expecting anything in return — that was the Flamm motto," Judy went on in a choked voice. "To thank Hashem for what we have, for the gifts He's given us for free. He doesn't owe us anything! That's what my poor father and mother taught us. But I let frustration and bitterness dig deep into my soul. So, Someone comes along and asks, 'You're not satisfied with one eye that sees like two? Maybe you should try getting along without it for a while. Then, if you get it back, you'll be happy!' "

Tami was taken aback. "Judy, what are you saying?"

A pair of well-known Israeli political figures across the aisle stopped chatting to stare at them. Judy's shoulders were shaking with sobs. "What a Jew is supposed to say. I thank you, Tami, for waking me up and helping me recognize where I've gone wrong. I was ungrateful. Hashem gives us, measure for measure, what we deserve. Our own behavior determines the results."

Tami had a question. "Why do you call your rich parents 'poor'?"

At that, Judy was consumed entirely by grief. A black cloud descended on her as she tried to speak. "The ones you saw back at the airport are my adoptive parents — wonderful, wonderful people," she whispered. "My real mother and father disappeared in India 13 years ago, together with Shlomo, my little brother. He was only 11 at the time. We've never heard of them since."

Stewardesses circulated constantly, offering fine drinks and every kind of delicacy. Judy hardly tasted a bite. Tami checked her bag of medicines, murmuring to herself the names of the various antibiotics, ointments, and eyedrops to which she might have recourse during the trip.

As for Judy, she closed her good eye and fell asleep. She didn't open it again until the plane had landed at Kennedy Airport in New York.

23

Rav Anshel beamed with pleasure as the yeshivah's entire student body sang Shabbos *zemiros* in melodious, two-part harmony. The dining room was filled to capacity on this Friday night. For this "in" Shabbos at Aish Aharon, a large group of public high school students from Jerusalem had been invited as guests. Two or three of these non-religious students sat at each table. For many, this was their first taste of a traditional Shabbos.

Adina Goldenblum had outdone herself in the food department, providing a superlative traditional meal of stuffed carp, chicken soup with feather-light *kneidlach*, chicken in wine, and a delicious fruit compote for dessert. But the guests were hungry for another sort of nourishment. As they listened to the yeshivah students' slow, uplifting song, their expressions were rapt. A small door opened in their hearts, so long starved of spiritual fare.

Rav Anshel had been waiting for this moment. He stood up and cleared his throat. Instantly, silence fell over the large dining hall. The high school students gazed with interest at the *rosh yeshivah.*

"*Shabbat Shalom* to all our guests. We're very happy to have you here, and hope that you'll join us again in the near future. Right now, I'd like to introduce a young man who embodies all the good qualities to which our students aspire — a truly outstanding member of our yeshivah." He paused, glancing to his right."Eliyahu Flamm will say a few words." Rav Anshel returned to his seat.

Eli blushed. "Are you trying to finish me off?" he whispered to Rav Anshel.

The *rosh yeshivah* smiled. "Is *hakaras hatov* worth nothing? You gave me a new lease on life, turned me into a new man. Permit me the pleasure of praising you now and then."

"But I'm not prepared to speak."

"That's why I asked you. You're at your best when you improvise."

Eli had no choice. Dozens of boys were waiting. He stood up and began to speak, off the cuff. Rav Anshel had been right. As the words poured from his lips, Eli stood revealed as an electrifying speaker. He began with a few words on the *parashah,* moving quickly from there to a discussion of the yeshivah's role in modern-day life. He depicted Torah students as guardians of the walls that have protected Israel down through the centuries. Twenty minutes passed as he provided the young secular visitors with much food for thought.

After the meal, Eli led a tour around the yeshivah campus. The sky was cloudless and black, dotted with millions of tiny lights. Though the night was frigid, the guests preferred to bundle up in their warm coats and endure the cold rather than miss out on the night walk with the yeshivah's founder. Through grass and trees they strolled, enjoying the scent of invisible flowers and the tinkle of water falling among the stones in the natural pool.

As he led his tour, Eli narrowed his eyes and saw a form dip into the water. Despite the darkness he managed to make out Akiva Tamiri's face. Abashed at this sudden meeting with so many strangers, Akiva abandoned his original idea of immersing himself 310 consecutive times. He dressed hurriedly and disappeared into the night.

"A brave boy," Michah, one of the guests, remarked. "I wouldn't have believed anyone could do it — to dip into freezing water on a night like this. Brrr... He's got guts. Is he from the yeshivah?"

"Not at all," Eli said firmly. "He's not one of our boys."

"Why do you say it that way? What's wrong with what he was doing?" asked Leor, another of the high school boys. "Isn't it considered holy?"

Eli debated how to answer. "In this case, the path to holiness is distorted."

A boy named Gadi asked, "Why? Don't religious people dunk in the *mikveh* all the time?"

"The goal here is rather unusual." Eli told them about the Friends of the Mikdash group and its dreams of rebuilding the *Beis Hamikdash.* "They've chosen to live here at Anafim partly because of this natural pool. One of the prerequisites for entering the Temple Mount is immersion in a *mikveh.*"

His guests were soon engaged in a hot debate over the Friends of the *Mikdash* and their goals. Some justified them; others thought them deluded. Eli walked the boys back to the *beis midrash,* where he introduced them to the weekly *sidrah*. The young people quickly became interested, asking many questions. It was nearly midnight before he sent them off to the dorm. Eli himself remained at his *shtender* until his eyes closed of their own accord. It was after 1 a.m. when he finally went to find his own bed.

He was just dozing off when he remembered Judy's eye surgery, scheduled for Sunday. A wave of fear seized him. Covering his head with his pillow, he whispered, "*Ribbono shel olam,* He Who restores vision to the blind, please open my sister's eyes — Yehudis bas Margalit — and let her see again!"

"It's a difficult operation, but not an especially risky one," his brother Benjy had assured him. Why, then, did he feel this dread in his heart, as though a tragedy, Heaven forbid, was waiting in the wings?

The surgeons might wield their scalpels, but it was Hashem Who would decide whether or not Judy would be able to see again. Only *tefillos* could help her now.

On Sunday, he would take the entire yeshivah and travel to Jerusalem, to the *Kosel Hama'aravi*, where they would storm Heaven's gates with one voice, to rouse Hashem's mercy.

The eastern sky was a strip of pale blue when Eli's eyes finally closed.

◆ ◆ ◆

At 5 p.m., the port at Kronshtadt was as dark as the dead of night. Strong spotlights followed the *Charlotta* as she weighed anchor and moved slowly away from the pier, picking her way carefully among the ice blocks.

Arkady's nerves were unraveled by the long wait. He suspected Captain Breinen of postponing their departure intentionally. Even after the ship had sailed into open seas, Arkady remained tense and nervous. How long would it take Israel to pick up his trail? Would speed be enough to break him free of their shadow, or would he end by engaging his pursuers in a battle of wits, a deadly chess game? He despised himself for his fear, but justified it at the same time. "Not everyone has cargo — or opponents — like mine."

"Gray Cap" had promised to be in daily contact via the ship's radio. Arkady prayed for nothing but routine news. He thought again of the lead barrel and its horrific contents. How many years had he been on the most familiar terms with such things? Forty years or more. Arkady closed his eyes and drifted back to happier days, when he was at Mayak.

He had been 45 years younger then, a brilliant and promising young scientist at the start of his career in the secret nuclear plant. Like all his fellow workers at the Mayak reactor, he was filled to the brim with utopian ideals and glittering socialist dreams.

It was a busy time. The slogan at Mayak was "security, security, and security." They wore special clothes to work and underwent periodic blood tests. Anyone found with a REM of greater than 40 units was removed from the reactor area at once. The reactor itself bore numerous dire warnings: DANGER! RADIATION! Skull-and-crossbone symbols decorated many areas, along with the internationally recognized symbol of the atom, complete with whirling electrons. Caution was bred into their very beings.

And then the young Arkady had noticed a dangerous paradox. In the past, radioactive waste used to be placed in lead barrels and deposited on the floor of the Tacha River. Then Stalin issued orders that dispensed with the barrels. From 1948 through 1956, lethal nuclear waste was introduced directly into the river's waters, affecting an area populated by some 124,000 citizens. Between the years 1954 and 1961, thousands of residents were evacuated, and their villages razed to the ground by tanks. Only the town of Moslemova, some 87 kilometers from Mayak, remained standing and fully populated. The authorities claimed that this town was simply too large to evacuate.

Local doctors and bureaucrats, however, had a different — and far more sinister — explanation. They argued that the town had been left intact deliberately, to serve as a research resource for the study of the short- and long-term effects of radioactive poisoning. And so, the village of Muslimova continued its existence for years on the banks of the radioactively polluted river.

When the river overflowed periodically in local flooding, the poison spread into the fields, in which the village animals continued to graze. Sporadic testing of the villagers brought to light individuals whose blood carried more than 400 REM units — more than 10 times the amount permissible for reactor employees.

Arkady and his colleagues knew what was happening, but were rendered blind, deaf, and mute by orders from the Communist leadership. They continued to develop weapons of destruction targeted at the enemy, while destroying their own fellow citizens on the side. Thousands of their more courageous countrymen — villagers from the region — demonstrated publicly against the radioactive pollution of their river, and were rewarded with wholesale slaughter by the Red Army's legions of tanks.

In recent years, Arkady knew, dribbles of information had begun to leak out of the old KGB files, telling a horrific tale of some 60 million Soviet citizens murdered during Stalin's infamous "re-education" campaign between the years of 1937 and 1955. Even if those figures were inflated, the number of victims had clearly ranged in the millions. When dealing with destruction of such vast proportions, how significant was the radioactive poisoning of a "mere" 124,000 villagers? The Communist boot trampled all underfoot, while consciences slept.

"What happened then is now going to happen again," Arkady thought. "How many people will pay with their lives for the contents of this barrel?"

Arkady's Communist boot trampled, and his conscience remained soundly asleep.

◆ ◆ ◆

Three bullets flew simultaneously at the target. They ended in three soft *plops,* like a dry cough, swallowed by the noise of cracking ice in the nearby trees. The wooden target came detached and slid silently into the snow, where fresh snow proceeded to cover it.

There was an eerie silence on the hilltop at twilight. The place was deserted except for the three Israeli agents practicing their target-shooting. The spot offered the best panoramic view of Moscow. The city lay spread out below them, glorious in the lights that were being turned on to greet the night.

Uzi Saraf was fluent in Russian, and it was he who read the signpost attached to a wooden fence at the site. "It says here that before the Revolution this place was known as Freedom Hill. Amazing how little freedom you can find here today."

"Freedom in Russia was canceled by the Communist Revolution," Yossi Katri remarked as he returned his pistol to its underarm holster.

"Hurry up, guys, I'm freezing to death!" Yoni Dor's knees were literally shaking with cold, despite his heavy fur-lined parka. To his chagrin, he had come down with the flu immediately upon their arrival in Moscow, and was coughing and sneezing almost constantly.

The three men descended the hill and returned to the car they had parked at the side of the road, close to the Luznikowski Bridge. Yossi Katri took the driver's seat and began warming the engine. "Guys, we have to coordinate our efforts — decide who does what."

"No problem," Uzi Saraf said. "Our respective jobs were assigned back in Israel. You meet tomorrow with your counterpart in the Moscow police — investigative customs officer, Michael Spiro."

"Customs?"

"An internal name for an elite group operating inside the Moscow police department." Saraf smiled. "Incidentally, Spiro is Jewish, a supporter of Israel. He'll be happy to help you." He paused. "Next. I'm going to check into the nuclear angle. I'll look into Arkady's previous places of work, whom he's met with recently, etc. Yoni —" He turned to the third in the trio — "assuming the flu doesn't ground you, or at least that you can refrain from sneezing more than 10 times a minute, you'll tackle the hotels.

"We start work in the morning. Tomorrow evening, we meet to report."

◆ ◆ ◆

"Have you ever seen such snobs?" Dani Devash was outraged. "Who found the newspaper ad? Who raised the suspicion that we're dealing with an enormous story? Who discovered that he ran off to Russia?"

The clearing of a throat from the other side of the desk halted the angry monologue in midstream.

"All right, all right," Devash conceded irritably. "Border control is your purview. But who started the whole investigation, who insisted that he didn't drown as everyone supposed — who but me? And now they've neutralized me, put me out of the picture."

Ari Naot, chin cupped on the heels of his hands, nodded in agreement. A rare empathy had sprung up between the two slighted police officers.

"I called Shimi Tzipori this morning for an update on the investigation," Devash continued. "You know what he said? 'Don't ask.' "

"I won't," sighed Naot.

"But before he said that, he got angry at me, asking who gave me his private number! I reminded him that the last time I called, to report my suspicions in this case, I called this number. He snapped at me not to call him again. 'Stick with your police work, officer, and don't poke your nose into matters of national security. The case is in good hands and is being properly handled.' "

"And what did you answer?"

"Nothing. Before I could even assimilate what he was saying, he slammed down the phone. Hung up on *me,* Dani Devash, chief inspector of Bat Yam!"

Ari's chin lifted fractionally. "If it had happened to me, I'd have called him back once more and said just one sentence."

"What?" Despite himself, Devash was interested.

"We'll see who catches the scientist first, the policeman or the detective."

Devash was silent for several moments. Suddenly, he sprang up. "Brilliant! Ari, you've just given me an incredible idea!"

"Naturally." Naot was smug.

Devash ignored the barb. He began to pace the room, speaking as he went."I'm going to set up a brain trust to deal with the Arkady Bogdanov case. In my opinion, the way they're handling things is doomed to failure. Israel stands in danger of a nuclear holocaust, and those fools are busy fighting over their petty egos.

"I'm going to call the first meeting tonight, at my house. What was it you said — we'll see who catches the scientist first? The policeman or the detective."

24

In Uzi Saraf's mind, the word "archives" conjured up a picture of an old, dusty office, rusted bars, and faded black file boxes. He was surprised, therefore, by his first view of Moscow's Interior Department archives office. It was situated in a complex of large halls, well lit and heated. There were no paper files. Instead, a network of computers held information on millions of people.

The archives director, a thickset, middle-aged man wearing a red necktie that appeared to be choking him, presented himself to Saraf. "Gregori Zislin, at your service. Whom do I have the honor of addressing?"

Saraf showed his identity card. Zislin motioned for him to follow. "We must preserve confidentiality," he whispered, his eyes inspecting their surroundings. He led Uzi to his private office at one side of the archives hall.

It was an ornate office by any standard. The furniture was Baroque.

A large oil painting of former Soviet Prime Minister Leonid Brezhnev graced the wall behind Zislin's desk. The archives director took his seat and reached over to shake Saraf's hand warmly. "Now we can talk. You're from the Israeli Mossad! We are colleagues, then. As a young man I was an agent, and later a senior interrogator, in the KGB How can I help you?"

"I need details on Arkady Bogdanov."

Zislin creased his brow. "I recall that name — just a moment — of course! He was the top administrator at Mayak. What's your problem with him?"

The Israeli agent related the events surrounding Bogdanov. When he was done, Zislin inclined his head. "Let us see." He tapped a few keys on his computer keyboard. Some 30 seconds later, the screen was filled with a plethora of information on the scientist, including photographs of Arkady at Mayak.

"Who can swim in such an ocean of information?" Zislin joked. "We have to search now for the name of a person who was close to him."

He peered at the screen, muttering to himself as he scrolled down. Uzi tried to read over Zislin's shoulder, but that shoulder proved too broad — and the Cyrillic letters too closely packed — for easy reading. At last, Zislin said, "Here's one name that keeps coming up: Yevgeny Morozov, Bogdanov's personal secretary at Mayak. I'd suggest that you speak with him." His hand hovered over a light-blue phone featuring many buttons.

Saraf hesitated. "Will he agree to speak over the phone?"

"Certainly. He'll talk, my friend. In this country, people have learned to keep silent at home and to talk in the KGB cellars."

"You led me to understand that the KGB was history for you."

Zislin's face beamed with pleasure. "Good, good, let's get at the truth. In honesty, my 'past' is not exactly in the past. I am still employed in the service of my country." He jerked a thumb at the portrait of Brezhnev. "You see Leonid? It's because of him that I'm here. He drafted me for life. Ah, that was a leader. See the intelligence and strength shining from his face! Today we have weak rulers, chatterboxes and compromisers and pleasers who are worth about as much as an old onion peel!"

As he spoke, the thick fingers were punching in Mayak's telephone number. He spoke with the secretary at the reactor; just seconds later, Morozov himself came on the line.

Morozov's first tactic was to try, diplomatically, to shake the caller. When Zislin allowed a harsher, more peremptory note to enter his voice, Morozov changed his tune. "I'm not the person you want. If you want details on Arik, ask Svetlana Shesuyov."

"Arik?"

"That's what Arkady was called here at Mayak."

"And who is Shesuyov?"

"She was Bogdanov's assistant. Today she runs the nuclear reactor at Zaporozh'ye, in the Ukraine."

"Many thanks."

Zislin leaned back in his swivel chair. "You've got a trip to the Ukraine ahead of you."

Uzi was taken aback. "I'm here on a very tight schedule. How will I fit in a trip to the Ukraine in that short a time?"

"You Israelis," Zislin said, shaking his head, "are used to working fast — and that's why your country is going down the drain. You won the Six-Day War in a lightning victory, so now you think that that is how everything works. It doesn't. If you are in a rush, you will leave Russia empty-handed. You must take your time and work slowly and thoroughly, as we do in the KGB"

Uzi's heart sank. "In all my training for the Mossad, I never learned how to infiltrate a nuclear reactor and get its administrator to confide in me. Maybe you can help by flying me there?"

Zislin boomed with laughter, saying, "Give me one good reason why I should."

The Mossad had equipped its agent for such a contingency. Uzi Saraf whipped a roll of dollars from his pocket, wrapped in clear plastic.

"Would 10 be enough?"

"T-t-ten?"

"Five thousand right now, and another five when we return."

Zislin struggled up from his seat, moaning, "Oh, my poor bones!" He went to the windows and quickly lowered the shades. "Now we can talk."

Uzi unwrapped the roll of bills and counted $5,000 into the Russian's hand. Gregori Zislin smiled from ear to ear. "I will fly to the Ukraine with you. I like a man who is direct and to the point. In fact, I like Israelis — wonderful people, energetic and charming."

"Thanks," Uzi said dryly.

"You're welcome. Oh, you're going to enjoy this. I will prepare a tour for you, hundreds of kilometers of lakes, forests, and rivers. So peaceful — so wholesome! You can travel in the Ukraine for days on end without meeting a sick person. Everyone is healthy there."

"Like in Chernobyl," Uzi murmured.

"Excuse me? You said something?"

"Nothing. When do we leave for Zaporozh'ye?"

Gregori Zislin pulled a gold-tipped pen from his desk drawer and wrote a few words on a square of paper. "Here are my phone numbers, at home and in case of emergency. We meet tomorrow morning and fly to the Ukraine, to meet with the good scientist, Svetlana Shesuyov."

Kum, Iran

Yusuf Abu Rabia gazed out the window at the desert panorama spread out below. It was only an hour since the plane had lifted off from Teheran's airport; in another hour and a quarter it was scheduled to land in the Islamic holy city of Kum. Yusuf would be put up at a Shi'ite palace and begin preparations for the biggest operation of them all.

Impatiently, he tugged at the ends of his black mustache, then pinched his nose, as was his habit when particularly elated. He hadn't felt this good in a long time. The plan was advancing right on schedule. The Zionist enemy was about to feel the full brunt of an attack that would put an end to the independent Israeli state. It would still be several years before Iran developed a nuclear warhead that would reach Tel Aviv, but Yusuf's "missile" was already in existence, and much smarter than all the Tomahawks and "smart bombs" in America. His "missile" had legs and a human warhead. His missile was a man. A nuclear man.

The original idea had not been his own, but he had contributed the twist of using a human atom bomb. Yusuf had always been considered the wonder child of the Abu Rabia family.

The fax was sitting in a secret pocket in his jacket. Yusuf put his hand in the pocket just to feel it, then irresistibly pulled the page out and read it for the 10th time:

In the name of the merciful Allah, and under the rulership of the exalted leader Ayatollah Ali Rafsanjani,

At a meeting of the Revolutionary Council that took place two days ago, it was decided to request that you return to Iran to personally oversee the final stages of Operation "Lightning and Thunder."

The Council's secretary, Mullah Adal Palhavani, read aloud the progress report, and the Council members expressed great joy at the good news. Toward the end of the meeting, I suggested that you return here to supervise on the spot, and everyone burst into vigorous applause and shouts of support. We all know of the large part you played in devising the brilliant plan behind "Lightning and Thunder," and agree that there has not been another Moslem since Mohammed's days capable of causing such vast quantities of Jewish blood to be spilled.

Return to us, be with us and help us to recapture what is ours. Together we will chase the Zionists from Jerusalem, Tel Aviv, and Haifa. We will raise the Arab flag proudly over the Knesset, and build a new Palestine — to your credit!

Your courage instills pride in every man who has noble Arab blood in his veins.

The fax was signed by his good friend, Ishmael Kadar Issawi, father of "Lightning and Thunder," the plan that Iran had initially rejected outright, and then accepted with reservation. If it succeeded, it would be Iran's plan. If it failed, Iran would never have heard of it.

But the plan would not fail. Abu Rabia thought of the young Sulimein Halil, eyes blazing with dedication and purpose. Yusuf had last met him two months before, on a trip organized by the Shi'ites. Sulimein had been photographed against a backdrop of miles of gas pipes in the Saudi desert. Two things about the photograph immediately caught the eye: the endless lines of pipes snaking through the sand, and the burning eyes of Sulimein Halil.

The eyes had impressed themselves on Yusuf much more strongly than the miles of pipes. Those eyes held the cunning and poison of the deadliest of snakes.

Operation "Lightning and Thunder" would not fail.

◆ ◆ ◆

Uzi Saraf hated admitting it, but Zislin had been right: The Ukraine's natural beauty was truly breathtaking. As their train sped southward, Uzi saw miles of plains and valleys, forests and lakes, leaping waterfalls and rocks split asunder as if with a giant knife, sparkling in the sun like chunks of glass. Here, nature was still triumphant over progress. There were panoramas as yet untouched by man's hand, great tracts of land with only a sprinkling of human population: a village here, a small town there.

Three hours after setting out from Deniproptrovsk (Yektrinoslav of old), the train approached the city of Zaporozh'ye, site of the largest nuclear power plant in Russia. The train stopped at the edge of what was labeled a restricted military zone. Saraf and Zislin were the last two passengers to leave the train.

Uzi waxed philosophical. "From the purity of nature to its destruction — the death-dealing atom." He shook off the mood as a government-issue Chaika rolled up to collect them. At three separate checkpoints, Zislin was asked to display his official pass.

Finally, they stood at the portals of the gargantuan plant, marveling at its proportions. "Bigger than your Dimona, eh?" Zislin boasted. "It's a whole city."

There were three nuclear reactors at Zaporozh'ye. As giant and menacing as the site had appeared from a distance, it was infinitely more imposing close up. Electric fences and vicious guard dogs halted them some 500 yards from the main plant; two armed soldiers accompanied them the rest of the way. Zislin's pass clearly specified his aim: a meeting with the plant manager.

Uzi had expected an atmosphere that was cold, remote, almost devoid of life. What he found was exactly the opposite. Inside the gates of the facility, the landscape was adorned with well-tended flower beds, spilling an extravagance of multicolored beauty on every side. Clear plastic coverings protected the plants from the bitter winter cold. Life and movement abounded. Small buses transported workers to and from different points in the facility; Dobermans prowled at the end of chains, breathing heavily in the frigid air.

An orange, tractorlike vehicle made use of the snow chains on its enormous tires to bear Zislin and Saraf to the main office in the plant's western wing. They were escorted to a long room in which computer consoles covered an entire wall. An elderly woman awaited them there. Time had softened neither the cruel lines of her face, nor the animation in her sharp eyes.

They were facing Dr. Svetlana Shesuyov, manager of the Zaporozh'ye nuclear plant.

◆ ◆ ◆

With a few tepid words of welcome, she invited them to be seated in one corner of the large room, where an arrangement of brown leather chairs surrounded a glass coffee table. "Just like a living room," Uzi laughed inwardly. "There's even a thick rug to warm your feet! The only thing missing is a crystal chandelier."

"Gregori Zislin, archives supervisor at the Interior Ministry," Zislin introduced himself. "I see that you rule over a not inconsiderable kingdom here."

Svetlana permitted herself a small smile. "We have six reactors here," she said proudly. "The most advanced of their kind — the WER 1000. Right now, they provide for the electrical needs of all of the Ukraine — some 36 billion kilowatts."

Zislin did not allow the plant manager to become lulled into a false sense of security. Leaning forward, he said, "Dr. Shesuyov, perhaps my name is familiar to you from the past. I was a KGB interrogator."

A shadow crossed Svetlana's face. Almost immediately, she recovered her poise and stared at him with ice-blue eyes. Zislin went on, "Do you know a man by the name of Arkady Bogdanov?"

Svetlana nodded without speaking.

"Has he been here recently?"

A negative headshake. The woman's lips were tightly compressed.

The KGB man sighed, then said softly, "Madam, this attitude will quickly make you a *former* nuclear plant manager."

Svetlana hesitated a long moment. Then, she said decisively, "That despicable Arkady Bogdanov. Thirty years I worked for him, and I never knew who he was."

"Have the two of you had any contact in recent days?"

"Certainly. He met with me and asked me to smuggle out radioactive materials to him, enough for the construction of two nuclear bombs."

With his superior command of the Russian language, Uzi needed no interpreter. He was shaken at what he had just heard. Two bombs! What foul plot was in the making?

The manager's words had no such powerful effect on Zislin. "Did you provide what he wanted?"

"You are insulting me, *Tovarisch* Zislin! Do I look like a thief to you?"

Zislin answered calmly, "Yes, Dr. Shesuyov. Communism has made potential thieves of us all. Every thief has his price. A thousand dollars may not be enough to buy the cooperation of a nuclear plant manager; $100,000 is much more attractive. Bogdanov offered more."

He stated this as a fact. Svetlana had no way of knowing that he was actually probing, and that he had, as yet, virtually no facts at all at his disposal.

She was furious. "We met at Alexander Park, in Moscow. He didn't specify an exact sum, just spoke vaguely of compensation that would cause my son to bless his mother all the rest of his days. But I turned down his offer and sent him on his way."

Why is she afraid? the KGB man asked himself. *She's hiding something.*

"Where did he go after you rejected his proposal?" Zislin asked.

"Probably back to his hotel."

"And which hotel is that?"

"The Russia."

Zislin struggled to his feet. "Thank you for your cooperation, Dr. Shesuyov. We will go now."

An escort of three soldiers saw them off the grounds. At the gates of the power plant, they found the same government car waiting to carry them off to the train station.

"Well, we did not leave empty-handed," Zislin remarked. "The scientist you're looking for stayed at the Russia Hotel. That will be our first stop."

Uzi smiled sardonically. "As usual, it's a question of the stable doors being shut after the horses have bolted. Bogdanov won't be there anymore."

"You're in a hurry, young man?" Zislin was laughing at him.

"Yes! Two atom bombs threaten my country!"

"Nothing is exploding yet, and no horse has bolted. With Gregori Zislin at your side, the globe is smaller than a ping-pong ball!"

◆ ◆ ◆

Yossi Katri honked impatiently. Dusk was falling — the hour when thousands of Muscovites set out from their offices, bound for home — and the Moskevich he had rented was stuck in a long, long line of traffic on Gogol Avenue.

Yossi's reserves of energy were fast becoming depleted. Today's investigations had yielded no fruit. Uzi Saraf had flown off to the Ukraine that morning, leaving Yossi behind with Yoni Dor, who was flat on his back in bed with a high fever. Yossi had wanted to stay with him, but Yoni had waved him off. "You didn't come to Moscow to be a nursemaid. We have a job to do. I'm stuck in bed at the moment, but you can still do yours."

So Yossi departed, and tried to get inside the enemy's head. Arkady Bogdanov had stayed at a hotel. Which one? Common sense dictated that a man looking to buy an atomic bomb would want to keep a low profile. Accordingly, Yossi began his search with the Sevostopol, on Bolshya Yoshoneskaya Street, a three-star hotel with a dank, uninviting look.

Inside, the hotel was even grayer and drearier. Yossi imagined that he could hear the scurrying of mice in the lobby walls. Scrutinizing the place carefully, he saw nothing worthy of note apart from an extremely noisy group of Hungarian tourists. He approached the front desk and made inquiries. The name "Bogdanov" elicited no special response, not even when Yossi explained that his uncle, the former atomic scientist, had tried unsuccessfully to reach him from a room in that very hotel last week.

"Where now?" he wondered, discouraged, as his car crawled up Prospect Mira. "The Cosmos, not far from here, or the gorgeous Savoy, or the simple Sovietskaya — I'm going in circles. This city is so big, with every other street a Prospect — The snow is snarling up traffic, and I have to stop every few minutes to ask impatient drivers the way to some street. What next?"

Suddenly, he had the answer. Arkady Bogdanov must surely have wanted to get lost in a crowd. He would have sought out a large hotel — the largest.

The Russia Hotel was the anonymous traveler's dream.

Just as he pulled the Moskovich into the hotel's parking area, his cell phone rang. Uzi Saraf was on the line.

"Yossi, I have a scoop for you. I know where Arkady was staying. In the Russia Hotel, near Red Square."

"Thank you very much," Yossi said, smiling into the phone. "I'll be walking through the doors of that very hotel in about 30 seconds!"

25

Half an hour before the operation, Judy was anesthetized. Her thoughts grew confused and sluggish, detached from the activity around her. People wished her a successful surgery, and she nodded politely without really absorbing what they were saying. She couldn't understand why Benjy — accompanying her into the operating room — had red eyes. A few milligrams of some chemical had the power to turn fear and nervousness into peaceful indifference.

Nurses and doctors clustered around like bees around honey. Judy was transferred to the surgical table and strapped down, her head immobilized. Yesterday, she had expected to faint from terror in the operating room; now, she heard her own heartbeat amplified over the monitors and it was calm and stable — thump, thump, thump.

Masked faces hovered above her head. She saw a pair of eyes; they belonged to the surgeon, Dr. Schneider. For the 10th time, he asked, "Judy, do you hear me?"

"Ye-e-e-s." Her answer was weak.

"We haven't even put you under yet, and you're already asleep!" the surgeon joked.

"Where's my brother?" she asked thickly.

Benjy called from his place at one side of the room, "Here I am."

"I want you to stay for the operation. Don't go."

"I'll be right here."

He had not intended to witness the procedure firsthand. It would be almost unbearable to watch what would be happening to Judy's eye. But bear it he must. His only sister wanted him there!

"How do you feel?" Dr. Schneider asked.

"I — don't feel — anything." The anesthesiologist injected something into her veins. Her eyes closed.

◆ ◆ ◆

The operation was proceeding at a satisfactory pace. Dr. Schneider lifted Judy's eyelid to its maximum, exposing as much of the eye as possible. The eye muscle was manipulated to roll the eye as far downward as it would go. The surgeon made an incision in the cornea and penetrated to the shattered lens. All the fragments were removed and an artificial lens was implanted in their place. He bathed the new lens in a liquid solution that would suffice temporarily until the eye stabilized and began producing its own moisture again.

It was time to sew it up. Dr. Schneider stitched the cornea with nylon thread only one third of a hairsbreadth in diameter. He worked with the aid of a microscope and a magnifying monitor.

All went as it should. The surgery was nearing completion when, without warning, Judy's heartbeat weakened. Benjy was the first to notice. Before he could decide whether the situation was serious, there was a further deterioration. Karen, the head nurse, said anxiously, "Her blood pressure's dropping rapidly. She's going into shock!" A horrifying instant later — "There's no pulse!"

Within seconds, the O.R. was filled with all the urgent activity of a battlefield. Doctors and nurses raced in with emergency equipment. Judy was hooked up to a respirator, then given massive electrical shocks in the region of her heart. The medical staff scanned the monitors for her vital signs. She seemed to be slipping through their fingers.

Benjy's lips never stopped moving, reciting broken snatches of prayer. *Ana Hashem, hoshiah na, ana Hashem, hatzlichah na...* As Dr. Schneider passed, Benjy reached out to clutch his arm. "What happened?"

"I don't know. Maybe an allergic reaction to one of the chemicals. She went into sudden massive shock. It's something we never expected; all her tests were fine. Dr. Levinstam, in Israel, couldn't have known, either. He can't blame you."

"Blame me!" Benjy's grip on the surgeon's arm tightened. "Doctor, is — what are her chances?"

Dr. Schneider shrugged, and gently shook off the restraining hand. He passed by quickly, avoiding the sight of Benjy's frightened eyes.

◆ ◆ ◆

They reached the Western Wall at 2 o'clock in the afternoon. Eli and Benjy had synchronized their plan in advance: the time difference between New York and Jerusalem was seven hours. Eight a.m., when the operation was due to begin, was 3 p.m. in Israel. Eli wanted to be sure to have enough time to recite the entire book of *Tehillim* before, during, and immediately after the surgery.

The students of Yeshivas Aish Aharon stood together at the leftmost corner of the *Kosel* and quietly, with concentration, recited the *Tehillim.* Eli asked Tzvika Sofer to act as *chazan,* as his own throat became periodically too choked with tears to allow him to function in that capacity. Scores of times, he pulled his handkerchief from his pocket to dab at his eyes. His friends noted his inner emotion but were tactful enough not to comment.

Toward the end of reciting *Sefer Tehillim,* another large group suddenly joined them. It was the Friends of the Mikdash, headed by their spiritual leader, Rabbi Yonah Pinter.

"We heard that your sister is having a serious eye operation today, and we've come to be with you. Here, near the spot of the Holy of Holies, it's possible to call forth great salvations," Yonah said.

Eli made a gesture that asked, "How did you know?"

Yonah understood. "Some of my people saw a large minibus leave Anafim with all the yeshivah boys. They asked about it, and one of the workers at your yeshivah told him the story. We organized ourselves right away. We're good neighbors, no?"

The newcomers joined the yeshivah boys for the final chapters of *Tehillim.* The voices of Chemi Maimon, Akiva Tamiri, Sruly Egozi, Dekel, and the rest of the Friends of the Mikdash mingled with those of Yoel Goldfinger, Yitzi Winogradski, Giora Shaharabi, and the other aspiring students of Yeshivas Aish Aharon. They formed a giant choir that shook the very stones of the ancient Wall.

When they had finished *davening Minchah,* the boys kissed the stones and slowly backed away. Yonah Pinter called after them, "Hey, where are you running off to? A dance! A joyous dance can shatter a harsh decree!"

He seized Eli Flamm's hand with one of his own, and grabbed Rav Anshel Pfeffer's with the other. He left them no option but to dance with him. An impossible circle of Aish Aharon's finest, in their sober clothing, danced hand in hand with the colorful figures of the Friends of the Mikdash, singing all together for Hashem's mercy and compassion. But when Yonah Pinter began shouting, at the top of his lungs, *Adir Hu, nivneh beiso bekarov* ("He is great! We will build His House soon") — with the emphasis on the *nivneh — we will build,* the yeshivah boys began slipping away. The Friends were left on their own, dancing and singing as the Aish Aharon group shook their heads.

"I told you they were crazy," Shmulie Abrams said on their return to the minibus. "It's a pity we let them join us; now the yeshivah world will have something else to say about us. They'll say we've become corrupted by our neighbors."

The boys wanted to leave quickly, but Eli Flamm was missing. A moment earlier, he had been seen in quiet discussion with Rav Anshel Pfeffer. Now the *rosh yeshivah* was alone.

Asked where Eli was, Rav Anshel answered, "He's not a child. He probably had something to do and will be right back."

They waited in the minibus. When Eli finally reappeared, he did not say a word. He sat down beside Rav Anshel and sank into a deep, brooding silence.

Rav Anshel alone knew what had kept Eli. He was waiting for a moment when they could be private, away from listening ears. As they had been preparing to leave the Western Wall plaza, Eli had noticed David ben Avraham — "Dekel" — in a whispered conversation with one of the *Kosel's* Arab cleaning staff near the mouth of the tunnels.

"Why would a *ger tzedek*, hounded and persecuted by his former Arab brothers, be talking secretly to an Arab near the *Kosel* tunnels?" he muttered to Rav Anshel. Hastily, he had found a place where he could continue to observe Dekel. A few minutes later, Dekel had vanished into one of the tunnels.

As the minibus sped toward Anafim, the darkness in Eli's heart strengthened. He anxiously awaited word on Judy's difficult surgery, but Dekel's face intruded again and again, confusing his thoughts.

After *Ma'ariv*, the yeshivah boys sat down for their evening meal. Perhaps because Adina Goldenblum had been distracted that day, the food she had prepared tasted bland and uninteresting. Also unusual was the silence that reigned in the dining hall. More than one person present compared the dull gloom of this Sunday night to the lively and inspiring atmosphere that had filled that same room on Friday night, a mere 48 hours before.

It was a night of telephone calls. Eli made the first call immediately upon his return to yeshivah. He spoke a few words, listened a moment, then suddenly shrieked, "Benjy, tell me honestly — is she alive?"

That was how his fellow students learned that Eli's sister, Judy, had lost consciousness in the final moments of her operation. Her condition was not stable. Someone tacked a hasty note on the communal bulletin board: "At 9 p.m. we're meeting in the *beis midrash* to say the whole *Sefer Tehillim* for the *refuah* of Yehudis *bas* Margalit."

Eli closeted himself with Rav Anshel in the staff lounge near the dormitory. The telephone rang. This time, it was for Yoel Goldfinger.

"Good evening, Yoel," the caller said. "Do you recognize my voice?"

Yoel stuck a finger in his ear, the better to hear over the noise in the corridor. "No, I really don't."

"It's your Uncle Dani."

Yoel was astonished. "Dani Devash?"

Devash chuckled. "How many Uncle Danis do you have? Listen, I need you urgently this evening. My brother-in-law, who also happens to be your father, is always boasting about how intelligent yeshivah boys are, and he cites you as his prime example. He says you're a born analyst. Tonight I need an analyst."

He quickly gave Yoel the necessary background, then told him that he was convening a brain trust in his Bat Yam home in two hours' time. "Yoel, we're talking about the lives of millions of Jews in *Eretz Yisrael.* I'm sending a car to pick you up at the yeshivah."

Yoel didn't promise to come until he spoke to Rav Anshel. He found the *rosh yeshivah* sitting with Eli in the staff lounge. Eli was speaking in an earnest, agitated way. Rav Anshel looked perturbed.

Yoel approached tentatively. "Is anything wrong?"

Rav Anshel sighed. "You must have heard that Judy has lost consciousness. But what brings you here?"

Yoel passed on his uncle's story, and his request. "Should I go?" he asked.

Rav Anshel rose from his seat and paced to and fro, considering the matter. "The question is, are they trying to draft yeshivah boys through the back door? Also, what about tonight's *Tehillim* session?" He turned to Judy's brother. "What do you think, Eli?"

Eli sat with his hands on his knees, fingers taut as wires. "No. It's not a ploy. I believe what Dani Devash said. Yoel must go to Bat Yam tonight. Judy is only one person. Right now, millions of Jewish lives might be hanging in the balance."

The second recitation of *Sefer Tehillim* suppassed the first one, at the *Kosel.* The boys felt the weight of Judy's plight on their shoulders, and did their best to break through the *beis midrash* walls with the force of their prayers. This time, Eli himself led the others. He wailed without shame, and his tears proved contagious.

They finished at midnight. Most of the boys went to sleep; even the top students were exhausted after the full day. Normally, Yoel Goldfinger and Shmulie Abrams would have been at their *shtenders,* but not tonight. At 8 p.m., Yoel had been picked up by a car his Uncle Dani sent. Shmulie, having stayed up all of the previous night learning, had tumbled into his bed.

Eli was left alone in the *beis midrash.* At 1 a.m., he had risen to return to the dorm when the public phone in the corridor rang. He flew to the phone and snatched up the receiver.

It was Benjy.

"She's still unconscious," Benjy said, "but her condition has begun to stabilize. For the first time since she went into shock, the doctors are being cautiously optimistic."

"*Baruch Hashem,*" Eli breathed.

"Yes. What really surprises them is the way Judy keeps mumbling in her sleep. That's not consistent with people in a coma — and that's what gives the doctors hope. The neurologist, Dr. Seligman, told me that the formula goes: A brain that isn't asleep is a brain that isn't damaged."

"What is she mumbling about?"

"How can anyone understand what she's saying?" Benjy was surprised by the question. "Her face is covered with an oxygen mask."

"A pity." Eli yawned in complete exhaustion. "At times like these, the brain releases all kinds of things that may have been buried for years."

Benjy had caught the yawn. "Go on, get some sleep. If it's 6 p.m. here, it must be 1 o'clock in the morning over there. Go to bed."

Eli slowly descended the *beis midrash* steps. A light wind rustled the leaves of the evergreen trees, their sharp scent wafting to his nose. Despite his overwhelming fatigue, he decided to stop at the cattle pen belonging to the Friends of the Mikdash.

The goats and sheep had been herded into two enormous corrals. Most of them were asleep under night lights, looking sleek and fat. From the second pen, where the younger lambs were kept, a plaintive bleating issued. Eli saw that the pen was substandard. "It's *tza'ar ba'alei chayim,* he thought. "How can they keep babies in these conditions?"

He pulled up a handful of grass and held it out to the small animals, who bounded over to eat it hungrily. They licked his hands and begged for more. "There's something to this task — one Moshe *Rabbeinu* and Dovid *Hamelech* both held. They were both tested through their devotion to these pure creatures," Eli reflected as he continued to feed the lambs. When he grew too weary to continue, the animals bleated sadly. "I have to go to sleep now," he whispered. "Maybe I'll come back tomorrow night."

He was puzzled."Is this how Dekel cares for future *korbanos* for the *Beis Hamikdash*? At this rate, they'll be dead long before he plans to use them." The vision of the poor hungry lambs wouldn't leave him. He walked slowly across the settlement toward the yeshivah's quarters.

A white car came up the road and turned into the gates. Yoel Goldfinger emerged, saying a few words to the driver. He started when he saw Eli waiting for him in the dark.

"How's your sister?" he asked tensely.

"There's been a slight improvement."

Yoel burst into tears. He loved Eli like a brother. He patted his friend on the shoulder as though to give him strength.

"Nu, what have you brought with you?" Eli asked.

Yoel collected himself. He turned to Eli, saying seriously, "Eli, you were absolutely right. The situation is not simple. I don't know how I'll be able to close my eyes tonight — or any night. We're on the verge of great danger. Two atom bombs are on their way to Israel, and no one knows where they'll land."

In the course of the ensuing hour, Yoel described to Eli what had taken place that night in the brain trust meeting at his uncle's house in Bat Yam.

26

The hours crawled by with maddening slowness. Instead of traveling home to Flatbush to sleep in his own bed, Benjy sat beside Judy's hospital bed, a small Gemara in his hand, and learned silently by flashlight.

He had used his standing as a doctor at Mount Sinai, as well as his ties with Dr. Schneider, to get Judy a private room in the intensive care unit. Judy was still unconscious, but the oxygen mask had been removed once her breathing became regular and less labored. She lay attached to various machines which monitored her breathing, blood pressure, and heartbeat. All her vital signs were stable — and yet, no one knew when Judy would wake. Or *if* she would wake.

He stared out the window at the nighttime view of Manhattan. This part of town was lit up with neon signs and shifting electronic billboards. The streets hummed continuously with traffic. Youths with headphones sang along raucously to the music they were hearing. Benjy turned away and drew the curtain closed. He had never liked the city at night. Flatbush was different, much quieter, with young Jews hurrying to their *shiurim* and boys running to be on time for *Ma'ariv.* "They run, and we run," Benjy thought. "But how different the running." His eye fell on Judy. Would she ever run again?

He felt uncharacteristically helpless. His sister looked as fragile as a baby bird in the high bed. There was nothing he could do for her. The most sophisticated technology was right here at hand, but none of it could restore Judy to consciousness. Many times, he had pointed out this very thing to his atheistic colleagues. "Don't you see that there must be a Higher Power behind nature? You're busy treating live, conscious patients. Try taking just one unconscious one and waking him up." It was an ongoing debate that had suddenly become extremely relevant to Benjy's own life. Neither he, nor the world's top neurologists, could do a thing to restore Judy to consciousness.

But there was something he *could* do, and that was to *daven.* Yesterday, he had spoken of Judy to one of New York's renowned rebbes. The rebbe had promised that Judy would wake within a short time. Benjy clung to this promise with all his might. The last thing the Flamm family needed was another tragedy.

From the moment his sister had landed at Kennedy Airport, Benjy had neglected his clinic entirely. He had not seen any patients for three days. This very morning, a competing eye clinic had opened near his own facility in a new Manhattan medical center. Benjy was not worried; Hashem is the One Who supplies a livelihood to His children, and He could easily provide enough for both Benjy and his competitors. He refused to let himself be troubled by the fact that many of his patients had canceled their appointments as soon as they heard he would not be at the clinic. His secretary at the People's Clinic had asked whether, in his concern for his sister, he wasn't overdoing things.

No, he wasn't overdoing things. His father had always taught him, by personal example, how important it was to sacrifice oneself for another's sake. Abba had done it himself, on many occasions. One of the last, and most impressive, was the way he had acted upon the discovery that his old friend had been toiling to produce a scholarly work on the very same topic that Aharon Flamm himself had been laboring over for years. Without hesitation, he had handed over the fruits of his labor to his friend. "Abba was willing to lose something for the sake of a friend," Benjy thought. "I can stand to lose a little for my own sister's sake."

At 3 a.m., Manhattan was more subdued. Exhausted, Benjy leaned his head back in his armchair and dozed. Suddenly, he jumped up as if a snake had dug its fangs into him. Judy had said his name!

"Benjy..."

Leaning closer, he saw to his disappointment that his sister was still unconscious. She was talking in her sleep. She had babbled earlier, but this time Benjy could make out words. Judy had returned to scenes of her childhood, murmuring of Eli, Dovy, Moishy. She referred to Moishy by his earliest baby name, "Mickey," which the family had fondly called him until the little boy had returned home from nursery school one day complaining that his friends were calling him Mickey Mouse. Judy wove whole scenes that had taken place 15 years earlier, things Benjy had forgotten. She talked of his, Benjy's, bar mitzvah. She spoke of her mother, father, and Shlomo with a raw longing that squeezed Benjy's heart and made him weep silently with a nostalgia that cut like a knife.

Several times, he was certain that Judy had awakened, but each time he was doomed to disappointment. Her breathing remained even, as in sleep, and when he called her name she did not answer. She was locked inside her own world — an unconscious world.

Suddenly, he heard something that made him lean forward to listen. He placed his ear directly above her mouth, the better to catch every syllable. Judy was apparently reliving the many meals the family had shared with various guests, including fundraisers — *meshulachim* from Israel. One name kept cropping up, again and again. The name was "Rabbi Pinter," or, occasionally, "Yonah Pinter." He was someone Benjy had never heard of, and didn't think Judy knew, either. Then he heard her say, "Rabbi Pinter, what are you saying? Danger.... I work for the State Department, I know what I'm talking about. Danger, danger..."

Benjy understood. Judy was speaking in their father's voice. Aharon Flamm was warning Rabbi Pinter about something.

When had they spoken, and what was it all about?

◆ ◆ ◆

There were five men present besides himself. His uncle, Dani Devash, introduced Yoel to his assistant, Ari Naot, and to officers Ruby Albert, Chaim Nachmias, and Benny Turiel, head of police intelligence.

When Yoel arrived, he found the others aimlessly thrashing over the topic of the night. It was a mediocre group, far from being the "brain trust" his uncle had described. The only one who deserved that name, apart from Yoel Goldfinger himself, was Ari Naot, whose keen logic and power of analysis were obvious from the start.

Yoel had to smile inwardly at the sight of the analysts sprawled at their ease among the sofas and plush armchairs in his uncle's living room, cracking sunflower seeds with their teeth. The piles of discarded shells on various plates told him that the meeting had begun some time ago. Yoel took a seat on one side and listened as his Uncle Dani rapidly reviewed the case for him. Seven minutes sufficed for Yoel to understand the whole picture.

Devash noticed the flash of comprehension in his nephew's eyes — the spark for which he had been vainly waiting these past two hours. "It seems to me that our young guest has something to say," he remarked.

Yoel said quietly, "Yes. The net that the security forces has spread is excellent — but the fish has already slipped away."

"What do you mean?" The question erupted from several throats at once.

"I mean," Yoel explained, "that Arkady, the scientist, is not stupid. In my opinion, he got the stuff he came for and left Russia as fast as he could. Searching for him there is useless, with all due respect to Yossi Katri, whom I understand is one of your own men." This last he addressed to Turiel, whose eyes darkened.

"What are you suggesting?" Turiel asked coldly.

"Simply this: to cast the net in the area where the fish is swimming."

"In other words?"

"To have agents waiting at every port in Lebanon: Tripoli, Beirut, Tsur, and Sidon. This time, the fish mustn't be allowed to slip through the net."

Dani Devash felt a rising exhilaration. His nephew was right! Yoel had certainly justified his presence at this gathering. But not all the others agreed with him.

"Pure speculation," Chaim Nachmias snapped. "What makes you so sure of yourself?"

Yoel answered calmly, "Is it possible to see a map of Europe?"

Albert leaned back in his chair. "There's one on the wall right behind you. And if you don't mind, speak to the point, not in riddles. You're not in yeshivah now."

Yoel swung around to find a large map of Europe tacked to the wall behind his back. His uncle apologized,"This meeting was organized very quickly. If there'd been enough time, I'd have gotten hold of a modern map with all sorts of digital and electronic information lit up on it. Unfortunately, this is all there is at the moment."

"What's wrong with it?" Yoel asked in surprise. "If Hannibal and Napoleon had had a map like this, history would be different." A wave of laughter met this sally. Ignoring it, Yoel continued, "My contention is based on two points. One, that we have a tough and wily opponent who established a goal and achieved it. And second, that it's impossible to smuggle an atomic bomb, even a small one, onto a civilian plane. The chances of Russia supplying him with the bomb and putting a plane at his disposal seem remote. So what are we left with?" He answered his own question: "A sea route."

With the aid of Devash's laser pointer, Yoel shone a red dot on the city of Petersburg. "Petersburg, the former Leningrad, is a port. Let's assume that Arkady sailed from there with his bomb a few days ago, on his way to Lebanon."

"Lebanon? Why not Cyprus?" Turiel objected. He seemed intent on playing the obstructionist.

Ari Naot decided to set himself up as the defender of Yoel's idea. "Ben, I don't understand you," he scolded. "Put yourself in Arkady's place. If you wanted to smuggle an atomic device into Israel, wouldn't you look for a neighboring country that has ports?"

Turiel fell silent. Yoel continued moving the laser across the face of the map. "I'm drawing a line that runs from Petersburg and the Baltic Sea, through the North Sea, passes near Holland and France, goes around Spain and Portugal and reaches the Mediterranean Sea via the Straits of Gibraltar. Once in the Mediterranean, he'll pass near Malta,

Greece, Cyprus, pass by Nikosia, and arrive at one of Lebanon's ports."

There was a burst of talk when Yoel finished, one conversation cutting into the next until no one knew who was saying what. Devash raised his voice, so that he could be heard through the confusion. "We can't go on like this. Ruby, what did you want to say?"

Albert's eyes twinkled. "It seems as if our guest here is in cahoots with Arkady. I'm surprised that he doesn't know exactly which port the scientist will be bringing his bomb to, including the date and time."

Yoel's face turned pink. Helplessly, he said, "I'm not a *navi.* I just deduced things from the facts I heard from all of you. Studying Gemara helps me learn to analyze things."

All at once, the atmosphere lightened. There was friendliness in the air, even murmurs of appreciation. Yoel, relieved, was about to add something when he saw that not all the opposition had surrendered. Benny Turiel rose from his armchair in one smooth movement, fixed a stony eye on Yoel, and said, "I don't get it. Educated men like us are supposed to listen to what a yeshivah student says — someone who hasn't even served in the army? What he's told us is guesswork at best, and a pile of nonsense at worst. I don't buy a word of it."

Yoel's heart dropped with a leaden thud. He felt the color drain from his face. His support, Uncle Dani, was silent. Yoel didn't catch the swift exchange of glances between Devash and his lieutenant, Ari Naot.

Ari stood up, brushing minute cracker crumbs off his navy pants. "Gentlemen, the meeting is adjourned. Time to go home. Your cars are freezing in the parking lot, their wheels sticking to the ice." It was for all intents and purposes a dismissal to the participants in the secret meeting.

"But we're not done here," Turiel protested.

"Tomorrow night," Ari promised, clapping him on the back.

Slowly, the small group made its departure. When the sound of their footsteps and their voices had faded, Dani Devash let out his breath in a sigh of exasperation. "Good riddance to those fools. What idiocy — I wanted a brain trust, and ended up with a pile of pumpkin heads! All I really need is you, Ari, and you, Yoel."

"Especially since I do such a good job as your broom, sweeping out the undesirables," Ari said. He began collecting bowls of empty shells. "I agree with Yoel. Tomorrow I'll see about sending agents to stand guard at all the Lebanese ports."

"The main thing is to keep this from the Mossad and the GSS," Devash warned. "This is our own private project. The Mossad won't be taking credit for this one."

◆ ◆ ◆

It was 3 a.m. by the time Yoel finished relating the evening's events to Eli.

"So what do you say?" Yoel asked. "It's a critical situation, no? We might as well break our heads over it till morning. The night is already shot."

A series of awesome yawns brought tears to Eli's eyes. "No, go to sleep! *Shacharis* and saying *kriyas Shema* at its proper time are also critical."

Slowly they walked toward the darkened dorm building, skirting a large puddle that the last heavy rains had left behind.

27

It started snowing just before dawn. New York is experienced in dealing with snow, so the city was by no means paralyzed. Subways roared underground, sanitation trucks collected trash, and most of the fast-food outlets remained open. Still, the cloak of white muffled the early-morning Manhattan bustle, so the music of the city was playing in a minor key.

The first light of day found Benjy dozing in his armchair beside his sister's hospital bed. He did not react to a soft voice calling his name once, twice, three times. Then he woke with a start, to hear Judy saying, "Benjy, are you here?"

In his surprise and joy, his answer came in a near-shout."Judy, you're awake!"

"Is the operation over?" she asked weakly.

"Yes, it's over." Judy did not understand why Benjy's voice sounded as if it were clogged with tears. Actually, he was alternately laughing and crying. The waiting was over! After lying unconscious for four days, Judy had experienced a gradual wakening. She had begun to speak more clearly — though still in her sleep — several hours before. Now she was fully conscious. Just as the rebbe had promised him yesterday!

He approached the bed in a turmoil of emotion. "Judy, how are you feeling?"

She plucked fretfully at the bandages covering her eyes. "My head hurts, and I'm very dizzy. Why are these bandages still on?"

"Don't take them off! Wait a second, I'm going to get a doctor." He burst into the corridor, whipping his cell phone out of his pocket as he went.

His first call was to Eli in Israel. The second was to his home, to tell his wife, Shulamis, the good news. The third was to Dr. Seligman, the neurologist. In his happiness, Benjy hadn't bothered to check the time. He wrenched the doctor from his sleep to shout, "She woke up!"

Seligman asked, "Who did?"

"My sister Judy!" Not even when his firstborn son was born had Benjy felt this measure of joy. Judy had come back to life!

His emotion was contagious. The normally phlegmatic neurologist promised enthusiastically to come to the hospital as soon as he was able, to examine Judy and ascertain that her neurological systems were working properly.

Less than an hour later, he was there. Seligman was a short man with unruly white hair. Just now, his shoulders were also white, with snow, and his glasses opaque with condensation. Wiping them with his handkerchief, he boomed, "Let's see what we have here." He approached the patient's bed. "So she really *is* awake! And how is the young lady doing this morning?"

"Why are you all so excited?" Judy asked in wonder. "Wasn't I *supposed* to wake up after the operation?"

Seligman's head wagged to and fro as he considered whether or not to tell Judy the truth. His eyes scanned the monitors. "Her pulse is perfectly normal, as are her respiration and blood pressure. We can tell her." He turned to Judy. "Actually, you didn't hurry to wake up after the operation, so we're a little excited now. But everything's okay. You'll be back to yourself in a few days."

Benjy followed the neurologist into the corridor, where they walked to Seligman's office. "Your sister will undergo a few basic tests. She appears very weak."

"The main thing is, she's conscious." Benjy refused to let anything dim his happiness.

"True, but our attitude must be cautious until we've checked out everything."

Judy underwent the tests later that day. Seligman was satisfied. Dr. Schneider checked her eye and he, too, liked what he saw. "The eye looks good, and recovery is advancing at a nice pace," he told Benjy. "Interestingly, the period of unconsciousness actually helped. Other patients worry about their bandages and feel anxious and stressed, thus slowing the healing process. I'll test her vision tomorrow. If that checks out okay, we'll send her home within a couple of days."

Judy was taken to Dr. Schneider's clinic the next day. Benjy was tense as a spring, pacing back and forth, cracking his knuckles. Schneider had explained to him that he had no intention of testing the lazy eye, whose vision would always remain at about 10 percent. He was going to check the vision in the eye he had operated on, and emphasized that this was the crucial test — the one that would tell them whether Judy would rejoin the ranks of the seeing, or remain almost blind for the rest of her life.

Carefully, Dr. Schneider removed the bandage, lightly stained with a residue of blood. The entire clinical staff held its collective breath. Would she see? The doctor had turned off the lights beforehand, to give Judy's eyes a chance to adjust.

Judy opened her eyes slowly. She was deathly afraid. Heart pounding, she tried to see, but all that met her vision was a murky gray. Her heart sank like a block of lead.

Then, gradually, the darkness started to clear. Various shapes began to outline themselves in front of her. Out of the fog she identified her brother's anxious face.

"Benjy, I see you. I can see!"

Benjy tried to answer, but his throat had constricted. Dr. Schneider and his staff saw the young ophthalmologist burst into uncontrollable sobs.

Forty-eight hours later, Judy was discharged from Mount Sinai Hospital.

◆ ◆ ◆

"Unconscious for four whole days! I don't believe it!"

They were sitting in Benjy's dining room. Shulamis, Benjy's wife, hovered around Judy incessantly, spoiling her as much as the girl would allow. While they ate dinner, Shulamis told the story of her husband's visit to the rebbe's house, and his blessing.

"And I thought I had just woken up from the surgery," Judy said with wonder."I didn't know a thing."

"Meanwhile, Eli has been overturning the world in Israel," Benjy said, squeezing some fresh lemon over his lettuce salad. "I just found out that he fasted all day long, every day that you were unconscious — fasted and *davened.*"

Judy's fork was arrested in midair. "Eli's a *tzaddik,*" she exclaimed softly, a tiny tear trickling down her cheek. "His prayers were answered."

"You babbled a lot while you were unconscious. You reminded me of all the nicknames we used to call each other when we were little," Benjy laughed. "Remember Moishy's? He was Mickey — sometimes known as 'The Mouse.' "

"Did I really? I don't remember."

"You did. But let's leave nicknames aside for the moment. There's something else on my mind." His eyes probed Judy like a pair of searchlights. "Do you remember someone by the name of Yonah Pinter?"

"No."

"Does the name mean anything to you?"

"No."

"That's what I thought. Eli didn't tell you about him, did he?"

Judy shook her head."What's the matter? Why the interrogation?"

"You took the words right out of my mouth," Shulamis said. "What is it, Benjy?"

Benjy gazed out the window at the trees in front of his house, icicles dangling from every branch. He saw a small brown squirrel pop out of a hollow in one of the trees. It scurried down the trunk and up the porch steps. Through the glass door it stared at them with its beady dark eyes, swaying back and forth on its hind legs like a person praying.

"The Brooklyn squirrels have a lot of nerve," Judy laughed. "In Israel you only find them in zoos." She got up and went over to the glass. "Here, sweetie, have a nut."

The squirrel turned tail and vanished. Benjy tore his eyes from the window and returned to the interrupted talk.

"You want to know why I'm talking about Yonah Pinter? It's because of this. Just before you woke up, Judy, you quoted full sentences from an argument he apparently once had with Abba. Abba kept warning him not to do something, and shouted, 'Danger!' At least, that's what I was able to gather from what you said."

"*I* said all that? Benjy, you're pulling my leg, right?"

"No, I'm not. Really."

Judy could make nothing of it. She thought a while, then suddenly sat up. "Benjy, I just remembered something — before I left Israel, Eli said something to me about a secret memo that Abba had written."

"We'll walk over to the house tomorrow to get it," Benjy promised.

Arkady spent the evening on the upper deck playing cards with Christian, a massive sailor who was at least partly drunk. A martini jug stood on the table, which in turn was covered by a tablecloth stained with beer and grease. From time to time, the sailor drank noisily straight from the jug. "Have some, too," he invited Arkady, smacking his lips. "It's a good martini — a cocktail of vermouth and gin, smooth and cold."

"Thanks, I'm not drinking anything but vodka." The sight of his companion guzzling out of the jug nauseated Arkady.

Christian shrugged. "If you won't, you won't. All the more for me." He scooped the cards up from the table. "I told you, friend, vermouth and gin sharpen the brain. I drank and I won. You owe me $100. Go get the money."

"On the contrary," Arkady said. "*I* won. You owe *me* $100."

The sailor stared at him with alcohol-glazed eyes. "You won? I must have gotten mixed up, sorry." He burst into laughter and left the table, rather unsteady on his feet, singing a drunkard's song. "By the way," he called back over his shoulder, "Clement said to tell you that there's an urgent message waiting for you in his cabin."

Arkady blanched. He leaped up and ran after Christian. "When did you speak with the captain?"

The big sailor shook him off as though he were a fly. "Hey, friend, forget about the money. I spoke with Clement this morning. Say good-night and get out of here before I eat you for supper. Martinis give me an appetite!"

Arkady didn't linger to hear any more. He sprinted to Clement's cabin, breathing hard and wondering anxiously. An urgent message! And that drunken fool had waited until night to casually inform him of it.

He found the captain leaning over a large map, marking arrows in red chalk, an unlit pipe between his teeth. "You finally got around to coming, did you? Why are you out of breath?" he asked sardonically. "The world is turning upside down, and you have all the time there is."

"I was just playing cards with Christian. It was only when he lost the game that he remembered to give me your message," Arkady gasped. "What happened?"

Clement reached into one of the heavy drawers that lined one wall of his cabin, and pulled out a folded sheet of paper. The scrawled message was legible enough:

They're after you, waiting at every possible port. There's some risk of a sea chase. Clement will take care of that.

The note was signed, *Gray Cap.*

Fear turned Arkady's insides to liquid. "This is how the message arrived? Any ignorant seahand could have read it!"

"What's the matter with you?" Clement said coldly. "It was in code. I decoded the transmission myself."

Arkady relaxed slightly. "I understand that the Israelis are tracking me and preparing a reception in Lebanon. What do we do?"

The captain tapped some tobacco into his pipe and lit it with a long match. Puffing peacefully, his head resting against his chair's high back, he ignored Arkady's question. For a while, his eyes wandered over the map, with its red lines. Suddenly, he swung around to face Arkady, and his eyes were hard.

"Your boss, the one you call Gray Cap, has asked me to change my route for your sake. I've spent the last six hours working on it — calling various coastal authorities in different countries to request permission to weigh anchor and unload cargo. And you, old man, have time to play cards?"

The contempt in his voice made Arkady double up his fists. No one had ever spoken to him that way! He, a respected scientist, was being treated with less respect than the lowliest deck hand. A stinging retort sprang to his lips.

He decided to keep his mouth shut. Slowly, he unclenched his fists. He needed Clement. Swallowing the insult, he said coolly, "Lazy sailors like that Christian put this whole crate — this miserable *Charlotta Simpaya* of yours — in danger."

Clement didn't mind letting Arkady blow off a little steam. He bent over his map again. "See, instead of sailing the usual way, we'll have to swing around all of Britain. And after we pass the Straits of Gibraltar we'll have no choice but to approach Algeria, Libya, and Egypt."

Inexperienced seaman as he was, Arkady understood only that a long detour was being planned. He studied the red arrows on the map. "How much time will all of this take?"

"A lot longer than you think."

Arkady passed a hand over his hair and said, "No, I can't have that. From now on, forget about Gray Cap. You'll take your orders from me. I'm the one who is paying you, not him. Return to the original route and rescind the cancellations you made with the ports at Holland, France, and Spain."

Clement eyed him steadily. "Gray Cap promised me $100,000 for the change. What will you give?"

Mourning in his heart, Arkady answered, "One hundred and fifty." His tone left no room for argument.

Clement said, "Two hundred."

Arkady was ready to gamble the whole ante. His eyes turned frigid, and his voiced matched them as he said, "My friend, either you accept my terms, or you can go down to the bottom of the sea together with your *Charlotta*. I'm not arguing any more, and I'm ready for any visit by the police."

"What will you do with your cargo?" the captain sneered.

"I'll throw it into the sea!"

The mocking smile vanished. Clement saw that the scientist meant what he said. Arkady's manner was that of a man with nothing to lose.

Clement stopped arguing. Silently, he erased the red lines he had drawn, and pulled out the original map with the former route. His manner became genial. He offered Arkady a cup of strong coffee and chatted with him of long-ago journeys and their dangers, and of the pearls he had harvested from the sea. He lifted a mother-of-pearl shell from his drawer and held it out to Arkady, asking, "What do you see?"

Lifting the shell so that it caught the light, Arkady waxed poetic. "I see a rainbow of color, emerald shifting to diamond and back to ruby... The shell is whispering secrets to me, old secrets and sailors' songs, of ancient storms, tempestuous waves, the screams of the drowning and ships sinking down into the sea."

Clement doubled over with laughter. "You're some poet! Actually, you were not far off. This thing really does hold a secret. It was my great-grandfather, Jorgen Breinen, who pulled this out of the ocean when he was young. It's been passed down through my family as a sort of charm. Before every trip, I hold it up to the light and look inside. If it appears blue, I sail that very day. But if the light is red, it's a bad sign and I wait till nightfall."

"Oh, come on. Is there anything to that nonsense?" the scientist scoffed.

The captain's expression grew somber. "I'm sorry now that I shared the secret of the shell with you. You are not worthy of hearing it. I've sailed hundreds of times on the basis of this 'nonsense,' as you call it."

Arkady bit his lip. Clement looked so serious about what he was saying. "Tell me," Arkady asked, with real curiosity."What color was the shell on the eve of our trip?"

The captain was quiet for a moment. Then he pursed his lips and began whistling an aimless tune. With a chill of fear, Arkady suddenly remembered that the *Charlotta Simpaya* had sailed from the Kronshtadt port only after night had fallen.

28

"I can't even bear to see the outside steps," Judy said in a choked voice."I haven't been back here for so many years. All the memories are waiting — I'm beginning to wish I hadn't come."

Benjy understood how she felt. "I know what you mean, Judy. It's hard for me, too, even though I've never lived very far from here. But now that you've come this far, don't stay outside."

Slowly, they climbed the stairs of the three-story Flatbush house. Like most of the others on the block, it was constructed of red brick and wood. An iron gate insured the residents' privacy.

Shulamis's brother was currently renting the place. Benjy used his key to let himself and Judy in. The moment she stepped through the door, Judy knew she had made a big mistake. As she breathed in the air of the house she had grown up in, the very essence of her childhood, a thousand memories came at her all at once: memories of happy times, basking in the shelter and security of loving parents who always seemed to be smiling. Voices from the past rose up to engulf her: peals of laughter, babies babbling, children playing, parents scolding, siblings squabbling, the sweet chant of Gemara, Abba teaching his children "*komatz alef — aw*, reciting the *Shema* before falling asleep... All blotted out, obliterated in Amritsar, India. From that day on, the memories had turned from sweet to bitter. As children, they had loved this house; after the tragedy, they hated it.

Judy had expected to be mature today, almost indifferent — after all, she wasn't a little girl anymore. But the pain overwhelmed her and a sob rose up inside. She leaned her head against a wall and cried.

Benjy waited patiently, silent in his understanding. He had been afraid of something like this, but it had to be faced. Yesterday, while Judy slept, he had spoken at length to his brother in Israel. Eli had postulated a theory which Benjy tended to think was correct. It remained for him to find the proof.

"It's all stayed just the way it was," Judy said, when the tears had slackened. "The same wallpaper, the hat stand, the pictures on the wall. There's the picture that Abba took in front of the *Kosel* when we all went to Israel that summer. It's still here."

Benjy explained, "The house was unoccupied until about a year ago. When I rented it to my brother-in-law and his wife, I stipulated that they couldn't change anything."

"Where are they now?"

"Shmuel learns in *kollel* and Debby is a school secretary. I have their permission to come here today, and there's no chance they'll be back before we're done."

They went into the large dining room where their parents had entertained guests at countless meals over the years. How many pleasant moments they had enjoyed here! This was where Abba would tell the children stories of *tzaddikim* as a reward for their eating a sardine sandwich. Here was where Abba would discuss anything and everything with them, guiding their philosophy and turning them into little intellectuals. Here was where they had eaten their Shabbos meals, listened to Abba's words of Torah, sung *zemiros* in three-part harmony. Judy felt as though a golf ball were stuck in her throat.

Benjy was not happy with the way things were going. He had not brought his sister here to inflict pain, but to prod her memory. It was Judy's mind he wanted to stimulate by this visit, not her emotions. He had hoped that the sight of the house would help lift the veil from some long-dormant recollection.

It worked!

The wave of nostalgia and sadness prodded a portion of her memory that had long lain dormant. One minute she was standing quietly at the dining room table, and the next she was crying out, "What was the name you mentioned yesterday? Pinter? Yonah Pinter — Oh, Benjy! I remember that man, and the shouts, as if it all happened yesterday."

"Tell me," Benjy urged.

"When I first heard the name yesterday, it didn't ring a bell at all. Pretty soon, though, I began to feel as if the name was a part of me — part of my childhood. And now that I see this table and chairs, it's like a door has opened up in my mind. I remember the argument Abba had with that man. Rabbi Pinter was from Israel. Abba held me on his lap, and the shouts were deafening. I was scared. In the end, Abba was so mad that he got up abruptly, and I fell to the floor and cried."

Benjy sucked in a lungful of air. Eli had been right!

"What did they argue about?" he asked urgently, terrified lest his sister lose her grasp on the frail thread of memory. But Judy was almost in a hypnotic trance at this point. She said, "I want to sit in Abba's chair, where I sat then. May I? I need to actually relive those moments."

Almost of their own accord, her feet took her to her father's seat. She sat, and said dreamily, "Pinter yelled first and Abba answered him calmly. But in the end, Abba was yelling, too. 'Rabbi Pinter, what are you saying? Danger! I work for the State Department and I know about these things. Danger, danger! ' "

Waves of hot and cold washed over Benjy as he listened. "They're the same words she said when she was unconscious," he thought. Aloud, in a fever of impatience, he asked, "Well, what were they talking about? *What was it?*"

With furrowed brow, she tried to tug more from her memory — and failed. "I was a little girl, just 8 years old. How much could I have understood?"

"A pity," Benjy sighed. "All right, let's go into Abba's study. You need to take something from there and hand-deliver it to Eli."

◆ ◆ ◆

Aharon Flamm's study door was locked. "This room was not rented out along with the rest of the house," Benjy explained. He turned a key and they went inside.

The room was the same as it had been on the day their father left it. Pictures of the generation's Torah greats lined the walls: Rav Aharon Kotler, Rav Moshe Feinstein, the *roshei yeshivah* of Flamm's yeshivah, Torah Vodaath, Rav Shraga Feivel Mendlowitz and Rav Yaakov Kamenetzky. The glass-covered desktop held a lamp, several pens, and an old-fashioned computer. Everything was just as it had been. A melancholy half-light filled the room. Brother and sister stood silent, communing with the memory of their beloved father. This had been his sanctum. This had been where he had labored over his life's work, the complete *Tosafos* on *Bava Kamma,* that he had subsequently handed over to his friend.

"Where is it?" Judy whispered.

"In his secret drawer." Benjy was also whispering. "I only saw it once."

He unlocked a drawer in the desk and pulled out a pile of black binders. When the drawer was empty, he reached inside again and felt around. There was a click, and the drawer lifted up.

"False bottom," he murmured. Carefully, he removed a thin white binder with TOP SECRET emblazoned on the outside in red.

"This is a copy of the memo he sent to the Secretary of State," Benjy told Judy. "You have to get it to Eli."

Benjy opened the binder. The first page was hand written:

> *I want to preface my remarks by saying that the following thoughts have been on my mind for a long time. I was finally prompted to write them down after having a disturbing conversation with a man who stayed as*

a guest in my home. His words strengthened my very real fears for what the State of Israel can expect, should a certain Jewish extremist group attempt to blow up the mosques on the Temple Mount. In the months that followed that conversation, I conducted a thorough investigation, with the help of the CIA. I learned that the "speculation" was not speculative at all. There exists an Arab plan that fits, in uncanny detail, the scenario I have outlined here. This constitutes a grave danger for Israel — danger of the highest order!

◆ ◆ ◆

"It's the memo that Abba handed in to the State Department. They reassigned him immediately afterward," Benjy said bitterly. "Till today, I don't know what he did wrong."

"Show me," Judy said with curiosity. He handed the binder to her and she flipped through its pages. At the very end, tucked between two pages dealing with Flamm and Mantel's finances for the year 1982, was a folded piece of paper. "What's this?"

"I haven't a clue," Benjy said, surprised. "I never noticed that page. It's actually two — no, three thin pages. Let's see what they say."

The pages were written in Aharon's Flamm's handwriting.

I must set down here, for my own safety, the episode that led me to send that crucial memo to the State Department. It was an extraordinary incident, which I will describe in full detail, step by step.

As Benjy and Judy perused the pages, they were transported back 13 years.

◆ ◆ ◆

New York, May 1983

Three guests were enjoying a lavish breakfast at the large dining room table. Their meal included several types of breads, a tempting variety of hard and soft cheeses, both soft-boiled and scrambled eggs, smoked fish, raw vegetables, olives, butter, and jam. An individual pancake in caramel syrup sat at each diner's elbow. Margalit Flamm wanted her guests to feel right at home.

The front door opened, and Aharon Flamm entered with another guest. "Good morning, good morning!" Flamm greeted them. "I want you to meet Rabbi Yonah Pinter, from Jerusalem." He was not aware that the newcomer needed no introduction.

"Yonah! Shalom aleichem! So you've come to pick up a few dollars in America?" Zevulun Blum laughed.

Shaya Garfinkel boomed, "What's the matter, Yonah? You gave up on Har Habayis and have come to build the Beis Hamikdash in Brooklyn?" The others grinned in appreciation.

"I see that you know each other," Aharon Flamm smiled. "I'm glad. Who doesn't know Rabbi Pinter, world-renowned expert on the Beis Hamikdash?"

"Expert? Not exactly," Yonah corrected modestly.

"It's true," said the third visitor, Saadia Ben-Hayim. "Yonah Pinter is the only man in our generation who will know how to guide the Mashiach when the time comes to build the Beis Hamikdash. He'll know precisely where the *Mizbei'ach* is supposed to go, and the Menorah, the Kodesh Hakedoshim — exact to the last centimeter!"

The three finished their breakfast, recited the Birkas Hamazon, and departed for their day's fund-raising. Aharon lingered at the table after they had left. It was a Sunday, the day when New York stopped working. He was interested in continuing his talk with the intriguing Rabbi Pinter. A little girl came skipping downstairs, dressed in a pleated skirt, with a red ribbon in her long blond hair.

"Ah, here's my little angel!" Aharon exclaimed and lifted his daughter onto his lap. "Rabbi Pinter, meet my daughter, Judy. Young in age, but great in wisdom. She's a real bookworm. Have you met another 8-year-old girl who doesn't like dolls? Judy doesn't."

"But Abba, what are dolls, anyway?" the small girl asked. "A little plastic and fake hair, wrapped up in a piece of cloth. I'm supposed to hug the plastic and sing it to sleep?"

"Nu, what do you say about my princess?" Aharon asked his guest, beaming.

Pinter had finished his meal and was sipping scalding coffee from a mug. His eyes were fixed on a distant point. "I disagree with Saadia Ben-Hayim. I won't help the Mashiach build the Beis Hamikdash. Definitely not!"

"Why not?" Aharon asked, startled. "You're the only person in the world who could do it, and now you say you don't want to. Hey, that reminds me of a joke. A university lecturer noticed one of his students reading a newspaper in his astronomy class. He called, 'Johnny, you may explain to the class what sunspots are.' Johnny was unprepared for the sudden question that tore him away from the news. He scratched his head. 'Uh, I knew but I forgot,' he said. 'What a pity,' the lecturer retorted. 'The world's top scientists have been breaking their heads over the nature of sunspots. At last, someone comes along who actually knows — and he forgot!' "

Yonah Pinter was clearly at a loss to grasp the connection between himself and Aharon's story. "Perhaps you did not understand me. I myself am going to build the Beis Hamikdash!"

Aharon recoiled. "What are you saying?"

A fanatic light gleamed in Pinter's eyes. He pushed his plate away and waved his hands in the air. "Three times a day, we pray for the *Beis Hamikdash* to be rebuilt. Does anyone even pay attention to what his lips are saying? You're hypocrites, all of you. You talk about the *Mashiach* but your souls are bound up in your worldly affairs. You want to live pleasantly in a materialistic world for 80 years, and just before your death you'd like the *Mashiach* to show up, along with eternal life!"

Aharon's efforts to interpose even a word into Pinter's monologue were unsuccessful. The Israeli ranted on, "You end every *shiur* with a plea for the rebuilding of the *Beis Hamikdash,* speedily in our days — but you do nothing beyond that! You and I have a place to live, but *Hakadosh Baruch Hu* has no House. Since the destruction of the *Beis Hamikdash,* He cries all night for his destroyed Sanctuary. Do you hear Him crying, just before dawn, or do you just burrow deeper into your quilts? Ah?"

"What can we do beyond *davening*?" Aharon asked placatingly.

Yonah Pinter set his mug down with a disgusted thud. When he was in this exalted mode, food and drink revolted him. "We must go up to *Har*

Habayis to offer *korbanos*, destroy the impure mosques, and build the new *Beis Hamikdash* with our own hands!"

Little Judy was mesmerized by the charismatic visitor. Her blue eyes watched every movement of his hands as he spoke. He was like someone out of a storybook! But her father did not seem very excited. He merely said, "Your intentions are admirable but the actions you're suggesting are not good ones. It is forbidden to go up to *Har Habayis*."

Yonah Pinter raged, "You're just like all the others, boors and ignorant fools who don't know where it is permissible to walk on *Har Habayis*. I could take you up there and draw you a line at the exact spot."

"That's not the point." Aharon waved a hand as though chasing away a bothersome fly. "We're all considered impure these days, and there's no red cow around whose ashes we could use to purify ourselves. I wouldn't risk the chance of being punished with *kareis*."

"You're evading the issue!" Pinter exploded. His bellow woke Dovy and Moishy, who had been asleep upstairs. "The Rambam says that we are required to bring all the *korbanos* even though there is no *Beis Hamikdash* standing! Didn't the Rambam know your answers? But he states that we have a positive commandment to build the *Beis Hamikdash*. Understand?"

In his excitement, he seized Aharon's hand and shook it forcefully. To young Judy, the charisma she had enjoyed had dissipated. The stranger seemed very threatening.

Aharon Flamm extricated his hand, reached for the teapot, and poured himself a cup of fragrant tea. Settling Judy more comfortably on his lap, he set about demolishing Pinter's points, one by one.

"Perhaps you'd care to explain to me why not a single Torah leader today, or throughout the ages, stands with you on this?"

"Next, what you say about permissible and forbidden areas on *Har Habayis* contradicts your primary goal of building the *Beis Hamikdash* yourself. If you know exactly where you'd deserve *kareis*, how will you be able to build the *Beis Hamikdash* with your own hands?

"Apart from that, your words smack too much of 'taking our fate into our own hands.' That denies the kingship of Hashem, and His power to rebuild the *Beis Hamikdash* Himself."

Yonah Pinter opened his mouth as though to speak, then clapped it tightly shut. His lips twitched nervously. Aharon went on, pointing out the fatal flaws in Pinter's reasoning.

"It seems to me that the reasons for the Temple's destruction haven't gone away — causeless hatred, for example. You and your friends heap abuse on anyone who doesn't agree with you. Just a minute ago, for example, you called me, your host, a boor and a fool. Not even great Rabbis escape your barbs. If you are genuinely fighting *l'shem Shamayim,* for Heaven's sake, then why mock those who don't agree with you? Also, if you're so determined to fulfill Hashem's will, why not concentrate on becoming better Jews? To do the mitzvos, to learn Torah, to improve our characters, especially when relating to our fellow man. Our tradition tells us that our good deeds will merit the coming of the third *Beis Hamikdash,* which will descend from Heaven completely built."

"But we have to bring *korbanos!*" Pinter screamed, his eyes glittering with a strange light.

Aharon absently stroked Judy's hair. "*Korbanos?* A humble spirit is the form of sacrifice Hashem wants from us today until *Mashiach* arrives. You want another kind of sacrifice? You just ate a hearty breakfast, managing to cram in the caramel pancake at the end, even though you were full. Our holy books tell us that when a person stops eating in the midst of a meal, while his appetite is still strong, his act is considered equal to a *korban* in Hashem's eyes."

Pinter was speechless. The American was speaking sense! Aharon, noting his distress, smiled. "The main thing about a *korban* is the intent and the goal — where it brings a person. It's meant to humble the arrogant spirit. Have you learned the first *perek* of *Yeshayahu*?"

Yonah paled. In one voice, he and Aharon recited, "*Lamah li rov zivcheichem? yomar Hashem....*

"Why do I need your numerous sacrifices? says Hashem. I am sated with elevation-offerings of rams and the fat of fatlings; the blood of bulls, sheep, and goats I do not desire. When you come to appear before Me... to trample My courtyards?"

When they finished, there was a heavy silence in the room. Judy jumped when Pinter suddenly broke it by shrieking, "Yeshayahu is talking about evildoers!"

"Certainly we eagerly await the rebuilding of the *Beis Hamikdash*, but in the meantime, have we all done *teshuvah*?" Aharon laughed wryly. "Who has stamped *us* with His approval?" His voice softened. "I'll tell you something. From the time the *Beis Hamikdash* was destroyed, we've been left with the following tools: Torah, fear of Heaven, good deeds, and repentance. These are Hashem's 'House,' the dwelling that He has in every Jewish heart. How does the song go?" Aharon burst into the melody he liked to sing with his children on Friday nights:

"Bilvavi mishkan evneh

Lehadar kevodo

U'lemishkan — mizbei'ach asim

Lekarnei hodo."

(*"In my heart I will build a sanctuary for His glory, and in the sanctuary I will place an altar to His radiance."*)

Pinter's lips began trembling as he listened to the song. Every word pierced his heart like a needle:

"U'lener tamid ekach li

Es eish ha'akeidah

U'lekorban akriv lo es nafshi

Es nafshi hayechidah."

(*"And for the eternal flame I will take the flame of the Akeidah, and as a sacrifice I will offer my soul — my one and only soul."*)

Yonah felt as though the American had caused the ground from under his feet to crumble. He stared at Aharon as the latter continued speaking.

"From the time the physical *Beis Hamikdash* was destroyed, we have been building it in our hearts, our souls. Sacrificing on the *mizbei'ach*, if not accompanied by a heartfelt intention, becomes an empty, meaningless act. The same applies to prayer. *Hakadosh Baruch Hu* has no desire for empty gestures. That's why He poured out His wrath on stones and wood. If our deeds had found favor in His eyes, He would not have destroyed the *Beis Hamikdash* at all.

"Do you know why the Arabs are so fervent about the area around *Har Habayis*? The thing that draws them to that spot is the very reason that the *Beis Hamikdash* was destroyed. A Heavenly Hand guides all of history; the prophecy of foxes prowling on the Temple Mount came true with the building of the mosques there. They are an integral part of the destruction. When we will be deemed worthy, the mosques will vanish as if they had never existed, and a fully built *Beis Hamikdash* will stand in their place. Right now, it looks like things have to remain the way they are. That's why *Har Habayis* was declared off-limits — so that a few misguided people would not take it into their heads to rebuild the *Beis Hamikdash* with their own hands."

Yonah seized the chance to attack. "Are you calling me misguided?"

"What you're talking about doing is misguided and foolish," Aharon answered implacably. "Building a *Beis Hamikdash* in our present reality would be nothing but a caricature."

"I can't bear hearing the *muezzin* on *Har Habayis,*" Yonah cried. "It's a desecration!"

"I don't understand you — are you blind?" Aharon raised his own voice. "You want to fight the entire Moslem world? True, in Israel itself we're in the majority. But there are at least 100 million Islamic believers in the world. A hundred million people who will want to murder you and every other Jew if you destroy those mosques! It would be suicide on a global scale, a mortal danger heaped upon every Jewish head."

"How would they react?" Yonah asked, in a subdued manner. This was the point that worried him — a question he normally swept under the rug and refused to consider.

"I don't know," Aharon returned somberly. "But it would be serious."

Pinter hardened his resolve. "We must destroy the center of the contamination. We pray three times a day for the idols to disappear from the world."

Aharon warned, "Rabbi Pinter, what are you saying? I work for the State Department and know about these things. This is a very grave danger. Danger, danger!" He leaped up from his seat so abruptly that Judy slid off his lap to the floor. She burst into tears. She had no way of knowing that a spark had been ignited in her father's mind at that moment.

Late that night, Aharon Flamm sat in his study and drafted the memo outlining the scenario to be expected should extremists attempt the destruction of the Temple Mount mosques. His prediction: The Arab reaction would be an attempt to destroy the entire State of Israel, and maybe every Jew on earth!

29

Yossi Katri searched for the exact word to describe the way he was feeling.

"Frustrated," he decided. That was the word. He was feeling bitter and chagrined over the way his plan had so rapidly gone awry.

The trip to Russia had been unlucky from the start. Some setbacks were to have been expected, but Katri had never anticipated such a colossal failure. He blamed it all on Uzi Saraf, whose desire for glory had ruined everything.

They were an unlikely trio of agents — an impossible combination. The Mossad man, responsible for handling Israel's security problems abroad, the GSS agent who dealt with Israel's internal security, and the police representative who, it seemed now, was deemed utterly superfluous.

In the first few days of their mission they had worked well together, confident that success was waiting to crown their efforts. It was, after all, a fairly uncomplicated mission, one that did not require a large measure of courage. All they had to do was uncover the scientist's trail, like bloodhounds, and then follow him the way a lion might stalk a wounded deer. Israel had undertaken far more daring operations in the past, and triumphed.

But things had begun to grow strangely complex. Yoni Dor, the GSS man, lay in his hotel room with a raging fever. The doctor they had called insisted that Yoni be hospitalized, and only by the skin of their teeth had the other two managed to prevent this from happening. In terms of their mission, Yoni was definitely out of the picture.

Uzi Saraf had elected to strike out independently. He had managed to conduct an interview at the atomic reactor at Zaporozh'ye, leaving Yossi Katri behind in snowy Moscow, far from the action. Now, triumphantly, he had phoned Yossi to tell him about Arkady's stay at the Russia Hotel. To his surprise and disdain, Yossi had mockingly informed him that he was sitting in the hotel's parking lot even as they spoke. Uzi had just found out, to his displeasure, that his fellow agent had not been idle in his absence.

"Don't do anything without me," Uzi warned.

"I'm just going in to see the beautiful lobby. Maybe I'll have a little drink while I'm there." Yossi shut the motor. He did not mention his intention to grill the hotel staff about Arkady Bogdanov.

"No!" That little policeman wouldn't steal *his* glory! "Return to our hotel, the Hyatt, and wait for me. Tomorrow we'll work together." Saraf waited for the inevitable question: "In that case, why did you call me with this information?"

But Katri made a more pressing point: "Uzi, we're chasing a man who has an atom bomb in his possession. Every minute is bringing the danger closer to Israel — and you're talking about 'tomorrow'!"

Uzi laughed. "Yossi, what's gotten into you? You're much too serious today."

"That's right, I *am* serious. Two atom bombs are heading for our neck of the woods, and we don't even have an inkling where they are."

Uzi kept on laughing. "With Zislin of the KGB on our side, the whole globe is like a little ping-pong ball." He spoke with a heavy Russian accent, and Yossi could hear Zislin chortling in the background.

"I'm glad you've found such a patriotic friend for Israel," Yossi said dryly. "But with all due respect, it's not Zislin's home that's being threatened."

At that, Saraf sobered. "Yossi, don't argue with me! Leave the hotel at once. You have no experience with Russians and could ruin everything!"

Yossi was forced to yield. The Moskovich shot out of the parking lot with an angry screech of tires.

◆ ◆ ◆

Uzi Saraf returned early the next morning, after a sleepless night. His flight from the Ukraine had been delayed six hours due to an unexpected glitch in the plane's workings. Uzi was nervous and irritable as he confronted Yossi Katri. He eyed him with suspicion, as though trying to determine whether his fellow agent had defied orders and returned to the hotel without him. Apparently satisfied with what he read in Yossi's face, he led the way to the car Zislin had put at his disposal. Together they drove to the Russia Hotel.

As they approached the magnificent Red Square, Yossi had his first glimpse of the Kremlin's dome. "Slow down," he requested.

"No time," Uzi answered curtly. "At a time like this you have the leisure to gawk at pretty buildings?"

Yossi glowered silently.

The Russia Hotel was bustling as ever. It boasted 21 stories, four wings, four entrances, its own theater hall, an impressive lobby, thousands of rooms — from the most simply furnished to deluxe suites with a piano — and an overabundance of shops and restaurants. They entered through the main entrance on the hotel's southern side, crossed the lobby, and approached one of the reception desks. Uzi addressed the clerks in fluent Russian, presented his credentials, and began firing off a number of questions. Yossi didn't understand a word, but the clerks' negative headshakes needed no translation. Uzi tried again, with the same results. The clerks advised him to take his questions to the manager.

"Bureaucrats," Uzi muttered angrily.

"Surprising. I'd have thought they'd be bowled over by your powerful Mossad personality," Yossi deadpanned.

Saraf didn't answer, but his eyes spoke volumes.

They began traversing one wing after another in search of the elusive manager's office. "We'll get ourselves lost in this jungle," Uzi complained, when they had stopped for the 10th time to ask for directions.

They found the office at last, and learned the manager's name — Oleg Marchenko — from a brass nameplate on the door. Oleg was a tall, robust man with small, hard eyes. Grudgingly, he allowed them into his ornate office. As they approached the desk, the Israelis' shoes tapped loudly on the polished parquet floor.

"You have five minutes," Oleg announced.

"Five whole minutes?" Uzi returned in mock-wonder.

"I'm not joking. I have little time to spare for troublemakers like you. Time is precious." On the desk stood an old-fashioned hourglass. The Russian upended it and watched the sand begin trickling down.

For his part, Uzi set his watch to beep in five minutes. Briskly, he asked about Arkady Bogdanov. Marchenko checked his computer for the relevant dates, and said immediately, "The name appears here. He stayed in this hotel for four days and paid in cash. There are no other comments in the record. Nothing out of the ordinary."

"Where did he go from here?" Uzi asked.

The last grains of sand were pouring down. The top portion of the hourglass became empty two seconds before Uzi's watch beeped. Marchenko's face grew colder.

"A stupid question," he snapped. "Are *you* in the habit of informing a hotel where you'll be going after you leave? Your time is up!"

He followed them to the door, the beady eyes never leaving them until they could no longer be seen.

◆ ◆ ◆

They sat in the car in the hotel parking lot, watching their breath mist in the freezing air.

"He's hiding something, our *tovarisch* (comrade) Oleg," Uzi Saraf said. "There are still thousands of fervent Communists in Russia, and Oleg Marchenko is one of them."

"Those beady suspicious eyes," Yossi agreed.

Uzi tapped a finger impatiently against his cheek. "What next? What next? Hmm... Wait a minute, I just remembered something. There is someone who can help me."

"Gregori Zislin to the rescue!" Yossi saluted.

"Are you a mind reader?" He whipped out his cell phone and punched in Zislin's number.

An hour later, they were back with the hotel manager. This time, they sat on comfortable armchairs in Marchenko's private office, behind his official one. Zislin was with them.

"*Tovarisch* Marchenko," Zislin said in a tone of reproach, "my good friend Saraf tells me you didn't welcome him properly."

Oleg Marchenko, like many of his fellow countrymen, knew of "Zislin the Terrible" from KGB days. Rumor had it that Zislin could extract secrets from the dead. Others said it was he who had caused them to die in the first place.

But the KGB's day was over. "I told him everything he wanted to know," Marchenko said. He reached out and flipped over his hourglass.

"What's that?" Zislin demanded.

"Something to measure five minutes for visitors." Oleg did not know Zislin well enough to recognize the signs of rage gathering in his face. Zislin seized the hourglass, flung it against the wall, and watched it shatter on the parquet floor in a shower of glass and sand.

"*Tovarisch,* I'll sit here for five minutes, too — until you hand over the cassette tape."

"C-cassette? What cassette?" Oleg's lips whitened.

Zislin gave a small laugh. He strode over to an illuminated aquarium on one wall. Colorful fish darted peacefully about in the clear water —

until Zislin pounded his fist on the glass. The fish scattered in panic.

"Don't tell me you didn't bug Bogdanov's room," he thundered.

"*Tovarisch* Zislin, perhaps you haven't heard the news. Hotels no longer record their guests. You know, Boris Yeltsin and all that...."

Zislin regarded the aquarium thoughtfully. "If something should crack this glass and all the water spills out, would that ruin the floor?"

"I beg your pardon?"

"Just curious. By the way, why do you keep poisonous fish in your aquarium? I see one here" — a pudgy finger tapped the glass — "whose slightest touch would finish you off."

Oleg Marchenko knew when he was defeated. Slowly, he rose from his chair and walked over to a bank of drawers built into the far wall.

A minute later, he laid two cassettes on the desk.

◆ ◆ ◆

Late that night, three telephone calls were made.

"Number Three?"

"Yes."

"This is Mr. Coates in New York. What's new in Tel Aviv?"

"Nothing new."

"And what's the news from Moscow?"

"Slow. Zislin is talking, but not enough. Our budget's too limited."

"I spoke to our friends in Washington. They're willing to finance this business — to the end."

"No limits?"

"No limits."

"Excellent. There's a chance now that the plan will proceed to completion."

"Good luck, and good night."

Click.

"Uzi?"

"Yes."

"Tzipori speaking. What have you found out?"

"We've listened to tapes of the scientist. They recorded him all over the Russia Hotel."

"Well?"

"He had contact with someone named Anatoly Sarmatiev, identified as a member of the 'operation' in St. Petersburg. The trail is leading to St. Petersburg."

"Don't waste any time. Go there tomorrow."

"It's not that simple, but Zislin is willing to help. I'll need to grease his palm with a few more thousand."

"You have a fat budget — grease away. The main thing is that that pest from the police department doesn't go there with you. I understand that Yoni Dor is still sick?"

"That's correct."

"Good. We don't need to share the glory."

"I understand."

Click.

"Yossi?"

"Yes?"

"This is Ari Naot. Your boss, Benny Turiel, has authorized me to speak to you."

"Yes, he told me."

"What's happening?"

"It's bad. The scientist has a 10-day start on us. Ten days ago, he spoke to someone from the Petersburg Mafia and traveled there to buy the materials. Apart from that, I'm constantly running after Uzi Saraf. He's hooked up with a bulldozer by the name of Zislin, a KGB man, who manages to open all doors for him."

"I have an idea. Do you have money on you? A lot of money, I mean."

"'Don't leave home without it.'"

"Pardon?"

"That's the American Express slogan. I have one of their credit cards, and an open account at the Chase Manhattan bank."

"Benny Turiel takes good care of his men. Well, it seems all three of you are well padded. You're staying at the Hyatt Regency—"

"You wanted to tell me something?" Yossi prompted.

"Yes."

Clearly and succinctly, Ari Naot outlined his plan. Yossi listened carefully, answered, "Got it," and concluded with, "It shall be done."

Click.

Uzi Saraf's car turned into Anna Karenina street and found a place to park. This looked nothing like Russia. A distinctly Western flavor pervaded in this area. The streets were broad; the cars parked at the curbs and in private parking slots were new. Most of the houses were opulent and surrounded by pleasure gardens, now covered with snow and waiting patiently for spring. Uzi had halted in front of a two-story corner house.

Gregori Zislin welcomed him affably, inviting him to have a little drink. Outside, the weather was frigid; here all was toasty warm. Zislin selected two crystal goblets from a small antique table and poured a clear liquid into them from a crystal decanter. "You'll drink vodka?"

"No, thanks."

"Afraid of alcohol? Alcohol is good in the winter, it quickens the blood. If it were summer, I'd have offered you some *kvas*. It's the typical Russian drink, made from black bread and yeast, with a sweet-sour taste — and it doesn't make you drunk."

Uzi was not interested in drinking. "I'm worried about that scientist," he said impatiently.

Zislin tilted back his large head and guzzled down his liquor. He sighed contentedly and set down the goblet. "Good vodka. You're in a hurry, I see. While you were sleeping last night, I was hard at work. I managed to get in touch with my best sources of information. I know everything: what Arkady bought, and how much he paid."

"Excellent! I need that information as quickly as possible. Every hour is crucial." Uzi had no idea, as he spoke those words, that he had just ensnared himself in a very expensive trap.

Gregori was silent. He smiled.

Suddenly, Uzi understood. "What an idiot I've been!" he thought grimly. "Who knows how much he'll want? This man is the king of the greedy."

Aloud, he said, "I'll pay you handsomely for the information, of course."

Gregori continued smiling in silence. Uzi felt around in his pocket for his wallet.

◆ ◆ ◆

Some two hours later, Yossi Katri ordered the taxi to pull up in front of Zislin's house.

"Do I know you from somewhere?" Zislin asked, grinning. "Ah, yes — you're Saraf's friend. I forgot." He switched to broken English. "Forgive me, you do not understand Russian."

"We can both break our teeth on English," the Israeli said with a grim smile. "I've come to ask you for all the information you have about the missing scientist, Arkady Bogdanov."

"You're not working together with Saraf of the Mossad?"

"No! I'm a representative of the Israeli Police, working independently."

"Ah!" Zislin rubbed his hands with pleasure: here was a contingency he had not expected. If these Israelis were working separately, they would also pay separately.

"I want to know everything," Yossi continued. "I overheard Saraf talking to his superior in Israel. You didn't reveal exactly how Bogdanov is planning to bring the bombs to Israel." He pulled a wad of cash from his pocket.

A cunning gleam lit Zislin's eye. "Ah! You're smarter than he is, I see.

He was being cheap, so I held back part of the story. But you'll pay well, right?"

Yossi paid very well. Zislin was happy to offer the additional information. Thus, the police agent learned what the Mossad had not: that Arkady Bogdanov hoped to land in Lebanon with his lethal cargo.

When Yossi had taken his leave, Zislin stood at the window watching the departing taxi. He mused, "Both the KGB and the CIA have something to learn from the Israelis. How each one works behind the other's back.

"But I, Gregori Zislin, need not be more patriotic on behalf of Israel than they are. I need only concern myself with my beautiful house and my pension." He licked his lips and laughed aloud. The Israelis were doing a fine job of providing for Zislin's old age. Ha, ha, ha!

He looked forward to his next meeting with the Israelis. This was beginning to be interesting! And the smell of money was growing stronger by the minute.

30

Shimi Tzipori was one of the Mossad's most brilliant lights. He had entered the army from his kibbutz in Emek Yizrael, where he had been considered a top student. But the actual scope of his talents became known only after a series of psychotechnical tests revealed his superior intelligence. He served in an elite army corps, and after his service ran its course he naturally found his way into Israel's security arm.

His advance through Mossad ranks was meteoric. After a number of years in various Mossad branches abroad and more years of staff work inside Israel, Tzipori had attained the highest level of the Mossad's hierarchy and was considered a strong prospect for its eventual head of operations.

There was no arguing with his formidable analytical powers. Thanks to his thick dark glasses and nondescript physical appearance, Shimi Tzipori might easily have been mistaken for a bank clerk. The glasses masked his sharp penetrating stare from the world. Though his thoughts flew along at lightning speed, his manner and gait were measured — except where the

Mossad's honor was involved. When that was threatened, Shimi's calm was transformed into a hurricane — a volcano — a typhoon.

It was 4 a.m. when Shimi finished going over the routine reports he had received from Mossad agents worldwide, jotting down quick instructions where necessary, and he finally went to sleep. His exhaustion urged him to switch off his cellular phone; the State of Israel could survive without him for a couple of hours. But Shimi had a change of heart. He left the phone operational. Five minutes later, he was to regret it.

The dark curtains of sleep were drifting down on him. His breathing became slow and even. He was at the edge of some sweet dream when the thin shrill of the phone penetrated his consciousness. Groggily, he pulled the phone out of its base, listened a moment, then flushed angrily.

"You! Just wait until tomorrow, you'll see what you'll get from me. I'll send you into early retirement! I *told* you never to call me on my cell phone!"

Dani Devash said apologetically, "They said you could be reached 24 hours a day."

"Not by you!" Tzipori whispered furiously, trying not to wake his wife. "My men can reach me if necessary — not a small-time cop from Bat Yam!"

Dani swallowed the insult. "True, I'm only a small-time cop. And there's an even smaller cop who serves as my lieutenant, Ari Naot by name. He has something important to relay to you."

"His 'something important' can wait for the morning," Shimi snapped. "The nerve, calling me now." He disconnected the line with an angry jerk of his thumb. Turning over in bed, he let the waves of rage wash over him. In cases of genuine emergency, he had other means of communications in his home — means these troublemaking policemen knew nothing about.

By noon the next day, he was regretting his outburst. It was not in keeping with the facade he liked to present to the world. After some thought, he did the unexpected. He phoned Devash.

"Listen, Devash, you really were out of line last night. But what did you want?"

Dani restrained himself from hitting the ceiling. Masking his jubilation — the great man had called *him* — he said, "My lieutenant and I would like to meet with you."

"You say you have something important to tell me?"

"Something that can't wait."

"All right." Shimi named a restaurant on Frischman Street in Tel Aviv. "We'll meet there in —" he consulted his watch — "40 minutes."

◆ ◆ ◆

Dearest Eli,

Would you believe it? I can write again! Just two weeks ago I was sure I'd be blind forever, and today I can sit down and write my brother a letter. Benjy has a friend who's traveling to Israel tonight, and it was his idea that I find out if I can write. "A letter's much better than a fax," he said. "It's your own handwriting, a part of you that can be in Eli's hands in just a day or two." I took his advice and sat down to write by hand, just like in the Middle Ages!

To tell the truth, my vision does blur occasionally. At those times I'm surrounded by a white cloud and can't see a thing. When that happens, I lose my cool completely. Benjy says it's a reaction that sometimes occurs after an operation, but it reminds me of Humpty Dumpty. Remember that fat doll we used to have when we were kids? We would throw it down and it would rock back up again — down and up, down and up. Davey, our sweet nephew, has two of them. I think in Israel that kind of doll is known as a Nachum Takum. I told Benjy that I feel just like that old Humpty Dumpty of ours: half an hour up, half an hour down. Benjy gets mad when I talk that way.

Yesterday we traveled to Manhattan to see Dr. Schneider. He checked my eye, sighed with relief, and told Benjy, "The cataract hasn't returned." That's how I found out what they'd been afraid of all along. "So why is there a fog sometimes?" I asked in alarm. Schneider laughed and said, "It's nothing serious. We'll get that cleared up in no time." He gave me some eye drops with a 17-letter name, and my eyesight is really improved now, Baruch Hashem.

I have another appointment scheduled with Dr. Schneider next week. If all is well then, I'll be back on a plane to Israel as soon as I possibly can!

L'hitraot — see you soon!

Your sister, Judy

◆ ◆ ◆

Shimi Tzipori satisfied his hunger with a portion of grilled chicken and a tall, foaming, ice-cold beer. He patted his mouth dry with his napkin and told Ari Naot, "Sorry, but it's pure nonsense."

Ari took it calmly enough. "Why?"

Shimi toyed with his fork, shifting grains of rice from one side of his plate to the other. In a bored voice, he replied, "You ask why? A person would have to be mad to prefer such a long route over a much shorter, quicker one — if, that is, we accept the premise that Bogdanov has an atomic bomb at all. In short, this meeting was a waste of time."

Dani Devash and Ari Naot exchanged a chagrined glance. They had spent a fruitless half-hour trying to explain their position to the Mossad man, but he was firmly convinced that the police had no business poking their noses into matters of security. Dani ground his teeth, close to exploding. "I was the one who started this investigation," he burst out. "I'm entitled to be involved!" He had been harping on this theme, in vain, for days.

"The Mossad was bound to uncover this plot in any case," Tzipori stated. "Thanks for your help, but it is no longer necessary."

Ari pushed the plates aside. He had expended a great deal of energy trying to get Tzipori to buy his theory. He tried one more time. "Put yourself in the scientist's place. He knew we'd immediately think of the shortest possible route and reject the longer land route."

Tzipori's fork was suspended in midair. "Well?" he asked with interest.

At last, Ari got to finish explaining his theory. "So he opts for the overland route — lengthy, roundabout, entailing considerable switching of cars and trains. He moves slowly, but with confidence, knowing that there's no one on his heels. The Israeli Mossad is waiting patiently for him at the ports of Lebanon —"

Eyes closed, Tzipori thought this over. "There might be something to that," he admitted grudgingly. "I'll check it out." Though he tried to sound relaxed and indifferent, it was clear to Naot and Devash that the Mossad man's confidence was beginning to fray.

It was with satisfaction that the two police officers presently made their way back to Bat Yam. They had accomplished what they had set out to do: they had sowed a seed of doubt in Tzipori's mind. The Mossad would waste valuable time and manpower trying to trap Bogdanov on the Armenian-Turkish border, trying to outrun the wind, while their own boss, Benny Turiel, would scoop up the scientist and his horrific cargo at one of the Lebanese ports.

For once in Israel's history, enemies of the State would meet their downfall not at the hands of the mighty Mossad and the all-powerful GSS, but at those of the lowly police!

◆ ◆ ◆

He was sitting in a small bungalow together with some of his friends, consuming a light supper. The smell of frying was awful: the oil had scorched, but Chemi Maimon insisted on using it to cook sunny-side-up eggs. "It's a *segulah* for a good memory!" Chemi laughed, flipping a finished egg directly from the pan onto Akiva Tamiri's plate.

"Hey, quit that," Akiva shouted. "You know I hate burnt eggs!"

But a mischievous spurt seemed to have taken hold of Chemi. Laughing, he fried another egg and flipped that one, too, onto Akiva's plate — and a third — and a fourth. Akiva lunged from the table with a roar of rage, aimed the egg-filled plate at the cook, and threw it in his face. Egg yolk dribbled down Chemi's nose, cheeks and chin, but still he laughed.

Pandemonium broke out. Everyone was yelling at the top of their voices when the door opened. Abruptly, silence fell. Dekel had entered the room.

He took in the scene in a few tense seconds, then strode over to Sruly Egozi.

"It's all your fault, Sruly! You didn't want to learn in yeshivah, now look where you've ended up! It's all your fault — your fault — your fault —"

Sruly woke with a start, sweating and trembling. "What an awful dream," he muttered. "Crazy!"

Strangely, the scorched smell persisted. Sruly sniffed, and finally identified the smell. It was the pungent aroma of burning meat.

He leaped out of bed and turned on the light. *Baruch Hashem,* his room was not on fire. Switching the light back off, he went to the window and opened it. Immediately, he began coughing and his eyes started tearing from the smoke that flew into his face. He rubbed his watering eyes and tried to understand what he was seeing. The vision in the clearing outside his cabin made his nightmare pale by comparison.

A circle of men surrounded Yonah Pinter, who stood beside a stone altar, praying aloud. On the altar burned chunks of wood, from which tongues of crimson flame licked at what appeared to be a young lamb. The red glare was reflected on the watchers' faces. But Sruly's attention was riveted to Pinter. There was something odd about him, though for a moment the youth couldn't put his finger on it.

Then, suddenly, he understood. Yonah Pinter was dressed in the attire of the *Kohen Gadol!*

The attire was one that Sruly had seen only in drawings: a *choshen* with its twelve colored gems, the impressive turban, the white flaxen coat and pants, and the embroidered tunic that flowed out behind like a wide apron. On his forehead Pinter wore a thin gold circlet engraved with the words "*Kodesh L'Hashem.*" Though the clothes were only an imitation of the ones the true *Kohen Gadol* used to wear, they had been beautifully, and devotedly, sewn by hand — by Pinter himself.

Sruly felt a nearly uncontrollable urge to burst into hysterical laughter. He wished he had someone with whom to share this scene. He dressed quickly and ran out to join the circle of men watching around the *mizbei'ach.* Yonah Pinter was speaking, eyes closed with spiritual concentration: "Just as we sacrifice this *korban olah* here tonight, may we merit bringing all the holy sacrifices in the *Beis Hamikdash.*"

"Amen," the others responded, in a shout that echoed afar. In ecstasy, Pinter continued, "In order that we may rebuild the *Beis Hamikdash,* we must destroy the accursed mosques on *Har Habayis.* In a month's time, the desecrations calling themselves the Mosques of Omar and of Al Aksa will crumble and fall. On that day, we will begin the work of building the Holy Temple."

Abruptly, Pinter turned and began walking away. A strange sound accompanied him. In a moment, Sruly saw what it was. As part of the *Kohen Gadol* outfit, Pinter had small gold bells sewn to the hem of his garments, which tinkled as they swept the grass and stones.

"He's really gone over the edge," Sruly thought. This time, he couldn't contain his laughter, but managed to turn it into a harsh bout of coughing instead.

The Friends of the Mikdash lingered around the altar until the lamb was reduced to a pile of charred ash. As they began to scatter, Dekel approached Sruly.

"You were very soundly asleep, weren't you, Sruly? We tried to wake you but apparently you did not merit being present at the sacrificing of the *korban*." Dekel accompanied his words with a long, searching look. Sruly, taken aback, didn't know what to say.

Dekel handed the youth a note. "Pass this around to the other members," he commanded, and strode away.

The note contained a single line: "Meeting in half an hour in Dekel's room. First briefing."

◆ ◆ ◆

Fifteen young men entered Dekel's room in the building adjacent to the Friends of the Mikdash dormitory. The *ger tzedek* had furnished the room lavishly, with a comfortable sofa and armchairs, a handsome coffee table, bright halogen lighting, and luxurious plants. But none of those present noticed the decor. They stood at attention before Dekel, whose leadership shone forth in a powerful and charismatic speech.

"I've asked you to remain standing, because tonight we are going to swear an oath of loyalty to the *Beis Hamikdash*. From the day the *Beis Hamikdash* was destroyed, foxes have roamed *Har Habayis* — the Temple Mount — two impudent foxes, named 'Omar' and 'Aktzah.' They've been sitting in the Owner's seat, not permitting Him to enter His own House. Isn't that outrageous? A maidservant has become her mistress' heir! Whoever sees those polluted mosques on the Temple Mount and does nothing to get rid of them will be held accountable."

His burning eyes seared the listeners' very souls. "After 120 years, we will each have to answer for that in the Heavenly Court. Do you know what they will ask us there? 'Why did you not erase the desecration of Hashem's Name that stood there day after day, year after year on *Har*

Habayis? Why did you not destroy the abomination with bombs and explosives? How could you stand by to see the Holy of Holies desecrated, and keep silent?'"

The young faces were contorted with fear. Akiva Tamiri looked like he was close to bursting. Dekel went on, "Come, let us prepare our answer. Let us sanctify the Name of Heaven — even at the cost of our very lives!" His thundering voice dropped. "One night soon, we will penetrate the tunnels of the Wall. I have found a secret opening that no one knows about, somewhere near the southern end of the Wall. Through a deep route from the days of the Hashmonaim — a British archaeologist showed it to me — we will reach the Well of Winds, beneath the Mosque of Omar, and then the Black Well, under the Mosque of Al Aksa."

Dramatically, his voice dropped even further. "Simon Gibson, the archaeologist, was here on a research grant from Britain. He explored deep beneath the Temple Mount, and found its foundations to be in deteriorating condition. And so...."

Dekel's face shone as he finally unveiled the details of Operation Mikdash. His smile was filled with the joy of vengeance as he described the way the mosques would collapse like houses of cards, burying thousands of Moslem worshipers as they did so — his Arab brothers who had turned into his bitterest enemies, and who had issued a sentence of death against him.

The next morning, in the boiler room at the Aish Aharon yeshivah, Sruly Egozi passed on to Eli Flamm the full particulars of the secret meeting that had taken place the previous night, and of the sacrificial ceremony that had preceded it.

31

"I'm telling you, I've never had the flu in my life," Yoni Dor complained, bringing a tissue to his nose in time to catch an enormous sneeze. "I need bedsheets for this nose of mine, not tissues. This is just not normal!"

On this, the fifth day of his illness, Yoni was still running a high fever. His nose was deep red and sore from constant blowing and wiping, and his cough had worsened. Yossi Katri prepared yet another in an endless round of cups of tea, using the electric kettle the hotel had provided. "Some hot tea with lemon will be good for you," he said encouragingly.

Yoni coughed. "What did I come here for?" he asked plaintively. "To drink tea? I must have drunk a million cups so far, and I hate tea. It's an old man's drink! How did I get sick, anyway? I'm always as strong as an ox."

These words rang an alarm bell in Yossi's mind. "What did you say?"

Yoni sipped some tea, then repeated, "I said I've never had the flu in my life."

"And now you got sick — here in Russia," Yossi finished slowly.

"On the very first day."

Yossi weighed his suspicion, then decided to share his thoughts. "Doesn't it seem a little strange to you?"

"It sure does!"

"Maybe someone did this to you on purpose."

"Who — the KGB?" Yoni said, blowing his nose. "Come on, Yossi. Those days are over."

Yossi went to the door, opened it, and peered along the corridor. Uzi Saraf was nowhere in sight. Returning, he said, "You're fluent in Russian. From the first, I've been shunted to the side, but no one's really worried about *me*. I don't speak Russian, and in any case they think of me as an intellectual lightweight."

"What are you trying to say?" Yoni stared.

Yossi hesitated, then said obliquely, "Did Uzi offer you anything to drink on our first day here?"

"Not here," Yoni said, remembering. "It was on the plane coming to Moscow. The stewards were busy serving a meal, and Uzi insisted on going to the galley and making me a cup of coffee."

"And there, with no witnesses looking on, our kindhearted friend no doubt introduced a few virulent influenza germs into the cup. He could easily have gotten rid of the dropper and container in the galley's waste receptacle."

"It *was* odd," Yoni said slowly. "He practically forced the coffee on me. I was willing to wait for the stewards."

"A clever and efficient agent, our friend. If you'd had occasion, earlier, to look through his attache case, you would have found a bottle of some mysterious fluid. But Uzi was smart. He got rid of the evidence while still on the plane, and managed to neutralize you even before the mission began." Yossi laughed, but it was laughter without either amusement or warmth. "Uzi was probably hoping you'd infect me with the same germ. Yoni, the strain of flu you're suffering from is a particularly virulent one — a laboratory strain."

Yoni took his time absorbing Yossi's theory. "But why would he do such a thing to me — to us?"

Yossi rose and went over to the balcony's glass door, looking out over Moscow. "Uzi is jealously guarding the Mossad's glory. He was given instructions to get us out of the way, and he readily obeyed."

He left Yoni in the room agonizing from his flu and from the complex discovery of their colleague's duplicity. "No matter," he consoled himself as he rode down in the elevator. "The tables are turned now. Uzi and the Mossad are farther away from Arkady Bogdanov than ever."

He found his car in the parking lot and set off in the direction of Gregori Zislin's house on Anna Karenina Street.

◆ ◆ ◆

At that precise moment, Uzi Saraf was sitting in the living room of that very house.

"I hope you have some new information for me, Mr. Zislin," he said as he prepared to give his host some money. "As you are probably aware, we at the Mossad don't suffer from an excess of funds, and the sums you're demanding are unbelievable. A hundred thousand dollars for a piece of information? All I'm asking for is Arkady Bogdanov's route to Lebanon, and a few dates."

"How much did you put down?" Zislin asked. His expression soured when he saw that the amount was only $5,000. "A gang of cheapskates," he thought contemptuously. "I did well, dealing with the Israeli police behind the Mossad's back. I'll cook the Mossad a pretty mess of porridge, see if I won't! Something they'll remember for a long, long time."

He opened a small notebook and studied the cramped Cyrillic writing for some moments. Looking up at Uzi, he said, "I spoke to my contacts in Petersburg today. I had to throw my weight around to get them to open up; they didn't want to talk."

"But they did talk, in the end?" Uzi asked eagerly.

"Yes. They did me a favor. Arkady Bogdanov set out 10 days ago."

Uzi paled. "Oh no," he whispered. "We've lost him."

"Wait," Zislin smiled, holding up a hand. "You'll calm down when you hear the rest. There's still a chance for you to catch him. He took a long,

long route. He is in no hurry. It's an overland route, crossing the Caucasian Mountains, Armenia, and Turkey. Then he'll cut through Syria to reach Lebanon." He handed Uzi a page on which details of the itinerary were jotted.

Uzi looked disbelieving. "That sounds like the most insane plan I've ever heard! Why would a 72-year-old man undertake such a difficult trip by land?"

Zislin said mockingly, "Now, now, such talk does not become a professional agent. I don't know what they teach you in Israel, but the KGB always emphasizes that the enemy will do exactly the opposite of what you expect from him. You're thinking of an old man who enjoys comfort and security, so you expect him to choose a sea route. Therefore, he takes the overland route. True, it's a hard journey, long and tiring — trains, trucks, constant border checkpoints — but he can relax, knowing that the Israeli Mossad won't be on his heels."

"The Mossad will get its man, never fear. I was just surprised that a man of that age can muster the strength for such a hard journey."

Zislin folded the check and inserted it into his wallet. "Not only cars, but people, too, have engines. From the beginning of time, money has been the engine that has driven man. See me? I'm 68 years old and believe in only one thing: the power of money. I grew up very poor. When I'd ask my mother for a boiled egg, she would say, 'There's no money.' A toy, a new coat? 'No money.' That's all we ever heard. Two of the most frustrating words in the world! Words that leave you feeling forever hungry.

"Arkady had a similar background, so he has the same religion as me: he worships the great god of money. Money makes him younger, stronger, and healthier, and gives him the energy to do what he must."

"But he's really old!"

Zislin was tired of arguing. He leaned back in his voluminous armchair and closed his eyes. "Arkady is young in spirit and healthy as an ox. The only old one here is you! You have a young body but an aged brain. If you were my son, I'd soon whip you into shape. You're 40 years younger than I am, yet my mind is fresher and more flexible than yours. I obtained this information — not you, old man. If you'd thought like a young man, you'd have traveled down to St. Petersburg yourself to find out what you needed to know."

A series of emotions crossed Uzi's face as he listened to this tirade: insult, repudiation, doubt, and finally acceptance. He clapped Zislin on the shoulder, saying, "You're right. It's actually very logical. I'm becoming more convinced of it by the minute: apparently, Arkady chose the overland route, via Turkey and Armenia."

Zislin's booming laughter echoed through the room. "Apparently? What is this, a theory? It's precise information! I got it straight from my old friend Sasha Smoleni, who is right-hand man to Victor Maximov, leader of the 'organization' in St. Petersburg. I'm only passing it on. Had I obtained the opposite information, I'd be sitting here convincing you that Arkady chose a sea route because he knew you'd suspect him of taking the overland route. But it all starts with hard facts — from the excellent information I get!"

"All right." Uzi went to the door. "I can't afford to waste any more time. Thanks much, my friend."

Saraf's car sped away just seconds before Yossi Katri's Moskovich turned into the opposite end of Anna Karenina Street.

A short time later, Yossi left Zislin's house, well satisfied. He knew now, with certainty, that his people held the winning card. The greedy KGB officer would cooperate with them all the way down the line, and would make sure to deflect and deceive the Mossad for as long as necessary. Zislin was a real find — the goose that laid the golden egg.

As for Gregori Zislin, he, too, was satisfied. His surprise visitor looked like he was becoming a treasure-trove — a veritable goose laying golden eggs.

Yoni Dor did not hear the footsteps as Uzi approached the hotel room. The thick carpet muffled all sound. But he did catch the scrape of Uzi's key in the lock. Quickly, Yoni pulled the covers up to his nose and feigned deep sleep. Yossi's theory had seemed the height of paranoia when he had first broached it, but the more Yoni thought about it, the deeper his own suspicion became.

He sensed Uzi's presence at the side of his bed. Yoni relaxed his breathing even more, never moving a muscle. After a moment, Uzi turned away, went into the bathroom and closed the door behind him. Quiet as a mouse, Yoni slipped out of bed and pressed his ear to the bathroom door.

He heard a series of beeps as a cell phone was dialed. A short silence, then Uzi's voice: "This is Number Four. I just received updated info from Zislin." Another short silence, then Uzi said excitedly, "I have Bogdanov's exact itinerary. He left Petersburg 10 days ago with a lead barrel, painted green. Inside are two bombs, one of them 10 kilotons and the other only a third as strong. I repeat, the second is limited, only three and a half kilotons.

"Bogdanov traveled by express train from Petersburg to Moscow. There he switched trains and went on to Rostov. From there he went by truck to the Caucasian Mountains. He's supposed to be crossing the border into Georgia, passing through the cities of Kobuleti and Batumi, then crossing again into Armenia."

Yoni Dor stood transfixed on the other side of the bathroom door, prepared at any moment to leap back into his bed. Uzi continued talking into the phone: "I asked all the same questions, but believe me, the information is reliable. Zislin got it straight from the horse's mouth — the 'organization' at Petersburg. Bogdanov will continue through Armenia in a Mack truck, using a local driver, then cross into Kurdistan near the Tigris River. From there he heads for Syria and southern Lebanon.

"Yossi Katri's not here. I got him out of the way. Yoni Dor is holed up in the hotel with a tough case of the flu; right now he's sleeping like a log. The plan is going beautifully."

When Uzi emerged from the bathroom, Yoni was neatly arranged in bed, trying to look like a log. Uzi crossed to the minibar and poured himself a glass of orange juice. Then he poured another for Yoni and left it on the night-table beside the bed. He dimmed the lights and left.

When Yossi returned half an hour later, Yoni related the conversation he had overheard. A strange light gleamed in Yossi's eye. He smiled, but didn't say much.

"You were right about my flu," Yoni sighed. "I wouldn't have believed it — he deliberately infected me. By the way, isn't it highly irresponsible of him to spill all that information over a cell phone like that?"

"Not really." Yossi made light of Yoni's contention. "If not for you, no living creature would have heard what was said. If anyone had stumbled onto their wavelength, all they'd have heard was a jumble of voices, and even that only for a brief time. The wavelength changes every five seconds."

Yoni placed his hands under his head and yawned. "In the GSS they trained us in methods of concealment that must date back to the Turkish era. Before I left Israel, they warned me not to speak on the phone at all."

"Well, Uzi has made sure you won't have anything to talk about," Yossi grinned wryly. He poured Yoni a scalding-hot glass of tea, squeezed in some lemon, and left the room. The elevator took him down to the parking level.

Seated in his car, he dialed a number in Israel. Ari Naot answered. Yossi wanted to enjoy the battle of the spies that was sure to follow on the heels of the information Uzi Saraf had just relayed to his superiors back home.

32

Uzi Saraf sipped coffee in the hotel lobby, immersed in his thoughts. Abruptly, he seemed to come to a decision. He set aside the coffee cup, stood up, and caught the elevator back to his room.

He barely avoided a head-on collision with Yossi Katri, approaching the room from the other end of the corridor. Both had been walking quickly, and both were too caught up in their thoughts to notice where they were going.

"Oh, Yossi, it's you!" Uzi exclaimed. "Good. I want to talk to you."

Yossi grimaced. "All of a sudden you're happy to have me around? What happened?"

"You'll understand in a minute."

They entered the room to find Yoni Dor standing at the glass balcony door, enjoying the rooftop view of Moscow. Hearing them, he turned. "Here's the latest news update," he said with a broad grin. "Yoni Dor's health has improved to the point where he can actually stand on his own two feet!"

The other two burst into laughter that obscured, for the moment, the tension between them. Mimicking Yoni's newscaster style, Uzi intoned, "Uzi Saraf reports that GSS agent Yoni Dor will be returning to Israel tonight on an El-Al flight."

Yoni joined in the continuing laughter. Gradually, the words sank in. He stopped laughing. "Just a second. Don't tell me you're serious."

"I am." Uzi waved at a chair. "Sit down, please. I have an important message for you."

"I'd better lie down," Yoni decided, stretching out on his bed. "I don't think I even have the strength even to sit, not with that ominous look on your face!"

Uzi considered how best to soften the blow, then made up his mind to be direct. "All right. I've received instructions to send you back home. Yoni, you've been down with the flu from the first day. You're not able to help here, and besides, it would be better that you receive proper medical attention in Israel. Our mission has already met with success. There's no further need to run around all over Russia. The follow-up will be done by our regular agents stationed in this country."

The other two regarded him in silence. "If he only knew the truth," Yossi thought. Suddenly, doubt seized him: "Maybe Uzi *did* know. Who is Zislin betraying, him or me?"

Uzi continued, "We know Arkady Bogdanov's entire route now. And it was all accomplished by one man in the field — you can guess who!" Smug did not even begin to describe Saraf's manner. But neither Yossi nor Yoni reacted to the implicit insult. Quietly, Yossi asked, "Is it possible to hear some details?"

"What a question!" Uzi was magnanimous in victory. "You two are involved in this business, after all. Well, by exhaustive work through the various ports, Gregori Zislin and I have managed to uncover Bogdanov's route.

"Arkady Bogdanov is a smart man. A very smart man — and a creative one. The scientist, carrying two atom bombs capable of destroying half of Israel in an instant, has decided to make our lives harder for us by choosing the most arduous and complicated route. He's 72 years old but strong as an ox. We've got a number of tips on Bogdanov's movements through the 'organization' in Petersburg. He's wily as a snake, but the Mossad will trap him like a bird at the right time and in the right place. Most likely, that will be within the next day or two. You can count on us: He won't reach Israel with those bombs!"

Yoni's eyes flashed. "And where does that leave us? Why did you keep us in the dark?"

"You?" Uzi repeated contemptuously. "Who are you? You've been down with the flu from day one. And Yossi? With all due respect, Yossi, you're not cut out for this kind of work. You have neither the talent nor the background."

"Thanks for the compliment," Yossi retorted heatedly. He made a masterful attempt to control the fury that leaped up inside him and made him want to lunge at Uzi.

"Are you insulted?" Uzi taunted. "Have you ever undergone espionage training? You're just a policeman — no, excuse me, not just a policeman, a police security officer! You have experience with hardened criminals, of course. Frankly, the Mossad didn't understand why the Prime Minister let Benny Turiel persuade him to include one of his people in this business. That's why I couldn't let you in on what I was doing. Don't get offended, now, but you've been nothing but a fifth wheel. Okay, that's all. We've reached the end of the road. I've got to get back out into the field."

"And what about me?" Yossi flared. "Why am I wasting my time here?"

"I've been asking myself the same question," Uzi said frankly. "But what can I do? I'm not the one who makes these decisions. Really, Yossi, you'll agree with me that Yoni is totally superfluous in this operation. How will he travel alone in his condition? You don't have anything to contribute here, either; and what you've contributed already is questionable, too. You've been going around in circles while I've broken new ground. It's only right that you let me finish the job alone. It's time to part ways."

A blue glass vase stood on the dresser. Yossi snatched it up and approached Uzi. With each step, his hands trembled more violently, with the effort to contain his rage. The hardest thing he had ever done was keeping himself from hurling that vase right into Uzi Saraf's complacent face.

When he spoke, Yossi's voice shook with fury, pain, and the insult that had been heaped on him.

"Uzi, I'm fed up to here with you and our so-called teamwork. I thought we were on the same team, motivated by concern for our people and our homeland under threat of destruction. For that, I was willing to overlook your arrogance. I'm prepared to sacrifice more than my own ego for the sake of life itself! For the sake of my people — for Israel. But if I'm superfluous here, I'll fly home with Yoni tonight."

Coldly, Uzi snapped, "Wonderful. You'll finally be doing something useful."

Yossi replaced the vase gently on the dresser. "I'll pack up right now. We'll leave you a clear field. But you might as well know now that I plan to lodge a strong complaint when I reach Israel." He thought for a moment, then shook his head. "On the other hand, I might as well save my breath. The fish is rotten from the head down. We have a critical situation here, danger of genocide — of a nation's destruction — and you in the Mossad are playing Russian roulette with millions of lives for the sake of a few extra moments of glory."

◆ ◆ ◆

Mossad agents, in a rare show of cooperation with the KGB, exerted tremendous effort in the following days in a futile attempt to track down Arkady Bogdanov. They boarded trains and swarmed over highways, inspected border crossings, and interviewed hundreds of people. At the checkpoints between Russia and Georgia, between Georgia and Armenia, and even between Armenia and Kurdistan, the agents were everywhere, showing Arkady's picture. They had the scientist's passport photo as well as drawings compiled by Mossad artists, depicting the various guises Arkady might have assumed: Arkady with a mustache and short beard; with the mustache alone; in a Western suit; in traditional Kurdi costume; Arkady as an elderly Japanese tourist, and as a Buddhist monk. The Mossad ran its agents ragged. Gregori Zislin, for his part, worked like a bulldozer, bringing in dozens of his own men to help in the chase. But four days of hunting brought no result. The scent was cold.

"What do you say to that?" Uzi Saraf fumed, when the final reports had come in. "Your information wasn't worth a ruble!"

Glaring, Zislin shot back, "And what did you want? You give me a few cents and expect full information? Your money was barely enough to buy a couple of herrings for the stray cats in Red Square. Apparently, we missed out on a few details in Bogdanov's itinerary. He's slipped through a hole in the net."

"What are you babbling about?" Uzi exploded.

"I'm talking about the Israelis' stupidity. They find money for every silly thing, and then get stingy when the lives of their citizens are at stake. My information is usually very accurate, down to the smallest detail. But with the minute amount of money you gave me, what could I do? I told you that a lot of money was needed to grease various palms. My contacts are men of the world — the underworld, that is. It's not love of Israel that motivates them, it's love of money. A *lot* of money. You have money, you get accurate information. You don't have money — the scientist slips away! Arkady is no fool. He's managed to camouflage his tracks."

Uzi left the meeting with the sour taste of defeat in his mouth. "Where did I go wrong?" he wondered as he stalked out into the street. "Zislin's made a fool of me!"

It was a depressing thought.

◆ ◆ ◆

"I'm about ready to explode," Shimi Tzipori said to Gadi, head of the Mossad, after four days of fruitless hunting for the vanished scientist. "We've turned over every stone. We've visited every place Bogdanov was supposed to pass through and lots of places he wasn't. We've spoken to railroad supervisors — both passenger and freight — in four countries: Russia, Georgia, Armenia, and Kurdistan. We've never launched an operation on this scale before. We've combed Armenia and sniffed through Turkey. We've even put out feelers in Syria, through you-know-who — but no Arkady Bogdanov. It's impossible!"

The Mossad chief looked at him with inscrutable eyes. "The conclusion: you've been had. They sold you a bill of goods and you bought it." He paused. "Have you thought about investigating the alternative?"

Beads of cold sweat stood out on Tzipori's upper lip. "I understood that to be unnecessary."

"You understood incorrectly! You overlooked what was in front of your nose and ran after illusions. You forgot that it's a very bad idea to put all your eggs in one basket. I want you to start immediately on an investigation of all ships that sailed from St. Petersburg in the past two weeks. Maybe we can still salvage something from this mess."

Tzipori got up to go, his entire face now bathed in perspiration. But the Chief waved him back into his seat. "Just a minute — don't run away. Have you recalled those two losers from Moscow?"

Tzipori nodded.

"That's one positive thing, at least," the Mossad head mused. "The Prime Minister forced our hand in making us send along those two. We provided five-star sickroom accommodations in Moscow — though neither one is worth even one star."

◆ ◆ ◆

Benny Turiel and Dani Devash were of the opinion that Yossi Katri was worth much more than one star. From the time they received his detailed report through Ari Naot, the police had launched a discreet logistical operation, far from the eyes of "Big Brother" — the Mossad. It had begun with a phone call from Devash to his superior, Turiel, immediately upon receiving Yossi's news from Moscow.

"We need people in Lebanon," Devash had said, swaying to and fro in his swivel chair. "People to keep an eye on all the ports. Do we have such people?"

Benny Turiel said quietly, "Exactly one week ago, I spoke to Nikko Patel, captain of the border police stationed in central Lebanon. Nikko told me he has a network of dozens of villagers ready to do business with him — some of them pretty talented guys."

Dani Devash sighed contentedly. "That's exactly what we need. Tell him to activate his network today. We've got work to do!"

◆ ◆ ◆

The phone call came very late at night. "Number Three" called Mr. Coates. "The fox is creeping very near the chicken coop."

Mr. Coates understood the reference at once. "Excellent. Is everything secure?"

"No. I can't locate him now."

"How did you lose him?" Mr. Coates raged. "This is a catastrophic development. I know *Tovarisch* Zislin. The man is floating on a sea of information and sells it to the highest bidder. If you'd paid him the way we agreed, Bogdanov would be ours by now."

Click.

Mr. Coates's anger was actually just an act. He knew more than Number Three did and he had sources of his own to help him track down the missing scientist. He had been reserving these for an emergency. Well, it looked like emergency time was here.

◆ ◆ ◆

Ten combat guerrillas crouched in the dense undergrowth near Jazin, in southern Lebanon. A heavy downpour fell continuously on their motionless bodies, but they did not move; they hardly breathed. These were 10 of the most daring men that Hizballah boasted.

They had already achieved great victories in their ongoing war against the Israelis, and their daring increased with each new success. Just a month before, Hizballah had inflicted heavy damage on Israeli troops with a powerful explosive set to go off as army jeeps rumbled down the road.

Right now, the guerrillas were poised to raise the level of terrorist violence by a few notches. According to information they had received from the Hizballah command, an Israeli helicopter was headed in their direction with dozens of soldiers aboard. The terrorists were prepared to fell the helicopter with the help of hand-held antiaircraft guns.

Like snakes lying in ambush for their unwitting prey, the men lay perfectly still. Thanks to their camouflage gear, they were invisible even close up, except to the experienced eye. In the distance, the Lebanese hills brooded above them, indifferent to their doings.

This was one of Israel's biggest trouble spots. In an attempt to protect its northern citizens from attack by the Palestinian terrorists that infested Lebanon, Israel had taken over a "security strip" in the southern region of that country. All too quickly, however, Israel had found herself sinking into a quagmire of guerrilla warfare. The terrain was hilly and rocky, with areas of natural undergrowth that provided perfect cover for Hizballah's surprise ambushes.

The hum of the helicopter reached them from afar. It quickly grew louder. Group leader Azmi Abu Negima held a pair of field binoculars to his eyes. He saw a small black dot approaching swiftly. A few seconds later he could make out the whirring propellers.

"Get ready," he whispered tensely. "In one more minute, we shoot!"

A sibilant rustle accompanied the lifting of 10 antiaircraft guns.

33

Raintorms lashed the sea into a frenzy. The waves rose to terrifying heights, then fell, smashing against the *Charlotta Simpaya*'s sturdy hull. Charcoal skies flooded the empty decks with sheets of rain. Beneath the onslaught of the elements, the last of the sailors had fled below.

The two of them were alone, wearing knee-high rubber boots and bundled into heavy anoraks, hoods pulled low on their foreheads. In silence they watched the raging sea.

Clement shook his head. "I don't like this weather," he shouted, cupping his hands around his mouth to be heard above the roar of the rain, the shriek of the wind, and the crash of the waves.

"Are you afraid for the *Charlotta?*" Arkady shouted, too. The din was deafening. "Can seven-meter waves sink her?"

Once again, Clement shook his head. He yelled, "No. She's weathered worse storms in her time. But for you, it's a blessing."

The wind sank a fraction. The relative quiet was beautiful. "I ordered this weather," Arkady said, smiling. He pointed at the black and brooding sky, adding, "I know you prefer blue skies and calm seas, but I need a clear field."

Clement pulled back the sleeve of his anorak to check his watch. "They'll be arriving at 4 p.m. You have two hours to pack your bags." He placed a special emphasis on the last words, as though to lend them a deeper meaning, and drove the point home by giving Arkady a meaningful glance. Arkady remained impassive. He was not sure how much Captain Breinen knew about the contents of his luggage, but any betrayal of nervousness would only strengthen whatever suspicions he already had.

It had been well after midnight, last night, when Clement had tapped on Arkady's cabin door. "I've received an urgent message," he whispered. "Come at once."

Arkady had been about to climb into bed. "Why didn't you just bring it here with you?"

"Your contact, 'Gray Cap,' sent a transmission over the ship's radio. He's going to be in touch with us again in five minutes."

Arkady threw on a robe and thrust his feet into his slippers. He followed the captain up through the ship to a small room with the words "Do Not Enter" on the door.

"This is the radio room," Clement told Arkady. "We updated it a year ago and put in state-of-the-art equipment." He passed a magnetic card over a slit in the door, which opened soundlessly.

Two radio technicians sat at their consoles, headphones clamped over their ears. Arkady gaped. In gleaming array before him was ranged the most sophisticated communications equipment he had ever seen. Clement noted his bemusement. "The world marches on, Bogdanov," he said jovially.

A digital beeping led to one of the technicians passing a pair of headphones to Arkady. "It's for you."

Gray Cap's deep voice was authoritative as ever. "Arkady, I needed to speak with you directly. Don't worry, this broadcast is electronically garbled. The Israeli Navy's radio people would give a lot to understand what we're saying, but all they can hear right now is a sort of squawking. I'd like to see their faces — "

Arkady smiled at the image the words conjured. But before he could reply, Gray Cap's tone changed as if with the punch of a button. In a hard voice, he said, "Before, we had only a suspicion. Now we know for sure: the Israelis are waiting for you at all the ports."

"What do we do?" Arkady asked anxiously.

"The plan's changed. You won't leave the ship at the shore, but rather in mid-ocean. A yacht will pick you up at 4 p.m. tomorrow, manned by our good friends from the Hizballah. They will take you ashore to a remote location. You and your cargo will be taken to a secret place in one of the coastal villages. Stay there until you receive further instructions."

That had been last night. Now, Arkady studied the waves rising furiously around the ship and crashing repeatedly into her sides. In sudden anxiety, he tugged at Clement's sleeve. "Two questions. First of all, how will the yacht manage to cut through those monster waves? And, second, in this wind my barrel could fall overboard!"

Clement threw off his hood, tilted his head back, and opened his mouth to meet the rain. "Have you ever tried drinking rainwater?" he asked mockingly. "If you try it once, you'll be hooked. This is the purest water in the world — You asked me two questions; I'll give you two answers. In approximately one hour, the winds will drop. The eye of the storm is behind us. Second, Christian is prepared to accompany you ashore — for a small sum."

"Who, that drunkard?" Arkady had not forgotten the card game with the burly sailor.

Clement took another mouthful of rainwater. "If you don't mind letting your barrel wash overboard, be my guest. I'd advise you to take along 'that drunkard.' He's strong as an ox, and it would be well worth your while to have him at your side for a paltry thousand dollars."

Arkady muttered sourly, "Another thousand?"

Clement burst into raucous laughter. "A thousand more, a thousand less, what does that matter in the long run? You've already invested so much. Now, when it's only a question of pennies, you're getting cheap."

They entered the ship's central stairwell and descended to the lower deck. Arkady's heart had commenced a loud pounding in advance of the upcoming adventure. Everything that had happened until now had been child's play compared to operation "Lightning and Thunder."

Clement had been mistaken: the eye of the storm had not yet passed. On the contrary, it was moving closer with each passing minute.

◆ ◆ ◆

The clacking of propellers came closer. The men were standing at attention with their shoulder-guns poised to fire, when Abu Negima's transmitter sprang to sudden life. "Abu Negima, this is Farouk al Atrash. *Do not fire!* Repeat, do not fire at the helicopter!"

Abu Negima grabbed the radio and pleaded into it, "It's in our hands. We've never downed an Israeli helicopter before."

The answer that erupted from the communicator shocked all 10 men in the camouflage unit. "I will terminate your lives with my own hands if you fire on that helicopter! I have a big job for you. Be here in one hour."

Farouk al Atrash, the Hizballah commander for the Jezin area, was the caricature of a fighting machine: cold, cruel, and calculating. He set his goals ruthlessly, studied every relevant factor thoroughly, and was careful to stay away from braggadocio and empty rhetoric. If he said he had a "big job," he meant it.

Muttering in disappointment, the men watched the helicopter pass safely overhead and come to a landing on the plain opposite their hiding place. The doors opened, discharging 20 Israeli soldiers — all oblivious to the enemy commandos watching them from afar. If not for Farouk al Atrash's order, they would have been nothing but smoke and ashes by now.

The guerrillas slithered through the mud until they emerged from the undergrowth at a paved road. Two jeeps, engines muffled, drove up to collect them. An hour later, they were passing through the gates of the local field command.

Farouk al Atrash was a stark contrast to the guerrillas. Educated in Germany, he was clean shaven and dressed Western style. Privately,

Farouk despised his primitive Arab brothers and wanted to turn his soldiers into a civilized band of fighters. He received them coolly, as always, and said, "There's big action waiting for you. Right now we must keep a very low profile. You could have ruined everything."

"I don't understand what's going on," Abu Negima complained. "You're giving us contradictory orders. First you send us on a daring mission, on a scale unknown to Hizballah till now. We spend weeks drilling and learning the terrain. Then, at the last minute, with the target in sight and ready to fall into our hands, you cancel everything and talk about big action. What could be bigger than downing an Israeli helicopter carrying 20 soldiers?"

Farouk's eyes narrowed. "All that is child's play compared to what is about to take place." His voice rang out confidently. Abu Negima was filled with curiosity as he asked, "What do you mean?"

"You'll all know soon enough. Right now, we need to lie low. If you had harmed that helicopter, all the bears would have come running out of the woods. The Israelis would not have taken such an attack lightly."

"And you didn't know that ahead of time?" one of the commandos burst out. He was still angry about the operation that had been snatched out of their hands.

"Silence!" Al Atrash snapped. The single word and the expression in those ice-cold eyes were enough to subdue any signs of incipient rebellion among the others. Farouk continued immediately, giving them no time to think. "A great adventure awaits you. You are Hizballah's elite unit in this region, and you have been selected to carry out a difficult and important mission. In three hours, you will board a yacht for a trip into the sea, and you will bring this man back with you" — he showed them a picture of Arkady Bogdanov — "along with a green lead barrel. Remember, both the man and the barrel must arrive safely and in one piece." He broke into laughter. "Seriously, you must guard that barrel as you would your only daughter. It is 'Hitler's Weapon' — the final solution for Israel's destruction!"

The fighters waited, but no further explanation was forthcoming. Farouk al Atrash signaled that the briefing was over.

Two Land Rover jeeps transported the guerrilla unit over rough terrain to the coast. On a deserted strip of shore, they awaited their yacht.

As they waited they speculated about the nature of "Hitler's Weapon" concealed in the green lead barrel. Whatever it was, they were determined to carry it, and its owner, safely back to headquarters before the day was over.

◆ ◆ ◆

Captain Breinen's weather forecast proved accurate. At 3 o'clock in the afternoon the wind abated dramatically. The high waves settled down. Only the rain continued to lash the deck, and heavy clouds continued to darken the skies, blotting out what little light remained.

"That's it, my lad," Clement said with satisfaction. "You've got ideal conditions. The waves have subsided and the yacht will arrive on time, but the rain and the dark will hide you from unfriendly eyes."

Christian the sailor, after a stern talking-to by the captain, had managed to refrain from drinking. The talk had ended with $500 passing into his hands as an advance on the day's work.

There was plenty of work for him to do. First, he had to assemble and lower the ladder that would allow him, Arkady, and the barrel to descend into the yacht. Christian carefully oiled the screws that held the different components in place, to prevent their jamming at a critical moment. Then he carried all of Arkady's belongings from his room. Lastly, he carried the lead barrel, as easily as if it weighed nothing at all. He performed these tasks quickly and efficiently, biceps bulging beneath the sleeveless shirt he wore despite the rain. "He's worth every penny," Clement noted in a whisper to Arkady. "You're investing in the right man. Without him, I would have had to hoist the barrel with a crane, which offers many more possibilities for an accident. To operate a crane over a tiny yacht on a stormy sea is practically impossible."

Tiny pinpoints of lights signaled the yacht's approach while it was still some distance off. It reached the ship exactly 50 minutes after the appointed hour, by which time Arkady's nerves were stretched to the breaking point. The clumsy maneuvers with which the yacht's crew tried to align her to the ship attested to their inexperience. At last, the yacht was docked alongside the much larger *Charlotta*, looking something like an ant beside an elephant. A shadowy figure in dark clothes stood up in the bow and said into a megaphone, "We've come to take the Russian scientist."

Arkady's nerves, already stretched to their limit, snapped. "Why are you announcing it like that? Might as well take out ads in the newspapers, too!" But his furious cry was lost in the noise of the rain and the churning sea.

Clement pounded Arkady's shoulder encouragingly. "Your nerves are shot; you need a good rest. You're afraid of the megaphone? For a radius of 20 kilometers all around, there's no one to hear us but the sharks."

"And the sailors — is it necessary for them to hear everything?" Arkady asked querulously.

"They've been with you for two weeks now," Clement roared with laughter, "and you don't think they know who you are? Don't worry, apart from drink and money, nothing much interests them."

There were new lines on Arkady's face, giving him a look much closer to his own age than when he had left Israel for Russia several weeks earlier. His shoulders slumped tiredly as he said, "You're right. It's just this tension — it's killing me." He glanced with some apprehension at the dark yacht waiting in the waters below.

But his fears proved unfounded. Everything went as smoothly as clockwork. Christian performed wonders, carrying Arkady down the ladder on his shoulders to spare him the precarious trip down 80 bobbing rungs. The sailor returned up the long ladder to bring down the lead barrel. When that was safely stowed aboard the yacht, he made yet another return trip for Arkady's personal belongings.

The yacht chugged away from the big ship, into the waves. Arkady looked back at the *Charlotta Simpaya,* marveling that he had come all the way from Kronshtadt aboard her. "All this way, and no one's even tried to stop me. Who would have believed it?"

The yacht was old, and its progress to Lebanese shores was slow. After two hours, they finally sighted land. The crew pulled into a strip of deserted beach, where the two Land Rovers were waiting for them. Arkady and his baggage were transferred to one of the jeeps, which traveled without lights to Hizballah regional headquarters.

At 10 o'clock that night, the lead barrel was resting securely in an underground vault, by orders of Farouk al Atrash.

34

Kum, Iran

Sulimein Halil was preparing in earnest for the role of the world's greatest *shahid*.

"You will be a greater warrior than Samson," his ayatollah teachers had promised. "Samson killed more people through his death than he did in his lifetime, but no *shahid* has ever succeeded in killing more Jews through his death than you will. When you rise to Heaven, the Prophet Mohammed will embrace you in Paradise and call you 'son.' No, no — 'My *dear* son.' You will merit a life of eternal pleasure."

Year after year, Sulimein absorbed these messages. The brainwashing did its job. He was ready for the great mission he was called upon to do.

Had a Western tourist been allowed to set foot in the *shahid* headquarters in the Dishti-Karnad quarter of the holy city of Kum, he would have rubbed his eyes in wonder. The building was new, and appeared from the outside to be a typical Iranian structure: domed roof, arched windows, a large sandy courtyard with its decorative fishpond, tiled in pink and light- blue mosaic. Iranian anti-American fanaticism, however, stopped at the door. Inside, the house was a replica of a Beverly Hills mansion. In this house, where young *shahids*-in-training received their indoctrination in murder and mayhem, no creature comfort was lacking. Sulimein's every wish was granted. He spent the days wallowing in pleasure in the company of his fellow zealots, merry young Iranian men so brainwashed that their own expected lack of longevity did not depress them a bit.

This morning, Sulimein was excited. An exalted visitor was coming to see him — one of the chief planners of "Operation Lightning and Thunder." The excitement helped to temporarily distract him from the inner turmoil that plagued him night and day. In contrast to his friends, Sulimein had a sharp mind and liked to use it. His superior intelligence often led him to question many things that his friends took for granted.

Yusuf Abu Rabia arrived at 10 o'clock that morning, all smiles. His fingers played constantly with the edges of a luxuriant black mustache. Fervently he embraced every one of the young men, kissing their hands and calling them "Khomeini's holy *shahids.*" Over and over, he told them how proud he was of them. "And I am especially proud of *you,* Sulimein Halil — the greatest *shahid* in history!"

Sulimein lowered his eyes, blushing crimson from collar to temples. "Don't be embarrassed, my brother!" Abu Rabia boomed. "Mohammed, in Paradise, will offer you even greater praise!"

When the tumult over his arrival had subsided, Abu Rabia closeted himself with Sulimein in the younger man's room. It was a luxurious room — the most luxurious in the house. His friends envied him, not knowing that Sulimein rarely bothered making use of the many electronic games or the computer that had been provided for him. He would sit for hours, staring at the wall and wiping away the occasional tear.

"The fateful day is fast approaching," Abu Rabia said, tapping a cigarette out of a pack he'd pulled from his pocket. "We're waiting for the final signal, and then you'll set out."

"When will that happen?" Sulimein's eyes darted quickly to his visitor's.

"Soon, my brother." Yusuf's cheeks shone with such pleasure that Sulimein had to quell an almost irresistible urge to slap them. "Tomorrow you fly to France, switch identities and clothes, and continue on to Israel. There you will receive your instructions for activating 'Operation Lightning and Thunder.'" Abu Rabia rubbed his hands together. "Oh, how I wait for that day! The entire Arab nation has been waiting a thousand years for it — and you, Sulimein, were chosen to carry the banner of Arab liberty. You, and no other!"

◆ ◆ ◆

The interoffice intercom on Shimi Tzipori's desk phone buzzed. A secretary's voice came through apologetically, with the news that "Gadi wants Shimon Tzipori in his office immediately."

Shimon Tzipori? Not even "Shimi"? Gadi had become very businesslike all of a sudden. No doubt he was about to aim a thorough scolding at Tzipori's head, or perhaps even enter a comment into his personal file, making it much more difficult for Shimi to inherit Gadi's title in time. There was a bitter taste in Tzipori's mouth, and his stomach hurt.

He had known that this unpleasant moment was coming and he had tried to prepare for it. His letter of resignation was composed and typed, nestled in his pocket in case it should be needed. But now that the moment had actually arrived, Shimi was finding it difficult to face.

Gadi, the Mossad chief, had hard gray eyes, a stubborn chin, and a face that seemed to have been poured from molten steel. He had requested from Shimi Tzipori a full report on the Russia-Iran-Hizballah triangle. When the report was delivered, Gadi had stamped it with a single word: "Failure." The simple mission of locating an elderly scientist and his lethal baggage had turned into a circus of bumbling errors — and an expensive circus, to boot. The Mossad's shining gems stood revealed in all their flaws.

The chief was waiting for Tzipori in his private office. His elbows were on the desk, fingers steepled. He issued curt instructions to his secretary to hold all calls. She nodded her comprehension and hastened to leave the room, shutting the door behind her. Years of experience had sharpened her antennae, and they told her that the scene about to be enacted in Gadi's office would not be a pretty one.

For several long minutes, the chief remained sunk in thought. Shimi waited nervously. Finally, Gadi looked up and said coldly, "Just between the two of us, what happened? Bogdanov is coming closer and closer, with a holocaust in his suitcase, and the great Mossad has turned into a crew of clumsy idiots. Who's to blame?"

Shimi felt suffocated. He tugged at the knot of his tie and tried to breathe normally. Finally, he found his voice. "It's true, I failed. I'd like to submit my resignation." He pulled the prepared letter from his pocket and placed it on the bare desktop.

The unexpected gesture seemed to take the wind out of Gadi's sails. Smiling slightly, he said, "Your resignation is absolutely rejected." He picked up the still-sealed envelope and handed it back to Tzipori. "The truth is that you deserve to be fired. You failed! But I'll give you a chance to make it up. Right now, I want absolute clarification of the situation, leaving out nothing. Let's put our thoughts in order, step by step."

Shimi Tzipori breathed a sigh of relief. "Okay. To review the Mossad's part in this operation ..." He spoke for half an hour. Gadi listened with complete attention, occasionally jotting something down in a small notepad. When he was done, the chief rested his chin on his palm.

"I heard you, Shimi. I make out four salient points. First, Zislin tricked us and sold us false information — apparently because we didn't pay him enough. Second, someone else bought the true information from him. Third, that 'someone' is the police. And fourth, the police have succeeded in fooling us."

"How did you reach that conclusion?" Shimi asked in amazement. "I haven't even dropped a hint in that direction."

"The head of the Mossad has to be able to read between the lines." Once again, a half-smile appeared fleetingly on Gadi's lips. "Devash and Naot met with you and suggested that you consider the possibility that Bogdanov chose a complicated land route. Zislin said virtually the same thing to Uzi Saraf. I have to conclude that there's a guiding hand behind both of these things. How can it be that you didn't consider that?"

"I did consider it," Tzipori said defensively. "But I thought that if everyone was pushing for the land route, it must be right."

"Have you lost all your wits, Shimi? In that case, maybe you *had* better resign. Is this how the second-in-command at the Mossad thinks? For the past week, rumors have been circulating that Benny Turiel and Dani Devash have been hand-in-glove over this matter and are preparing an ambush for us in Lebanon. And you're sound asleep!"

A heavy silence descended on the room. It was beyond doubt the harshest reprimand Tzipori had ever received. He tried to salvage what remained of his pride.

"Let the police sink in the mud of Lebanon," he said with fierce determination. "We — not they — will catch the scientist."

The cold, metallic words rained down on him like an icy shower. "And how, may I ask, do you plan to accomplish that?"

Tzipori was regaining his equilibrium. He straightened his tie, stood up to his full height, and smirked confidently. "We will wait for the barrel at the border, at the route the drug smugglers use."

Gadi considered this, then asked, "How do you know he'll use that route?"

"You would use it, too, if you were an enemy agent trying to pass from Lebanon to Israel with a barrel full of atom bombs. There's no other way. The other crossing points are just about totally sealed."

Thinking out loud, as though he wanted to be convinced, Gadi said, "And what about the sea? He might reach the port of Akko or Haifa, for instance."

Tzipori laughed. "If I were an enemy agent, I wouldn't try to pass even a pair of shoes through the Israeli Navy's net."

"All right. Let's say the barrel arrives along the route you suggest. What do we do, sit around twiddling our thumbs?"

"No! Here's how I see it. The barrel will probably arrive at the gate in the usual way, at 2 o'clock in the morning." He coughed. His throat was dry, but Gadi did not have so much as a pitcher of water set out for this meeting. "We can't betray our presence in any way. We don't want to disturb their efforts to bring the barrel into Israel. I will plant a few of my agents on the drug route. On the very night the barrel comes through, my men will get it."

"Bravo, Shimi. You've come shining through. Late, of course, but shining nevertheless." At long last, Gadi's steel-hard demeanor relaxed a little. "If you manage to get hold of the 'holocaust in a suitcase,' I'll erase what I wrote in your file."

◆ ◆ ◆

The TWA jumbo jetliner lifted off at exactly 8 p.m. Spread out below was a twinkling panorama of lights that grew steadily smaller. Judy recited *tefillas haderech*. Then she sat back in her seat and gazed out the window at the never-ending sprawl of New York below. A million tiny lights bid Judy farewell.

How good it was to see them. How good it was to *see*!

On her way to this country she had seen almost nothing. One eye was "lazy" and the other injured. Now she could gaze upon sky and earth. *Baruch Hashem.*

The last days in New York had been the hardest. Her longing for *Eretz Yisrael,* for her family, her close friends, had kept her from fully enjoying the love with which Benjy and his wife had flooded her. She ached to *daven* at the Western Wall, to pour out her heart in thanksgiving and pleas for the future. On her next-to-last night, she had woken suddenly from a deep sleep, about to order a taxi to the *Kosel.* Suddenly, she had remembered that she was in Flatbush, not Jerusalem. The realization had brought home to her the terrible distance between her and the holy place where she longed to be. Seizing her *Tehillim,* she had poured her emotion into a fervent recitation of her favorite psalms. That had relaxed her enough to let her put aside, for the moment, her unquenchable thirst.

The passenger in the adjoining seat was a religious American woman with a pleasant manner, whom Benjy had asked to watch over his recovering sister. "My name's Penina Kahn," she'd introduced herself. "In America they call me Penny, but when I visit my married children in Israel I'm Penina. How wonderful to have children there, so I can leave the *galus* for a little while!"

They chatted comfortably for a while, then drifted off into a doze, from which they awoke when the plane began its descent into Paris for what was supposed to be a one-hour refueling stop.

That was when the troubles began.

First, a wave of heavy fog swam before Judy's eyes — and then another, and another. "I can't see anything!" she cried hysterically to Penina. "Maybe the difference in air pressure in lifting off and landing is doing something to my eyes!"

"Calm down," Penina ordered. "Breathe deeply and it will pass."

The plane lifted off again. Presently, the "Fasten Seat Belt" signs were turned off. Judy turned to Penina. "I'm in trouble. It hasn't gone away. I want to go wash my eyes, maybe that will help. Please walk me to the bathroom."

Penina stood up and assisted Judy down the length of the plane to the lavatories. She waited outside the tiny cubicle until Judy had finished washing her eyes and irrigating them with eye drops.

The treatment helped. Slowly, Judy's vision began to return. Through gaps in the fog she began to see again.

"Thank you," she said warmly to Penina as they proceeded back down the aisle. "I can see now. You don't have to hold on to me."

"Better to be safe than sorry," Penina insisted, not letting go. Judy walked carefully, in case the blindness should suddenly return. Penina stopped, studying a young man who was sitting in an aisle seat, reading the airline magazine. In his three-piece suit and silk tie, he looked like the son of a prosperous banker — a nervous and restless son. His feet tapped out a constant rhythm and his knees knocked together erratically. Feeling Penina's eyes on him, he glanced up from his magazine.

Penina had seen young men like this before, rich and spoiled. But she had never seen eyes like those.

A blazing flame burned in those eyes. It was a fanatic flame, uncompromising, prepared to burn down the whole world. There was great rage there, along with great sorrow. The eyes glared at Penina, making her step back in alarm.

"What's the matter? Why did you stop?" Judy asked.

Penina tore her eyes away with an effort and continued walking. "I'm scared," she whispered. "I'm afraid that man's a terrorist. Only terrorists have crazy eyes like that."

They returned to their seats, stealing surreptitious glances at the young man in the three-piece suit sitting three rows ahead on their right. As if he felt them watching him, his nervousness increased. From time to time he twisted in his seat to glare at the two women.

"Maybe we should say something to the stewards?" Judy whispered anxiously.

"No! Lots of hijackings begin when one of the passengers starts showing suspicion. We have to ignore him."

Judy didn't know if they were doing the right thing. They did not tell the stewards, but neither did the young man reveal himself as a terrorist. Three tense hours passed. Judy only began breathing easily again when the plane's wheels touched down on the tarmac of Ben Gurion airport. It was noon in Israel.

"The flight's over," Penina sighed with relief. "I was sure we were going to be hijacked to Iran or Syria."

"The nightmare's over," Judy agreed. "And the fog is completely gone, too, *Baruch Hashem.*"

They did not know that the nightmare had not yet begun.

35

As they waited for their luggage at the revolving airport carousel, Judy again noticed the young man with the burning eyes. As before, she was thrown into alarm and confusion. She tried to calm herself: "It's probably just my imagination. He's probably just an ordinary tourist." Penina, busily searching the carousel for her own and Judy's suitcases, did not see him.

As he passed them, the man took in Judy's frightened and suspicious glances. He walked straight ahead, calm and cool, a large suitcase in hand. At a mirror beside the restrooms, he paused to check his appearance.

The Jewish girl's attention frightened him. Any second now she could be screaming down the airport, calling for security, and bringing to an ignominious end years of careful preparation. But there was something else — an indefinable pain much more powerful than his fear. Beads of sweat dotted his face.

"If this is how you begin, Sulimein, you won't be getting very far," he told himself. He rubbed a hand across his forehead as though trying to erase the mark of Cain. "What's wrong with the way I look? How did that Jewish girl latch on to me so quickly?" He thought he looked exactly as he should, from head to toe. His suit was an Armani, his tie a fine Italian import, his white silk shirt a Ralph Lauren. He wore a Tiffany watch and Gucci shoes. Moreover, his face was light complexioned and his eyes blue-green. It was his Western looks that had won him, among some 300 other candidates, the privilege of blowing up Tel Aviv.

It suddenly seemed to him that everyone was looking at him — accusingly. As he scanned the crowd in the airport, he realized that the men who had planned this operation had forgotten one crucial point: the human factor. They had no understanding of the Israeli scene. These expensive clothes were more likely to call attention to him — and ring a warning bell — than anything else. It was a good thing they had thought to provide him with a change of clothing. He hurried into the restroom and switched his clothes to a white cotton T-shirt with some innocuous slogan scrawled across the front, faded jeans, and sneakers. Hastily he bundled his former apparel into his suitcase, heedless of creases. He passed his hand through his hair to ruffle it, and he emerged from the restroom with nothing to identify him with the elegant young man who had entered a few minutes before. Once again he checked his appearance in the mirror. He was satisfied. Now he looked no different from any of the hundreds of tourists passing through the airport.

How many costumes have you worn in your day, Sulimein? If his mentor, Sheikh Abid al Hunud was to be believed, his greatest one was yet to come. "The Prophet Mohammed's red cloak is waiting for you Above," the Sheikh had promised as he bid farewell to Sulimein before his trip. To tell the truth, it was neither the prospect of meeting the great prophet nor of wearing his cloak that excited Sulimein. His whole being awaited the instant of the big blast that would blow him up and expiate his great sin — the heavy sin that he had been dragging about all his life, making each day, each hour, more bitter than the last.

He joined a stream of young tourists past the no-customs zone, and emerged at last outside. Had the customs officials stopped him, they would have found nothing suspicious in his luggage.

An Arab taxi driver was waiting. "Welcome to Israel," he said, inviting him inside. Sulimein got into the taxi and leaned back on the comfortable seat. "Take me to Tel Aviv," he said in English. "Stop at the Shalom Tower."

"Shalom Tower?" the driver laughed. "Don't you have enough skyscrapers in America?"

"On second thought, take me to Dizengoff Square — No. No, not Dizengoff. Take me to the Dan Panorama Hotel." Sulimein yawned, the perfect picture of a traveler suffering from jet lag. The driver shrugged. "Wherever you say." Under his breath — almost — he muttered something in Hebrew about tourists. Sulimein smiled to himself. The cab driver had no way of knowing that Sulimein was fluent in seven languages, including Hebrew.

He left the taxi at the hotel entrance, which had a view of the sea. At the reception desk he exhibited his American passport, in the name of Cliff Dillar. In short order he was depositing his suitcase in a large, clean room. He left the hotel again, going down to the boardwalk and from there to the center of town. He strolled leisurely through Tel Aviv's busy area: Dizengoff Square, Shenken Street, the Shalom Tower. He crossed streets, looked at buildings, stopped to make small purchases in various stores, and window-shopped. His eyes raked the men and women going about their business, walking beside him on the sidewalks, and the children playing and laughing. "I am your Angel of Death," he thought, "and here I am, walking among you!"

Tomorrow, he thought, he would travel to Jericho and begin his actual preparations. Right now he would just observe — to see what he was shortly going to destroy.

Look carefully, Sulimein. This is the city you are about to reduce to rubble. "Operation Lightning and Thunder" will not leave a single stone intact. Not only Tel Aviv; the entire Gush Dan area will disappear as if it had never been. And the radioactive waves following on the heels of the first mighty blast would continue to spread further and further afield.

The ayatollahs had etched the words on his mind in expressions of blood and fire: "Death to the Jews!" "The Jews are sinners in their very essence. Only death can serve as their atonement," his teachers had taught him. He would help them atone for their terrible sin, and at the same time make amends for his own personal one. Wonderful!

Experts in Iran had pored over topographical maps of Israel, seeking the most destructive spot, the place where the radioactive cloud would cause the most damage without spreading westward to dissipate over the sea. And the ayatollahs' final word had been — Tel Aviv! Nearly two million souls made their home in the Gush Dan area. And Tel Aviv was the heart of Gush Dan.

It did not matter where the explosion would occur, in a busy intersection or a quiet side street. Hundreds of meters were insignificant beside the nuclear bomb's awesome power. The important thing was that the explosion take place somewhere in central Tel Aviv — in the heart of the city that represented proud Zionism. Then, and only then, would the collective Arab dream be realized at last.

And Sulimein would be the one to realize it!

◆ ◆ ◆

"Now I regret not having warned the stewards on the plane," Penina fretted, as they pushed their laden luggage carts ahead of them. "I'm sure he's a dangerous man. I'm a psychological counselor by profession, and there's no mistaking the hatred in those eyes. Actually, it was more like self-hatred — or rather, self-flagellation on an awesome scale. I recognize that look. It belongs to a person whose values are truly perverted. A person like that is ripe for martyrdom — for becoming a suicide bomber."

"I saw him here in the terminal. He disappeared in a hurry," Judy said nervously. "Who knows what he's planning?" Something was troubling her, even beyond her fear, but she could not put her finger on what it was.

◆ ◆ ◆

On Monday night, after supper, Dekel passed among the tables in the dining hall, dispensing a succinct message: "Meeting in my room at midnight exactly."

Sruly Egozi, still chewing on a tuna sandwich with olives and tomato, hurried after him. "Dekel, wait up," he called.

Dekel continued to stride along at a rapid clip. "Dekel!" Sruly called again. "Wait!" It was only when they reached the copse of cypress trees that the wind carried his voice to Dekel's ears. He stopped and waited for the boy to catch up. "Sorry — I was thinking about something and I didn't hear you. What is it?"

Sruly dabbed tuna from his lips. "Last time, you chose me to hand out notes to everyone. How come you don't have a job for me today?"

"Last time you were all still under probation, so to speak. At this point, I can count on you. There's no need for notes." Sruly was good material, he thought with satisfaction. A little childish, but that was all to the good for Dekel's purposes. He had no way of knowing that that impression was precisely what Sruly, on Eli's orders, had been trying to cultivate.

Stroking his short black beard, Dekel continued, "Sruly, since you're so committed to the idea, I'm going to let you in on what we'll be talking about at tonight's meeting. In a few days, we'll be leaving for our first active mission. Operation Mikdash — shaking up the layers of earth beneath the mosques on the Temple Mount."

Sruly whistled. "Finally, some real action. I can't wait!"

Dekel waved a finger in front of the boy's face, saying sternly, "Sruly, don't get too excited. This is no game. We could be killed, you know."

"Those engaged in doing a mitzvah aren't harmed," Sruly answered confidently.

Dekel shrugged. "Just don't forget the first rule."

"I know, I know. Our lips are sealed." Sruly returned to the dining hall, humming happily. Dekel trusted him implicitly. Sruly's act was perfect.

As the hour approached midnight, the membership of the "Friends of the Mikdash" began to converge in Dekel's room — 20 young men in all. They waited idly, chatting, and cracking sunflower seeds with their teeth. As soon as Dekel saw this he put a stop to it, demanding a solemn and respectful attitude in honor of their holy mission. At two minutes to 12, Chemi Maimon and Akiva Tamiri went to the doorway, silver trumpets in hand. At exactly midnight, they blew a mighty blast.

"The *Kohen Gadol!*" a voice cried. Yonah Pinter came toward the room with a proud, measured stride. He was the ideological spearhead of the "Friends," and in that capacity had arrived tonight to fan the flames of enthusiasm in the group. In the interests of dramatic effect, once again he had come dressed in the *Kohen Gadol* costume.

Had he but known it, the effect was the opposite of what he had intended. In his flowing garments he looked like nothing more than a graceless scarecrow. It was all Sruly could do not to laugh out loud. He bit his lips till they bled. Somebody nudged him in the ribs. Glancing sideways, he saw that Chemi Maimon was suffering from the same trouble. Sruly winked at him, but whispered warningly, "Watch out. Yonah'll get mad."

But Yonah Pinter was above paying attention to these commoners. He had been transported to another sphere and was floating in another world. The dream he had nursed from childhood was about to become a reality! With his mind's eye he was able to see the third *Beis Hamikdash* standing on its hilltop, in all its glory.

"My dear friends," he began portentously, eyes bright and cheeks blazing, "the Jewish nation is beginning a new page in history today. Starting tonight, we are setting in motion active preparations for the rebuilding of the *Beis Hamikdash.* From this day onward, we will no longer greet one another with 'Shalom,' but rather with the words '*Yibaneh hamikdash*' — let the Temple be built!" His penetrating gaze swept the room. "Is that clear?"

"Yes!" the others shouted with one voice. "*Yibaneh hamikdash*!"

Now Dekel stepped in to add a word. "In order to make that slogan come true, we must first shout the slogan, '*Yicharev hamisgad*' — 'Let the mosque be destroyed!' One thing cannot come about without the other." He began singing the new slogan softly, to the tune of the popular song, "*Yibaneh hamikdash.*" The others joined in, mesmerized.

When the song eventually died down, Yonah Pinter spoke again. His voice was lower now, less dramatic and more practical. "We start work tomorrow night. We will all go to the *Kosel* tunnels. One of the laborers there is a friend of ours. At 2 a.m., he will secretly open one of the gates. At 2:30 we will all gather at the tunnel. Dekel will show us a hidden entrance to the inner portion of the tunnels — the part they never show."

A buzz of surprise went through the room. Yonah smiled. "What, didn't you know that secret? Our wicked government gave the Moslems control over all of *Har Habayis*, above and below. Did you know that *Har Habayis* is full of springs and natural pools — 37 of them, to be exact? They say this water could supply all of Jerusalem's needs for a year! They're huge holes, and most of them are interconnected. We will penetrate these secret tunnels to reach the underside of the Mosque of Omar.

"In one week, the Moslem holy month of Ramadan will be drawing to a close. On the last Friday of that month, approximately 200,000 Moslems are expected on the Temple Mount. That number of people weighs down the hill by about 15,000 tons, or 15 million kilograms. The bottom of *Har Habayis* is riddled with cracks, as Dekel has already reported to us. He has his information from British archaeologist Simon Gibson, who explored it to its depths. All we need to do is shake up those foundations a little more. We'll accomplish that by 'shaving' old layers of stone and undermining the mosques' foundations.

"Next Friday, the ground beneath the mosques will receive a prod during the Moslem morning prayers. The mosques will collapse onto the 200,000 worshipers inside." Pinter's eyes gleamed with mad glee.

Chemi Maimon raised a hand. "May I ask a question?"

"Please."

"We're getting ready to do something that will anger the whole world," Chemi said evenly. "What do we do if the Arab nations join forces against Israel after this attack on their holiest spot?"

It was Dekel who answered. "I have news for you. The holiest Islamic spot is the black stone at Mecca. After that comes the famous mosque in the city of Medina. The Mosque of Omar comes in third. For your information, neither Jerusalem nor the Temple Mount are mentioned in the Koran."

"True, but the Temple Mount and the Mosques of Omar and Al Aksa *are* holy to Islam, only slightly less holy than Mecca and Medina — possibly because of traitorous Jews telling the Moslems about the importance of the place to Judaism," Chemi insisted. "The Mosque of Omar is called the 'Dome of the Rock' because it was built on a huge stone, the *Even*

Hashesiya. In the month of Elul 5729 (August 1969), a young Australian by the name of Michael Rohan lit a fire in the Mosque of Al Aksa, and the State of Israel was engulfed in a flood of recrimination from around the world. Apparently, Christianity also has a stake in keeping the Temple Mount out of Jewish hands.

"The Church sees the destruction of the *Beis Hamikdash* and its continued nonexistence as a triumph of Christianity over Judaism. To them, the destruction symbolizes the Jewish loss of national independence, both religious and political. According to Christian theologians, it serves as proof of our loss of standing as G-d's chosen people — with Christianity as our heir.

"That's why I have to ask again: What happens if the Arabs — with the passive support of the Christian world — react by waging total war against Israel in retaliation for the mosques' destruction? And, by the way, how will we manage to rebuild the *Beis Hamikdash* in the face of a harsh Arab reaction?"

A great deal of water had flowed in the Hudson River since the day Aharon Flamm had posed that same question to Yonah Pinter. Yonah's face turned crimson. He seemed close to exploding, when Dekel passed him a small note. As Yonah read it, his eyes lit up.

"Yes, that's clear. We thumb our noses at the Arabs." His voice grew stronger. "Dekel and I have heard from Kabbalists that when impurity loses its grip on *Har Habayis,* the Mount of Olives to the east will split in half, the dead will return to life, and *Mashiach* will come."

Sruly felt a pang of revulsion and alarm. He looked around to see if any of the others felt the same way, but they were all gazing raptly at Yonah Pinter. The leader continued his thought. "I recently found proofs of this in old books."

"Telephone books?" Sruly muttered.

"Solomon the Small" spoke up for the first time. He was a huge man, nearly seven feet tall, and one of the first members of the "Friends of the Mikdash." He had a reticent nature and was self-effacing despite his great bulk. "The Gemara, in *Maseches Succah,* says that when King David dug the foundations for the *Beis Hamikdash*, the underground waters rose up and wanted to flood the whole world. We're planning to destroy the Mosque of Omar, which stands on the *Even Hashesiyah* — the Foundation Stone. Isn't there a danger that the waters will rise again?"

Flames leaped from Pinter's eyes. "You know only half the story! How does the Gemara continue? King David wrote Hashem's secret Name, the *Shem Hameforash,* on a piece of pottery, and tossed it into the deep. Immediately, the waters descended 16,000 *amah.* Then King David recited the fifteen "*Shir Hama'alos*" psalms and the water rose back 15,000 *amah,* bringing it back to a level just beneath the surface. I, too, will come prepared with a piece of pottery bearing the *Shem Hameforash!*"

"And what about the *Kosel?*" The question burst from Rafi Gamliel, the Israeli soldier who had beaten an Arab youth near the Lion's Gate and lost his whole world in an instant. From his corner, he insisted, "Those mosques are strong buildings. If they fall, so will everything around them — including the Western Wall!"

Shock registered on every face. "He's right! Rafi's right," the young men began muttering excitedly. "The *Kosel* will fall!"

Yonah Pinter favored Rafi with a scornful glance and said, "You seem to have a problem understanding what you hear. We're planning to rebuild the *Beis Hamikdash* — all four walls of it, understand?" He crowed with laughter. "And you're worried about the outer wall of the Temple courtyard?"

A shower of questions rained upon the leader. Dekel intervened, silencing the group. "Gentlemen, I can calm you all. The *Kosel* will not fall. The ground beneath *Har Habayis* will be affected at some distance away. You don't seem to understand — in order to build the *Beis Hamikdash,* we are obligated to strike at the Arabs. To do so, we will rely on a simple psychological effect." A confident smile played about his lips as he added, "I was born an Arab. The Arab mentality is not unknown to me. When you drop a bombshell on an Arab's head, he respects you. While they're licking their wounds, we'll use the momentum of surprise to build the *Beis Hamikdash.*"

Sruly Egozi spoke up. "How will we go up to *Har Habayis* if we're all impure and don't have the ashes of a *parah adumah*?"

Impatiently, Yonah Pinter said, "Again the same stupid questions. I've already told you a million times, I know ways that are permitted. The boundaries between the permissible areas and the forbidden ones are engraved on my brain.

"Tomorrow we will all immerse ourselves in the natural pool here in Anafim. After that, no one is to touch another person. Don't go near anyone, not even the students of Yeshivas Aish Aharon."

Suddenly, he slammed a fist down on the table. "In fact, stay *especially* clear of those yeshivah boys." His eyes raked over Sruly Egozi and the others. "If they get wind of our plan, they might try to stop us!"

36

The Israeli-Lebanese Border

The green lead barrel made its way from Farouk al Atrash's stronghold, via the Lebanese drug routes, into Israel proper. The Hizballah routinely smuggled large quantities of drugs into Israel along these routes, as part of Iran and Syria's campaign to undermine Israel's infrastructure by introducing the addictive poison into its populace.

That night, three GSS men were waiting near the border fence between Metullah and Kibbutz Misgav-Am. Actually, only two were GSS; the third was a Mossad agent who had joined them on this critical night watch. Uzi Saraf had been flown to this point by the Mossad chief himself. The GSS men were not enthusiastic in their welcome to the man who had neutralized their agent, Yoni Dor, in Russia — but orders were orders. As for Uzi, he had the hide of an elephant in matters like this.

They waited a short distance from the fence, in a car concealed behind a mammoth oak trunk, gazing at the border through infrared binoculars. The sky was cloudless and the winter's freezing grip had given way to the slight warming that heralded the approaching spring. At 1:45, a commercial pickup truck appeared on the Lebanese side, lights extinguished as it drove along the border fence at a distance of two meters. It stopped. Six dark figures stepped out, carrying small canvas knapsacks. Then two more figures descended from the jeep, carrying a large barrel between them.

"That's it!" Uzi Saraf whispered, almost beside himself with excitement. "Get ready, guys — we have some business with a couple of nuclear bombs tonight. What a joke! I turned Russia upside down to find that thing, and in the end it falls into my hands right here, near Metullah. Fate must be laughing its head off."

The Israeli agents crept slowly toward the border, commando knives clamped between their teeth. Their right hands rested on the handles of their guns; their transmitters were set on the frequency that connected them with the backup team in the fields behind them. The backup team had been joined by three top nuclear experts. Tonight, Israel would grapple with one of the most complex and dangerous missions in its history.

When they were 100 meters from the border, the three agents halted with bated breath to watch the scene unfolding before them. "I want to catch them red-handed with the barrel," Saraf whispered. "Don't make a peep until they've finished hauling it."

Shadowy figures were nearing the fence from either side of the border. The fence was massive, reinforced with steel pillars and topped by specially piercing barbed wire. The smugglers knew that one touch of the electric fence would send a signal shooting its way to the Israeli military outpost nearby and alert the formidable Israeli security forces. But they were experienced by this time, and worked calmly. Two of them picked up a bundle, wrapped in waterproof black plastic, and threw it over the fence to their cohorts on the Israeli side of the border. The barrel was last. "I'm curious to see what they'll do," Uzi whispered.

The smugglers had perfected a simple technique. Two aluminum ladders appeared out of the darkness. The men opened them near the fence. The watchers' breath caught in their throats as one man, built like a stevedore, climbed the ladder with the barrel tucked gingerly under one arm.

His progress resembled that of a man tiptoeing through the jungle knowing that a hungry leopard prowled nearby. He reached the topmost rung and handed the barrel over to a similarly well-muscled man waiting at the top of the ladder on the Israeli side.

The trio of Israeli security agents stared, fascinated. These three were only the tip of a vast iceberg that included the entire Israeli cabinet, the heads of the Mossad and the GSS, and the Knesset's Subcommittee for Intelligence and Security Services. They all knew about the transfer that had been slated to take place that night.

A great many details had been taken under consideration in planning this operation, but one had slipped through the cracks: the unit of dogs employed by the border patrol to sniff out drugs. Someone had forgotten to lock them in their kennels that night.

Four enormous dogs lunged suddenly out of the darkness. They exploded into a furious barking as they stormed the ladder. Gripping its aluminum legs in their mouths, they shook it violently.

"What's going on?" Uzi Saraf fumed. "That barrel's going to fall and that'll be the end of all of us!"

The man at the top of the ladder held on for dear life. He managed to maintain his footing — but the heavy barrel slipped inexorably from his grasp. With a mighty crash, it fell onto a large stone below.

◆ ◆ ◆

The whole family, except for Eli, was waiting for Judy at the airport's exit. The reunion was emotional and inundated with a good many tears. Adina Goldenblum was almost incoherent with joy, saying over and over again, "My Judy's back, would you believe it? My Judy's back!" She pressed the girl to her heart and could hardly bear to let her go. "Judy, you look wonderful!"

"I *see* wonderfully," Judy corrected, with a wide smile. A few tears welled up in her eyes, too. Though not usually one to exhibit her feelings in public, the emotional turmoil she had undergone recently — especially the tension of the Paris-Tel Aviv flight, with its fears of a terrorist attack — combined with exhaustion, to produce a highly sensitized and weakened state. Falling into Adina's arms, she gave free rein to her emotions.

After a few moments, she wiped her eyes and turned to her loving brothers. Only Eli was missing. He and Judy had arranged to meet at Anafim, where she would show him the secret memo their father had written all those years ago.

Mark Goldenblum's big car made quick work of the drive up to Jerusalem. On the way, the car turned left off the main highway to drop off Judy at Anafim. She stepped out and turned to wave an affectionate farewell to the rest of the family, who were to proceed to Jerusalem.

There was a hint of spring in the air. The fields were beginning to wear a mantle of pastel color. Judy drank it all in hungrily: the wildflowers sprouting in the young grass, the honeybees sipping their nectar, the trees showing off their new green coats. Everything seemed as vivid as a painting come suddenly to life. She had eyes — she could see!

Eli met her a few minutes later, a small violin in his hand. As a child he had shown signs of musical talent and had become proficient at the violin. These days he rarely played, except when in the grip of strong emotion.

"Hi, Judy! I composed a special song in honor of your recovery," he told her exuberantly. "There's a secluded little valley not far away where I can play in peace, without disturbing a soul."

Together they walked over to the valley along a path bursting with poppies. Eli led his sister to a wide boulder in the shade of a date palm. He tuned his strings. "This is my new song. It's called 'Forever Light.' Listen." His fingers passed gently over the strings, and a delicate melody wafted into the fragrant air. Leaning against a tree trunk, Eli sang softly, and with great feeling, "May it be Your will, Hashem, that we stand forever in Your light — and never in the dark. Do not sadden our hearts, or darken our eyes."

The words were heartfelt, and brought fresh tears to Judy's eyes. When her brother was finished singing, he turned to her shyly. "Do you like it?"

"Like it? There are no words, Eli! It's so beautiful — so moving. When did you compose it?"

"On the nights I couldn't sleep." He placed the violin tenderly on the grass. "Judy, how can we thank Hashem for restoring your vision? How do we tell Him, 'Thank You for the light'? How can we thank Him for bringing you back to consciousness after the operation?"

"Really, how?" Judy murmured. She imagined a large thanksgiving feast at her adoptive parents' home, a party overflowing with guests and an abundance of food. But Eli's aspirations were different, and much more modest.

"Tomorrow we'll go to the *Kosel.*"

"Great!" Judy's face shone. "I miss it like crazy."

"We'll go up together," Eli promised. "But right now, the important thing is — where's the document?"

She searched through her small traveling bag, finally pulling out a plastic folder. Judy extracted the memo that their father had written 13 years before. Eli gazed with awe at the handwriting. He read the pages closely, his face growing progressively more clouded. Judy sat and watched him in silence, fear and anticipation making her heart pound.

Nature was providing a veritable symphony all around them. Bees and gnats zoomed around a puddle with a vigorous buzzing; a pair of thrushes sang on a branch; a chorus of swallows chirped merrily, and white doves cooed overhead. But Judy heard only the rustle of the pages as her brother turned them.

"I'm amazed at Abba's powers of prediction," Eli said finally. "There was ample reason for the State Department to pick him to head the Middle Eastern desk and to submit his forecasts. He accurately predicted political trends and their geopolitical ramifications."

"I read it, too," Judy said anxiously. "It seemed kind of farfetched to me."

"What's the matter with you?" Eli snapped, plucking his violin out of the grass. "Everything Abba wrote here is coming to pass these days. Down to the last detail!"

◆ ◆ ◆

The Israeli-Lebanese Border

A fraction of a second after the atomic bomb fell, a fireball rose into the sky like a meteor. A giant pillar of fire and smoke formed in an instant. When the phe-

nomenon achieved a state of equilibrium, a giant mushroom cloud appeared, growing rapidly to a height of about 15 kilometers. In seconds, the clouds detached from the pillar and was sucked into the upper atmosphere. The area was darkened by an enormous rolling cloud of smoke and dust. Large drops of water began falling onto the ground — drops of condensed moisture from the tower of dust, heat, and particles floating above....

Strange, how many thoughts can flit through a man's mind in a single second. Uzi Saraf saw the worst-case scenario unfolding in an instant. He saw the large green barrel fall to the ground and heard the sound of the terrible explosion as lead met stone.

"It's the end of the world," Uzi thought, his blood freezing. He felt suffocated. "A nuclear holocaust!" Photographs he had seen as a child, of Hiroshima and Nagasaki after the atomic attacks at the end of World War II, flashed before his eyes. For a split second he pictured himself as a skeleton. He was vaporizing, turning into a million discrete molecules, into a speck of dust blowing across the vacuum of space....

He opened his eyes halfway and took a cautious breath. It had not happened. The barrel had not exploded on impact. There was no radioactive mushroom cloud hovering over his head, no wave of million-degree heat. It had all happened only in his imagination.

For a moment, shock and panic had paralyzed everyone. The area was like a picture of Pompeii after the volcano buried it forever under a layer of molten lava.

Then the northern border sprang to life. Searchlights raked the ground, while helicopters churned overhead, dropping additional flares. The smugglers on the other side of the border tried to escape, but the Israeli Border Patrol collared them. This is not to mention what was happening on the Israeli side of the fence.

It was like a well-staged ploy. The stage was this small section of the border, but the audience was widely spread: in the battlefield, in army headquarters, in a security pit in Tel Aviv, in the offices of the Prime Minister and Minister of Defense in Jerusalem, and in the subcommittee room in the Knesset. Never before had Israel confronted smuggling on this scale. Two nuclear bombs had crossed the border from Lebanon into Israel, to be detonated at an unknown time and place. The atomic experts who had been waiting tensely in the background came tearing up in jeeps to investigate the barrel's contents.

The shock in store for the Israeli security forces was complete.

The captured barrel contained scores of waterproof plastic bags. Each bag contained white powder. There were some 200 kilograms of heroin all told. And not even a sign of an atomic bomb.

◆ ◆ ◆

The successful ploy staged on the northern border was Gray Cap's brainchild. It had been preceded by a transatlantic phone call in the small hours of the night, between "Number Three" and Mr. Coates in New York.

"The equipment is ready to pass into Israel on the drug route," Number Three reported in a dry, businesslike tone. "It will be attached to the first shipment of drugs to arrive from southern Lebanon, and they will cross the border together at 2 a.m., three kilometers north of Metullah."

Mr. Coates stood at his office window, looking out on the twinkling lights of Manhattan. He was due to finish work at 6 o'clock, and had been preparing to leave for his home nearby, but the news he heard electrified him. The lead barrel was slated to pass into Israel. The Israeli security forces knew this. Therefore, the route must be altered.

"Very good, Number Three. Thank you very much for the information. I don't know what I would have done without you."

Number Three was amazed at this unaccustomed warmth from his superior. Mr. Coates continued, "I think I'll recommend a special payment for you — something in the seven-figure range — for the excellent service you've rendered us."

Number Three uttered a short bark of laughter. "Seven figures? I hardly know how to thank you."

"Don't. Just continue to be vigilant. Our job's not over yet. In fact, it's still just beginning. There'll be plenty of sweating to do before we hear the big boom." Coates paused. "By the way, does anyone suspect you?"

"No." Number Three spoke firmly, but the question disturbed him.

Lately, things had been getting complicated.

Mr. Coates was ready to hang up. "Good-bye, Number Three," he said. "And watch your back."

Coates's next call was to Gray Cap. "Your route is no good," he said bluntly. "Israel's onto it. They'll be waiting for you tomorrow night, at 2 a.m., at the designated spot."

"Is that so?" Gray Cap sounded unruffled. "I'm prepared for such a contingency. I will put the alternative plan into action. Israel will capture a barrel tomorrow night, but it won't be *our* barrel." He laughed.

Gray Cap laughed a good deal that night. His ploy worked to perfection, and succeeded beyond expectation.

And in Israel —

Mossad agent Uzi Saraf's chagrin knew no bounds. "How many times can we be made fools of?" he asked himself. Then a strange and frightening thought entered his mind. He amended the question, "How many times can *I* be made a fool of?"

Tomorrow, he decided, he would start digging around. He would not stop until he had followed the trail of his suspicion to the bitter end.

37

On the night after the aborted border capture, at precisely 2 a.m., the Friends of the Mikdash penetrated the *Kosel* tunnels. "The plan is ticking along like clockwork," Yonah Pinter crowed as the inner gates swung open for them.

"Sssh, they can hear you all the way to the *Kosel,*" Dekel warned. "With all due respect, do you want to ruin everything?"

Cool, clammy air met them in the tunnels. The men trembled with excitement and a sense of the moment's significance. "We're about to do something historic," Yonah stage-whispered. "To destroy the mosque!"

"Destroy the mosque!" came the echo in a sibilant whisper.

Rafi Gamliel poured cold water on the celebratory mood by asking, "How will the mosque be destroyed without any weapons?"

The others look at each other in bemusement. How had none of them thought of that? Sruly Egozi bit his lips and forced himself to swallow the sharp comment trembling on the tip of his tongue.

Dekel did not allow the question to hang in the air for long. "I've taken care of that. There are air drills waiting for us inside."

Rafi faced him in surprise. "Compressors? That's awfully noisy. We'll be heard!"

Yonah Pinter hastened to calm him. "I have a holy name to counteract noise. The angels will protect us."

It was all Dekel could do not to laugh out loud. He was the only one who knew why they did not have to worry about this particular noise. He decided to provide his fellow members with some details.

"We're going to penetrate a pool called, in Arabic, *Bir al Aswad* — that is, the Black Pool. It's a giant hole, approximately 30 by 40 meters, carved completely out of a huge stone beneath the plaza between the Mosque of Omar and the Mosque of Al Aksa. The underside of the Temple Mount is carved out of soft stone, and the builders left the upper, harder stone as a roof. The hole can hold some nine million liters of water." He kept one detail to himself: The hole was located 14 meters beneath the plaza — 14 meters of solid rock.

Chemi Maimon was astounded. "You say the roof is made out of hard rock. If we manage to scratch out two or three centimeters tonight, it will be a world record!"

"Nonsense," Dekel said crisply. "You don't know what you're talking about. I've gotten hold of air compressors with Japanese drill bits made of a titanium-steel alloy. They're sharp as knives, the last word in state-of-the-art tool technology. I've conducted an experiment, and it was pure pleasure — the drill sliced through the stone as if it were butter. Four to five hours of work by all of us, and we'll peel through the stone to the top. We'll leave some 30 centimeters of rock, no more. We'll perform a series of cuttings like this all along the underside of the mosques; I have a good map of all the holes and water pools beneath the Temple Mount.

"This much I can tell you: On the last Friday of Ramadan, the earth will open up and swallow the mosques — along with the hundreds of thousands of people praying inside."

◆ ◆ ◆

Dekel's men followed him to a concealed entrance leading to an unknown part of the tunnel. Using his map, Dekel guided them beneath the Temple Mount to the giant pool he had described.

"We've arrived," he said with satisfaction. "We're standing at the site of the largest water pool under *Har Habayis* — the Black Pool. Its proportions are gigantic. On the last Friday of Ramadan thousands of Moslems will be standing above this spot, praying for Paradise. Well, we'll help them get there quicker than they might ever expect."

Right now, the pool was lit with fluorescent lighting that Dekel had prepared beforehand. As the group waited expectantly for the signal to start drilling, Dekel drew Akiva Tamiri aside to confer with him privately. He was not afraid of being overheard: the small generator that supplied the electricity for the lights was making enough noise to drown out his voice. The tunnel walls muffled the generator from the world outside.

Akiva Tamiri glowed with pride at this sign of Dekel's favor. Dekel, it seemed, had taken him aside in order to teach him a passage from history.

"Akiva, I want you to understand what's involved here. The Moslems, led by the Caliph Omar, captured Jerusalem some 1300 years ago, in the year 638. They turned immediately to the Temple Mount, to the *Even Hashesiyah* which, according to their tradition, contains the secrets of the Creation. They dug around the huge stone — it measures 17 by 13 meters — and exposed it in its entirety.

"Fifty-three years later, in the year 691, the ruler of Jerusalem, Abd el Malik, built a lavish structure on top of the rock. He called it *Kuvat-a-Tzachkrah* — the 'Dome of the Rock.' The building was meant to demonstrate respect for the rock. It was not originally intended for prayer.

"Only later did the place become a mosque. The popular name, 'Mosque of Omar,' is misleading: it's neither a mosque nor was it built by the Caliph Omar. But this is the third most important site in the Islamic world, after Mecca and Medina. This is exactly where we must strike."

Akiva watched him, waiting for the point of this homily. It was not long in coming. "Akiva, the *geulah* can only come if we eradicate this mosque! The world is becoming more sophisticated every day. Computers, and especially the internet, are wrapping up the world like a spider's web. Supersonic planes can cross the world at unbelievable speeds — 2.5 Mack, or two and a half times the speed of sound! Man has traveled into outer space. Intelligent robots are poised to leave the factories and run our lives for us."

Akiva was shaking violently. This vision of the 21st century induced in him overwhelming terror. He longed for the days when electricity and telephones had not existed, when there were no cars or superhighways — a Biblical world that moved slowly, a world where water was drawn from wells and flocks of sheep roamed the hills and fields. Dekel continued to speak, playing on Akiva's fears. "Soon everything will be computerized. The instant your son is born in the hospital, they'll map out his brain with an electronic laser. There won't be a drop of individuality or privacy left. Ultraviolent rays will track us everywhere.

"The hole in the ozone layer is growing larger every day," Dekel went on. "The globe is warming every year. The North and South Poles are melting. Great big chunks of ice — 300 kilometers across — have broken off from the Poles and have floated into the open sea. The whole world may be covered in ice one day — if we don't burn up first from the global warming!"

Akiva's eyes bulged in their sockets. It was hard for him to breathe. Dekel leaned closer, whispering, "Do you want that to happen?"

"No. No! I can't stand it — Dekel, tell me what to do."

"Blow up the mosque," Dekel whispered. "The logic is simple: the mosque is destroyed, we build a new *Beis Hamikdash*, and the *Mashiach* comes! That will mark the end of electricity's rule. No more planes, telephones, or computers. The unholy internet will vanish. A couple of volcanoes in the Philippines will explode, cooling off the globe. The hole in the ozone layer will contract. The breakup of the Polar icecap will stop. Hashem will rule the world — and you're His messenger!"

"B-but how can I blow up the mosque? Bombs are modern weapons, and I like only natural ones. Give me a match, and I'll *burn* the mosque down!"

"Matches are also a modern invention," Dekel said urgently. "Better to take two flint stones and rub them together. "

"Excellent!" Akiva enthused. "Where can I find flint stones?"

Dekel sighed. "Akiva, can't you overlook your principles just this once? Just once! Afterwards, you'll have the world exactly as you like it

— no electricity. No one will ever be electrocuted to death again, as your poor father was. It will be a wonderful world, filled with flowers and butterflies, waterfalls and birds. Akiva, we'll live the way our forefathers did — Avraham, Yitzchak, and Yaakov."

"That sounds good," Akiva said, his face shining. He glanced at his friends, who were testing out the air drills. "Just a second. If there's to be an explosion, why do we need to peel back the layers of stone?"

"I told you. Right above us, tens of thousands of Moslem worshipers will gather on Friday. We'll drop them into the hole. But you'll have the most important job, Akiva. You will destroy the Mosque of Omar. The center of gravity is located in the Well of Winds."

"The Well of Winds?"

"Directly underneath the Mosque of Omar, in a straight line from the *Even Hashesiyah*, there's a large cave. It's over seven meters long, 1.40 meters wide, and 2.60 meters high. Its ceiling is natural stone, but the floor is lined with slabs of marble. Listen closely, now. Underneath that marble is a deep hole that the Arabs call the 'Well of Winds.' Understand? There are three levels. The mosque is on top, the cave is underneath, and the Well of Winds under that.

"On Friday, at 4 a.m., you will stand by the locked gate of the *Kosel* tunnels. A friend of mine will open the gate from inside and lead you directly to the Well of Winds. There, you will activate the timer on the detonator, leave the tunnel, and return to Anafim. An hour later, you'll hear on the news that the Mosque of Omar is no more."

The Friends of the Mikdash were restless. There was an air of mingled fear and anticipation among the group at the Black Pool. Suddenly, the generator fell silent. The lights went out.

Producing a flashlight, Dekel calmly bent over the generator. The huge hole was silent as a tomb, broken only by the occasional sound of a small stone being dislodged by the men's feet and slipping into puddles. After a few minutes, Dekel brought the generator back to life.

The men activated the air drills. The noise they made, on top of the generator, drowned out all other sound. Yonah Pinter's eyes glowed like coals. They did not merely reflect the artificial lights; they were a source of light in themselves. He passed among the laboring men, clapping them on the shoulder to encourage them. "Friends, you are making history. You are building the third *Beis Hamikdash*." His head held high, he pronounced, "In the Black Pool, I laid the foundation of the third *Beis Hamikdash*!"

The titanium-steel drill bits were sharp and strong, but an hour's backbreaking labor left no more than a small hole in the stone — a hole 30 centimeters deep and a meter and a half wide. Many of the men raised the same troubling question: "At this rate, we won't finish the job in a year!"

Dekel said firmly, "Friends, holiness and impurity are locked in battle right now. Whoever asks questions and sows doubt is only arraying himself on the side of evil."

Yonah Pinter took charge. Smiling mysteriously, he said, "Gentlemen, it has been revealed to me that we are not obligated to do the whole job ourselves. We are only obligated to begin it. Heaven will complete what we start."

The Western Wall plaza was still empty as the men stole out of the tunnels. They piled into a Ford Transit that took them back to Anafim. As they went, Dekel tried to rouse their enthusiasm with rallying words. When he saw that he was speaking to nodding heads and drooping eyes, he, too, fell silent.

◆ ◆ ◆

While the Israeli security forces had their attention firmly riveted on the smuggled drugs at the Lebanese border, the Syrian air force contributed its bit to the deception. A Russian Komov-50 helicopter lifted off from a military base, cut past the Lebanese mountains, and crossed into Syrian airspace. For a considerable time the helicopter flew over Syrian deserts, heading always southward, toward Jordan. After crossing the Jordanian border, it veered west and continued until it reached the eastern side of the northern Dead Sea. The helicopter landed on the yellow sand in a temporary circle of flares. The hills of Moab rose to the east, their peaks piercing the night.

The helicopter door opened, and out stepped Arkady Bogdanov and Yusuf Abu Rabia. Two powerfully built Syrian soldiers quickly unloaded the green lead barrel, which had been strapped onto the helicopter floor. In silence, the soldiers retreated from the barrel and hurried back into the helicopter, which lifted off for its trip back to Syria.

"That's it," Arkady sighed with relief as he watched it go. "The baby birds are finally nearing the nest. All we have to do is cross this water, and it'll all be over."

Abu Rabia eyed the barrel. "Both bombs are in there?"

"Both."

The other man was incurably suspicious. "Can I have a look?"

Arkady dismissed the request with a wave of his hand. "You know nothing about atomics. What will you see? Two black attache cases, nothing more. But the power that's hidden in them — " He chuckled. "Save yourself the pleasure for when one of them explodes."

Abu Rabia's communicator crackled into life. "We're coming for you in three minutes."

The Palestinian Authority had delegated three of its policemen in a jeep to provide them with safe passage. The jeep collected them exactly three minutes later and drove them — and their lethal cargo — to the edge of the east bank, where a motorboat, engine muffled, awaited them. In silence, the boat cut through the Dead Sea waters from east to west.

As they drew closer to the Israeli side, at Kalia, the policemen's nervousness grew. They gazed at the far shore through infrared binoculars. "The Israeli army has a command post on the Kalia beach," Yusuf explained to Arkady. "If they sense our approach, the whole operation will be down the drain. But they won't sense us," he hastened to add, at Arkady's panic-stricken expression. "We're far away, and the post is manned by reserve soldiers long on fatigue and short on training."

The boat brought them cautiously in to the shoreline. The transfer of the barrel was executed smoothly and in total silence. P.A. police vans waited to whisk them away. Ten minutes after touching land, there remained no sign of their presence.

The barrel and the scientist, together with Yusuf Abu Rabia and the

Palestinian police, reached a safe house in Jericho before the first hint of dawn touched the sky.

◆ ◆ ◆

"So, you've recovered from the flu?" Uzi Saraf asked, his tone sarcastic. Yoni Dor waved a dismissive hand, but Uzi grasped it in midair, pumping it earnestly. "Sorry, Yoni. What we all need now is perfect trust and honesty. Otherwise we'll all just flounder in the mud — as I gather the GSS and the police have been doing in Lebanon."

Yoni was not quick to forgive. "Look who's talking about honesty and trust! Were you thinking of them when you put flu germs into my coffee on the plane?"

"I'm sorry," Uzi acknowledged. "I was stupidly patriotic. I received an order and I carried it out. Let's return to the present. What happened in Lebanon?"

They had bumped into each other, as though by accident, at the entrance to an expensive Tel Aviv clothing store. Yoni had no way of knowing that Uzi had been following him and had carefully orchestrated the "chance" meeting. Now they were pacing slowly to and fro beneath the shade trees on Rothschild Avenue.

Yoni burned with anger as he remembered the Israelis' futile efforts to capture Arkady Bogdanov in Lebanon. Resting one foot on a bench, he said, "We have exact and reliable information. You know that Gregori Zislin sold the accurate information to Yossi Kaduri, not to you. The police paid him more than the Mossad. We knew the precise day and hour when the Norwegian merchant ship, the *Charlotta Simpaya,* was due in Beirut. Still, we took no chances. A complete network of agents were waiting at every port in Lebanon — in Tsur, in Sidon, in Tripoli. But our boy wasn't there. Can you imagine our frustration? The *Charlotta* arrived at Beirut harbor, but without Arkady Bogdanov or the bombs. We invested millions in the operation, and —"

"The same thing happened to us at the Israeli-Lebanese border," Uzi broke in. Briefly, he described the foiled capture attempt at the border fence. "Someone keeps on fooling us. Everything is spoiled at the last minute. It's as if there's a leak somewhere."

Yoni looked at him. "You suspect someone?" His sudden movement startled the pigeons pecking nearby. They rose with a rush of wings.

"Yes, I do — and how!" Uzi leaned closer and whispered something in Yoni's ear. "I need your help," he said.

"Happy days are here," Yoni said dourly. "Cooperation between the Mossad and the GSS"

"And the police," Uzi insisted. "I need Yossi Kaduri, too."

Later that day, the three agents — so recently divided in competition and animosity — made a pact of friendship for the purpose of destroying their common enemy. He was a tricky enemy, and a sophisticated one, who had succeeded in tripping them up again and again. They were determined to lay a trap for him.

38

Sulimein was in his room on the 16th floor of the Dan Panorama Hotel when the call came.

"This is Crystal," said a familiar voice. Crystal was Yusuf's code name. "The packages are waiting for you."

Sulimein rented a blue Peugeot 306 at the car-rental desk in the hotel. Two hours later, he was passing into Palestinian Authority territory, using his American passport under the name Cliff Dillar. It seemed to him that the Palestinian police winked at him as if they shared a secret.

"Impossible," he told himself. "I'm imagining things."

Sulimein would never have described Jericho as a city. It was more like a small neighborhood in a large city. He drove through dusty streets, lined on each side with architectural ruins. When he reached the main street, he flipped open his cell phone and received further instructions. He drove into a narrow side street, shaded by date palms which provided an air of calm and leisure. Sulimein, in contrast, was coiled tight as a spring, his heart galloping. Nine years of preparation had been leading up to this very moment!

His car passed a row of small shops that had urns and clay drums in the windows. He counted the shops and parked in front of the fourth one. "Go into the fourth shop on the left," Yusuf Abu Rabia had instructed. "Ask for a glass of cold water. The shopkeeper will invite you inside. Cross through the store and open a brown door at the back. We'll be waiting."

Sulimein did as he'd been told. Opening the brown door, he found Abu Rabia waiting inside, as he'd promised. He wasn't alone. There were four others present: a giant of a man with a bulldog face and highly aggressive manner; a man of about 40 who strongly resembled Yusuf; a spectacled older man with Slavic features who had a nervous habit of raking his fingers through his thinning hair; and a pleasant-faced man with the benevolent air of a trusted family doctor.

The small table was covered with glasses, bottles of soft drink, platters of dates and ripe bananas, bowls of chocolates, and honey-dipped cakes bursting with cinnamon and nuts.

"Help yourself," the giant told Sulimein. "Eat while you can, you won't be around much longer." His evil laughter echoed through the room.

"This spread is all in your honor," Yusuf told Sulimein. He stood up, clasped the younger man's hand warmly, and planted a kiss on his cheek. "Sulimein, my brother. The greatest *shahid* of them all! The eyes of the whole Arab world are raised to you today. No, no, don't be afraid — no one knows a thing. But soon, every Arab nation will be proud of you. Your name will be etched in letters of gold on every Koran, next to those of Mohammed and the Caliph Omar."

Sulimein shrugged lightly. He was too tense and too choked with emotion to speak.

"Let me introduce you," Yusuf continued, gesturing at the four men with him. "They have come here especially to meet you. This is a great honor for us all." He pointed at the men, one by one. "This is Mahmud Talel Nadir, chief of our unit in Gaza. And this is Faud Halil, one of Hizballah's senior men. The man standing next to him is my brother, Issam Abu Rabia. The Israelis would give a fortune to get their hands on him. His cover name is 'Gray Cap.' He was a grocer in Gaza until I drafted him into

Operation Lightning and Thunder. Issam, how long have you been waiting for this moment?"

"An eternity," Issam said, seizing Sulimein's hand and kissing it reverently. He pointed at the dark circles under his eyes. "For a week now, I haven't been sleeping from excitement. I was waiting for the chance to kiss the hand of the man who will realize the Arab dream."

"And this," Yusuf ended, "is Gray Cap's prime draftee — Professor Arkady Bogdanov."

"The Israelis are dying to meet me," Arkady grinned. "Some of them would pay more for the chance to be standing here in your place than they would for Issam!"

"Arkady is a modest man," Yusuf said. "He isn't telling you who he is. Well, I will tell you. Arkady, among his other jobs, has served as a KGB agent, as a senior nuclear scientist, and as administrator of a nuclear reactor in Russia. He is the one responsible for bringing those two atom bombs here." He pointed at a corner of the room.

Sulimein turned his head. A pair of black attache cases sat on the floor in the corner. "How long I've waited for this," he whispered, and hoped that the others present would not notice the weakness that overcame him suddenly. He found his way to an armchair and pretended to study the cases with interest. But Yusuf Abu Rabia had sharp eyes. He came over with a glass of cold raspberry drink. "What's the matter?" he asked, bending over Sulimein in concern. "Why are you so pale?"

With an effort, Sulimein pulled himself to his feet. "It's just excitement — and joy. I have no strength to wait any more. When do I go into action?"

"Not so fast," Issam Abu Rabia, or Gray Cap, spoke for the first time. "We have to wait for the green light."

"That won't be long," his brother put in. "I spoke with Daoud Abu Nimar. Their portion of the operation will go forward on the day after tomorrow." He turned to Arkady. "Professor — explanations, please."

"Stand back," Arkady ordered hoarsely. Slowly, he approached the black cases.

The other men took a rapid and fearful step backward. Arkady broke into mocking laughter. "You fell into a fool's trap. First of all, if one of those should explode, there would be no difference between this room and a room 30 miles away. Everything would be equally destroyed. Secondly, the bombs are not yet armed. And, third, I can't simply open these cases. There is a double-delay mechanism, and half an hour's wait before they open."

"So we'll wait half an hour," Issam said.

"There's no need to wait. There's no need to open the cases," Arkady laughed again. "All the instructions are right here. I will ask the rest of you to leave now so that I can instruct Sulimein, with precision. All except for you, Talel Nadir. You stay."

"Me?" Talel pulled himself up, conscious of the honor.

"Yes, you," Yusuf thundered. "When you grow up, you'll understand."

They filed out into the street, leaving Arkady, Sulimein, and Talel Nadir poring over the instruction manual. "This is the fuse," Arkady explained, showing Sulimein a picture of a cigarlike cylinder with a diameter of three centimeters. "In professional terms, it's an activating cylinder with a plutonium core. The core is surrounded by tiny detonators, giving us a bomb within a bomb. Incidentally, the bomb is equipped with a double relay, in case of primary relay failure. When the tiny detonators explode, they set off a chain reaction. In order to arm the bomb, you have to insert the red 'cigar' into this hole. The instant you do that, this innocent-looking attache case is transformed into a destroying angel."

"And what is this?" Sulimein asked, heart pounding like a drum.

"This is the digital activating mechanism. When you press this blue button that says 'ENTER,' the mechanism is activated. Think well before pressing that button: it's irreversible. Press — and explode."

"Immediately?" Talel asked, his breathing rapid and shallow.

"No. You have a four-minute delay, time enough to close the case and leave. It's a pointless exercise. Where can you run in four minutes? But you people are suicide bombers — *shahids.* A *shahid* is ready to lay down his life for an ideal, no?"

"I'm not the *shahid,*" Talel shrilled. "He is!" He pointed a finger at Sulimein.

"True," Sulimein smiled proudly. "This attache case will take me straight to Paradise." His face darkened. "Just a minute. What about the delay factor in opening the case? That'll hold me back."

"Tomorrow, after I leave the country, at 3 p.m., you will receive a message from me. The messenger will give you the codes for these time-delay locks. The first one entails a wait of 10 minutes, the second 20 minutes."

"A long time," Sulimein remarked.

"Such a short time," Talel said, white as a ghost.

Arkady said, "Sulimein, remember this. Half an hour's wait, and you will possess power like that of the President of the United States — or maybe even greater. He gives orders to others, while you operate alone. He holds a briefcase with codes and buttons for activating nuclear warheads; you hold live ammunition in your hand. Life — and death.

"Remember, Sulimein: from the instant you arm the bomb — four minutes to explosion!"

◆ ◆ ◆

Anafim, Friday, 3 a.m.

At 3 a.m. on Friday morning, Dekel woke Akiva Tamiri. "Akiva, wake up. It's late."

Akiva's eyes flew open, wide and bewildered. "What happened?"

"Have you forgotten? You're going to the *Kosel* now. Go immerse yourself in the spring and purify yourself for the great mitzvah you'll be performing today."

Akiva slipped out of bed. "The Well of Winds, the explosion — It's going to be an interesting day." He got ready quickly and strode down the dirt path to the spring.

Shivering, he emerged from the water some minutes later. He had begun to pull on his clothes when a whisper came from behind. "Pssst!"

Sruly Egozi was waiting for him in the dark. Akiva had never seen him so excited. "Akiva, it's a miracle that I caught you! You're going to the *Kosel?*"

"You scared me," Akiva gasped. "I should throw you into the water."

"Forget that nonsense. You're going to the *Kosel,* right? To the Well of Winds?"

"How did you know?"

Sruly had no patience. "Never mind that. Do me a favor. I want to give you a *kvittel* to put into the Wall. Mention my name at the *Kosel, daven* for me." He handed Akiva a small, brown-paper-wrapped package. "Hide this so Dekel won't see."

"What is it?" Akiva was astonished. "A little heavy for a *kvittel.*"

Sruly cracked his knuckles nervously, scratched behind his ear, tugged at a lock of his hair. "Akiva, don't ask questions. It's a surprise. You'll see, it'll be worth it."

"A surprise? I'm opening it now."

"No, no!" Sruly was adamant. "The surprise has to stay secret until you get to the *Kosel.*"

"Great!" Akiva's eyes shone. "I love surprises. By the way, how did you know about the Well of Winds?"

Sruly blurted, "When you read it you'll understand. Don't tell Dekel you saw me." He turned in the direction of the yeshivah dormitory, stealthy as a cat. Akiva hid the small package in his *tefillin* bag and walked down to the road. As he entered the car, Dekel noted Akiva's damp hair with approval. "Excellent. It's important to immerse in a *mikveh* before doing an important mitzvah. Have you brought the *tallis* and your *tefillin*?"

"They're right here." Akiva wanted to tell Dekel about his meeting with Sruly and the surprise Sruly had prepared for him, but something made him swallow the words.

"Wonderful," Dekel smiled. "As we said, you'll sneak into the Well of Winds, put on the *tallis* and *tefillin,* and press the delayed-activation button — just like the *Tanna'im,* the *Amora'im,* all the greats throughout the generations."

Dekel let Akiva out near the Dung Gate at 3:45. After watching him disappear through the gate, Dekel drove on, his laughter echoing through the Silwan Valley.

◆ ◆ ◆

Akiva stood by the Western Wall. The place was nearly deserted at this hour. "A minute here, no more," he told himself. Dekel's friend would be opening the gate for him in just a few minutes.

But before anything else, the *kvittel* and the surprise. At last he was alone and could open the package. He was bursting with curiosity! He unzipped his *tefillin* bag and felt the package. It was too hard to be just paper. Carefully, he ripped open the wrapping. In the palm of his hand, wrapped in several layers of paper, lay a tiny tape recorder with wire earphones.

"What?" Akiva's face twisted in revulsion. "This is the surprise? Sruly wanted to make me mad. He's giving an electronic tape recorder to *me?* I'll break it right now!"

Then his eye fell on the long note Sruly had included in the package. Curious, Akiva began to read.

"Akiva, forgive me. I had to find indirect ways to reach you. There was no choice — I had to be careful around that murderer, Dekel."

Murderer? What was Sruly babbling about?

"Akiva, don't be surprised by my harsh words. Yes, Dekel is a murderer. He is not a ger tzedek, as he pretends to be, but a Palestinian terrorist whose hands are red with Jewish blood. He never converted. Yonah Pinter is naive, and Dekel leads him around by the nose. He is ready to kill you, too. If you enter the Well of Winds you'll never come out alive. You'll press the button, activate the delay mechanism of a powerful bomb — two-and-a-half tons — that the Wakf hid there with the help of the Palestinian Authority. Do you remember Dekel talking about an 'earthquake'? He was referring to this big bomb, which will create an effect like an earthquake. Do you want to cause that to happen?

"When you try to leave the Well of Winds you'll find you can't, because it will be locked from the outside. You'll be stuck inside until the bomb goes off and puts an end to your life. The bomb is meant to destroy the Mosque of Omar, wholly or partially, at noon. Today is Friday, the last day of Ramadan, when 200,000 Moslems will be praying in the mosque. The bombing will incite the entire Arab world against Israel in a holy war of revenge. The Hizballah, and their masters in Iran, have been planning this provocation for a long time now — an excuse for the Arab world to rise up and destroy the State of Israel. Dekel was the one who built up the Friends of the Mikdash. He was the charmer who gathered in all the snakes with his magic flute.

"He insisted that you wear tallis and tefillin in the Well of Winds. Why? It's simple. When they find the body of the 'terrorist' who destroyed the mosques and killed tens of thousands of Moslem worshipers on the Temple Mount, there will be not even a shadow of a doubt that he was a Jew.

"Now you can understand how Dekel knows so much about the secret places under the Temple Mount, and who is opening all the gates for him, and why he didn't mind the noise we made drilling. His friends in the Moslem Wakf have been helping him all along. We followed, like sheep to the slaughter.

"If you're still not convinced — play the tape I've sent along. I know that you hate electricity and electrical appliances, but your life is your most precious possession."

Akiva hurriedly wrapped himself in his *tallis* and leaned against the *Kosel* in utter confusion. With trembling fingers, under cover of the *tallis*, he placed the earphones in his ears and pressed the "Play" button on the recorder. His heart was slamming in his chest like a machine gun.

"Hello, Akiva." It was an unfamiliar voice. "This is Eli Flamm, from Yeshivas Aish Aharon. We met in the yeshivah on the night you provided us with a total blackout, remember? Sruly Egozi is my friend. You can trust him. I planted him in the Friends of the Mikdash because I had my suspicions of Dekel. In the following recording, you will hear two people speaking together in Arabic. You'll hear Dekel speaking with his contact, a man by the name of Issam Abu Rabia. You'll certainly recognize Dekel's voice. In order to understand what they're saying, you'll hear my own translation as well. Here goes —"

His face as still as the stones on which he leaned, Akiva listened to the taped conversation. He did recognize Dekel's voice. The other voice was deeper and slightly raspy.

Dekel: Listen, Issam, everything's in place. On Friday noon the bomb will go off.

Issam: How powerful?

Dekel: Two and a half tons of plastic explosive. Our Wakf friends worked hard and prepared something nice and big, just like you asked.

Issam: Ah, I'm afraid to face Mohammed. He will ask me, Issam Abu Rabia, why did you destroy my mosque?

Dekel: Mohammed will forgive us. A building can be rebuilt, but an entire state — no!

Issam: Who will activate the bomb?

Dekel: The crazy kid who hates electricity, I told you about him. His name's Akiva Tamiri. I've never met a bigger fool. I managed to convince him to wear a tallis and tefillin for the job. Get it? Just think of the horrible pictures in every newspaper in the world: the mosque in ruins, a hundred thousand corpses or more, but the Well of Winds below still intact. There they'll find the bomber's body — a Jew wrapped in his tallis and tefillin. It'll be a fine photo opportunity. The world will certainly understand if we respond very harshly to the Jewish violence!

Issam: Even with atomic weapons?

Dekel: Even with atomic weapons. The Christians want to be rid of the Jewish state as much as we do; we're just more daring. The countries of the world will stand in line to thank us....

Akiva trembled like a leaf. It was completely unbelievable! Dekel's voice was unmistakable. Akiva was able to identify the exact Arabic words that derided him so mockingly. *I've fallen into a trap, like the world's biggest fool,* he thought. *Or rather, I haven't fallen. Sruly Egozi has saved me.*

But where to go now? He had nowhere to go. Back at Anafim, Dekel would be waiting.

He quickly divested himself of his *tallis* and stumbled drunkenly away from the Wall. For two hours he walked the Jerusalem streets, trying to make up his mind what to do. He did not want to betray his companions in the Friends of the Mikdash, but he did want to rescue them from Dekel's clutches. He climbed up Jaffa Street, passed Davidka Square. By the time he was standing opposite the Machaneh Yehudah police station, a resolve had formed in his heart.

◆ ◆ ◆

The Western Wall Plaza, Friday, 7 a.m.

At 7 o'clock in the morning, Eli and Judy stood on the steps overlooking the Western Wall plaza. "Let's soak up the atmosphere for a couple of minutes," Eli said. "Prayer is completely different when you stop and think about Who you're about to daven to. The early chassidim would wait a full hour before beginning their davening."

Judy gazed out over the broad expanse to the *Kosel,* waiting impatiently for the longed-for reunion with those venerable stones. She carried a small *Tehillim* which she reserved specifically for special occasions such as this. It was the *Tehillim* that her father had given to her brother Shlomo, just a short while before the tragedy in India.

Eli wanted to prepare himself for *tefillah,* but he found himself too tense to concentrate properly. He cast repeated glances at the top of the Wall, beyond which stood the mosques. Judy turned to him at last with a gentle smile. "Eli, I would have liked to hear your new song again, to feel the way I did the first time I heard it. Too bad you didn't bring along your violin."

Eli was silent. There was nothing further from his mind at the moment than the desire to sing. Fervently, he hoped that Akiva Tamiri liked surprises, that he had read Sruly's letter and been persuaded to listen to the tape. He prayed that Akiva had not entered the *Kosel* tunnels. One hope infused his entire being: Maybe, if the planned-for provocation did not take place — if the mosques were not destroyed — then the nuclear revenge would be put aside. There was too much depending on a pair of earphones —

"You look worried," Judy said. "What are you thinking about?"

"I don't really know," Eli answered evasively. "I guess we can go down to the *Kosel* now."

As they began to traverse the plaza toward the Wall, a young man crossed their path. He was blond and blue eyed, wearing a green polo shirt and khaki pants. His right hand carried a black attache case. For some reason Judy could not explain, she watched him walk over to the steps leading up to the Temple Mount and slowly begin to climb.

He lifted his head to observe the plaza below. Judy's blood froze. The earth seemed to open up under her feet. Where was Penina when she needed her? Those eyes were even more frightening now — no longer blazing with hate, but simply cold and menacing as ice.

It was the young man from the plane. The terrorist.

39

The Western Wall Plaza, Friday, 7 a.m.

"That's him!" Judy whispered agitatedly. Her forehead was bathed in perspiration, her hands clenched into tight fists.

"Who?" Eli asked.

"The terrorist who boarded our plane in France. The one I told you about."

Eli had listened — albeit dismissively — to Judy's description of her fellow passenger, and her account of Penina's diagnosis. In his opinion, if every young man who appeared angry or frustrated was to be labeled a terrorist, the prisons would soon be bursting at the seams.

Now, he suddenly was not so sure. The threads came abruptly together in his mind. This was the exact scenario that his father had described in his memo — the link between the Temple Mount and the nuclear bomb in Tel Aviv. Maybe that man *was* a terrorist — the terrorist assigned to scout out the scene of the upcoming provocation: the destruction of mosques. The provocation that would justify Arab nuclear retaliation — Eli had been wondering what his next step should be, and here was the answer, walking right up to him on two feet!

He studied the young man climbing the stairs to the Western Wall plaza. Even at a distance of several yards, he was struck by the intensity of the other man's eyes. The army checkpoint at the top of the stairs would not prove much of a challenge to a determined terrorist; the bored Israeli soldier in the little booth, busy fixing an electrical extension cord with the aid of a nail clipper, did not strike Eli as Israel's answer to the worst threat it had ever known — if, indeed, the man on the steps was the terrorist Eli suspected him to be.

As the stranger climbed closer to him, Eli peered again into his face. There was a stab of recognition — a painful stab. "That's impossible. I can't know him."

Judy was thinking the same thing. Her legs felt glued to the ground and her heart hammered with fear, but something about the frightening young man was strangely familiar, and she didn't have a clue as to what it might be.

Judy glanced at her brother. Both turned again to look at the approaching stranger, who became aware at that moment of the two young Jews gazing openly at him. He, too, felt suddenly that he'd seen them somewhere before.

"Very strange," Eli murmured. "Do you see what I'm seeing?"

Judy said slowly, "That man, in a slightly different version, could be you..."

Their eyes met again in a long, appraising glance. All three pairs were blue-green, framed with thick dark lashes. Eli and Judy exchanged a quick, incredulous look. Together, in a single voice that echoed across the plaza, they cried, "*Shlomo!*

It was a surrealistic scene, something out of a different dimension, a different planet. The young man froze in place for an instant, eyes darting in panic. Then he recovered himself. Looking past Eli and Judy as if they were made of air, he sprinted toward a twisting lane leading to the crowded Arab shuk.

Eli and Judy followed at a distance. "I've got to talk to him," Eli muttered. The young man's steps slowed as he entered the shuk. At a small perfume booth, at which bottles of scent were arrayed to tempt buyers, he paused. To the followers' astonishment, he began sniffing at the bottles, one by one.

"What's he doing?" Judy asked. The drifting fragrances were prodding a memory — the memory of some terrible experience, buried deep in her bones.

But Eli was no longer standing beside her. He covered the distance between himself and the other, who whirled around to face him.

"What do you want?" he demanded.

"I know who you are, and I have to talk to you," Eli whispered into his ear.

The young man stepped back, nearly losing his balance. Throwing some money down on the shopkeeper's table, he grabbed a bottle of lavender and plunged rapidly into the heart of the shuk. From time to time he looked back over his shoulder, his face the picture of confusion. The cold, metallic gleam had disappeared from his eyes. Eli hurried after him.

Judy did her best to keep up, but they were walking too quickly for her. Was it really possible that her brother, Shlomo, who had vanished without a trace in India 13 years before, had suddenly resurfaced in Jerusalem's Old City? A moment earlier, Judy had been calling him a terrorist; now she thought he was her long-lost brother. It was enough to blow her mind.

They had lost Shlomo in the Amritsar marketplace; now they were pursuing someone who might be Shlomo in Jerusalem's Arab marketplace. Was the resemblance anything other than coincidence? Judy panted for breath as she ran after Eli. The two young men were no more than two meters apart, striding through the crowded shuk, bumping into people they passed in the narrow lanes.

The differences between them were obvious. One wore a dark suit and white shirt, *peyos* tucked behind his ears and *tzitzis* dangling from his belt. The other wore a green polo shirt and a sports jacket, jeans, and sneakers. But beyond these surface details, the similarities were startling. Their foreheads were alike, and their noses, mouths, and the color of their hair. It was the same face — except for the expression, which in Eli was sweet and in the other embittered. Both had the same lanky legs and long stride. Most of all, they had the same eyes. All the Flamm children had those eyes.

These days, it was possible to prove blood relationship through genetic testing. She would approach him with a needle, saying, "Excuse me, would you mind donating a little blood so that we'll know whether or not you're our brother Shlomo, whom we've missed so much for 13 years?"

No, she couldn't do that. She could not realistically approach him with a needle — but she *could* approach him.

She broke into a run and darted ahead of him, blocking his way.

"Excuse me," he said politely, moving to his right. But Judy stood her ground, gazing intently into his eyes. Now she was sure.

"Shlomo! You're Shlomo Flamm!" she said emotionally. "It's me — your sister, Judy! I was only 8 when you got lost in the marketplace at Amritsar. And that's Eli — your twin!"

The young man's eyes nearly bulged out of their sockets. He rubbed his head as though a sledgehammer had just fallen on it, looking at Judy and Eli in turns. "What? It's not possible!" he muttered in English, apparently to himself.

Eli moved slowly closer. "It *is* possible," he said shakily. "This is no mistake."

The other's lips trembled and his eyes grew damp and overbright. "Impossible," he said again. "You're dead. You're not really them — just their souls. The devil sent you to get in my way." He waved his hands as though to erase their image from his vision.

"We're real," Eli whispered. "We're very much alive. You can pinch yourself a thousand times, and you won't find any other reality. We've finally found our lost brother."

The other young man shook his head from side to side, and said,

"Mullah Ibn al Hunod warned me that the devil would try to stop me at the last minute. Here, he's doing it now."

He began walking very quickly, leaving Eli and Judy gaping after him.

"Shlomo, don't run away from us!" Judy wailed. She ran after him with all her strength. "Shlomo, don't go! We've waited for you for so many years. We've worried about you, *davened* for you, dreamed about you day and night. Benjy, in New York, Eli, Dovy, Moishy, and me. We're all alive. Come back to us!"

Eli closed in on his other side, also on the verge of tears. "Shlomo, what have they done to you? Don't you recognize me? We're flesh and blood. I'm Eli, your twin brother!"

The other stopped. For a moment he wavered, confused and exhausted. Eli and Judy came cautiously nearer. Around them the shuk scrambled and bustled noisily, leaving the trio to form an island of silent suspense. Then, without warning, the young man broke into a run, wheeling off to the right into one of the side streets leading to the Christian Quarter of the Old City. Eli dashed after him, calling, urgently, "Shlomo, come back to us! We'll be waiting for you at a settlement called Anafim. Remember the name — Anafim. It's on the road to Tel Aviv."

The young man disappeared into a tangle of courtyards and clotheslines. With bowed head, Eli trudged back to the Jewish Quarter. He said not a word to Judy, and she asked no questions. Together they returned to the *Kosel* to *daven.* Judy found her thanksgiving prayers tinged by a deep bitterness. Shlomo had disappeared again, like an illusion she could never grasp.

As for Eli, he was suffering from more than just disappointment. He was consumed by a despairing anxiety such as he had never known. The young man who might be his brother had been holding a long black attache case in his hand — a case he had never for a instant let out of his grasp. Even when buying the bottle of lavender scent, he had kept one hand on the case.

In a flash of understanding, Eli knew what that attache case contained. He prayed from the depths of his heart that his brother would turn around before it was too late — that the flicker of a bond that Eli and Judy had tried to forge with him just now would be fanned into a flame before tragedy struck.

◆ ◆ ◆

Jerusalem, Friday, 8 a.m.

He left the Old City from the other side and walked for a long time through the quiet Jerusalem streets. Though the night's cold still lingered, the sidewalks were bathed with the golden sunlight of early morning. The Peugeot was waiting for him in the parking lot. He slipped behind the wheel and picked up his cell phone.

"Yusuf — Sulimein here. I'm in the center of town now. Is everything all right?... What? I know — you sent two people after me, but I brushed them off.... I'm not agitated, just very angry. I asked you not to send people to watch over me. I know exactly what to do. They trained me for years to be ready for this moment. If you want the operation to succeed you're going to have to let me operate in peace. I know how to guard the briefcase. Everything will go smoothly. I'm just waiting for your signal."

As he cut off the connection, he saw that his hands were shaking. Yusuf was right — he *was* agitated. How could it be? Eli and Judy, alive... Eli, my twin brother... Judy, my sweet little sister. The last time I saw you, you were a little girl. But they're alive — there's no doubt about that. Those eyes! Those unique, Flamm family eyes....

Impossible, he thought sadly. For 13 years he had known they were dead. The Sikhs had shot at the car and killed the whole family. No one had been left alive.

Sitting in his rented Peugeot, he bowed his head over the steering wheel and wept. For 13 years he had been suffering for his sin, every hour of every day. If only he could know for sure that they had lied to him! If he knew that they had all remained alive: Eli, Judy, Dovy, Moishy. And Benjy? Had he gone insane, as they'd told him? Or — or had they tricked him about Benjy, too?

How he longed for them all. Thirteen years had passed since that family trip to India had ended in tragedy in the Amritsar marketplace.

Amritsar, India, 1983

Shlomo got out of the car and ran along the main street. He knew that his mother had ordered him not to leave the car until she and Abba returned. As a rule, Shlomo was neither wild nor impatient. But, of all the Flamm children, he was the most sensitive, and the most closely bound to his mother. He was an adult in a child's body, delicate and introverted, thoughtful and quiet, intelligent and full of feeling. He was afraid of being a boy who was "tied to his mother's apron strings," and he made every effort to hide his feelings so that no one would make fun of him. But beneath the surface, his emotions led an active life. Only his mother knew the depths of his attachment to her. She could read it in the intensity of the child's large, wise eyes.

"Okay," he thought. "I already passed the place where we saw them last." He stopped at the mouth of an alley lined with fragrant oils and perfumes. Cautiously, he entered, head moving left and right without pause. The gloomy alley was completely empty.

"Where could they have gone?" He was frightened. The Sikh demonstration, which Abba had gone to study at closer range for the State Department, was taking place some hundred meters away, near the locked gates of the Golden Temple. Could his parents be there?

Retracing his steps to the top of the alley, he peeked out into the main street. He saw hundreds of impassioned Sikh extremists listening to a speech being delivered by a hoarse man in a turban. Every few seconds, the speaker would chant a slogan that sounded to the boy's ears like "Gunda la hunda," and the crowd would erupt in a raucous echo.

"Well, I won't find them there," Shlomo decided, and ran back to the farther end of the alley, ears still ringing from the chanting outside. Suddenly, he caught the sounds of a scuffle. His eyes widened in horror as he took in what was happening. The thunderous crowd outside had distracted the local police, drawing all their attention and providing two men with complete freedom of action.

Abba and Ima stood in a hidden corner of the marketplace, some 50 meters from where Shlomo cowered. Their hands were tied, their faces drained of color and covered with a deathly fear. Abba's hat had been knocked off and his hair was standing on end. His glasses had rolled into the dust, and twisted out of shape. Ima had not been treated with any more respect. Two gargantuan Sikhs stood over them with threatening expressions, guns in hand. Shlomo saw his father, a man who wouldn't hurt a fly, plead for his life: "What do you want from me? I haven't done anything to you. Free us, and we won't call the police, I promise."

Shlomo stood frozen, his eyes wide and unblinking. It was a scene out of a nightmare. "What are you waiting for, Shlomo?" he thought, as though in a dream. As happens often in dreams, his legs refused to move, refused to carry him to the place where he was needed. "Run and help Abba and Ima!"

But the words had no power to make him move. His own thoughts were as unreal as the rest of the dream. He was paralyzed.

Then he heard his mother scream, "No, no! We have children. Don't shoot!"

The rest was a merciful blank.

◆ ◆ ◆

When he came to several hours later, he found himself lying on the floor of a dim room. A dense fog surrounded him. He wanted nothing more than to bury himself in its depths.

As he became more fully awake, he began to remember what had happened outside the Golden Temple. Shlomo opened his mouth to scream, when footsteps reached his ear from the courtyard. He pulled himself up to the window and peeked outside. What he saw cast into shadow even the terrible scene he had witnessed in the marketplace.

The two Sikhs had been busy — digging a couple of large holes. They flung two bodies into the holes, covered them quickly with dirt, and loaded several cartons onto the fresh graves in the courtyard.

Crouched by the window, Shlomo wept silently. Any minute now, he was certain, they would come for him. His grave would be dug next. Some time later, still sobbing, he fell asleep.

When he awoke, he heard voices in the next room. The boy was not quite sure if they were human voices.

"What do we do with the kid?" one voice asked.

"The same thing we did to his parents."

"Are you sure they're his parents?"

"Yes. Said Tarabashi knows what he's talking about."

"Said wants the kid for his brother."

A short silence ensued, followed by the tread of heavy feet. The door opened. To Shlomo's terror, the two men who entered were the same turbaned Sikhs who had held guns to his parents in the market alley — and the same two who had buried them in the courtyard. He screamed, scurrying in fear to a corner of the room. The Sikhs regarded him with small, hard eyes, laughing.

"Where do you think you're running to, boy?" one of them asked in thickly accented English. "We'll catch you in that corner, too."

They moved closer. The taller of the two produced a gun. Shlomo began to tremble uncontrollably from head to toe, positive that his end was near. Then the door opened a second time, to admit an Arab in a red kaffiyeh. Though his walk was youthful and springy, the lines on his face belonged to an older man. A white robe covered him from throat to ankles.

"Rotek, Arjune, leave the boy," he snapped. "He belongs to my brother, Afnadi Golam Tarabashi."

Under his glowering gaze, the two giant Sikhs were transformed into a pair of jellyfish. "We were only j-joking, Said," Rotek stammered.

"Fool!" Said shouted. "Look at him — he's nearly dead of fear. I want to take him to Iran, give him to my brother. You know he has no children. This boy will be his son. A nice-looking boy, with light eyes and pink cheeks. A Western child, the kind Golam likes." He stepped closer to the corner where Shlomo huddled, appraising him. "Come with me. We'll leave these boors who killed your mother and father. We don't have much time — tomorrow you're coming to Iran with me."

He took Shlomo's hand in his own surprisingly gentle one and led him, still trembling, from the room. Outside in the courtyard, he bundled the boy into a long brown cloak and covered his head with a dark cloth turban so that only his eyes peeked out from underneath. Poor Shlomo did not know that the local police and American CIA agents were combing the city for him and his parents. Furtively, he raked the building and courtyard with his eyes, as though committing them to memory.

Said took the boy for a walk among the shade trees, urging the youngster to get some fresh air. After that, Shlomo was returned to his Sikh guards, who were harshly warned not to harm a hair on his head. The guards were afraid of the Arab. Still, he hadn't told them they couldn't tease the boy.

"Why did you get out of the car?" Rotek taunted. "Your parents returned to it and would have driven away, but then they turned back to search for their son, who had left the car. We heard them. They went back to the marketplace, and that's how we caught them."

"But — but *I* went to find *them!*" Shlomo blubbered.

"We followed them. They went back to the car and almost slipped out of our hands. Suddenly, we saw them get out again, all excited because their son was missing. That's how they fell right into our trap." Gloating, Rotek poured salt on the young prisoner's wounds.

Shlomo was bereft of speech. He did not even think of asking why these two had been following his parents in the first place. From time to time, he slipped over to the window and looked for the twin mounds of dirt among the cartons in the courtyard.

The next day, Said Tarabashi took him to Iran. Shlomo left India with a passport that identified him as Sulimein Halil Tarabashi.

40

Golam Tarabashi paid the two Sikhs a fortune for the merchandise they had supplied via his brother, Said. The murder of the American couple and the sale of their son turned Arjune Singh and Rotek Singh into overnight millionaires.

The boy himself did not fare as well. Immediately upon his arrival in Teheran he fell ill, and wavered for several weeks between life and death. The awful adventure in India had broken his spirit. He looked death straight in the eye and did not wish to live any longer. But his body was young and resilient and, with the help of Iranian doctors paid handsomely for their labors by the wealthy Tarabashi, the boy triumphed over the sickness.

When the youngster had recovered enough to be discharged from the "Martyrs of the Revolution" hospital, Golam Tarabashi and his wife, Fatima, took him home. There, they showered him with all the love that 20 years' yearning for children had stored up inside them. Shlomo was officially renamed Sulimein Halil Tarabashi.

He rejected every attempt on the part of his adoptive parents to come close to him. For days at a time he would not speak a word. He stayed shut up in his room, brooding in the dark behind closed shutters.

After half a year of this behavior, Golam and Fatima gave up. They handed Sulimein over to Ibn al Hunod, a mullah, or religious teacher.

Ibn al Hunod was a subtle man. He knew that force would never succeed in winning over the clever Jewish boy. For a long time he treated his charge with cool indifference, taking care only that he eat the minimum required to sustain life. He observed the boy carefully all the time, seeking the chink in his armor. But day after day Shlomo continued to sit, sealed as a stone, in his dark room.

And then, one afternoon, the mullah's luck turned. He found several pages that the boy had written and hidden under his mattress. They were the emotional confessions of a sensitive and brokenhearted child with an unusually developed conscience for his age — a child who blamed himself for his parents' bitter end, and he pleaded for a sign that he was forgiven.

Silently blessing his good fortune, al Hunod carefully returned the pages to their hiding place beneath the mattress.

A week later, a guest appeared in the Hunod home. He wore a large skullcap and introduced himself as Avraham Halevi, an elder of Teheran's Jewish community. Shlomo drank him in with every fiber of his being. He saw a man who behaved as a pious Jew, reminding him sharply of his home. The youngster had no way of knowing that the man was actually a rabidly Jew-hating convert to Islam — or that his feigned piety was no more than an act designed to win Shlomo's trust.

The pretender did not have to try very hard. The very presence of an observant Jew in such a setting was a sign to Shlomo that his prayer had been answered.

"I'm a good friend of the Mullah al Hunod," Halevi explained to Shlomo. "Al Hunod is a good man who wants to help you grow into a healthy human being, despite the tragedy that has befallen you."

For the first time in months, Shlomo spoke. "I want to go home."

Halevi was silent. The following day, at dusk, he took the boy out for a walk. In the course of their talk, Halevi gently broke the news that Shlomo no longer had a home to which to return. The Sikhs, he said, had murdered the entire Flamm family, from the parents down to his youngest brother.

"I want Benjy!" Shlomo sobbed.

"Who's Benjy?"

"My oldest brother. He stayed home in the United States."

Drowning in a sea of hatred and strangeness, Shlomo clung to Halevi as to a life-giving rope. He believed every word the man said. Halevi was quick to take advantage of the situation. In a pain-filled voice, he informed Shlomo two days later that an investigation by the Iranian ambassador to the U.N. had brought to light the sad fact that Benjamin Flamm had become mentally unhinged from grief, and had been admitted to a psychiatric hospital in critical condition.

This was the final blow. Once again, young Shlomo shut himself in his dark room. Weeks passed, then months. Al Hunod continued to observe him secretly and, when the opportunity arose, to search beneath the boy's mattress. A satanic smile played about his lips when he found what he was after. Yet another heavy stone had been added to the penitential necklace hanging from the boy's neck.

"Forgive me, Hashem, for causing the deaths of my family, and for making Benjy go crazy. If only I would have listened to my mother! I would have stayed in the car and they would still be alive." The words were written with his heart's blood. Al Hunod was satisfied. The groundwork had been laid.

The next day, Avraham Halevi paid the mullah, and Shlomo, another visit. In a roundabout way, he succeeded in transmitting the message he had come to deliver: It would be a good thing for Shlomo to befriend the mullah. Al Hunod would heal his broken heart. To prove Al Hunod's goodwill, Shlomo's diet would henceforth be strictly vegetarian, in order to avoid problems of *kashrus.*

The boy was hungry for healing. Halevi's message pierced straight to his core. From that day on, al Hunod began to find his path much smoother. He gave the boy free reign to do more or less as he pleased, and enveloped him with warmth at the right moments. Shlomo was never exposed to anyone from Teheran's Jewish community. His only companions were ayatollahs and mullahs.

From the middle of his twelfth year, Shlomo — who had gradually become accustomed to being called Sulimein — underwent a continual brainwashing by Moslem religious teachers. These men played ceaselessly on his feelings of guilt, honing them into weapons for their own ends. He learned that he was not the only one responsible for his family's deaths. His parents were responsible, too. Their sin had been — their very existence. "The Jewish nation sinned, and that is why their Temple was destroyed," the ayatollahs explained. "There is no atonement for a Jew except through his death."

Al Hunod was a member of Iran's Revolutionary Council. When the question of the destruction of Israel arose, he submitted a proposal that the Jewish boy be trained as a *shahid*. A *nuclear shahid*.

"He looks completely Western, and his state of mind is such that he will believe that the only way to atone for his personal sin, and for that of his people, is by dying along with the rest. What a nice punishment for the Israelis — to have one of their own sons serve as their executioner!"

The ensuing years proved Al Hunod correct. Sulimein received his daily dose of anti-Semitic poison, in the form of diatribes against the State of Israel, the Zionists, and Jews in general. If he resisted such propaganda at first, lengthy exposure to its foul repetition wore the defenseless boy down. After a number of years, he identified completely with the brainwashing, and was selected from among 300 other candidates to become the first nuclear *shahid*.

1996 — Jericho, Friday, 9 a.m.

Yusuf Abu Rabia and Talel Nadir were worried. The men they had sent to shadow Sulimein had phoned to report that Sulimein had shaken them off near the Western Wall plaza.

Talel fumed for a full hour over this news blackout. He was quick to blame Yusuf. "A hole in the plan!" he screamed. "Now you won't get the signal from the Revolutionary Council. Nine years of work, and millions — down the drain!"

They were sitting in the control room of Operation Lightning and Thunder, behind the Jericho pottery shop. Yusuf knew how to quell the mountain of muscle seated opposite him with one cold look, but he preferred to reserve that for a more difficult moment.

"What would you have me do?" he asked pleasantly. Talel, not perceiving the shielded barb in the words, retorted angrily, "I thought you'd hide a microphone or some other gimmick on Sulimein. Where is all your wonder technology? We hardly have two telephones in here!"

Yusuf's eyes were half closed. Resting his feet on the table, he purred, "No technological wonders will help. I can call Mr. Coates in New York, ask him to get his NASA or Defense Department friends to get us an airborne tracking device that can measure nuclear radioactivity in the vicinity of Jerusalem's Old City. I don't suppose there's more than one atom bomb in that area today."

"Then do it — now!" Talel lunged from his seat and went to the phone.

Yusuf sat up. "What I wanted to tell you," he said slowly, "is that no such tracking devices will help. We can't force Sulimein to explode the bomb from 30 kilometers in the air."

"Then what?" Talel pounded his fist on the table.

"We have a much more efficient weapon: Sulimein himself. For nine years we've been grooming him for this moment. He is a programmed creature, from head to toe — not a man, but a robot. Sulimein is locked on target and nothing will deter him from it.

"This telephone" — Yusuf pointed a finger at one of the two instruments that Talel had disparaged a moment before — "is sufficient. One word from me, and Sulimein will activate the bomb. Because that is what he *must* do!"

◆ ◆ ◆

"And you'll be the second one," Yusuf said suddenly to Talel.

"The second what?" Talel asked, startled.

"The second nuclear man — what else? Why do you think you were asked to stay behind with Sulimein? You learned how to activate the bomb."

Yusuf spread a large map of Israel on the table. "Sulimein took nine years of training because he was born a Jew. You, on the other hand, are an Arab from birth. A couple of months should suffice."

"True," Talel said, his face impassive. He was by no means enamored of the idea of becoming a nuclear *shahid*. At the last minute, he decided, he would send his oldest son to Paradise in his place —"What do I have to do?" he asked.

Yusuf studied the map with concentration. "I'm still trying to choose the best location. Right now I'm debating between Yodefat and Moshav Zechariah. Both are good; we'll have to make up our minds where you're to go. At any rate, tomorrow — Friday at noon — the 'Friends of the Mikdash' will blow up the mosques of Omar and El-Aktzah on the Temple Mount, with expected casualties of about 150,000 Moslems. World reaction will be swift and harsh. The Israeli government will be eager to appease and to apologize, but our anger will be too strong. The world will easily forgive whatever we do. We will have full support, a world coalition in essence — even to a nuclear attack on Israel.

"For tactical reasons, we wanted to postpone our revenge for a month, or two weeks — a week, at least — but in the end we decided that the world would be understanding even if we wait no longer than a mere four hours before exacting our revenge. And so, a small atomic bomb will be set off in the heart of Tel Aviv. It will cause widespread destruction — but this, remember, is still the smaller bomb. Once the radioactive cloud has settled, we will present an ultimatum to the State of Israel, or what is left of her: to return to her November 1947 borders. Israel will, of course, refuse. We will then explode the larger, 10-kiloton atomic bomb" — He pointed to the second attache case that Arkady Bogdanov had brought, resting in a corner — "near their nuclear base at Yodefat, or their other base near Moshav Zechariah, which is not far from Beit Shemesh."

"Moshav Zechariah is better," Talel Nadir remarked, smacking his lips with pleasure. "I saw what you wrote in the file you prepared. Zechariah is Israel's central nuclear arsenal. According to experts, there are some 50 Jericho-2 warheads there, in chalk caves. Security is insufficient. Israel, it seems, prefers to invest in the creation of more warheads rather than protect the ones it has."

"That's it exactly." Yusuf's pleasure matched Talel's. The picture of destruction his imagination drew bathed him in an almost physical glow. "International protocol calls for nuclear warheads to be stored in underground bunkers, protected by doors that can withstand a nuclear attack. These do not exist at Moshav Zechariah. According to a report published in the English journal, 'Jane's Intelligence Review,' the storage caves at Zechariah are riddled with cracks and would not stand up to a nuclear attack. Therefore, we will explode our second bomb near that base." Yusuf rubbed his hands together. "Just think of what will happen when 50 nuclear warheads go off at once. Israel will disappear from the map! Nadir, imagine it — Israel no longer exists! And all because of you."

His eyes gleamed with a maniacal light as he lost himself in his fantasy. After a moment, Talel Nadir got up and walked quietly from the room. Yusuf was admittedly brilliant, but no one could force Talel to sit by and watch as the other man's consuming hatred erased every vestige of humanity from his face. It was an almost nauseating sight.

Contrary to Yusuf, Talel did not rely on Sulimein to get the job done. He phoned Uzmi Shalallah, liaison to the Islamic Jihad cell in Jerusalem's Old City, and ordered him to send a couple of men at once to follow a blue Peugeot 306, license plate number 28-700-04, presently parked in the lot near Mishkenot Sha'ananim. Sulimein had been instructed to wait there for the mosques to explode.

◆ ◆ ◆

Jerusalem, Friday, 9 a.m.

Yusuf had been right. Years of systematic brainwashing had turned Sulimein into an emotionless, preprogrammed robot.

Almost.

The ayatollahs had nearly succeeded in burying, under layers of anti-Semitic ideology, the Jewish spark that belonged to the old Shlomo. But his meeting with Eli and Judy had fanned that spark into a small flame and helped to peel back the layers of dust that had settled on his soul.

He was torn between intellect and emotion.

Intellect stated: "You're done for in any case. From the time you were 11 years old you've been stuck on a dead-end street, and now you've reached the end. You lost your mother and father, you lost your world. The Jewish people won't have you back, and the Moslem world sees you only as a nuclear *shahid*."

Emotion argued: "They tricked you. They murdered your mother and father and lied about killing the rest of the family. The truth has just been thrown into your face. They're alive and well! Benjy, my twin brother Eli, Judy, Dovy, and Moishy. I missed them for years, even when I thought they were dead. Now that I know they're still alive, I'm choked with longing. I want to see them before I press the button."

Have you ever seen a robot cry?

Sulimein wept a long time. His face was hidden in his handkerchief and his shoulders shook with grief and despair. What to do, what to do? The ayatollahs had made it very clear that only his death could atone for his terrible sin of leaving the car and causing his parents' death. They had also hammered home the message: "The Jews are sinners in their very essence. They can find atonement only in death." He wanted to please his teachers, but a powerful longing for his brothers and sister was slowly ripping him to pieces.

He decided to find a compromise between intellect and emotion. He would meet with Eli and Judy one more time, and then travel to Tel Aviv. Eli had mentioned Anafim, which was on the way to Tel Aviv. He would ask until he found the place. It was 10 a.m. when Sulimein switched on the engine of the Peugeot and left in the direction of Tel Aviv.

The two Arab youths sent by Talel Nadir were waiting in the parking lot, concealed inside a silver Mitsubishi. They pressed the gas, making sure to keep the Peugeot in sight at all times. One of them turned to the other and asked, "Why was the *shahid* crying?"

"He has to go to Tel Aviv," the other explained knowledgeably. "He cried because he knows that his life is about to end."

The first one shook his head. "Something doesn't smell right to me. Let's report to Uzmi Shalallah."

◆ ◆ ◆

Jerusalem, Friday, 8 a.m.

Second Lieutenant Giora Abuksis gazed with boredom at the two stone lions mounted in front of the Machaneh Yehudah police station. "They haven't changed their angry expressions since they were placed there a hundred years ago," he thought, yawning.

This precinct was responsible for maintaining security at the bustling Machaneh Yehudah shuk, a magnet for terrorists. The morning had started out quietly enough. Apart from two early pickpockets and one lost toddler, nothing of import had come into the station.

This was something of a surprise. On the last Friday of Ramadan, there was generally a rise in the number of complaints to the police. Those with an ear to the ground had heard rumors of high tension in the inner circles of the GSS and the IDF of late, but the prevalent feeling was that today, too, would pass uneventfully.

A youth wearing an outsized yarmulke and very long *tzitzis* came running breathlessly into the station. Lieutenant Abuksis perked up. "Yes, how can I help you?"

The boy — he was little more than that — took a seat. "My name is Akiva," he gasped. "Akiva Tamiri. I want to lodge a complaint about an attempted bombing!"

"What are you talking about?"

Akiva put the small tape recorder on the desk and switched it on. "Listen to this," he said. This day had seen him betray more than one of his principles.

Giora Abuksis did not get overly excited by the recording. "Anyone could falsify those voices," he told Akiva coldly. "You'll have to bring me better proof than that."

Akiva breathed deeply. Not for naught was it said that wisdom and the police always came after the fact. This particular police officer was causing his blood pressure to rise. "Sir, if you don't act soon, the mosques of Omar and El-Aktzah are going to crumble in a few hours, right on top of all the people inside. Please tell the police at the Temple Mount to check the cave under the Mosque of Omar. They'll find a two-and-a-half-ton bomb there. They should also check the 'Bir al Aswad,' or the Black Pool, under Aktzah. There they'll find some very sophisticated digging tools.

"And apart from that," Akiva added dramatically to the shocked policeman, "if you hurry, you'll be able to stop the leader of the Friends of the Mikdash — called Dekel, or David ben Avraham — in the settlement of Anafim, before he drags the entire innocent group into the Black Pool. They believe him to be a *ger tzedek*. I believed it, too, up until a couple of hours ago. They think Dekel wants to destroy the mosques in order to rebuild the *Beis Hamikdash*. Now I know better. The Arabs want to blow up the mosques as a provocation for terrible revenge against Israel!

41

Anafim, Friday, 10 a.m.

Eli and Judy sat on the grass in the shade of a tall cypress tree, one of the many that lined the entrance road to the settlement. Their nerves were at the screaming point; the tension was killing them. A book of *Tehillim* lay in each of their laps, and their lips never stopped moving. They hoped and prayed that the seeds they had sown in their brother's heart that morning would take root. Every car that passed had them leaping to their feet, only to sink down again in disappointment.

"He'll come," Eli said stubbornly. "He *has* to come."

"Because you want him to?" Judy did not want to crush his hope, only to inject a note of reality. "He ran away from us. Did you tell him clearly where we'd be?"

"Yes — as clearly as was possible under the circumstances. I yelled 'Anafim' after him a couple of times. But — he's going to come," he repeated with rock-hard conviction. "He has to come!"

They heard another car approaching, moving slowly. As it rounded the bend, they saw that the car was a Peugeot. Then they caught sight of a familiar blond head through the window.

"Excuse me, is this Anaf—?"

He recognized them in middle of the question, and suddenly could not say another word. His throat had closed. With a shaking hand he killed the motor and stepped out of the car. In slow motion, he walked toward them.

◆ ◆ ◆

The silence was deeper than any words could ever be. It contained a thousand impressions they would never share, a thousand laughs they had not laughed together, a thousand tears that had dampened their respective pillows through long nights of grief.

Eli and Judy looked at him with hearts filled to bursting. In a trembling voice, Judy said, "Shlomo, my lost brother."

He stood rooted to the spot, confused, and torn by an inner battle that showed itself clearly in his expressive eyes. A burning bitterness and hatred flared up in them for an instant, before giving way to profound suffering. He spoke as if in a dream: "I don't believe it."

For a moment, he said nothing more. Then, visibly shaking, he said, "I'm — I'm shocked. Eli, you're not dead. My twin — and here's Judy, my little sister. When I left, you were only 8. You look just like Ima now — alike as two drops of water. You're both alive.... I don't believe it!"

"Believe it, Shlomo. Believe it," Eli whispered, in an effort at self-control. "Shlomo, my brother — Shlomo Flamm. *Baruch haba.* I love you, Shloimy —" His voice broke, and a flood of tears welled up in his eyes. With arms outspread, he took two lurching steps toward his twin and hugged him tightly.

The youth in the sport jacket struggled for an instant, trying to break free of the powerful embrace. Then he surrendered to his own emotions. Laying his head on his brother's shoulder, Shlomo gave way to a flood of stormy tears. Judy stood to one side, crying quietly with love and pain. The three stood beneath the cypress trees, giving release to feelings locked away for years — longings that echoed from the depths of one heart to the other.

Shlomo recovered first. As he moved out of his brother's arms, he became aware that he was still holding tight to the black attache case. Sorrowfully, he shook his head. "It's not possible. For 13 years I've known you were dead. They told me that the Sikhs fired on the car and murdered the whole family — that none of you were left alive."

"Who told you?"

"The men who kidnapped me in the marketplace when I went to find Ima and Abba." Sobs rose up in his throat again.

"What happened to Ima and Abba?" Eli and Judy asked together, fists clenched with urgency. "Where are they?"

"In India," their brother said sadly.

"And what are they doing there? Are they in prison?"

"No!" The answer emerged in a scream, followed by more bitter tears. "Don't you understand? I'm torturing myself for my sin for the past 13 years — every minute, every day. It's because of me that they're buried in the courtyard of a house in Amritsar, under some vegetable cartons — And you ask me what they're doing!"

Eli whispered, "I knew it. My heart told me they weren't alive anymore. What was it Benjy used to say? The dead are gradually forgotten. If they were still alive, we wouldn't have been able to think of anything else."

They stood in silence for several minutes, like statues carved in the image of grief.

"But Ima and Abba *are* alive," Judy said, eyes brimming. "They're living in my heart and in yours. Whoever sees Eli and Benjy sees a carbon copy of Aharon Flamm. Our mother's heart is beating inside each one of us. Certainly in *your* heart, Shlomo. You carried the greatest burden all these years. You saw your pain through a magnifying glass."

"Yes, yes," Shlomo nodded. "The pain was too close. I was hurting for all of you."

Another silence, longer this time. Old wounds were reopened and old aches throbbed again in all their intensity. With great effort, Judy and Eli mastered their own distress in order to envelope their long-lost brother with love and warmth. Judy, like a good sister, offered to take the heavy-looking briefcase from her brother's hand.

"Where are you headed?" she smiled. "Such a big case, and heavy, too, I'll bet. Put it down — relax." She tried to take it from him, but his fingers remained clamped to the handle. Judy became curious. "What's in here?"

He took two steps backwards. All at once, he became unrecognizable again. The cold, frightening look returned to his eyes, and his voice, when he spoke, was metallic. "Don't you dare come near this briefcase. I have received my orders and I will carry them out faithfully."

His brother and sister recoiled. The young man standing opposite them was no longer their brother. He was no longer even a human stranger. He had reverted to a robot — a robot operated by remote-control.

"What are you talking about?" Judy asked. "What order?"

"This case," the robot said, "weighs only 43 kilograms, but it contains enough plutonium and uranium rods to turn this entire area into a desert. The time has come to arm it."

He began twirling the dials on the lock. "It's not very difficult. All I have to do is insert the detonator between the plutonium rods."

Judy screamed. "You're telling me that's an *atom bomb*?! It can't be! An atom bomb is as big as a house, not small enough to fit into *that!*"

"You're wrong," Eli said grimly, his eyes never leaving his brother. "Everything is scaled-down today, even nuclear weapons. That small case is a nuclear bomb in every respect. There are a hundred of them roaming the streets of the former Soviet Union."

Sulimein laughed at Judy's panic. "Don't be afraid. Until the bomb is armed, this thing is about as harmless as a banana. Well, maybe slightly more harmful, because there is a little bit of radioactive activity. I was very happy to meet you, my brother and sister, but the time has come to say good-bye. I'm on my way to Tel Aviv, and you'd better run in the opposite direction as fast as you can. You have a couple of hours to get as far away as possible from the eye of the storm."

Glistening beads of sweat appeared on Eli's forehead. "You're joking."

"No, I'm not joking." The answer shot back, cold and crisp. "I've been sent by the holy revolution. The Jewish nation sinned and must die to atone for its sins."

"Quit making those idiotic speeches, would you?" Eli shouted. "Israel's enemies in Iran have got you good and brainwashed. Snap out of it! You're no fanatic Arab; you're a smart Jewish boy. How could you fall for that nonsense? It's just not possible — our father predicted a nuclear holocaust, and his son, his own flesh and blood, is going to make that insanity happen?!"

Sulimein boiled with anger. "Don't call Arabs fanatics. They're a proud and noble nation!" He hefted the heavy briefcase ominously. "If you make me angry, I'll arm the bomb. It will explode four minutes later."

Eli froze.

With womanly intuition, Judy was pleased to see these signs of anger. It spoke of an inner struggle between the machine and the man — the Jewish man. A war between the 24-year-old Sulimein and 11-year-old Shlomo. She sensed that, despite all the brainwashing, he had not turned into a complete robot. How much of her brother was left?

The child Shlomo had been extremely sensitive. What remained of that sensitive soul?

"Shlomo," she said softly, "you see with your own eyes that they fooled you, filled you with lies. It's a fact that we're all alive and well. And you're not to blame for our parents' deaths. It's another lie that Ima and Abba came back to the car and then went out looking for you. They never came back. They didn't die because of you. It was premeditated murder. Their fate was sealed the minute they set foot on the plane to India. A traitor in the American State Department sent them to their deaths."

Sulimein didn't answer. Tensely, he glanced at his watch. Yusuf had not yet called. Without the code, he would not be able to unlock the attache case.

The mullah, Ibn al Hunod, appeared before his eyes. "My dear Sulimein," he said, smiling, "the Jews don't know what's good for them. We know. After you kill them they will thank you. You will send them to eternal Paradise. Death hurts only for an instant, and then the pleasure comes — a billion years of pleasure, and then another billion, and then another — "

Eli was near despair. No school has yet been founded that teaches how to deal with a brother who is a potential suicide bomber with his finger on the nuclear trigger. Eli's white shirt had become a wet rag. His fists clenched and unclenched helplessly. What could stop his brother? Who could stop him?

An idea, born of despair, came to him. Carefully, he began, "You know, Shlomo —"

His twin cut him off. "It's Sulimein to you. You can't turn back the wheel of time!"

"Okay. Sulimein." Eli was good at keeping his eye on the ball, at separating the essential from the trivial. "Our father was a learned and pious Jew. He learned a lot of Torah. Intuitively, without even knowing about his death, I opened a yeshivah on this settlement in his name. It's called 'Aish Aharon.'"

Sulimein retained his grip on the case, but Eli sensed a heightened interest. Encouraged, he continued, "The *rosh yeshivah* is Rav Anshel Pfeffer, a very outstanding individual who reminds me of Abba, even in the way he looks. Just imagine, Shlomo — sorry, Sulimein — Abba with a beard—"

Sulimein did not react.

Eli risked everything on a last gamble. The wisest of all men had advised: "A soft answer turns away wrath." He must wrap hard words in a soft wrapping. Eli prayed inwardly for the right words. Emotionally, he seized his brother's hand. "You're not Sulimein. You were Shlomo, and Shlomo is who you still are. A terrible tragedy happened — a tragedy that was not your fault. It's time to come home."

"I have a mission," Sulimein insisted. "And don't take a step closer to this briefcase. It's the angel of death."

Eli wiped the perspiration from his brow. "I'm not afraid of death. Rabbi Yosef Yitzchak of Lubavitch said that anyone who has one G-d and two worlds need not be afraid of a gun."

"Like me, for instance," Sulimein said coldly.

"No, Shlomo. You have only one world. You fantasize about an exciting meeting with Mohammed and his army of martyrs in Paradise. But a person who takes his own life and murders many others does not receive a portion of the *Livyasan* and the reserved wine. You'll go straight down to *Gehinnom* and your name will be carved in letters of shame forever."

Sulimein's hands trembled. "Where do you get that from?"

"From the holy writings. Shlomo, I have a suggestion for you. You have nothing to lose by meeting Rav Anshel Pfeffer for a quarter of an hour. He'll be able to explain much more clearly than I can exactly where you're mistaken."

"I doubt that. In fact, I'm sure he can't." Sulimein had his pride. "But if you say this rabbi resembles Abba, I guess I can spare him a quarter of an hour. But don't delude yourself that I can be budged from my mission even one inch. Fifteen minutes from now, I'm on my way to Tel Aviv!"

They got into the Peugeot and drove in silence to the yeshivah. Eli hoped that Rav Anshel was in the *beis midrash* and had not already left for home on this *erev Shabbos*.

◆ ◆ ◆

Anafim, Friday, 11 a.m.

Rav Anshel Pfeffer was in the Aish Aharon beis midrash, learning the weekly Torah portion, when a student came over to hand him a small slip of paper. Mystified, Rav Anshel opened it, and read: *I'm waiting for you outside. This is a matter of life and death. Come quickly to the clearing in front of the yeshivah. Eli Flamm*

Yoel Goldfinger received an identical note. What had been good enough for Dani Devash was good enough for him, Eli had reasoned. Like Devash, what he needed at this moment was a brain trust.

Rav Anshel rose in agitation from his *Chumash*. There were only 10 verses left in the *parashah*, and he made it a practice never to talk while learning it. Now he would have to start over from the beginning. But Eli was referring to a matter of life and death —

He stuck his hat quickly on his head, shrugged into his overcoat, and left the *beis midrash* together with Yoel Goldfinger.

Seeing them through the Peugeot's passenger window, Eli sighed in soundless relief. Sulimein, however, had the opposite reaction. "You said one person. I see two," he said suspiciously. He switched on the ignition. "I'm going."

"No, no, no!" Eli pleaded. "Don't go. That's a good friend of mine, very intellectual, no muscles to speak of. He's not coming to start up with you."

Rav Anshel stopped short at the sight of the strange car parked in the clearing. Where was the matter of life and death? Eli rolled down his window and called softly, "Rav Pfeffer, this is my missing brother, Shlomo Flamm. He's interested in meeting you. I told him that you look the way our father did."

Rav Anshel was completely bewildered. He didn't understand a word. "What did you say?"

"Nothing — Please, let's meet in my room at the dorm in two minutes."

"You plan on locking me in your room?" Sulimein flared. "Get out of the car, you and Judy. I'm going to Tel Aviv!"

Rav Anshel and Yoel Goldfinger had already started, at a rapid clip, down the path to the dormitory. Sulimein's shout stopped them in their tracks. Yoel's quick brain worked with lightning speed to consider the options. The stranger beside Eli was his brother, and he was threatening him with something. "We'd better go back," Yoel whispered to Rav Anshel. Together they returned to the car.

Eli was white as plaster, the driver appeared furious, and Judy was visibly shaken. In his gentle way, Rav Anshel leaned close to the window and said, "Let's go for a little walk among the trees. There's a small valley nearby, with many colorful flowers and lots of shade. Ah, Hashem's world is so beautiful."

"He really does talk like Abba. Even their voices are similar," Sulimein thought in astonishment. Aloud, he said, "You were right, Eli. He does remind me of someone. I'm going out to talk with him for five minutes."

Eli sighed with relief: the threat was in abeyance for at least five more minutes. That was something.

He and Judy watched the unlikely pair descend the path to the valley. Rav Anshel, in dark suit and hat, strode side by side with the wild-haired young man lugging the heavy attache case, from which he refused to be parted for even a second. A little way behind them came Yoel Goldfinger.

"You're not afraid for Rav Anshel?" Judy whispered anxiously.

"We're all in the same boat," Eli smiled sadly. "May Hashem have pity on us all."

◆ ◆ ◆

"I want you to understand something right from the start. This briefcase is a three-and-a-half kiloton atomic bomb. I have a cellular phone in my pocket and am waiting for the signal to act," Sulimein said.

Rav Anshel nodded thoughtfully. Now he understood — Eli had summoned him to deal with someone who was obviously mentally unstable. But what about all the talk of "life and death"? Wrinkling his brow, he came up with what he thought was probably the answer: this boy must have threatened Eli physically. With a pleasant smile, Rav Anshel said, "Nice to meet you. My name is Abraham Lincoln and I'm President of the United States."

"No! Rav Anshel, don't make fun of him," Yoel called urgently from behind. "That briefcase really is an awesome bomb!"

Sulimein smiled briefly over his shoulder at Yoel. "That's right — and I'm about to blow up Tel Aviv."

Yoel overcame his hesitation, crossing the short distance between himself and Sulimein in a few rapid strides. "Don't worry about me, I come in peace," he said mildly.

Rav Anshel turned back to Sulimein. "Who are you?"

In a few succinct sentences, Sulimein told them about himself, and about those who had sent him on this mission. Silence reigned for several moments.

"My heart goes out to you," Rav Anshel said quietly, tears running down his cheeks. "You have suffered the seven levels of *Gehinnom* in this world. You were completely alone. It's no wonder they were able to brainwash you, to turn you against your own people."

Sulimein lifted his head proudly. "There was no brainwashing. They simply opened my eyes so that I could see the truth."

The rabbi found himself bereft of words in the face of falsity on such a monumental scale, where black is white and the straight is crooked. Thirteen years of systematic programming had created and developed a hatred for his own people that it would be impossible to change overnight.

But Yoel would not give up. "Which truth did you see — that they murdered your whole family? Yet all your brothers and sisters are alive. Benjy has become a successful ophthalmologist in New York. Eli is an outstanding yeshivah student, the kind every mother should be blessed with. He's a carbon copy of your father, Aharon Flamm. Your sister, Judy, is a fine seminary graduate, and Dovy and Moishy are doing very well in yeshivah."

He watched Sulimein closely, hoping to find a spark of humanity beneath the robotlike exterior. In his most persuasive mode, he continued, "Which truth did you find in Iran? That it's possible to murder a fine couple who never harmed anyone, then kidnap their son and poison his mind with lies to make him believe himself responsible for their deaths? And then to teach him that his 'atonement' is death — for himself and two million other people! Where's the truth? Where's justice?"

Yoel's eyes were brilliant as he gently took Sulimein's hand. "The Islamic religion is based on murder and bloodshed. Yishmael tried to kill his younger brother, Yitzchak, and was banished by Avraham together with his mother, Hagar. From the dawn of time they have hated us, and will continue to hate us forever, until *Hakadosh Baruch Hu* rescues us from them."

Many thoughts jostled for dominance in Sulimein's mind. Yoel's logic was piercing and his own common sense told him that Yoel was right, yet he had been programmed to destroy the "Zionist enemy"— Why hadn't Yusuf called yet? Sulimein pulled the cellular phone from his pocket and saw, to his shock, that the instrument had been turned off. Quickly he pressed the power button and listened to the dial tone.

There were two conflicting messages waiting on his voice mail.

"Sulimein, this is Yusuf. I very much wanted to give you the green light, but there's been a slight delay at the Temple Mount. The Revolutionary Council in Iran is waiting for news of the explosion that will destroy the mosques. As soon as that arrives, Operation Lightning and Thunder will be given the go-ahead. Go back to your hotel room, Sulimein, and wait for further instructions. Don't turn off your telephone."

"Sulimein, this is Fadlallah from Jericho. An old Russian by the name of Arkady gave me a note yesterday, and asked me to phone you at 1p.m. today to give you the following numbers...."

Sulimein listened carefully and jotted down the numbers in his little notebook. This was it. Now it was up to him. There was no need to wait for Yusuf any longer. All he had to do was play around with the locks on the attache case, and then he could arm and detonate the bomb in four minutes.

42

Herzliya, Friday, 10 a.m.

Piano music wafted through the spacious living room, lapping at oil paintings of fjords and ships before drifting out through the half-open shutters at the windows. Galina Bogdanov knew how to get the most out of a piano; before moving to Israel she had won five awards for excellence at Moscow's musical academy. She sat on a swivel stool in front of the instrument, eyes closed, playing a mournful old Russian ballad.

Yefim, her husband, lay on the sofa reading a newspaper for Russian immigrants. From time to time he, too, closed his eyes, and sang along with the melody in a deep baritone. The couple's Fridays were always spent relaxing at home after a hard week's work.

As the last notes were fading, the doorbell rang. Galina rose and went to the door. An elderly religious Jew with a long beard and coat stood on the doorstep. "We don't give charity," she snapped, about to close the door in his face.

"Galina," the 'collector' said in a familiar voice, "aren't you going to invite me in?"

"*Aiiiy!*" She screamed and fell back two steps. "It's Arkady!"

"Very true." The man in the long coat smiled, stepping inside. He closed the door gently and then, before Yefim and Galina's eyes, peeled the mask from his face. Everything quickly fell away: the old-fashioned glasses, the long white beard and sidelocks, the large black skullcap. "Why are you looking at me as if I've returned from the dead?" he asked, breathing deeply. "Bring me something cold to drink, I'm dying of thirst." He threw off the dark coat and kicked off a pair of scuffed black shoes. "The name of the game is consistency," he remarked, bending to rub his aching feet. "You can't dress up as a *chassid* and then wear sneakers. But these shoes have just about finished off my poor feet."

Galina hurried to fetch the drink. Yefim came closer, peering at his father disbelievingly. "Father, how did you manage to get here? The Israeli police are doing everything in their power to catch you — and here you are!"

"They're looking for an old, clean-shaven Russian with thinning hair, not an Orthodox charity collector with glasses," Arkady returned. He sipped gratefully from the glass of cold vodka and club soda his daughter-in-law handed him. "Thank you very much, Galina. I invite you and Yefim to join me in the next drink, on the plane. It's lifting off for Moscow in exactly two hours."

Yefim and Galina stared at him as though he had lost his mind. "Where did you disappear to, Father? Where have you been these last three months, and what's all this about a plane to Moscow?"

Arkady produced three airline tickets. "I'll explain everything on the plane. There's no time now. Do you want to be here when the atomic bomb goes off?"

"What are you talking about?" Yefim fumed.

Arkady jerked his head toward the large kitchen, remarking, "You've taken good care of my house — What am I talking about? I'm talking about two atom bombs that I bought for the Hizballah from the St. Petersburg Mafia. One of them is due to explode in Tel Aviv a few hours from now. According to my calculations, the radioactive wave will reach this spot minutes after the explosion, reducing the house to ashes."

"You're joking." Yefim's face was drained of color. This was not the form his father's humor usually took. There were only two other possibilities: either his father had become senile, or his story was true.

Arkady took a step toward the bedroom. "I'm not joking. In a few minutes I'm going to send the suicide bomber the secret code he'll need to arm the bomb. For all I care, let this whole place burn."

This was a lie. He had already passed on the secret code through Fadlallah, a Jericho youth. But he wanted to stretch Yefim's tension to the maximum. He had a score to settle with his son.

Without asking permission, Arkady went into the bedroom. Yefim and Galina followed. He was making himself at home; after all, this house had been his, until these two had thrown him into the old-age home in Bat Yam.

On one bedroom wall hung a large picture of the Volga River. Arkady took this down, exposing the safe hidden behind. "All we do is take the money and diamonds, and then off we go to the plane." He twirled the combination to open the door. "Excellent!" he said, pleased. "Yefim, I hope you haven't taken anything. I placed $300,000 here in hundred-dollar bills. And where's my box of diamonds? Ah, here it is. Everything is in order."

Yefim and Galina stood behind him, dumbstruck. They had lived here for three months and never known that their bedroom concealed such a rich secret. They went back into the living room to consult.

"Did you see what your father's hidden there? And it could all be ours." Galina's eyes glittered with greed.

"I saw. But we'll get it in his will. He has no one else."

"Guess again," she said scornfully. "He'll take away this nice house, drag us back to Russia, and end up leaving us without a penny. I know that skinflint."

Clearly, the atom bomb story held no water with her. It was only a trick meant to lure them out of the house. She knew Arkady, the sly fox. He had undoubtedly planned this well, down to the last detail.

Very quietly, she tiptoed back to the bedroom door.

Arkady was engrossed in counting his money. When the safe was empty, he put the bills and the diamonds into a gray briefcase. "Excellent. It's time to fly out of here. Where are Yefim and Galina?" He went to the door, but it wouldn't open. "What's going on? What's wrong with this door?" He grabbed the knob with both hands and shook it like a madman, but it was locked from the outside. It was a strong door. The room had been built in accordance with the latest government specifications, to withstand the long-range ground-to-ground missiles Israel was threatened with from time to time.

In the next room, Galina had the phone in her hand. "Good morning, Lieutenant Devash. I'm happy to have caught you in. This is Galina Bogdanov, the wanted scientist's daughter-in-law... If you wish to lay your hands on him, send a car to my home in Herzliya. Yes... He's locked up here in the house."

◆ ◆ ◆

Anafim, Friday, noon

"It was good meeting a person like you," Sulimein told Rav Anshel. "But I have to continue my mission now."

Yoel Goldfinger had been eloquent and convincing, but they were dealing with a machine. Rav Anshel saw with sorrow how thorough the Iranians had been with Shlomo Flamm, and how efficient. The boy had become a rocket ship headed in the wrong direction, a ship that had lost contact with its origins.

To the rabbi's alarm, Sulimein began fiddling with the lock on the attache case. Rav Anshel's eyes flew upward in silent supplication. *Master of the Universe, how to stop him? It's not his fault, he's been brainwashed, but we're not obligated to die for his mistake. Please, give me a few words —*

He turned to the young man. "Sulimein, let's make a gentleman's agreement. I'll ask you two questions. If you can answer them, you go on to Tel Aviv. If you have no answer, then you give me the briefcase."

Sulimein smiled politely. "Let's hear."

"You agree?" Rav Anshel wanted to cry with relief.

"I'm listening."

"All right. The first question: The Moslems agree with us that G-d never makes a mistake. You are set to destroy a portion of the Jewish nation. Are you claiming that G-d created the Jews for no purpose?

"Second question: Even if we accept the argument that you were responsible for your parents' deaths, it was only an indirect responsibility. Yet you are prepared to murder your brothers and sisters — directly! What was *their* sin?"

Feebly, Sulimein said, "Let — let them escape in Issam and Yusuf Abu Rabia's helicopter." Even as he spoke, he knew that what he said was nonsense.

"Who are they — the terrorists who sent you? They'll really take good care of them — " The mockery was transparent.

Judy was hiding among the trees behind the men, watching and listening. She watched her brother especially closely as Rav Anshel posed his questions. The first question confused Shlomo. The second one, she could see in his eyes, disturbed him deeply.

"Isn't Rav Anshel right?" she asked sweetly, coming out into the open.

Startled, Sulimein glanced around at her. His eyes became riveted to the small *sefer Tehillim* in her hand.

He recognized it. It was his *Tehillim*! The one his father had given him just a short time before the trip to India. A small, leather-bound volume that had fallen from his hands in the Amritsar marketplace.

"Give that to me," he shouted.

Judy handed it over. He flipped it open to the first page. There was his beloved father's inscription. The image of Aharon Flamm swam before his eyes, as the son read the father's words:

To my dear son, Shlomo,

Tehillim has accompanied our people since the days of King David. In its merit, we have never lost our way. It will stay with you all your life, in times of joy and times of sorrow, on cloudy days and sunny ones. It will be your signpost should you ever lose your way — and your guide to bring you safely home again.

Your loving father,

Aharon Flamm.

"Abba! Abba!" Shlomo cried in a trembling voice, grasping the *Tehillim* tightly. Tossing the briefcase onto the grass, he began running among the trees. "Where are you, Abba? Where are you, my Abba? You see everything — you wrote everything. Abba, my Abba, you taught me to give everything without expecting anything in return. And now, look what I was about to do. Oh, Abba!"

His screams echoed among the tall trees. He raced back to the grass and flung himself down. "Abba!" And then, in a cry straight from the heart, "Ima! *Ima!*" The rest was lost in wrenching sobs.

The others stood to one side, under the trees, and wept along with him. Eli, Judy, Rav Anshel, and Yoel suffered with him and agonized in his soul's agony. They felt his torment, and all the bittersweet joy of a lost son who has come home.

When the tears had abated enough to let him see, he raised the *Tehillim* and kissed it with intense love. His finger traced again the words his father had written years ago.

Only then did he raise his eyes to them. The eyes bore no hatred now. They were good eyes. The dark cloud had dissipated and was no more.

He was their Shlomo again.

◆ ◆ ◆

Anafim, Friday, 10 a.m.

A ring of police officers circled Dekel's house, waiting for the order to break in.

The first thing Giora Abuksis had done was to have the suspect's phone line tapped, and to place two officers in charge of listening to every incoming and outgoing call. The pair were galvanized by a phone conversation between Dekel and Yusuf Abu Rabia:

Dekel was very nervous. He had been notified just an hour before that Akiva Tamiri had never put in an appearance at the Western Wall tunnels. Nothing at all was known of the boy's whereabouts from the time that Dekel had set him down in the Old City.

"Why didn't you prepare an alternate in case of emergency?" Yusuf berated him.

"There is a substitute — Abdullah, the kid who was supposed to open the gate for Akiva. But he's also disappeared. Apparently, the thought of blowing himself up with two-and-a-half tons of explosives scared him off. I assumed that they were both in place on the site."

"What's all this about 'I assumed'? Are these the kinds of things you leave to chance? I'm sick of your poor organization," Yusuf ranted. "I've worked like a dog for nine years laying all the groundwork for the big moment. I thought you were working just as hard. But something always comes along at the last minute and spoils everything.

"I'm leaving for Jerusalem now. In one hour, I will be at the cave under the Mosque of Omar. The bomb will go off at 2:30. We haven't missed the boat yet."

The line was disconnected at both ends. A moment later, the door burst open with a mighty crash.

Giora Abuksis and three of his men advanced toward Dekel, brandishing guns. "Daoud Abu Nimar, who calls himself David ben Avraham, or Dekel," Giora said in a grave voice, "you are under arrest for inflicting a serious breach of security in the State of Israel, and for planning a massive terrorist bombing. Everything you say can and will be used against you in a court of law."

Dekel was the picture of outraged astonishment. "What are you talking about?"

Without warning, Giora kicked a chair at the suspect. Dekel fell, and two police officers were upon him at once, beating him vigorously.

"Ow, ow, that hurts!" Dekel shrieked.

"Whose pain is worse — yours, or that of the 150,000 men you planned to bury on the Temple Mount?" One of the policemen slapped Dekel, hard. "That was just a dry run. Keep yelling like that, and you'll see what's in store for you."

"What have I done? What do you want from me?" Dekel shouted the words, then hid his face in his hands.

"Quiet!" The policemen kept hitting him. "Don't teach us how to deal with disgusting terrorists."

They yanked him to his feet and clamped handcuffs onto his wrists. Then they shackled his feet with chains. The room quickly filled with policemen.

"I didn't do anything!" Dekel wailed. "What do you want from me? You're arresting an innocent person. It says in the Torah to be kind to a *ger*. You should be ashamed of yourselves!"

"It also says in the Torah to wipe out the memory of Amalek," Giora shot back. Someone handed him a small tape recorder. Giora placed the earphones in Dekel's ears and let him listen to a replay of his conversation with Yusuf Abu Rabia.

Dekel's eyes raced like mice scampering to escape. He made a lunge for freedom, but when he saw the number of policemen blocking his way he understood that he had waited too long. Escape was impossible now. His spirit broke.

"I want a lawyer!" he yelled as he was taken to a waiting police van. "Get me a lawyer!"

At the time that Dekel was being arrested, another group of policemen were swarming over the Friends of the Mikdash quarters and arresting all its members. All of them would have faced several years in prison, had it not been for Giora Abuksis's recommendation that charges be dropped. "Akiva Tamiri," he maintained, "prevented the whole chain of tragedy from occurring." At a later stage, Abuksis brought forward supporting testimony from Sruly Egozi, to the effect that "all the members of the organization are unbalanced, and don't know how to distinguish between imagination and reality."

The police searched diligently for Yonah Pinter, spiritual leader of the Friends of the Mikdash, but he had vanished without a trace.

Yoel Goldfinger phoned his uncle, Lieutenant Dani Devash. "Uncle Dani, what's new?"

Devash wanted to shake off his curious nephew. "Nothing special."

"I heard that there's a big step-up in security at the Temple Mount. They're talking about something big."

Devash was astounded. For the past month he had had no contact at all with the boy. Where did he get his information from? Striking a light note, he replied, "We live in a small and gossipy country. Every secret is spouted from a thousand fountains."

Yoel wanted to stretch his uncle's nerves a little further. Mischievously, he asked, "So what do you think, have the two Russian 'dolls' made it into Israel?"

"There's something behind all this talk," his uncle said evenly. "What is it? What's happened?"

"Ah, that's the question I've been waiting for. I want to make a little deal with you. If you promise me something, I'll let you in on a big secret."

"How big?" Devash asked jocularly.

"About the size of an atom bomb," Yoel answered, suddenly very serious.

"I promise."

That was how it came about that, five minutes after the police van left with Dekel and the Friends of the Mikdash, another contingent of police cars appeared in the settlement. This time, they were Dani Devash's men. Ari Naot was there, and Benny Turiel, along with two nuclear experts and their radioactivity-testing equipment. The experts were brought to the hidden valley beneath Yeshivas Aish Aharon, and shown the attache case lying on the grass.

"Move back immediately!" The police ordered everyone present away from the scene, then made haste to disappear themselves.

The experts were taking no chances. The first thing they did was hold a Geiger counter close to the briefcase.

The digital numbers galloped like a herd of wild horses.

"Whew!" one of the experts whistled. "This is a live one, all right. We'll have to take it by special transport to the bomb pit at Zechariah. It's not far from here. We'll be able to check it out carefully there."

The police entered the yeshivah and waited. Devash took his nephew off to a corner. "Don't tell me that bomb flew down from Heaven. I want the truth, Yoel. Where's the *shahid*?"

Yoel took a deep breath. "You promised me something."

"True. I promised that I'd listen to the story you wanted to tell me, and that I wouldn't bother you or your friend Eli Flamm. To tell the truth, I didn't understand it, but I respected your wishes."

Yoel filled his lungs again, then said, "I'll do my best to make the story short. It's the story of an American family that took a trip to India...."

43

Eli moved closer to where Yoel Goldfinger and his uncle were standing. "No, Eli," he said, as Yoel was about to begin. "The story starts way before that. The trip to India is almost the end of the story."

Yoel introduced him to Dani Devash. "This is the main hero, Eli Flamm. Thanks to him, a terrible tragedy was averted."

"I look forward to interviewing him in great depth," Devash said, a professional glitter in his eye.

Yoel leaned over to whisper in his uncle's ear, "Uncle Dani, please don't put too much pressure on him. There's a delicate matter involved that could complicate things for the Flamm family."

Carefully and in detail, Yoel told him of Eli's role in the whole affair. Dani Devash nodded his head and tugged at his lip. "Thirteen years of brainwashing, you say?"

"Exactly," Yoel confirmed.

"Let's hear his story. We need to get things clear. Let him tell us what he knows, and Naot and I will fill in the gaps."

Eli sat on a chair that had been brought out into the clearing opposite the yeshivah. Around him were Rav Anshel, Benny Turiel, Ari Naot, and several other top officers who had accompanied Devash.

"The story started with a visit that Yonah Pinter paid to my father's house, about 14 years ago. Yonah spoke forcefully about the destruction of the mosques on the Temple Mount. His talk reinforced in my father's mind something that he'd been thinking about for some time.

"On the surface, the Arab nations seem to have come to terms with the existence of a Jewish state stuck in their midst like a bone in a throat. Secretly, though — behind the screen of diplomacy and political expediency — the old Arab dream of wiping out the State of Israel has never died. One day, a group of extremist fundamentalist Arabs would rise up and try to actualize that dream. But causing a second holocaust would require some justification — a pretext of some kind. For example, a Jewish attack on one of the holiest Islamic sites.

"Preferably, such an attack would take place under Israeli jurisdiction. The Temple Mount Mosques of Omar and of El-Aktzah spring immediately to mind. They're highly visible because of their size and the gold and silver domes, and they are accessible. To every believing Jew they are an abomination, just crying out to be uprooted. It would be understood that any terrorist attack against the mosques would be perpetrated by Jews.

"Until he met Yonah Pinter, my father had estimated the chances of such a thing actually occurring as remote. But he changed his mind when he heard Pinter speak. Pinter was a charismatic man, a man burning with a Messianic fervor. A person like him could easily draw the fringe elements, the rejects of society or dreamers who don't live in the real world. He would infect them with his Messianic message, to the point where they'd be willing and eager to attack the 'abomination' — without taking into account the very real possibility that such an attack could be used by fundamentalist Arabs as justification for an off-the-scales revenge attack on Israel.

"Such a group would find support in Iran. That extremist nation represents the greatest threat to Israel today — a marriage of fundamentalist Islamic beliefs with sophisticated, nonconventional weaponry. Such a nation could produce a horror like a suicidal terrorist armed with a nuclear bomb.

"Aharon Flamm did not rely on pure theory. He investigated the extent to which his projected scenario was rooted in reality. For several weeks he pored over thousands of files and documents, before finally flying to Iran. In the guise of an American researcher with leanings toward Arab extremists, he spent two weeks roaming the Iranian government offices, talking to senior ayatollahs — my father knew how to get people to open up to him — and by the time he returned home he had what he'd come for. Some very senior people in top government positions had told him about an existing plan that was waiting for the proper moment to be executed. The plan called for Israel's destruction through an atomic bomb, in retaliation for a so-called Jewish terrorist attack on the Mosques of Omar and El-Aktzah. One of these senior officials actually provided my father — in return for a hefty bribe — with a copy of the document in question. Aharon Flamm showed that document to just two people. One was Steve Mantel, his colleague. The other was a senior figure in the State Department.

"My father put the information down in writing as well, and kept several copies in different places. He sent an urgent memo to the American Secretary of State.

"Immediately after that, the State Department began backing away from him. Aharon Flamm was removed from his job at the Middle East desk and transferred to the Far East one instead. He agonized over the question of who had soured him with the State Department, and the meaning of the threatening phone calls his wife received from someone with an Arabic accent. He was worried about the trip to India, understanding that he was being removed from the center of activity in the States. He tried to get out of going, but the government insisted."

Eli fell silent. It was impossible to continue. The memories choked off the flow of words.

Dani Devash had been making copious notes in a small notebook as Eli spoke, pausing from time to time to shoot fleeting but keen glances at Eli. Most of what he was hearing was new to him, but it fit in perfectly with other parts of the puzzle. He commented, "In light of what I've just heard, Eli, I'm beginning to get a clear picture."

With Eli apparently unable to go on, Devash took up the thread of the story. "Following the breakup of the Soviet Union, everything went up for grabs — including atomic bombs. General Alexander Leved, the former Soviet Minister of Defense, warned that hundreds of small atom bombs, each one no larger than an attache case, were floating freely in the marketplace and were being sold by the Russian Mafia to any comers. I'll let you in on a secret: even before the General's warning, Israeli Intelligence was dealing with its own substantial fears of a hostile group such as the Hizballah or the Islamic Jihad getting their hands on one of these bombs. The Israeli government discussed this possible threat, but the Mossad chief decided that the chances of its becoming a reality were very low to nonexistent.

" 'And why is that?' the Prime Minister asked, in a special conference on the topic.

" 'Because these terrorist groups are backed by organized governments such as Iran and Syria,' Shimi Tzipori, second in command at the Mossad, explained. 'Syria and Iran will never dare use nuclear weapons without real provocation. The only provocation that could justify such a step would be an attempt on Israel's part to threaten those countries' very existence — and the chances of that happening are nonexistent.'

"We soon learned that Iran's Revolutionary Council had indeed begun to transform Iran into a nuclear power. Its military arm worked to create a ground-to-ground missile capable of carrying a nuclear warhead. At the same time, Iranian agents went to Kazakhstan, where they met with former Red Army officers. Apparently, the Iranians bought four to six missiles, each armed with a 100-kiloton nuclear warhead. A very substantial acquisition — but Iran wasn't satisfied. When the heads of the Revolutionary Council heard about the small atom bombs circulating in the Russian black market, they decided to buy some of those, too.

"It was at this point that the Council decided to pull their grand plan out of the drawer and actually implement it. They called it 'Operation Lightning and Thunder,' after the two primary features of atomic explosions. The operation had three stages: 1) acquisition; 2) provocation; and 3) revenge.

"The Abu Rabia family, in Gaza, who felt they had been ruined under

Israeli occupancy, boasted a youngest son, Yusuf, whose hatred of the Zionist enemy was legendary. After he was expelled from this country, Yusuf traveled to Iran, where he eventually became the main force behind 'Lightning and Thunder.' His first job was to acquire the nuclear bombs.

"Today, with the aid of our intelligence services, we know how this came about. Yusuf returned to Gaza, where he persuaded his brother Issam — a destitute grocer — to join the Hizballah. Issam took the code name 'Gray Cap,' and recruited the Russian scientist Arkady Bogdanov. Bogdanov was formerly both an atomic scientist, administrator of a nuclear power plant, and a secret KGB agent. The KGB was always very cooperative with Iran. In accordance with an old agreement, Bogdanov was to announce his readiness to act by inserting a small ad in a newspaper.

"Yusuf had been waiting for that ad for two years. Bogdanov had spent most of that time living idly and self-indulgently. It was only when his son kicked him out of his own house and placed him in an old-age home that Arkady developed a surge of adrenalin. He remembered his dormant mission, and decided to act.

"With Bogdanov taking care of stage one, acquisition, Iran moved on to the second stage of its plan: provocation.

"The Hizballah were on the lookout for people to carry out this portion of the program. In Nablus, they came across one Daoud Abu Nimar, a bright and talented young man with excellent leadership abilities. Daoud Abu Nimar 'converted' to Judaism, becoming for the purposes of the plan David ben Avraham, a poor, persecuted *ger tzedek*. When he wanted a shorter and more convenient name, he chose 'Dekel.' Dekel began recruiting Jews to pull the chestnuts out of the fire for him — to blow up the Temple Mount mosques and provide Iran with the excuse it needed to destroy Israel.

"The first thing he did was hook up with the charismatic Yonah Pinter, a naive and friendly dreamer. It never entered Pinter's mind that he was being used, set up as a provocateur for evil. Dekel searched for disaffected youths, young men without a future, people who had nothing to lose, who would embrace any strange new idea that might offer their lives meaning. These young men became the core of the group that called itself Friends of the Mikdash."

Here Eli broke in. "I have to make a little confession," he said. "On that last night in Amritsar, my parents were having an argument. They thought I was asleep, but I was awake and heard what they said.

"I realized from their talk that my father had been fired from his job because of a secret memo he'd written, in which he predicted that a visionary Jewish group would become unwitting pawns in the hands of Iran. I was just a kid; I forgot all about what I'd heard — until Sruly Egozi was kicked out of yeshivah and came crying to me. I supported him through his hardest hour, and I soon got my reward. Sruly told me that he'd received a message from someone named Dekel, inviting him to join a cult that was aiming to destroy the mosques on the Temple Mount and rebuild the *Beis Hamikdash*. A thousand alarm bells began going off in my head. I remembered my father's warning, in the memo that cost him his life —"

He turned to Rav Anshel, blushing. "Forgive me, Rav Anshel. I had the idea of starting the yeshivah for aspiring students even before that, and was really prepared to actualize it — though not necessarily in this remote and picturesque spot. But the Friends of the Mikdash were determined to stay in Anafim because of the natural spring here, and I had no choice but to stick close to them."

"I think you were right," Dani Devash said. "Your calculations proved themselves by what happened later."

Rav Anshel stroked his long beard. "First of all, we have a saying: *Mitoch she'lo lishmah, ba lishmah.* Things that were done for the wrong reasons at first, eventually come around to being done for the right reasons. Also, it's not possible to say that it was completely for the wrong reason, because it led to the establishment of a yeshivah. And third, the Torah preserves and protects. In the merit of the Torah we've learned here, we had the privilege of contributing something to save human lives."

"Contributing something?" Benny Turiel retorted. "What kind of modesty is that? Two million people owe their lives to you!"

Dani Devash went on with his story. "Iran, through its agent Issam Abu Rabia, or 'Gray Cap,' facilitated Bogdanov's efforts. Bogdanov was stupid: had he asked for $4 million, he would have received it. The budget for Israel's destruction was unlimited.

"Bogdanov faked his own drowning and fled to Russia. No one in Israel was supposed to know that the scientist was still alive, or that he was planning to give his backers the third part of their plan: the means of revenge. He was prepared to destroy his second home — and would have succeeded, if not for the alertness of one police inspector from Bat Yam: yours truly, Dani Devash — "

"*And* his second-in-command, Ari Naot, who spoke with Tzipori," Naot put in smugly. He was waved down by his boss.

"I still don't know how," Devash continued, "but only the intervention of the police in the Bogdanov affair succeeded in whipping the cards out of the Iranians' hands and upsetting Operation Lightning and Thunder. Israel was not supposed to know a thing about the trip to acquire nuclear bombs in Russia. Israel's interference forced Iran to revise and improvise, but not to abandon the plan completely.

"I have not yet found the answers to two questions. First, who is to guarantee that the second bomb Bogdanov brought home is not walking through one of Israel's streets this very minute?

"And, two, who is responsible for the fact that Israel's security services failed so dismally in this affair? Where, for instance, is the Mossad in all of this?"

No one had answers for him.

Gradually, the group dispersed — but not before Dani Devash set a date with Shlomo Flamm for a short debriefing, "for protocol's sake." The police acknowledged that he had suffered enough and promised that no harm would come to him at their hands. He would leave after the debriefing with a full pardon in hand.

44

Hadarim, Friday, 12 noon

Shimi Tzipori rushed out of his house and sped into the adjacent parking lot. Just a little while before, he had received an urgent phone call from the United States. "The business has been completed. Come at once."

He had been anticipating such a call; when the critical moment arrived, he was ready. Many years in the Mossad had taught him to be prepared for sudden moves. His passport and documents were scrupulously in order. Twisting the key in the Volvo's ignition, he began to back cautiously out of his parking spot. Time was short, and he would have to waste at least two or three precious minutes maneuvering around the crowded lot.

It was his usual time to leave for his office in Tel Aviv. No one would wonder where he was headed. His briefcase, beside him on the seat, held everything he might need in the States. He whistled gaily as he drove.

He turned onto the highway leading to the airport. Suddenly, out of nowhere, four cars blocked his way, two in front and two behind. One of the latter was the BMW belonging to the Mossad chief. The BMW moved up slowly until its tinted window was parallel with Tzipori's. The window rolled down, revealing Gadi's cold eyes. He signaled to Tzipori to pull over to the shoulder of the road.

Tzipori had no choice but to obey. Gadi motioned for him to continue along an upcoming side road that led to Moshav Hadarim. Together with his entourage, Tzipori did so. All five cars stopped in front of a flourishing orchard. Doors flew open and a number of men stepped out. In seconds, Tzipori was surrounded by Mossad agents. There was a sprinkling of GSS men as well. Three faces looked familiar to him, and he easily identified them: Uzi Saraf, Yoni Dor, and Yossi katri.

The group passed among the trees, leaving several agents to secure the area on all sides. Gadi walked beside Tzipori. At the foot of a well-laden orange tree, he stopped. Saraf, Dor, and Katri came up to join them.

"Well, have I ruined your flight?" Gadi asked impassively.

Tzipori was shocked into silence. He could not utter so much as a word in his own defense. Gadi went on, calm as ever, "You know, I'm not particularly surprised that this happened. History is filled with spies. Modern history, especially, is rife with 'moles' who succeed in reaching the top of their agencies. What pains me is the trust I placed in you. You always shone, were always at the head of the class. I'll admit, I was finding it hard to suspect you even now. I could not conceive of treachery from one of my top men. The ones who opened my eyes were these two." He pointed at Uzi Saraf and Yossi Katri, who stood immobile as statues.

Speech returned to Tzipori's strangled throat. "May I ask what you're talking about?"

Gadi smiled his famous half-smile. "Not so much as a flicker of embarrassment? You thought you'd flee the country, leaving the rest of us to go up in smoke?" His voice hardened. "I'm talking about unparalleled treachery — the second in command at the Mossad, the man being groomed to become chief one day — a spy!"

"I have no idea what you're talking about, Gadi," Tzipori said coolly. "If this is some kind of joke, let me tell you that I find it in very poor taste. I could drag you into court for slander."

"Really." The smile left Gadi's face. "May I ask where you were planning to fly today?"

"I have personal business to attend to in the States. I may add that I don't stick *my* nose into *your* business!"

The Mossad chief was beginning to lose his famous iron control. Through his teeth he said, "You are a brazen and bare-faced liar. You have no shame. At the very least, make a confession, plead for amnesty, saying something like 'I was blinded by the money'! But don't just stand there and deny everything."

Tranquilly, Tzipori returned, "I am innocent of any suspicion. My hands are clean. I've never taken a bribe in my life." All at once, his calm evaporated, flaring into anger. "You're the one who should be ashamed, Gadi! I've devoted my best years to the State. I am a loyal Israeli citizen. No one in any Israeli security agency has foiled as many security breaches as I have."

"Your hands may be clean but your conscience is black as tar!" Uzi Saraf exploded. "Do you want to know who you are? I'll tell you."

"He knows it better than you," Gadi stopped him. "He's a low traitor who's been hand in glove with our worst enemies — all for money. The proofs, please."

"The proofs?" Uzi pointed at Yossi Katri. "He'll be happy to supply them."

Yossi moved closer to join the field trial Gadi had instituted in the flowering orchard. Slowly, he began, "When a watchdog joins the thieves and bites his own master in the leg instead of barking out a warning — that's a situation that cries out for an explanation.

"The Mossad should have been first to uncover Operation Lightning and Thunder, but someone managed to suppress it very well. That 'someone' was Shimi Tzipori, planted in the Mossad with the job of making very sure that Israel did *not* prevent Operation Lightning and Thunder from taking place. He did his job well, burying any and all intelligence reports from our men in Iran that warned of this threat to Israel. That's how it happened that it was the police, and not the Mossad, that learned of the scientist Bogdanov's disappearing act.

"The Mossad continued to lag behind all along. The search for Bogdanov became a farce, with Mossad agents looking more and more like lost sheep wandering in circles. Tzipori directed the search into all the wrong channels and neutralized two agents who had been sent into Russia. Everyone knew that Tzipori was a fanatic about the Mossad's honor. In reality, the opposite is true.

"Tzipori was afraid of Uzi Saraf and Yoni Dor. Both speak fluent Russian and would undoubtedly have found Bogdanov's trail in no time. They could have become a serious obstacle to Bogdanov. So what did Tzipori do? He persuaded Uzi, under the banner of Mossad loyalty, to put Yoni Dor, the GSS man, out of commission with a virulent flu germ. In order to prevent Uzi himself from learning the truth about Bogdanov, Tzipori personally ensured that the KGB agent, Zislin, would not provide him with the correct information under any circumstances. He did this by cutting back by 90 percent the Mossad's budget for purchase of information, leaving Uzi with a few miserly dollars with which to try and bribe that greedy Russian. It was like throwing a few crumbs to a hungry lion. Naturally, Zislin was not satisfied. The ploy was ingenious, and succeeded in sending agents to pursue the scientist over a bogus land route.

"Tzipori, when Dani Devash and Ari Naot met with you at the restaurant and suggested that Arkady Bogdanov had chosen the land route to Lebanon, their purpose was to mislead the Mossad and take the glory of Bogdanov's capture for themselves. You wanted to mislead the Mossad just as much, but in order to divert suspicion from yourself you pretended not to believe the police. At the same time, you 'reserved judgment,' and later 'capitulated,' pretending that you now accepted the overland scenario. It was a brilliant maneuver, whereby the straight became crooked, and the crooked — completely upside down.

"The Mossad, like a pack of fools, bought the story. They swallowed the incredible notion that Bogdanov, rather than take the quickest possible route to Lebanon, would choose the long, arduous overland trip while lugging along his radioactive luggage. Tzipori got what he wanted. He managed to turn the Mossad's nose in the opposite direction, and bought Bogdanov a peaceful trip by sea.

"In an investigation that we undertook a few days ago, Zislin reported that the Petersburg Mafia had given him Bogdanov's exact itinerary. Instead of selling it to Uzi Saraf of the Mossad, he sold it to Yossi Katri for a much more generous price. The information he provided was totally accurate — except that Bogdanov's sudden departure from ship in mid-sea was not planned ahead of time. It was quickly improvised when the enemy learned that we were waiting at Lebanon's ports. How did the enemy find that out? A difficult question. All at once, we became aware that somebody was consistently thwarting us *from the inside*. The only two in the know about the whole picture were the Mossad chief — and you. Because it was you, and not the chief, who actually supervised the entire operation, eventually all suspicion fell on you.

"In short, Tzipori — you're a traitor!"

Tzipori's eyes shot flames at Yossi. "You can't prove even 1 percent of this pack of lies!"

Gadi smiled thinly, and said, "Shimi, you hung yourself with your own words. When I called you into my office to scold you for the mess you'd made of the mission, threatening to put a negative note in your file, you played the wounded subordinate and offered to tender your resignation. Then I forgave you, and you were eager to prove yourself. What did you say? That the Mossad — and not the GSS or the police — would lay its hand on the lead barrel near the border, by the 'drug route.' During our whole talk, you spoke only of the barrel, the bomb. Not once did you mention Bogdanov. In other words, you knew that the barrel would reach the border alone, without Bogdanov — and that was actually what did happen.

"No one outside of the security services knew about the secret operation on the northern border, yet what occurred that night was solid proof that someone was talking. Someone was giving messages to the Hizballah and to the Mossad, back and forth, synchronizing times, and making sure that whatever I knew, they knew. For example, who passed on the information about the exact hour that the barrel would be smuggled? Who was it? It had to be either you or me. Apparently, it wasn't me. *I'm* not rushing to the airport a few hours before an atomic explosion is due to reduce Israel to rubble."

Gadi hammered the final nail into Tzipori's coffin. "We've checked your bank accounts, and discovered that you have several of them, both here and in Switzerland, containing sums that none of us here will have even after 50 years at the Mossad. The origins of that money are well covered, of course. All of it came from abroad through different routes and using various dummy names as fronts." He paused, then added softly, "We have reliable information that two days ago, your account at the Swiss Bank in Geneva received a deposit in the amount of $1 million. Does that tell you something?"

The day was not warm, but large damp patches appeared on Tzipori's shirt. The game was over.

◆ ◆ ◆

The Temple Mount, Friday, 11 a.m.

Yusuf Abu Rabia left Jericho and passed without incident from Palestinian territory into Israel proper. He continued on toward Jerusalem, foot firmly on the gas pedal. Twice he was stopped at Israeli military roadblocks — a warning had been issued of a possible impending terrorist bombing — but Yusuf's papers were in order and he was waved through.

He parked a short distance from the Old City walls and entered the Temple Mount through the usual wooden gate. To throw off possible watchers, he went south first, to the Mosque of El-Aktzah. Mingling with a large group emerging from the mosque, he turned left, across a large tract of land, toward the Dome of the Rock. At the foot of the steps leading to that mosque, he squinted in the sun at his wristwatch. He entered the Mosque of Omar.

In both mosques he had to make liberal use of his elbows to forge a path through the masses of worshipers who had come to celebrate the final day of Ramadan. An impassioned sermon in Arabic was being piped through loudspeakers.

Abu Jaffar was waiting for him, knees shaking in trepidation. Yusuf gave him a cynical smile. "My heartfelt apologies to the holy worshipers. In half an hour, their bodies will tumble among the ruins. The time has come for the earth to tremble." He shrugged, adding, "That's life. The masses are the oil in the wheels of the Revolution's machinery. What is happening with the sermon?"

Abu Jaffar's eyes darted in panic. "The mufti ran away a quarter of an hour ago. The people are listening to a tape. It will go on for about another 40 minutes. Everyone will be trapped here when the mosque crumbles."

Yusuf slipped into a hidden passage leading down to the cavern below. He had practiced so often that he knew the way with his eyes closed. But it had never occurred to him that *he* would be the one to activate the timer set to detonate the bomb that would blow up the Mosque of Omar and turn it into a pile of stones.

◆ ◆ ◆

To the left of the giant stone known as the *Even Hashesiyah* is a deep, circular depression. No one, apart from the Moslem Wakf and a few archaeological experts, had any idea that that depression leads directly to the cave beneath the stone. Yusuf knew. Flashlight in hand, he descended into the cave and sniffed.

He smelled danger. In rising tension he aimed the flashlight over the dark cave in every direction. The silence was profound. There was not a sound, not a rustle, to be heard.

Yusuf knew where the explosives were hidden. It was a large bomb, concealed inside a large wooden box. With pounding heart he sought the handle in the box's lid. His hand touched the bomb's delay mechanism.

Without warning, blinding lights dazzled him on every side. Yusuf was drowning in light. His hands went up in an instinctive effort to protect his eyes. Before he could cry out, he was surrounded by uniformed figures who kept him quiet with blows to every part of his body. His hands and feet were cuffed with no great ceremony.

"We could have had you sooner," one of the soldiers told him, "but we waited until our infrared camera got some very nice pictures to show the judge."

Yusuf was cowed but not yet defeated. "How did you get down here?" he demanded.

The soldiers were not inclined to hold lengthy dialogue with their prisoner. One of them replied curtly, "Every coin has two sides and every cave has two entrances."

His head was thrust into a bag, so Yusuf never got to see where the cave's second entrance was — the opening through which he was taken to an army truck, which drove him to a facility designed to hold the most dangerous of terrorists. His courage dripped away as he was interrogated roughly.

"Who are your masters?"

"Iran — Sheikh Ibn al Hunod — the Revolutionary Council — the Ayatollah Rafsanjani."

He screamed out the names between brutal blows from his questioners.

"Who else?"

Yusuf breathed harder, his mouth filled with bitter bile. "I can't talk—" A little more pain, however, revived his ability to speak. "Mr. Coates!" he gasped.

"Mr. Coates? What kind of name is that? Who is he?"

"I don't know."

He continued not to know, even as his interrogators used their tried-and-true methods for extracting necessary information from reluctant prisoners. Yusuf Abu Rabia could not identify the mysterious Mr. Coates for them. The name was clearly bogus. The interrogators marked it down for further investigation.

"Who are you working with?"

Finding it hard to breathe, Yusuf managed to say, "My brother — Issam Abu Rabia. Mahmud Talel Nader. Faud Halil. They're all in Jericho."

"Liar." The epithet came along with an iron fist. Yusuf was afraid that a few more blows like that one would take him to join his brothers who had been killed in Gaza after the Six-Day War. Broken, he spilled a great deal more of the story.

His interrogators were shaken. The danger was not yet past. Talel

Nader had received instructions to detonate the second attache case, even if the provocation — the destruction of the Temple Mount mosques — did not take place. Arkady Bogdanov had taught Nader how to arm the bomb.

The chiefs of Israel's security services now understood why the Hizballah had ordered Bogdanov to purchase two atom bombs, one limited in power, the other much larger. The first would be used in retaliation for the bombing of the Temple Mount mosques. The second was waiting in the wings, for blackmailing purposes at best, or for Israel's annihilation, at worst.

Near the end of his interrogation, Yusuf fainted. There was still one detail that his questioners had not succeeded in extracting from him. That was Talel's target — the nuclear missile base near Moshav Zechariah.

45

Manhattan, Monday, noon

The office door still bore the name "Flamm and Mantel, Statistics and Measurements," though even the lowliest State Department bureaucrat knew the title to be an empty one. After his partner's disappearance, Steve Mantel had risen to the position of bureau chief of the Middle Eastern desk. He was 54 years old now, at the zenith of his career. His friends expected to see even greater things from him in the years to come; he was making plans to try for a place on Capitol Hill. He was charismatic as ever, and very rich. Even by Manhattan's standards, his apartment on the other side of Central Park was worth a staggering sum.

He walked through the door of his office, unsmiling. He was returning from a meeting in Washington with Senator Richard Kirk. It had been a difficult meeting. Engrossed in his own thoughts, he hardly noticed the strange looks being directed at him from the other office workers. Had he paid attention, he might have seen the warning in their eyes — a warning that might have been translated as, *Run while you can!*

But he wasn't paying attention. And so, he walked into his inner office totally unprepared for what met him there.

Two uniformed police officers were waiting for him, along with a pair of FBI agents in dark suits. They remained completely silent until he had entered the office and closed the door.

"Good morning," he said heartily — Mantel had always been a master bluffer. "Will you have something to drink?"

"Black coffee for me, if you don't mind," one of the agents said.

Mantel gestured at the outer office. "The coffee machine is out there. I wouldn't mind a cup myself — one spoon of sugar."

"Let's forget about coffee," one of the policemen snapped. "Steve Mantel, you are under arrest."

Automatically, Steve protested, "I haven't broken any laws."

"Maybe you haven't broken the law with your own hands," the officer said grimly, "but you sure cooked up a nasty stew by remote control. Thirteen years ago, you sent your partner, Aharon Flamm, to his death — he and his wife and their five children, at the Golden Temple at Amritsar, India."

Mantel's lips turned white. He ran his fingers through his graying hair. "Excuse me," he said with suppressed fury, "but can I have that again? Those are wicked lies! You can ask the Flamm kids how devoted I've been to them ever since their parents were killed in India. I've poured tens of thousands of dollars into those kids, just to give them some peace of mind. I opened Benjy Flamm's office for him — his People's Clinic — and I still partially support it."

One of the FBI agents intervened here, his words like chipped ice. "You broke the law then and you've been breaking it now, by maintaining contact with an enemy of the state. You stand accused of accepting bribes, of using state secrets for evil purposes, and for your part in planning mass murder in a state friendly to the United States. Worst of all — and this is the reason we're here today — you sold state secrets to enemy agents. You handed over top-secret information to Iran, information that can endanger American lives. We are investigating a suspicion that you were also involved in selling information that aided in the bombing of the Twin Towers."

Mantel did not recognize his own voice as he answered, "Where did you get all that nonsense?"

The FBI man placed a small tape recorder on the desk and flipped a switch. During the next few minutes, Mantel listened to recordings of his phone conversations with someone he addressed as "Number Three." There was another talk with someone by the name of Issam Abu Rabia, and another... The recordings droned on and on.

Mantel tottered to his chair and sank into it. "I don't know what you're talking about. I don't understand anything." He could hardly get the words out of his suddenly parched throat.

The FBI agent flipped open his ID badge. "William Spear. I've been with the agency for 20 years. If you've forgotten what you did, I'll be glad to refresh your memory.

"It was no coincidence that you became Aharon Flamm's partner. You were planted here on purpose. The Arab lobby in Washington bought you — lock, stock, and barrel. You were placed in this office in order to keep a close eye on young Flamm, who had risen like a meteor in the State Department skies twenty years ago. The Arab lobby, headed by Senator Richard Kirk, was afraid of Flamm. You were Senator Kirk's golden boy — and he was the most pro-Arab of all the senators, with a burning hatred of Israel.

"When your partner, Aharon Flamm, uncovered a secret Iranian plan to incite an anti-Arab provocation in Israel and use it as an excuse for a vicious revenge attack, you took it immediately to Senator Kirk. The good senator began to see that you were repaying his investment very nicely.

"Senator Kirk wasted no time. Armed with papers and documents that you supplied, he walked the halls of the State Department. He managed to prove to the Secretary of State that Aharon Flamm's first allegiance was to Israel, with the U.S. coming second. The U.S. is very severe with its citizens who demonstrate patriotism to any other country. You succeeded in making poor Flamm smell bad in Washington. Not knowing, of course, that his loyal partner was stabbing him in the back, Flamm was shocked to find himself transferred away from the Middle Eastern desk. You cried along with him — crocodile tears, of course — and made sure he was moved to the Far Eastern division.

"You and Kirk were still afraid of Flamm's sharp mind. You knew he would never rest until he managed to neutralize the threat posed by the Iranian plan, and until he discovered who had ousted him from his old job, and why.

"So you planned a little trip for Flamm. A trip to India. You made it look like a pleasure trip, a family jaunt, but you sent off a telegram in the name of the State Department — which, as a bona fide State Department employee, you were able to do. The telegram requested that Flamm and his family be sent to Amritsar, 'in order to investigate the demonstration outside the Golden Temple.' The demonstration itself was a trumped-up affair, organized by your friends, the Iranians. It had one purpose, and one purpose only: to lure Aharon Flamm, and to finish him off. The noise of the chanting Sikhs was a bonus: it drowned out the dying screams of Aharon and his wife.

"Your part in Operation Lightning and Thunder began then. As you became more and more embroiled in Iran's attempt to destroy Israel, your nerve grew proportionately more outrageous. You were pulling all the strings from an office belonging to the American State Department!"

Mantel struggled to his feet, yanked off his tie and opened the two top buttons of his cream silk shirt. "You're a pack of idiots!" he yelled furiously. "You're wasting the taxpayers' money! I've never heard such garbage in my life. I'm prepared to stand trial. I have enough money to hire a team of lawyers to put you guys in your place."

The FBI man waved this aside. "We're also ready to go to trial. Your time is up, Mr. Mantel. We've got everything documented. Our evidence will be accepted in court. Get ready for what's coming."

"You're harassing an innocent citizen!" Mantel screamed.

"Let me tell you something," the FBI agent said coldly. "You have, no doubt, heard of the Iranian plan, Operation Lightning and Thunder, calling for Israel's destruction by atomic bomb? But of course you have. When that plan began to be put into action, you were told that the second in command at the Israeli Mossad, a man by the name of Shimon Tzipori, was actually a spy, planted in Israel from a young age. You went into partnership with this Tzipori. You called him 'Number Three' — why? Maybe because of the strange triangle that had been formed here: the U.S., Iran, and Israel. And he called you 'Mr. Coates.' You directed him in the most effective ways to neutralize the Mossad as it tried to defuse the most serious threat the State of Israel has faced in its history.

"Number Three was loyal to you — except for one thing. He did not tell you that much of the money you'd budgeted to the Mossad, for bribing KGB agents to provide false information, found its way into Tzipori's own pocket. Paradoxically, however, even this disloyalty played into your hands. Had Tzipori actually thrown all that money at Zislin, the Russian would doubtless have sung like a bird, leading the Mossad to capture Bogdanov and his precious cargo in Lebanon. Tzipori passed you information that you, in turn, passed on to 'Gray Cap' and your other partners in the Revolutionary Council — and vice versa. Whatever you knew, you relayed to him. Truly a wonderful example of cooperation among Israel, America, and Iran!"

Mantel snorted. "Nonsense. It's all nonsense! Any 5-year-old could fabricate a story like that to throw mud at a respectable citizen who's worked devotedly on behalf of his country for close to 20 years. I'd have expected something a little more original from the FBI."

"You want something original?" The agent smiled. "Here it is. The Israeli GSS has interrogated one of your partners, a Yusuf Abu Rabia. He's the one who pointed the finger at you. He told us everything."

The arrow found its mark. Steve Mantel's lips turned blue. Now, the agents judged, was the moment when the man would crack.

But they had forgotten that Mantel was German born and a master of self-control. He drew himself up and said, "Even if there were an iota of truth to all this — this pack of trash — even if this Yusuf — Yusuf — whatever his name is, identified someone, it was a 'Mr. Coates.' My name is Steve Mantel."

The agents exchanged victorious glances. "True," the agent said quietly. "It wasn't we who found you. It was Eli Flamm, Aharon's son."

"Eli Flamm?" Mantel whispered, appalled. "He's a smart boy — with remarkable intelligence."

"Keep that in mind," the FBI man said mockingly. "Yusuf Abu Rabia did not actually give us many details about you — but he did tell us everything he knew. One of the things he said was that a 'Mr. Coates' was his boss. His questioners didn't know how to take that further. Both the GSS and the Israeli police were at a loss. But a certain Israeli officer by the name of Devash was in touch with Eli Flamm who, as you say, is a very smart young man. He's demonstrated his abilities over and over again during this whole episode.

"Devash gave Eli all the details. Eli had his suspicions of you even before, because of what happened at Amritsar. After hearing what Abu Rabia had to say, his intuition went into overdrive.

" 'Coates?' he said. 'That must be Steve Mantel. Both names mean the same thing — a coat — in English and in German."

◆ ◆ ◆

Near Moshav Zechariah, Friday, 1 p.m.

Talel Nader studied the map. He was passing Moshav Sedot Michah and approaching, at a slow and steady speed, the outskirts of Moshav Zechariah.

The car was air-conditioned, but his clothes were soaked in perspiration. Talel Nader did not want to die. He was no green Arab youth who could be coaxed into sacrificing his life for an ideal. In fact, Talel Nader's personality was diametrically opposed to that of the typical *shahid*. He was 40 years old and a father of 10.

But for all that, Yusuf Abu Rabia had not erred in choosing him for the role of second nuclear *shahid*. He was banking on Talel Nader's hatred of Israel — a profound hatred that almost bordered on madness. Yusuf knew that Talel would struggle with himself, that he would find the decision a very difficult one to make, but that he would end by choosing the side of the holy martyrs.

To make doubly certain, Yusuf had informed Talel that he would not live to see the next day in any case. The Baretta in Yusuf's hand backed up this assertion. Yusuf had fired two shots at the wall above Talel's head. "I think you'd much prefer to end your life with the promise of eternal life in the shadow of the Prophet Mohammed," he said softly. Thin smoke curled out of the gun's mouth, and an acrid aroma tickled Talel's nose. "Understand?"

"I understand." Talel was trembling. Inwardly, he cursed the day he had joined the struggle against the Zionist enemy. That day had seen him embark on a road from which there was no return.

When he was close enough to Moshav Zechariah, he left the car, attache case in hand. He walked through fields until he glimpsed the moshav's green-gray security wall. The wall circled the hills that surmounted the chalk caves housing the missiles and their launchers. Batteries of the "Jericho" missile were to be found here — a missile 14 meters high and a meter and a half wide, capable of bearing a 2,000-pound warhead and of homing in on a target up to 5,000 kilometers distant. The missiles were programmed, Talel knew, for Libya, Syria, Iran, Iraq, and perhaps also for the Saudi Arabian oilfields.

His approach, black attache case in hand, represented an unprecedented threat to all of Israel. He hid behind an unused building and dialed Israel's news service on his cellular phone. Into the ears of the startled switchboard operator, he dictated his horrific announcement:

"The Islamic Jihad has sent a suicide bomber armed with a live atom bomb to the site of one of Israel's nuclear arsenals. We demand that the Israeli government declare the following within the next three hours:

"1. An immediate withdrawal to the November 29, 1947 borders.

"2. The establishment of a Palestinian state with Jerusalem as its capital.

"3. The return of all Palestinian refugees.

"4. Exclusive Arab control of water sources at locations to be named.

"5. Monetary compensation in the amount of $100,000 to each Arab family that lost a son or daughter in the wars against the Zionist enemy, dating from the year 1948.

"There will be no negotiation. There will be no extension of the three-hour deadline. This ultimatum is final. If, at the end of three hours, the imperialist Zionists do not inform every news service in every media of its complete agreement on every one of the above points, the suicide bomber will press the button."

Talel hung up.

At the other end of the line, the operator reread the announcement, and smiled sardonically. "Someone obviously thinks today is the first of April."

"What are you talking about?" the secretary asked her.

"The world has no lack of crazies," the operator giggled. "Some cuckoo has just informed me that he has an atom bomb and is going to blow himself up near a nuclear base!"

"What? Let me see that." Laughing, the secretary pulled the paper out of the other girl's hand. As she read, the smile gradually left her face. "You know something?" she said slowly. "I don't think this is a joke. Anyway, it's impossible to know when something's true and when it's not. If only for the thousandth of a percent chance that it's true, we have to let the management know. Let's go show this to the newsroom."

The news manager did not discount the message at once. Prudently, he phoned his military correspondents and asked them to make some discreet inquiries. Five minutes later, an army general phoned him with the unambiguous order to place a total blackout on the announcement. Under no circumstances was he to broadcast it.

"Is this for real?" The manager of the newsroom was a calm man as a rule. Now, he began to feel a very uncomfortable prickling sensation, as if a troop of ghosts were breathing down his neck.

The general tried to sound cool and collected, but it was impossible to disguise the panic in his voice. "No comment. Just this: We are attending to the matter."

The general hung up the phone, then glanced again at a secret memo that had been circulated that morning to every army, police, and security unit in the country. The first line said it all:

Section 21a. Protocol for nuclear incidents

1. Securing the area.

2. Damage assessment.

3. Evacuating the wounded.

46

Police Station, Bat Yam, Friday, 1 p.m.

Arkady Bogdanov was seething. His son and daughter-in-law had locked him in a room and then handed him over to the Israeli police!

Added to his fury was his fear that the bomb would go off, reducing all to dust. But when the hours passed and nothing happened, he understood that Sulimein, the *shahid*, had failed. The fear receded, and he allowed the full force of his anger — an anger such as he had never felt before, not even when he was admitted into the old-age home against his will — consume him once more.

He would have his revenge. He would implicate Yefim and Galina in the whole affair. Let them suffer, too!

He thought with gritted teeth of the other blow that had befallen him, the day before. 'Gray Cap,' Issam Abu Rabia, had surprised him at the last minute by paying only half the promised sum.

"What's this?" Arkady had demanded.

Issam rolled his eyes heavenward and lifted his palms. "The merciful Allah knows that I will pay you."

"But when?"

"After the bombs explode."

"But I am exploding already!" Arkady screamed in frustration. He felt like strangling the Arab.

"Understand me, please," Issam explained. "You take a million dollars, and what happens if it turns out that the cases were full of sand?"

"Fool! Open them for yourself and see the plutonium bars with your own eyes!"

"Sssh. Do not shout. I know nothing about atoms. Be happy that we trusted you enough to advance you half a million dollars. After all is settled, call me at a number I will give you, and we will arrange for the rest of the money to be transferred."

Arkady was disappointed and bitter and tired. He resolved to cooperate with his questioners even before they put pressure on him to do so, and to place some of the blame squarely on the shoulders of his traitorous son and daughter-in-law.

In a monotone, he explained to Dani Devash and Ari Naot — heading the special interrogation team — that Yefim and Galina had forced him into his nefarious acts. "They took advantage of the fact that I was a nuclear scientist in order to finance their luxurious lifestyle. Every day they put pressure on me to agree to deal with Gray Cap. When I didn't give them the answer they wanted, they had me locked up in the Golden Towers old-age home, promising that if I didn't do what they wanted I'd spend the rest of my life there. I had no choice. They forced me to buy that material in St. Petersburg."

Devash did not know which part of the scientist's story was true and which was false. Recalling Yefim's first visit to the police station, he thought there might be something to the old Russian's words. Arkady described his tortuous journey, ending in a back room in Jericho.

"They tricked me. Gray Cap — Issam Abu Rabia, and his brother, Yusuf. When I brought them what they wanted, they betrayed me. They promised me another million and gave me only half."

Devash wanted to clarify the details of the payment. "How much did they promise you initially?"

"Three million dollars," Arkady sighed. "They started with one, then raised it to two and finally promised three. I had planned to hide and not to hand over the bombs to Gray Cap until they also reimbursed the 300,000 dollars I lost in Petersburg."

"You're as crazy about money as a young man with his whole life ahead of him," Devash said mockingly. "Look at you — you're an old man already, and you'll be spending the rest of your life in prison!"

Arkady closed his eyes and leaned weakly against the back of his chair, arms hanging limply at his sides. Old age had indeed caught up with him these last few days. His wrinkled skin hung pouchlike on his face, and his shoulders were bowed. Feebly, he continued his confession. "Here's something in my defense. Maybe it will reduce my time in prison. I heard them talking in the next room — "

"Who was talking?"

"Yusuf Abu Rabia and Mahmud Talel Nedir. They were discussing the possibility of exploding the second bomb at the missile base in Moshav Zechariah. From what I understand, the arsenal there contains 50 Jericho-2 missiles. The entire Middle East would go up in flames. A small, three-and-a-half kiloton blast is nothing compared to one measuring 10 kilotons. Add that to 50 nuclear warheads exploding all at once, and who knows what kind of destruction would follow. Maybe the whole world would split in half!" The old scientist shivered. "I'm not such a wicked person. My conscience woke up and didn't let me cooperate with such madmen. And don't forget that they tricked me."

"Yes — that motivated you more than anything," Ari Naot said dryly.

"I decided to work secretly." A spark of life returned to Arkady's eyes.

Dani Devash roused himself from his thoughts to ask, sharply, "What did you do?"

"Last night, while they slept, I opened the case and neutralized the bomb."

"What do you mean?"

Arkady glanced at the table, where all of his personal belongings had been placed upon his arrest. "You see that pencil?" With his chin, he pointed at a metal cylinder, thick and red. "That's the detonator. That's what makes the bomb work — and I've got it! Without that detonator, there's nothing to cause the first atomic split, the split that brings on the chain reaction. I substituted something else in its place." Arkady broke into hysterical laughter. "I would give a fortune to see Talel Nedir's face when he tries to arm that bomb!"

◆ ◆ ◆

Near Moshav Zechariah, Friday, 4 p.m.

Talel Nedir trembled with fear. The fateful moment had come. Three hours had passed since he had announced his ultimatum. He had been listening to the news broadcasts in a state of spiraling tension, biting his lips with frustration when no mention at all was made of his threat. "They'll pay for this," he told himself.

The surrounding countryside had not changed in the intervening hours. Talel Nedir remained in place behind the abandoned building, darting nervous looks around him from time to time. The silence was total, and frightening. It betrayed no whisper of the elite commando group that was moving ever closer, taking cover behind bushes and undergrowth, and waiting for the signal to burst out of hiding.

He was a big man, and every inch of him shook. His mind grew numb, except for one longing. "I want to live," he moaned quietly. His heart contracted painfully and the adrenalin shot through his veins. "I have no chance to get out of this alive," he thought, trying to overcome his fear. "The Prophet Mohammed and all the holy martyrs are waiting for me to fulfill what the traitor, Sulimein, failed to do."

He opened the attache case — on the previous day, Arkady Bogdanov had removed the delay mechanism on the locks — and searched for the detonator.

A horror of death overtook him. "Am I crazy? Does life mean so little to me? If Allah grants life, how can I take it away? What do I need this for? Why did I ever agree to this insanity?" His limbs jerked and shook like a puppet's.

He wanted to phone the Israeli police and turn himself in. "Come save me!" he wanted to scream into the phone. "Abu Rabia forced me into this, he's trying to turn me into a *shahid*!"

But other things moved against this desire — his fear of Yusuf, his mighty hatred for Israel, and the hope of being known forever after as the greatest of all *shahids*. "You'll be a greater *shahid* than Sulimein could have been," Yusuf had told him. "You will kill a lot more people. Besides, Sulimein is a Jew, and the highest crown is reserved only for those in whom noble Arab blood has flowed for at least a thousand years."

As these thoughts were battling in Talel Nedir's frenzied mind, his fingers were traveling continuously through the case, in search of the detonator. He would not fail to carry out the glorious plan that would wipe out, at a single stroke, the blot on the Arab world that was Israel.

His fingers found something. "It's too thin," he thought, but fear and confusion made concentration difficult. Talel took two deep breaths and pulled the cylinder out of its casing.

His eyes grew round as saucers. In his hand was a Parker pen.

◆ ◆ ◆

Anafim, Friday, 3 p.m.

Yonah Pinter was in his underground workroom in Anafim when the police swarmed over the Friends of the Mikdash headquarters. While waiting for the abomination on the Temple Mount to crumble, he had been preparing himself for his role as the first *Kohen Gadol* of the third *Beis Hamikdash* after nearly 2,000 years of exile. "We will rebuild," he hummed to himself with pleasure. Suddenly, he heard a tumult upstairs, cries of confusion from the surprised youths and shouts from the police.

Pinter's shock was awesome. It took some time until the bitter realization was able to penetrate his mind. The "abomination" was still standing in all its mockery in the very heart of Jerusalem — and he and his faithful followers were in danger.

A terrible pain threatened to break his heart. His great dream had turned into a balloon that had burst in his face. How had it come to pass that this day of all days, the most important of his life, the day the mosques were to be destroyed, would mark the end of the road for the Friends of the Mikdash?

For a long time he wept bitter tears. Finally, he roused himself. This was no time for crying. He must prepare himself to meet the evil that was upon him.

Quick as a mouse, he slipped under his folding bed and waited there, trembling, for the police to come. To his astonishment, they never did. No one thought to search the basement for the group's leader. Yonah Pinter was divided between rejoicing over his continued freedom, and distress that he was held of so little account by the police.

He went to the small window above his head and stood on a chair, the better to see and hear. He heard the accusations hurled at Dekel. How had such a viper come to rest in his bosom? How had his eyes been so blind as to trust that man?

He saw the police drag Dekel into the waiting van.

"When all is said and done," he thought, "I am still the leader of this group. Whatever happens, I must represent it with honor."

As the hours passed, his depression turned into a crisis of despair. A thousand questions that had followed him from the days of his childhood leaped to the forefront now, dancing before his eyes. He remembered all the insults, all the people who had pointed meaningfully to their heads when they thought he wasn't looking. For the first time in his life, he asked himself if they had not, after all, been right. Had he perhaps gone too far in his efforts to bring on the end of days?

He had always laughed at the questions, dismissed them. He had been filled with certitude about the righteousness of his path. Suddenly, he understood that he had erred. All the question marks joined in one enormous exclamation point, calling out to him: *Wrong!*

His sorrowful glance encompassed the small basement room, filled with holy artifacts. There was his *Kohen Gadol* outfit, woven with his own hands on the small loom in the corner. There were his specially sharpened slaughtering knives. Against one wall stood a lovely scale model of the *Beis Hamikdash,* made entirely of maple wood to resemble stone. He had shown the model to only a few people, most of them experts on the *Beis Hamikdash,* and all had exclaimed over its beauty and precision.

Had it all been for nothing? The Moslems were proud of their Mosque of Omar, calling it one of the most beautiful structures in the world. But every Jew knew that — impossible as it was to even mention the two in the same breath — the mosque paled completely next to the glory that had been the *Beis Hamikdash.* "Why are You hiding Your Face?" he whispered, anguished tears trickling down his cheeks. "How long will the abominations be permitted to push aside the holy?"

He remembered his impassioned argument with Aharon Flamm, 14 years before. Looking back, he knew that Flamm had been right. Even then, in Brooklyn, he had known that Flamm was right. Flamm's reasoning had been incisive, his logic impeccable. But Yonah Pinter had let his madness overtake him, refusing to admit even the possibility that he might be mistaken.

"There is no desire like the craving for victory." Yonah understood now that his sense of victory had been a stumbling block, and had brought him and all the Friends of the Mikdash to the brink of disaster.

Slowly, gradually, over the course of the hours, a resolution formed in his mind. He crept out of his hiding place in the basement and ran, like a frightened rabbit, along the paths leading to the yeshivah dormitory. He searched for Eli Flamm's room.

When the yeshivah students saw him their eyes widened, as if he had dropped from the moon. To his agitated inquiries, they pointed silently out the window at Mark Goldenblum's big car, beside which Eli stood. Another young man stood beside Eli, looking exceedingly out of place among the human scenery of Aish Aharon.

Yonah ran out to the car. Eli was astonished to see him. "Yonah, where are you coming from? The police were looking for you." To his sister, Judy, he added quietly, "This is Yonah Pinter, of the Friends of the Mikdash."

She wrinkled her brow in an effort to remember. Suddenly, her brow cleared. "Oh, that's right," she called. "You're the one who argued with Abba at breakfast!"

◆ ◆ ◆

Mark Goldenblum had come to adopt another son.

That very day, the children had found their long-lost brother, and Mark had arrived to take him home. They would all spend Shabbos together. Dovy and Moishy, unable to wait for Shlomo to come to them, had traveled to the moshav with their adoptive father.

Shlomo had stood as if carved from stone as the Goldenblum minivan drove up. He knew himself to be the subject of every conversation at Anafim that day, and he was aware of the many surreptitious looks being thrown his way.

His paralysis began to thaw when he caught sight of the two boys leaping from the van and running directly at him, eager as young ponies. There was a brief moment of confused silence, as they met each other's eyes and measured one another. Dovy and Moishy seemed to be asking themselves whether this was truly their brother. Was it possible that it was all a ghastly mistake?

No, it was no mistake. "Dovy, Moishy!" Shlomo cried, spreading his arms as wide as they would go. They rushed into his embrace.

The three brothers stood locked together for a long time, clapping each other on the back, finding that the power of speech had deserted them, but not caring. The students who watched the reunion wiped their eyes with the backs of their hands.

It was Mark Goldenblum who roused them all. "Gentlemen, it's nearly Shabbos. Who wants a ride to Jerusalem?" His smile was inviting.

The entire Flamm family piled into the minivan. Only Benjy was missing. The yeshivah phone had worked overtime that day; Benjy was fully up to date on developments. He had spoken with Shlomo, cried with him, and immediately upon hanging up had bought himself a plane ticket to Israel for that very Sunday.

In the passenger seat, beside Mark Goldenblum, sat Rav Anshel Pfeffer. And at the very back of the minivan, quiet and embarrassed, was Yonah Pinter. With bowed head, he whispered to Eli, "They beat me."

"It's better this way," Eli consoled him. "Just think of what would have happened if you'd succeeded in blowing up the mosques. Sometimes failure is much better than victory."

Yonah beat his knees softly with his fists. "Oh, what have I done?" All the way to Jerusalem he kept up a penitent moan. "If only I'd listened to Aharon Flamm all those years ago, how much misery could have been averted!"

"It's good that you're able to admit your mistake now," Mark Goldenblum said. Then, determined to change the subject to a more pleasant one, he turned to wink at Shlomo. "You've missed so much, so much — where do we begin?"

Yonah nearly jumped out of his seat in his eagerness. "Let me have a chance," he pleaded. "Let me fix some of the wrong I've done. I volunteer to learn with Shlomo, to be his private teacher, without any pay. To start from the very beginning, with the alef-beis. Only if he wants me, of course."

"If you learn with him," Mark smiled, "I'm afraid he'll be ready to blow up mosques in a year or two."

"I'm through with all that," Yonah said, smiling for the first time in many hours. "I will wait for the redemption the way Jews have been waiting throughout the generations."

Rav Anshel nodded. Softly, he said, "We'll see. But I think that Yonah Pinter has learned the hard way that it is wrong to try to force the redemption. From now on, he will stop his wild ways and pray along with the rest of us. For 2,000 years, reality has thrown itself back in the face of all who tried to force the end of days before its time.

"All of Israel is waiting. In a long, long line, hundreds of generations have dreamed of the redemption. It has been a long process. But it is a Heavenly process. And it will conclude one day, we hope soon. And on that day, all our voices will be raised in song, and every eye will be filled with that which we have waited so long to see!"